"HEARTSTOPPING!"
Orlando Sentinel

"This"—he gestured to the room—"is not just a place of cruelty and pain." His face shone in the torchlight. "It was lovingly constructed by a man who saw it as a place of passion."

She took in the strange instruments that hung from the wall. How had she allowed herself to get into this situation? She had known that she might have to trade her body for information, but she was not prepared to lose her life.

He sat back. "You've proposed an exchange of intelligence. I'm testing that offer."

Elizabeth could feel fear creeping up on her. She had to remain calm, aloof. "What do you want from me?" she asked softly.

Triumph flared in his eyes. "The bizarre!"

Other Avon Books by
David Aaron

AGENT OF INFLUENCE

CROSSING BY NIGHT

DAVID AARON

AVON BOOKS ◆ NEW YORK

"*I Remember You*" by Johnny Mercer and Victor Schertzinger. Copyright © 1942 by Paramount Music Corporation; renewed 1969 by Paramount Music Corporation.

AVON BOOKS
A division of
The Hearst Corporation
1350 Avenue of the Americas
New York, New York 10019

Published in hardcover by William Morrow and Company, Inc.; for information address Permissions Department, William Morrow and Company, Inc., 1350 Avenue of the Americas, New York, New York 10019.

First Avon Books Printing: May 1994

For Chloe

Foreword

This book is a work of fiction based on the life and exploits of a real person, Elizabeth Pack, an American woman whose code name in the British Secret Service was "Cynthia." *Time* magazine described her as a blond James Bond who used "the boudoir the way 007 uses a Beretta." The British spymaster William Stephenson (*A Man Called Intrepid*) hailed her as "World War Two's greatest unsung heroine."

In dramatizing her story, I decided to focus on her remarkable adventures in the world of espionage in Europe in the 1930s and on why, at great personal risk, she left the comfortable world of a Washington debutante and diplomat's wife to lead the life of a spy. Although this is a novel, I have tried where possible to be true to Elizabeth Pack's spirit and the magnitude of her accomplishments. If this approach sometimes makes it difficult to sort out romance from reality, I apologize to the reader in advance and console myself with the hope that this is exactly as "Cynthia" would have wanted it.

In writing this book, I owe a particular debt to her colleague the late H. Montgomery Hyde for his many kindnesses and insights. I also want to express my appreciation to Corelli Barnett, director of the Churchill Library at Cambridge University, for facilitating access to her papers, diaries and other materials that otherwise remain restricted. And I must thank the many past and present members of the intelligence community on both sides of the Atlantic for their helpful and, as usual, anonymous assistance. Finally, I wish to record my gratitude to the late Count Michael

Lubienski for the opportunity to discuss his relationship with Elizabeth Pack. To my mind, he was a great Polish patriot without whom the world might have become a very dark place indeed.

PART ONE

July 24, 1935
*I think that I cannot quite
   understand
The depth of wanting unfulfilled
   desire,
And hating you to even touch my
   hand
When embers die where once there
   was a fire.*

—The last entry in Elizabeth
   Thorpe's childhood diary, written
   the day of her wedding to Captain
   Arthur Pack

Chapter 1

Windsor Castle, England—
April 12, 1937

"We can do business with Hitler, I assure you." Lord Halifax smiled at the king indulgently.

"You don't handle a bully by turning the other cheek," Churchill growled. He had his thumbs stuck in his waistcoat in the bulldog stance he used to address the House of Commons.

They stood on opposite sides of the fireplace in the library of the king's apartments in Windsor castle. George VI frowned with uncertainty and drew a lap robe more tightly around his frail body. Outside a spring gale howled. The tapestries shielding the windows and the layers of oriental carpet covering the stone floor could not keep out the damp.

It was an unusual group that the king had assembled at Churchill's urging. The tall and aristocratic Lord Halifax had recently become lord president in the cabinet of the new prime minister—Neville Chamberlain. As such, he was the second most powerful figure in Parliament. In contrast, Winston Churchill's star had been falling. He had been First Lord of the Admiralty in the Great War of 1914 and widely expected to become prime minister, but his opposition to the prevailing mood of pacifism in Britain had relegated him to the back benches of Parliament. Still, he retained influence with the king.

Two military men were also present. Sir Cyril Deverell, chief of the Imperial Defense Staff, sat to the right of the king, and Admiral Hugh Sinclair who was "C," head of the Secret Intelligence Service, was on his left. George VI turned to him.

"And what d-do our intelligence chaps say," the king asked.

"Your Majesty"—Admiral Sinclair shifted his bulky body forward—"we estimate that there is a grave likelihood of war in Europe within the next eighteen to twenty-four months, certainly by 1940."

The king's concern shifted to the chief of staff. "Are w-we r-r-ready?" George VI's stutter always became worse when he was upset.

Sir Cyril's face tightened. His hard angular features underscored his no-nonsense reputation. "At the current rate of defense production, we shan't catch up to Germany until 1946."

"And that," Churchill intervened, "is only if the Nazis make no greater efforts, which they well could!"

"Now you all know w-why," the king explained, "I asked you down f-for this ch-ch . . . talk."

"Speaking for the government, I don't think we're quite so gloomy as all that." Lord Halifax felt it was his duty to respond to his sovereign's concerns. "We don't think war is inevitable, and if it is, we don't believe Britain is fated to become involved. Hence our policy is to rearm at a pace that will not provoke Hitler further."

"But w-what if you're wro-wro . . . mistaken?" the king insisted.

"With all due respect, Your Majesty"—impatience had crept into Halifax's voice—"foreign and defense policy are the prime minister's responsibility, not royal prerogatives."

An embarrassed silence followed this oblique reference to the fact that the king had come to the throne only three weeks earlier, after the abdication of Edward VIII. The world believed that Edward VIII had resigned to marry the American divorcée Wallis Simpson, but everyone in the room knew that the previous British monarch had been pushed off the throne because he tried to force his way into making foreign policy.

But George VI was not so easily intimidated. "I t-take

it that I still have some authority over my s-secret s-s-service, isn't that s-so?''

Admiral Sinclair hastened to nod his agreement with the king. Halifax could not contradict him. By tradition, British intelligence was responsible first to the sovereign, only second to Parliament and the Cabinet.

"Your Majesty," Churchill spoke up again, "I may be only a lowly private member of Parliament, but it's my view that if the Prime Minister refuses to strengthen our defenses, then our secret service becomes all the more vital. Each day brings new German threats. First it's reports of Nazi plans to seize Austria, then it's Romania, or Czechoslovakia or Hungary or Poland. If we're to mobilize our meager resources against the Nazi juggernaut, we must know where and when the blow will fall!''

"Well, I wouldn't count on Sinclair's chaps," said Sir Cyril. "Eighty percent of his agents' reports prove dead wrong.''

"That's what happens when you've been brutalized by budget cuts," the chief of His Majesty's Secret Service replied angrily. He did not dispute Sir Cyril's numbers.

"Then what about the German codes?" Churchill asked. "If we could crack them, we would have the best possible source of intelligence.''

"Winston, you're living in the past." Admiral Sinclair dismissed him. "The Germans learned from the Great War. They have a new coding machine that creates unbreakable ciphers. We've tried everything to no avail.''

"William Stephenson believes it can be done," Churchill responded.

"I don't wish to take anything away from him as an inventor or a businessman"—Admiral Sinclair's jowels began to shake—"but Bill Stephenson is a rank amateur in this business.''

The snap and pop of the fire filled the ensuing silence. George VI raised his head and looked at C.

"S-So am I," the king observed. "But for the s-sake of the survival of the British p-people, I w-want my secret s-service to put on stronger g-glasses.''

Pier 48, New York City—
July 28, 1935

Elizabeth loved the waterfront. The Forty-eighth Street pier swarmed with burly men in caps and stained undershirts wrestling huge steamer trunks up a gangway and into the side of the Cunard liner *Berengaria*. Mounds of luggage and clusters of voyagers, well-wishers, and household staff created an obstacle course for the limousines, touring cars, yellow cabs, and Checker taxis that vied to deliver their passengers closest to dockside. A small brass band played on the promenade deck, which was festooned with crepe paper streamers hanging down to the dock. Overhead, tall booms lowered cargo crates suspended in huge nets into the ship's hold. The hot July morning smelled of sweat, steam, and the sea. To Elizabeth, it was the aroma of adventure.

At the age of ten, her Marine Corps family had sailed from San Pedro, California, to Hawaii, where she had climbed the volcanoes and explored the rain forest. A few years later, the U.S. Navy ferried Elizabeth and her parents to Cuba, where she had spent her days racing the Cuban boys through the canebrakes on horseback until her mother banished her to boarding school in Boston. After graduation, a tramp steamer carried her family to Europe, where they traveled for a year and where Elizabeth studied French at the Institution des Essarts in Switzerland.

Now, at nineteen, she was embarking on the biggest adventure ever, her honeymoon in England with Captain Arthur Pack, commercial officer in His Britannic Majesty's Foreign Service. Age thirty-nine, Captain Pack was twenty years her senior, old enough to have caught a dozen shell fragments in his left arm and shoulder from a seventeen-inch German "Jack Johnson" at the Battle of the Somme. He held that arm gingerly to his chest as he struggled with one of the trunks. Arthur Pack was far from any young girl's romantic ideal. He was only slightly taller than Elizabeth, with a thickset body, receding hairline, and a professionally unexpressive face that made him look even older than his years. But to Elizabeth, he represented both security and excitement.

Most of the "buds" of her debutante season had married into the dreary existence of Washington society, summers on the eastern shore, winters at the Greenbriar, bridge teas in the afternoon, bridge parties in the evening. Elizabeth looked forward to the romance of foreign capitals, the swirl of diplomatic life, and above all, starting a family. That she was already on the way was a surprise that she would reveal to Arthur when they were at last alone on the high seas. She could not imagine a better wedding gift to offer him.

Elizabeth Pack was a striking young woman with wavy strawberry blond hair framing an intelligent face: large, deep-set green eyes under a high forehead, prominent cheekbones, and a bold mouth accented by a mischievous cleft in her chin. Her traveling suit of shimmering green duvetyn did not reveal that she was "with child," but it still showed off her shapely and well-proportioned athletic figure. She stood waiting happily with her mother Cora, and her father George Thorpe, in the shade of the elevated West Side Highway, while Arthur counted their luggage for the third time. Arthur loathed travel; it interrupted his daily routine. But he relished the logistics. Elizabeth was comforted at how smoothly he had organized everything.

"You look awfully happy, dear." Elizabeth's mother managed to convey the compliment with a tinge of reproach. Dressed in a floral print dress that hung like a drape from her ample bosom, Cora Thorpe was still smarting from the way that the *Washington Evening Star* had treated the wedding. Her rage began when the event was ignored entirely by the Sunday society section and reached a fever pitch when, on the day of the wedding, the only picture on the society page was that of the daughter of the Nicaraguan ambassador.

"That's not even a real country," Cora had thundered. "It's a Marine Corps training camp!"

For a woman born before the turn of the century, Elizabeth's mother had gained a formidable education: a bachelor of arts degree from the University of Michigan and a postgraduate degree from Columbia. But after marrying George Thorpe, she had focused all her talents on promoting her husband's Marine Corps career and on the thankless task of moving the family from post to post around much

of the Western Hemisphere. Now that Colonel Thorpe had
retired from the military and become a Washington lawyer,
Mrs. Thorpe was conducting a campaign to advance the
family socially that was as relentless as Sherman's march
through Georgia.

Only the British, and prominent Republicans, moved the
mercury in Cora Thorpe's social barometer. She had almost
burst with pride when President Coolidge once came to
dinner at their home, but when Franklin Roosevelt and the
Democrats arrived in Washington, her social stock had
crashed along with the market. She not only considered
Roosevelt "a traitor to his class," but she eagerly participated in syndicating rumors that he was actually a Jew,
descended from a Colonel van Rosenfeld of Holland.

The ship's steam whistle let out an ear-shattering blast,
signaling fifteen minutes to sailing. "If we're going to see
your stateroom," George Thorpe said, "we'd better get on
board."

Colonel Thorpe's enthusiasm for his daughter's marriage
was under careful control. "Good God, Cora," he had exploded when his wife first broached it, "the man hasn't
exactly set the diplomatic world on fire. And he's a lot
closer to my age than hers."

"Now don't you go get jealous about your little girl.
She's a woman now."

"And I'm sure she'll attract a lot of admirers."

"That's precisely the point. She's too attractive for her
own good! Take that Antonio de Zaragoza who's been
skulking around. He's married! I told him to leave off or
I'd complain to his ambassador. Beautiful girls always end
up with the worst men."

"I guess we're lucky we didn't have that problem."

She ignored his sarcasm. "You have no appreciation,"
she had continued unabated, "for the lengths I've gone to
to find a suitable candidate like Captain Pack. He has dignity and a pension."

Flashbulbs popped as the ship's photographer caught the
wedding couple and the Thorpes climbing the crowded
gangplank. Cora was showing off the horsehair hat she had
bought for the wedding reception. Elizabeth, perspiring in
the heat, could not wait to get into her cabin to take off her

moleskin-trimmed jacket. The steward showed them to an outside stateroom on A deck. A magnum of Veuve Clicquot courtesy of the captain sat in a silver ice bucket. While Arthur opened a porthole and Elizabeth turned on the fan, George expertly popped the cork on the champagne.

"To a long and happy life together," he toasted them. George Thorpe was tall with hazel eyes and a firm jaw with a cleft in his chin that he shared with his daughter. Once tan and strongly built, her father now looked thin and gray, Elizabeth thought. She worried that having become a Washington lawyer did not agree with him.

"And take your time having children," Cora was saying. "I'm too young to be a grandmother." Elizabeth could feel herself blush. She had been right not to tell her mother.

The ship's horn gave two more blasts. They all gulped down another glass of champagne, then made their way to the promenade deck. Cora gave her daughter a hug. George put his arms around his daughter and kissed her on the forehead. Elizabeth could not hold back her tears.

"Betty, Betty." He rocked her back and forth as if she were still his child. He looked like he too might cry any minute.

"Thank you ever so much for everything," Arthur interrupted their moment together. He held out his hand and Elizabeth's father had to let go of her to shake it. Then they all said good-bye again, and the Thorpes made their way down to the dock. Elizabeth pushed to the rail and tossed them several white streamers. The ship gave a final three blasts on its horn, and the gangway was hauled aboard. The vibration under Elizabeth's feet increased as the vessel edged away from the pier. As the mass of the ship gathered momentum, Mr. and Mrs. Arthur Pack and Mr. and Mrs. George Thorpe held on to opposite ends of the streamers until they bowed, stretched, and finally snapped apart.

The ship swung out into the Hudson. George Thorpe followed them out to the end of the dock. Elizabeth could see him standing there in his handsome white suit, waving his panama hat as the ship moved down the river. When he disappeared, eclipsed by the stern of the *Normandie,* she had the sudden fear that she would never see him again.

Then the skyline of Manhattan opened up, and she ban-

ished any gloomy thoughts from her mind. The Empire
State Building towered above everything else, but other
skyscrapers looked like they might catch up. The sheer size
and vitality of the city thrilled her and somehow made her
proud to be an American. Despite the depression and its
problems, America was big and easy and open. For all of
England's rich culture, she knew that it exacted a price in
reserve and decorum. Well, Elizabeth vowed, she was up
to it.

As the closely packed spires of Wall Street and the tip
of the Battery slipped by, Elizabeth impulsively threw her
arms around Arthur and gave him a kiss. He staggered
backward with an embarrassed smile.

Arthur Pack had to admit things were going swimmingly.
The wedding at Washington's Church of the Epiphany,
draped with the Union Jack and the Stars and Stripes, gave
just the right touch of Anglo-American amity. His ambassador had been very pleased. At the luncheon afterward, he
took full credit for the marriage. Rising to propose a toast
he said:

"A year ago I offered Captain Pack some sound advice;
it was time he found himself a wife."

"Hear, hear!" the British guests responded.

"And do you know what Arthur replied?"

"Tell us!" several others called out.

"He said that he had never given much thought to
women!"

Laughter swept the room. Someone shouted, "A gentleman of the old school!"

"Quite. I, of course, commiserated fully," the ambassador continued to more laughter, "but insisted it would be
good for his career. Now even Arthur could see the point
of that!"

The audience chuckled again.

"But he was bewildered as to what sort of woman would
be suitable. So again I advised him. Being a diplomat's wife
was a daunting responsibility. We've always been proud
that the diplomatic corps gets two for the price of one. I
therefore urged him to find someone young who could be
properly molded. And so I lift my glass to Elizabeth, Mrs.

Arthur Pack, our newest member of His Majesty's Foreign Service!"

Looking at her now, standing at the rail with the stiffening breeze pressing her clothes against her body, Arthur had to admit he was proud of his accomplishment. She had taken off her hat, and with her hair blowing backward accentuating her profile, Arthur thought she looked like a cross between Gloria Swanson and Katharine Hepburn.

"Let's go to the bar for a drink." He rubbed his hands together.

"What about that wonderful champagne in the cabin? I want to stay here until I can't see land anymore." Champagne was just right for the news she had for him.

To Elizabeth, the wedding had seemed a blur and the ceremony a jumble of words. But this huge ship, gaining speed as it headed out to sea, made the change in her life feel irreversible. As Arthur disappeared into the hatchway, Elizabeth felt her affection for him rising. He could be stiff and standoffish, but she liked nothing better than breaking down his reserve. So what if he didn't ignite a grand passion. Such a thing scarcely existed outside of novels and the movies, her mother insisted, and at that, it was not altogether proper. Indeed, it was dangerous. Women who indulged themselves in love, women who made fools of themselves over men, ended up barefoot and pregnant. With Arthur, she was pregnant and safe.

The *Berengaria* steamed through the Verrazano Narrows before Elizabeth realized that she had missed the Statue of Liberty on the starboard side. Arthur and a steward reappeared at her elbow with the champagne. They clinked glasses.

"To the two of us," Arthur said. His normally square and stolid face took on a smile.

Elizabeth was bursting with her secret. "I have a surprise for you!"

"For me?" Arthur looked pleased. "Is it a present?"

"Definitely, but I promised myself I'd wait until we're on the high seas."

"Well, technically, we are already"—he smiled again—"so come across."

"You're trying to trick me," she said coyly. Elizabeth could still see land.

"Look at those ships, if you don't believe me." He pointed to several merchant vessels lying at anchor in the open sea surrounded by a number of small, sleek corvettes. "They're rumrunners sitting outside the three-mile limit. Cheeky, what?"

"Wonderful!" Elizabeth exclaimed. "You win!" She directed the steward to refill their glasses. He emptied the bottle.

"You're sure I'm going to like this?" Arthur laughed again.

"Are you!" She raised her champagne. "We're going to have a baby!" She touched his glass.

Arthur's smile froze, then became uncertain. "When?" he asked. "When is it due?"

"January, I think," she said happily, downing her champagne.

Arthur put his glass down on the rail. His face suddenly wore the look he had when dancing—he was counting in his head.

"It must have been the first time," she explained.

"I can't believe you kept this a secret from me." He was growing red. "Are you absolutely sure?"

"The rabbit died," she said anxiously. This was not what she expected.

"Oh my God!" He pressed the heel of his hand to his forehead.

"Aren't you pleased?" Elizabeth was stricken.

"January!" Arthur hurled his champagne glass overboard. "This could be an unmitigated catastrophe!"

Elizabeth reached out to him.

He pushed her away.

"What's wrong?" she cried.

"Leave me alone!" he shouted and stalked off.

Numb, dumbfounded, Elizabeth stood at the rail staring at the rolling sea until America disappeared over the horizon.

Chapter 2

Queen Anne's Gate, London—
April 20, 1937

"I want you to handle Bill Stephenson from now on," Admiral Sinclair told his deputy Stewart Menzies as they rode squeezed together in the tiny elevator that slowly rose to the fourth floor of his town house. "I'm handing him off to you at this meeting."

"A burden, is he?"

"He's been a good source on the European armaments industry, but he's full of harebrained schemes. Last month I had to quash his offer to shoot Hitler personally with a hunting rifle. Now, it's this German code machine foolishness."

The elevator stopped, and the two men passed through a door and into a corridor that linked Sinclair's residence to an office building in the rear that faced on Broadway. They emerged at the suite occupied by the Government Code and Cipher School, GCCS, the code-breaking arm of the Secret Intelligence Service.

British code breakers had achieved great success in the Great War of 1914–1918, most notably decoding the famous "Zimmerman telegram," which had proposed a German-Mexican alliance to attack the United States. When it was published, the public outcry helped bring America into the war, guaranteeing a quick Allied victory soon thereafter. But since then, British code-breaking had slowed to a trickle owing to budget cuts, and because the Germans had introduced an electrical enciphering machine called the Enigma.

William Stephenson sat waiting in an undistinguished conference room that had a blackboard on one wall, and a frosted window on the other. It smelled of stale pipe smoke. Stephenson had come late to the world of intelligence. Born near Winnipeg, Canada, he had impetuously volunteered for the Great War and gotten badly gassed for his trouble. But instead of returning home a disabled veteran, he talked himself into the Royal Flying Corps. He was accepted for two reasons: Small and wiry, he fit into the cockpit of a Sopwith Camel, and he was needed—the average life expectancy for pilots was only two weeks. Stephenson not only survived, he managed to shoot down two dozen German aircraft, including the brother of the infamous Red Baron.

His pugnacious spirit also led him into boxing, and by the end of the war he was the amateur lightweight champion of the world—a title he held until 1923 when he retired undefeated. By that time he was also well on his way to becoming a millionaire after having invented the modern radio photo that revolutionized journalism. With the royalties, he bought an interest in General Radio; helped found the BBC; and invested in Sound City Films, the construction industry, and Pressed Steel Ltd., the foremost British manufacturer of automobile bodies.

It was steel that brought him into contact with the British secret service. Through his dealings in Germany, he determined that the bulk of German steel production was being used in the manufacture of arms, in violation of the Treaty of Versailles. He shared this information with a friend, who put him in contact with Admiral Sinclair. The secret service chief arranged for Stephenson's reports to go directly to the Industrial Intelligence Center of the Imperial Defense Committee, where they came to the attention of Winston Churchill. With his support and influence with the king, Stephenson soon became a force to reckon with in the halls of the Secret Intelligence Service even though he was not formally a member of it.

Sinclair and Menzies entered the conference room accompanied by Alistair Denniston, head of GCCS, and the chief cryptographer Dilwyn Knox.

"Quex, it's good to see you," Stephenson exclaimed.

Sinclair cringed slightly at the use of his nickname.

"Good to see you too, Bill," he said perfunctorily. "You know everyone, so let's get started. We're intensely interested in your view that the Enigma can be broken."

"Anything that a machine can make," Stephenson declared, "a machine can break. Machines produce cycles," he added, "telltale patterns that can always be exploited."

A prolonged silence ensued.

"That's it?" asked "Dilly" Knox. A gangly and youngish-looking man with unkempt receding black hair, the chief British code-breaker paced nervously and with an awkward limp in front of a blackboard. "You've nothing more to offer than that?"

As a Canadian who had not studied at Oxford or Cambridge, yet who had the ill grace to make a success of himself, Stephenson was accustomed to being regarded askance by the British establishment. "We've been doing a lot of work at General Radio on signal processing," he explained. "Conceptually, it's a form of coding and decoding. With a vigorous research program, I'm convinced that we could get a breakthrough on the Enigma."

"You think we haven't tried?" Knox did not bother to conceal his irritation. C shot him a warning look to ease off.

"Have you seen this?" Knox lifted a small suitcase onto the table. Without waiting for a response, he opened the lid. It resembled a portable typewriter.

"Is this the Enigma?"

"Not exactly. This is the Scherbius machine. It was a commercial encoding device invented by a Dutchman and manufactured in Berlin to be used by banks. It disappeared from the market in 1922, shortly before we started intercepting unbreakable German signals. We believe the Enigma machine is a development of this design."

Stephenson looked at it closely. It had a keyboard like a typewriter, but above it were several rows of lights, each with a different letter of the alphabet. Where the carriage normally would be located, three cylindrical rotors were mounted crosswise to the way the roller would have been installed. The letters of the alphabet were inscribed around the rim of each rotor.

"Type your name," Knox suggested. Stephenson pushed B. The letter S lit up and the rotor on the right turned one stop. Then he pushed I, L, and L, the rotor advancing with each letter. The lights that winked on spelled SJXA. He was asked to do it again, and BILL came out NFZY.

"How does it work?" He was fascinated.

"When you press a key, an electric pulse travels through these rotors and comes out with a different letter. The way the wires inside each rotor are connected determines what you see. And each time the rotor turns it produces a different circuit for the pulse to go through, thus lighting up a different lettered bulb even if you keep pressing the same letter key." He then pressed Q four times and got PENL.

"And how do they decode it on the receiving end?"

"Decrypt it," Knox corrected him. "They use the same machine. They set up the rotors in the same way and do just the reverse." He turned the rotors back to their original position and typed SJXA. It came out BILL. "But if you're His Majesty's Secret Service and you don't know how the Enigma rotors are wired or how the Germans install them, or set them up to begin with, the number of possible combinations for each letter is twenty-six factorial!" Dilly went to the blackboard and wrote with relish: "That is the number 403,291,461,126,605,635,584,000,000!"

"Then you really do need a machine to sort through all the possibilities," Stephenson pointed out.

"But we don't know enough about how it works!" Exasperated, he limped back to a chair and sat down. "The Germans have made a number of modifications, perhaps changing the rotors, or the wiring, or scrambling the keyboard, anyway making it vastly more complicated. They obviously believe it can't be broken. And, despite your blithe optimism, Mr. Stephenson, I believe they're right!"

"Then I would think your highest priority would be to lay your hands on one of these machines, or at least the plans."

"From where, Nazi Germany?" Denniston spoke for the first time. Tweedy and balding, the head of the Government Code and Cipher School exuded the calm air of a university don.

"Where else?" Stephenson replied. "I assume you have spies in Germany."

Denniston looked over at C. Admiral Sinclair frowned, and a silence again descended over the room. "The plain fact, Bill, is that we have no high-level penetration of any kind in the Third Reich."

Stephenson tried to conceal his shock. "Well, then, that has to be your top priority," he allowed.

"It is"—C nodded—"and that's why we can't afford to waste our efforts on the Enigma. If you can show us that it can be broken, well and good. Until then . . ." He put on a smile that said that the meeting was over. "But do feel free to stay in touch with my deputy here, Colonel Menzies. . . ."

Bignor, West Sussex, England— August 5, 1935

The baby was never mentioned again until they had arrived at their honeymoon cottage in Bignor. When the *Berengaria* had docked in Southampton, no one had met them at the pier. Arthur had sent his parents a radiogram from the ship saying that he was canceling their visit to London and would call them to arrange dinner once they had settled in. He told Elizabeth that he wanted time to arrange a "proper" introduction to his family. When she asked if he had mentioned the baby, he looked at her as if she were quite mad.

That was it. He made no further explanations. No apology. No excuses. He simply lapsed into a void of silence that had enveloped him for the eight days since she had told him that he was going to be a father.

During the voyage, Arthur had become utterly remote, retreating into the security and sanctity of a nonstop bridge game in the men's bar. Stunned by his reaction, Elizabeth coped as she had in childhood when something awful occurred; she had pretended that it wasn't happening: She wasn't pregnant; she wasn't married; her life had not been changed forever. Elizabeth was on a holiday cruise. She would deal with everything else once she reached solid ground.

But inside, a smoldering core of panic would not be wished away. Elizabeth tried to smother it by eating six times a day, something she could do now that her morning sickness was gone. Breakfast was served from seven to nine A.M., bouillon on deck at eleven, luncheon at one, tea at four, dinner at eight, and a late-night buffet supper in the ballroom. She threw herself into the ship's social life. The captain had invited the Packs to his table the first night, dancing with Elizabeth into the small hours while Arthur, looking morose, excused himself to retire early. Thereafter, Elizabeth became the pet of many of the ship's most prominent passengers.

The financier Bernard Baruch taught Elizabeth to gamble at the baccarat and chemin de fer tables in the starboard lounge. On the rear deck, John Strachey, a leftish author who had been hounded out of the United States by the American Vigilance Association, showed her how to shoot skeet with a Purdy twenty-gauge "over and under" shotgun. The actor Leslie Howard and his wife accompanied Elizabeth to tea dances and fashion shows in the promenade lounge, while the poetess Vita Sackville-West invited her for swimming, calisthenics, and massage on D deck, regaling her with gossip and scandal about the other first-class passengers. The whole group went to the movies, and attended lectures in the forward lounge, and in the evening gathered again for the orchestra, floor show, and to dance the "continental" in the ballroom. By the time she returned to her stateroom late in the evenings, Elizabeth invariably found Arthur asleep in a cloud of Scotch.

The little car that Arthur had hired, an Anglia, looked like an icebox on wheels. After piling it high with luggage, the stevedores had warned that the car might tip over, so Arthur had to arrange to ship the steamer trunks by train.

Their destination and home for the next several months was to be Bignor, a small village outside the West Sussex town of Petworth. In an intermittent rain, they had set out from Southampton's Ocean dock, traveling north then east, along the edge of the South Downs. Elizabeth had felt anxious at leaving the ship behind. She and Arthur were now forced to be alone with one another. But he rarely talked

and hadn't touched her since she told him of the baby.
Tension filled the inside of the car like the fumes from the
manifold. Both were giving her a bad headache. They had
to talk about the baby. She vowed to have a showdown
when they got to Bignor.

After more than two hours of driving, Elizabeth had noticed the appearance of strange flat-topped pines reminis-
cent of the south of France. In the distance, a church spire
rising above the forest was the only sign of human habitation. Both America and the exciting new world she had
imagined seemed equally far away.

At Petworth they crossed the Rother River, then turned
east again onto a dirt road that led through the fields past
the ruins of an ancient Roman villa, finally disappearing
into a thicket of pine and beech that concealed the tiny
village of Bignor.

Consisting of no more than a few dozen houses, Bignor
had an oddly Mediterranean feeling. Dwellings of light-
colored stone crowded closely upon one another reminding
Elizabeth of hilltop villages in Italy, except that Bignor lay
in a hollow of damp shadows cast by the surrounding forest. The incongruity only increased Elizabeth's apprehension.

Next to the church, Arthur turned left onto an even
smaller and more deeply rutted track. It took them to the
edge of the village where the trees opened out into broad
sunny green fields of mustard. There, as if alerted by some
unknown rural telegraph, a heavyset woman in a sweater
and a tweed skirt was waiting for them. Cheery and red-
faced, she was Mrs. Willet, their landlady.

From behind a low stone barn covered in a patchwork
of moss, a large man in rubber Wellingtons appeared. She
introduced him as Mr. Willet. While he and Arthur un-
loaded the car, Mrs. Willet took Elizabeth through a
wooden gate and up a path toward a small cottage. Elizabeth realized that Arthur had never exactly described their
honeymoon cottage; he had kept repeating that it was "in
a beautiful area known for its grand homes." She felt a
wave of claustrophobia as Mrs. Willet proudly showed
them the three small rooms downstairs and the single bedroom upstairs tucked away beneath the eaves. When she

looked at the tiny sleigh bed in which she would spend her nights with Arthur, Elizabeth wanted to sit down on it and cry.

She had most of the luggage unpacked when Elizabeth heard a knock on the front door. Mrs. Willet had returned with tea, scones and clotted cream, biscuits, and little sandwiches. It all looked delicious and Elizabeth smiled, thinking how lucky she was to be able to eat for two. Then she felt depressed again.

"You look like you've had a long day, child," Mrs. Willet said. "I'll take this to the table on the terrace. The light at this hour makes for a lovely view."

"Won't you join us?" Elizabeth hastened to ask as she followed her out the kitchen door. She could not bear the thought of the coming confrontation with Arthur.

"Oh no, I'm sure you lovebirds would like a bit of privacy."

Arthur joined her under the grape arbor. As they drank their tea, Elizabeth tried not to stare at him. Finally, sick of his silence, she went to the edge of the terrace and looked out. From there, she could see across the open valley to the ridge several miles away that stretched from horizon to horizon. Not a house or a barn spoiled the sight of fields of wheat and rye and mustard and grass that rolled all the way down to the river hidden in a line of willows. Nearby, in a meadow, young lambs skipped and frolicked with one another. She couldn't take it any longer. She had to face him.

"Arthur, we must talk about the baby."

"Right." He got up and came toward her. "I've been thinking."

Elizabeth backed away toward the edge. She was ready to fight.

"I owe you a sincere apology," he said. "I behaved like a cad on the ship, and I'm terribly sorry."

Elizabeth dissolved. She threw her arms around him and buried her head in his shoulder weeping uncontrollably.

"There, there," he said awkwardly. "I didn't mean to be cruel. Let me explain myself."

He led her back to the table, where they sat down on a

rickety settee, knees touching, Arthur holding Elizabeth's hands in his.

"You'll learn that England's a strange country. Oh, we speak a similar tongue and share a common history, but under the surface similarities, you'll come to find that we are as foreign to you as if we were Levantines. It's merely more subtle."

Elizabeth did not want one of his lectures. This was a time he could be silent. She just wanted him to reach out and hold her.

"What I'm trying to say, if I may be direct," he continued, "is that we're not as morally relaxed as you Americans."

Elizabeth pulled away. She should have known that he had an agenda, that a simple apology was not the end of it.

"Don't be offended. It's true," he insisted, "particularly in His Majesty's Foreign Service and even more so if one is Catholic. The Protestants look down on us even more if we don't live up to our own standards.

"It's no bed of roses, being Catholic in England," Arthur continued. "In truth, we're descended from very old families, landed families, uncorrupted by the Protestantism spawned by Henry VIII's adultery and Oliver Cromwell's ambition. But prejudice over the centuries has deprived the finest Catholic families of their means. And of course it's not the least amusing to be asked constantly if one is Irish!"

"I'm part Irish." Elizabeth considered that her romantic side.

Arthur ignored her comment. "You might think that His Majesty's Foreign Service would be more sophisticated, since it must deal with foreign cultures, but that only seems to make for more suspicion, treating us as if we were secret agents of the Pope. If you've ever asked yourself why I've not advanced as far as some others, well I'm sorry to say that bigotry plays a part."

Elizabeth looked at him with genuine concern.

"There's a group of us in the Foreign Office, and we look out for one another. But to get ahead, we always have to be better than the others, and never, never make a mistake. My career is spent walking on eggshells.''

"Arthur, I forgive you about the boat, and I don't care about all that.''

"But I must make you understand. When you said the baby was coming in January, I suddenly realized what the others would say. Did you think they would be happy for me as they might in America? Did you think their wives would give you little parties with gifts for the baby—what do you call them?''

"Baby showers.''

"Right. Did you? Well, they wouldn't. My chums would whisper and laugh behind my back. The women would all be counting on their fingers.'' He wiggled each one like he was playing piggy goes to market. " 'Three months premature and over six pounds!' And they'd roll their eyes.''

Elizabeth had to laugh.

"It's not funny!'' Arthur said earnestly. "It's deadly important! The worst thing that can happen in the diplomatic service is to become an object of ridicule. Do you know what a *gaffe* is?''

"It's French for 'mistake.' ''

"Not just a mistake, an *embarrassing* mistake. Englishmen spend their lives desperately avoiding embarrassment. Everyone in Foreign Service lives in dread of the *gaffe*. And not merely for ourselves, oh, no! It's far worse to become an embarrassment to others. My God, my ambassador was at our wedding!''

"People may talk, but are you seriously suggesting that it will be a black mark against you that we made love before we were married?''

Elizabeth's directness made Arthur cringe. "I'm utterly serious. You don't know what scandal means until you've seen the English. . . . ''

"Scandal?'' Elizabeth couldn't believe her ears. "We're married!''

"It's still a scandal! That's how my fellows will see it! And I'll suffer. We'll all suffer! Look at this appalling little house. If I have to leave the service and become a clerk in some miserable business office, this is all I could ever afford. Abroad in the Foreign Service, one gets allowances for decent houses, servants, cars. I joined so that I might live beyond my cla—'' He stopped short of saying "class." Instead, he said "means." He squeezed her hand and stared at her. "I know it's hard for someone so young to understand, but this baby could destroy all that I've built and want for both of us."

"I'm terribly sorry. Is it all my fault?" A sense of dread swept over her.

"Of course not, I'm responsible too. That's why I feel I can ask you." Tears filled his eyes.

"Ask what?" The dread turned to panic.

"We can have more children, but I only have one career."

"What?" she cried.

"I wouldn't ask you to do anything illegal, but miscarriages happen all the time."

"You're talking about our child!"

"We have no choice! You must think of the future. Our whole life together is in jeopardy. So I've made a decision," he said firmly.

"No, no, no." She began to moan and rock from side to side.

"You must get rid of it!"

Chapter 3

Hotel Bar au Lac, Zurich—
October 11, 1932

From his breakfast table at the window of the Rotunda, Captain Gustave Bertrand could see the wind whipping up whitecaps on the lake. That should be to the good, he decided. It would reduce the number of passengers on the excursion boat and hopefully give him an opportunity for a private talk with his German agent "Asche."

Bertrand, a pudgy little man who was head of the decryption unit of French intelligence, known as Section D, had not recruited Asche. And like most of his colleagues, he had been quite suspicious of him at first. Asche was a "walk-in" who had approached a French intelligence officer claiming to work for the Reichswehr Chi-Stelle, the German Army's cryptographic agency. Originally, Section D considered Asche to be a plant, an *agent provocateur*, but in a series of meetings in Holland, Belgium, Denmark, and Czechoslovakia, anywhere Asche could get away for a weekend, he had been turning over secret material of increasing importance.

Thus far, he had supplied documents on the organization of the Chi-Stelle, various military codes including the German Army's code "black," and keys to several ciphers used by the army's signal corps. This meeting would be Asche's most severe test. At their last encounter in Marienbad, Bertrand had insisted that he supply information on the Enigma.

Captain Bertrand patted his lips with his linen napkin and signed the check. He picked up his camera bag and stepped through the polished brass doors into the hotel driveway. Waving away a taxi, he began to walk through the garden toward the lake, leaning against the wind. His watch told him he had less than five minutes until the steamer departed. He should not have taken the time for that second helping of *rosti* potatoes.

Ahead he could see that there was no line at the ticket window on the steamer dock. The ship's whistle gave three sharp blasts, signaling that it was ready to depart. Bertrand broke into a run. Already, the crew was beginning to unwind the hawsers that held the steamship fast to the dock. When the Frenchman reached the ticket window, he found it closed. The crew was starting to draw up the gangplank. Bertrand heaved his corpulent body over the gate and dashed for the ship crying "Stop!" in as many languages as he could remember. The crew hesitated, and in that second he leaped on board, colliding with the purser and almost knocking them both down.

Captain Bertrand apologized, paid his fare, and apologized again. He went to the rail and took several deep breaths to quell the nausea he felt as a result of his exertion. That was quite an arrival scene for a secret agent, he thought angrily to himself. Handling spies was simply not his line of work. He spent his days at a desk breaking codes. Yet if Asche had what they needed on the Enigma, even a heart attack would be worth it.

Twenty minutes later, with the peaks of the Oberland Massif rising in the distance, the lake steamer pulled alongside the pier at Mythenquai. Three passengers waited to board, an older couple with bicycles, and a tall thin man in civilian clothes but with the ramrod posture of a German military officer. Bertrand knew that Asche's real name was Hans-Thilo Schmidt but little else about him. He was deeply curious as to what would cause a man to spy against his own country but had been told by the professional spymasters never to ask that question of an agent.

The ship cast off again. There were less than two dozen passengers when the steamer could have held hundreds. At that midmorning hour, the burghers who used the ship for commuting to the center of Zurich were already in their offices, and it was late in the year for most travelers. Because of the wind, most passengers stayed in the lounge while Bertrand remained at the rail. The steamer was under way for ten minutes before Asche sidled up to him at the rail on the foredeck. They were alone.

"Any sign of being followed?" Bertrand spoke into the wind.

"I doubled back on the tram and walked for an hour in the park. I saw no one except the couple with the bicycles." His voice betrayed impatience for the games that spies play.

"And were you successful in getting what we asked for?"

"I don't think you'll be too disappointed." His diffidence was irritating.

"France is extremely grateful." Bertrand had been told to try to establish a personal relationship with Asche.

"*La France, c'est merde.* France is shit," he responded. "Do you have my money?"

"There is a bank deposit receipt in there." Bertrand glanced over at his camera bag that was sitting on a bench.

Asche passed him an identical one, then went to the bench and opened Bertrand's.

"Don't do that!" the Frenchman hissed.

"And the cash?" Asche demanded.

"After I develop the film. I'll see you at the cathedral at five-thirty."

The steamer was approaching Utoquai where a car would be waiting to take Bertrand to the French consulate. "Where will you be?" he asked.

"Spending the afternoon with several young ladies." Asche smiled for the first time.

Bertrand shook his head as he disembarked. Only a German, he thought, would find Swiss prostitutes amusing.

As he stood in the eerie red light of the consulate darkroom, Bertrand could feel his disappointment grow. The first roll of film provided keys to the manual ciphers used between military and civil authorities. The second consisted of ciphers used by the railway police. The third set of prints were more valuable, providing the German armed forces "B" and "D" codes. But suddenly Captain Bertrand became excited as the prints from roll four swam into focus in the developing tray.

The first set of pictures were labeled *Gebrauchsanweisung, H. Dv. g. 13*, and *L. Dv. 13*. They were the operating instructions for the Enigma! The next set comprised the keying instructions and a monthly table of army Enigma keys starting back in December 1931, and continuing through 1932, 1933, and into the first six months of 1934! The final roll of film produced an Enigma enciphered text with the corresponding plain text. It was a coup of the first rank! He would be a hero in his service! All he needed now to break the codes were the plans to the Enigma machine. And Asche could obviously get them for him.

The Grossmunster Cathedral sat on a hill on the right bank of the Limat River, not far from where it emptied out of the Zürichsee. As a French Catholic, Bertrand had never been inside a Protestant church and was reassured by the sight of a statue of Charlemagne sitting atop the south tower. Once inside, he looked about for water to bless himself and found none. Otherwise it looked like any other Gothic cathedral except that some bizarre modern stained glass was being installed in the windows.

There were few worshipers and Bertrand easily picked out Asche sitting halfway down the central aisle. He stopped at his pew and genuflected before sliding in next to him.

"You don't do that in a Protestant church," Asche whispered. After a moment, he added, "Were you satisfied?"

"It was a good start." Bertrand concealed his excitement.

"I want my bonus."

"I'm giving you half in cash." He passed over a leather pouch. "A thousand Swiss francs. The rest is on deposit." The most difficult problem with agents was their tendency to start throwing around their money wildly, calling attention to themselves.

"You don't need to worry about me," Asche said as if he could read Bertrand's thoughts. "I'm hiding the cash, not spending it."

"What for?"

"Terrible times lie ahead in Germany. You should know that. Hitler could win a majority in the next election."

"Will the army support him?"

"Most military men are just happy to be employed. But everyone complains that the politicians in Weimar give us no direction. They want to take orders. Most of the officers I know will vote for Hitler and his hooligans."

"And you?"

The pews were filling up for the six o'clock service. It was becoming more difficult to talk.

"Hitler means war," Asche sighed. "I've had enough of it. I'm preparing my own alternatives. That's why I want more cash."

Bertrand looked around quickly and dropped his voice to a whisper. "I can promise you much more if you can get me one thing."

"You want the plans to the new Enigma." He smiled with no trace of amusement.

"Yes," said Bertrand, slightly surprised. "There must be schematics, drawings, repair manuals, something of the sort at your headquarters."

"There are. In the commandant's safe. But I cannot get them. He would be instantly suspicious."

"Why is that?"

The answer, and his tone of voice, told Bertrand all he needed to know about Asche's motives.

"Because the commandant is my brother."

Bignor—
September 1935

As a child, dreams were the place where Elizabeth could hide from the pains and hurts of everyday life. Now, life itself was like a dream, but a bizarre and terrible one. The English days were unusually clear and sunny. They were filled with the sights and smells of the harvest: men moving slowly through the fields with their hand scythes, hay being heaped up in the meadows, women working through the orchards pulling down the apples, children gathering the last of the blackberries from the tangles along the roadside, and by the river, anglers drawing to shore the silvery salmon caught returning from the sea to spawn.

Elizabeth held fast to those images, trying to blot out the reality of what she was doing every day, riding hard across country, leaping ditches and stone fences, deliberately cantering like a beginner until she thought her bones would break. And when the truth forced its way through, as it often did, she fell back on blaming herself. She had let it happen. She had taken no precautions. She was the bad one.

Elizabeth knew the moment that she had become pregnant by Arthur. Her mother had arranged for them to go to a house party at the British embassy lodge in the Shenandoah. A freak spring snowstorm, however, kept the others away, leaving them stranded and without power in the huge summer house that was not insulated against the cold. Elizabeth built a tent of bedsheets to trap the heat from the fireplace while Arthur searched for food. All he came back with was a couple of bottles of 100-proof Scotch, one of which Elizabeth used to start a small blaze in the hearth; the other they drank to keep warm.

It was Elizabeth's suggestion that they take off their wet clothes. Their luggage was in the trunk of Arthur's Hudson Terriplane where it had slid off the road a half mile away. Clad in her underwear, Elizabeth had crawled into the tent next to Arthur, who, out of a sense of decorum, insisted on wearing his waistcoat and tie even though he had removed his pants. Warmed by the whiskey, she snuggled in his arms and began to fall asleep. Then, without warning, Arthur was on top of her yanking up her slip and pulling down her brassiere. He had hardly ever kissed her before!

"Arthur, no. . . . " She had started to struggle.

He tore her pants away.

Elizabeth became very calm. She could fight him, kick him, bite him. Or she could envelope him, smother him, steal his strength. When he forced himself between her legs, she had remembered thinking, Mother, is this what you wanted?

He plunged inside. Pain shot through her. He seemed desperate. And just as suddenly, released.

Elizabeth saw him gasp then shut his eyes, his power gone, overwhelmed with guilt. He tried to pull away, but she held on tightly with thighs now soaking wet. Finally, she rolled over on top of him, staring into his face.

It was full of shame and bewilderment. Tears gathered in his eyes and ran down his cheeks. In that moment, her pain at being violated was suddenly transformed. She'd found a new power. She made Arthur, of all people, lose control. He looked so humiliated she was moved to comfort him. She bent down and tenderly kissed his tears away. Never had she felt so close to anyone.

By the following morning she had persuaded herself that she must be in love with him. The next week, she agreed to be married. As the wedding approached three months later, jittery doubts began to arise in her mind, but she sternly suppressed them. And when she discovered that she was pregnant, Elizabeth rejected the troubling thought that her feelings for Arthur were merely the afterglow of conception. Now, she was imprisoned in a cycle of denial and self-justification. Through sacrifice she would convince herself that her marriage was no mistake. She would prove her love for Arthur by betraying her unborn child. So each day Elizabeth would ride until her horse nearly collapsed and she thought her insides would fall out.

It didn't work.

In early September, Arthur was called into the Foreign Office to plan for economic sanctions against Italy in the event Mussolini invaded Ethiopia. Each morning before he drove to the nearby train station for the commute to London, he left Elizabeth with instructions on her daily regimen. Growing increasingly anxious, he had added bicycle riding, jumping off walls and dips in the river, to the ordeal on horseback. At night, when he returned, came the interrogation. How many miles had she pedaled? How far had she cantered? How long a gallop? How had her body reacted to the icy water?

It still didn't work.

At the outset, she had begged to go back to America to have the baby. No one in England would know when the child was born. Arthur refused, claiming that everyone in Washington, including his colleagues at the embassy, would know. His real reason came out later; the passage, he said one night when drunk, "would cost a fortune."

Once a week, he would become maudlin with too much port and, through tears, beg her forgiveness. He would sob that it was all for her benefit. He was only insisting out of love for her. And the next morning, he invariably demanded that she push on.

Nothing worked, and she was glad. It seemed like the baby wanted her, and she wanted the baby. Elizabeth could feel the swelling in her abdomen. Running her hands over her body, she would sometimes stand in front of the mirror and examine how the veins were beginning to show through her growing breasts, and how the nipples were changing, and how the skin all over her body seemed to glow. She would feel joy and an awful vulnerability at the same time.

A few weeks after he started going to London, Elizabeth had begun to cheat by staying in bed. At first she told herself it was because of the pain. She would lie in bed most of the day, her womb aching, while Mrs. Willet brought her lunch and tea, looking concerned and perplexed but never invading her privacy.

Then she progressed to a deliberate and quiet rebellion. She had the groom ride the horse. She soaked her bathing suit in the sink. She even went so far as to give her bicycle flat tires—pinching the inner tubes with a pliers to make Arthur think that they had been cut by the rim on a rough road.

But she was unable to confront him directly. So weekends Elizabeth could not avoid the pounding of riding and jumping and the shock of freezing cold plunges in the river.

On Monday she would be back in bed and overwhelmed by loneliness. Her terrible secret kept her from reaching out to others who might help. What would Mrs. Willet and the villagers say if they knew what she was doing?

She thought of writing to her mother, but it was too humiliating. Besides, what would her mother say? Tell her to be practical. Probably agree with Arthur! No, she would rather not know her mother's advice.

She even thought of trying to contact Arthur's parents. But she'd never even met them. What would they do? Forgive him most likely. Furtive fantasies of Antonio de Zaragoza coming to her rescue, carrying her away to his castle in Spain, aggravated her sense that she deserved to be pun-

ished. So loneliness became her only close companion, and
her life a frightening and horrible dream from which she
felt she could not awake.

One rainy Saturday in October, Elizabeth gained a re-
prieve. To Arthur's surprise, they had received an invitation
to a dinner that evening at the country home of Harold
Nicolson and Vita Sackville-West, whom she had met on
the boat. Arthur felt put out that Elizabeth had attracted the
attentions of such socially and politically prominent people,
but he could hardly refuse their hospitality.

The drive to Sissinghurst took more than two hours over
narrow, winding roads through Piltdown and across the
Weald. Cramped in the front seat and afraid to move so as
to not wrinkle her full skirt, Elizabeth began to feel worse
than if she had been riding a horse. When they arrived at
their destination, she could barely stand up straight, but
having escaped Bignor, she was determined to make the most
of the evening.

Sissinghurst proved to be a restored castle with a brick
tower crowned by two cupolas rising from a central courtyard. The butler showed them into a drawing room with a
high vaulted ceiling where a baronial fireplace was ablaze
with huge logs and the cocktail hour well under way. Vita
Sackville-West appeared immediately to greet them. In her
early forties, Vita had the fine skin and delicate features of
a poetess, but the deliberately languid posture of the English aristocracy.

"How good of you to come on such short notice," she
said, seizing Elizabeth's hand and ignoring Arthur.

"We're quite honored by the invitation," he said stiffly.

"Let's get you some cocktails," Vita responded. "We're
all consuming these deadly tequilla stingers. It's a cactus
whiskey we discovered on our recent trip to Mexico. Then,
if the rain has stopped, I want to show Elizabeth my gardens while there's still a touch of light in the sky."

They left Arthur standing with a glass in his hand outside
a circle of men who were discussing the day's hunting.

"I've tried to make each garden like a room of the
house," Vita explained as she and Elizabeth stepped out-

side. There was a chill mist and she called for the butler to bring them shawls.

"This is the White Garden. It was quite literally a refuse dump only five years ago."

In the twilight, Elizabeth could see that it had been planted with a variety of white chrysanthemums.

"Each of my 'rooms' have flowers of a different color. The hedges will grow up to enclose the space. In fine weather, we live out here in a sort of roofless existence."

"That must be very seldom," Elizabeth could not help saying.

Vita laughed. "I see you're already familiar with English weather."

As they walked through the other gardens, Vita took Elizabeth's elbow. For the first time in months, she felt safe, and as Vita continued chatting, it required all of Elizabeth's self-control to keep from breaking down and throwing herself into her hostess's arms.

Suddenly, Vita paused and stared intently at Elizabeth. "Do you mind if I ask you a personal question? Normally, I wouldn't, but Americans don't seem to mind."

"Go ahead." Elizabeth tried to sound casual.

"What is it like, marrying a man so much older than yourself? How does your husband treat you?"

Elizabeth was taken aback. Did she know? Could she tell? "He treats me fine," she said defensively.

"It's just that Englishmen like your husband," she persisted, "can be very set in their ways. A young lady of my acquaintance married just such a gentleman. Right on their honeymoon he wanted to start coordinating their schedules. He told her that on Monday and Wednesday night, he always went to his club. And on Tuesday he attended evening lectures of the Ornithological Society. Thursday evening was set aside for business dinners with his solicitors and bankers, and Friday he liked to get away early to the country to dine with his fellows at the Hunt."

My God, was Vita telling her a joke? Elizabeth felt relieved.

"Now this gentleman considered himself very modern, and so he acknowledged that his new bride might have a

schedule of her own. 'Do tell me your plans,' he said after
his little presentation.

"'Well, they're really very simple,' she replied. 'At ten
o'clock each evening, I'm going to be in bed making
love—whether you're there or not!'"

Elizabeth burst out laughing. It had been so long she
found it hard to stop. Vita smiled back at her. "I want you
to know"—she took Elizabeth's arm firmly—"if that
should happen with Arthur, you can always come to me."

Before Elizabeth could fathom what she meant, dinner
was announced, and the other guests began trooping across
the courtyard to what Vita called the Priest's House. They
entered a gallery set with a long table. The candlelight
glinting off the silver was almost blinding.

To her surprise, she had a seat of honor near the center
of the table across from Vita, while Arthur was placed
down at the end below the salt. The meal was sumptuous,
and Elizabeth devoured everything in sight: the oysters, the
oxtail soup, the turbot, the champagne ice, the venison, the
potato croquettes, the green salad, the chocolate-covered
profiteroles, and several glasses of white burgundy and
claret.

Conversation with the gentlemen on either side of her
was not required. The member of Parliament to her left and
the earl of "Somethingshire" on her right entertained themselves by talking through her about the day's shooting, last
week's shooting, last year's shooting—paying her occasional notice only by glancing down her décolletage.

With the last course, the conversation turned more serious and inclusive. Addressing a cherubic-looking man next
to Vita, Harold Nicolson asked him to comment on recent
articles by an American journalist sitting farther down the
table, who had reported that in a new war with Germany,
Britain would surely face defeat.

The round-faced gentleman had been largely silent during dinner. He blinked slowly several times, and to the
evident surprise of most of the guests replied, "It may well
be true." He then picked up an unlit cigar and began to
stab the air for emphasis.

"It may well be true," he began again in a formal and
declaratory manner, "that this country will, at the outset of

this almost inevitable war, be exposed to dire peril and fierce ordeals. It may be true that steel and fire will rain down upon us day and night, scattering death and destruction far and wide. It may be true that our sea communications will be imperiled and our food supplies placed in jeopardy. Yet these trials and disasters will but serve to steel the resolution of the British people and enhance our will for victory."

Elizabeth nudged her companion from Parliament to ask who the speaker was.

"Old Winston," he said in a bored tone. "Winston Churchill."

"No, the gentleman of the American press should not have used that dreadful word defeat." Churchill aimed his cigar at the journalist. "Yet supposing that you were correct in this tragic utterance. It will then be for you, for the Americans, to preserve the great heritage of the English-speaking peoples. Nor should I die happy, were I not convinced that if we in this dear, dear island succumb to the ferocity and might of our enemies, over there in your distant and immense continent, the torch of liberty will burn untarnished and—I trust and hope—undismayed."

There were a few polite "Hear! Hear!"'s, but mostly coughs and silence. Elizabeth felt very moved. She had an urge to stand up and say, you can count on us, but realized that this would mortify Arthur. As the general conversation started to pick up again, her companion from Parliament said, "Such an old windbag and warmonger. I don't see why Harold and Vita put up with him."

On the long drive home, Elizabeth told Arthur that she had had a wonderful time. He responded by saying, "Yes, I noticed that you talked with everyone." She had seen him standing around in an embarrassed silence most of the evening.

By the time they reached Bignor, Elizabeth again felt cramped and sick. Arthur had to help her out of the car, and she was grateful to sink into her feather bed. As they turned out the light, Elizabeth mentioned that she might have found a friend in Vita Sackville-West.

Arthur snorted. "Of course she likes you. She's a notorious lesbian."

"You're joking!"

"Do you know Virginia Woolf?"

"The novelist?"

"They were lovers for years, still are for all I know."

"What about Vita's husband?"

"Harold? He's a famous poof."

Elizabeth lay silent for a while, pains shooting through her abdomen. "All that scandal," she said finally, "doesn't seem to have hurt them any. He told me he's standing for Parliament."

Arthur sat up. "You don't understand." There was anger and bitterness in his voice. "They're upper-class. They can do anything they want."

The next day, Sunday, was Elizabeth's birthday, and Arthur proposed a picnic. He dressed in corduroy pants and a tweed jacket and she put on a heavy sweater and a wool skirt. She was still in pain but decided an outing would do her good; whereupon Arthur drove the Anglia as fast as he could over the stony and rutted remains of an ancient Roman road that ran by Bignor. The car bumped and bottomed so hard that Elizabeth had to press her hands against the roof to keep from banging her head.

"For God's sake, Arthur," she finally shouted, "you're going to destroy the car!"

Their destination was an archaeological dig where a first-century Roman villa was being unearthed on a nearby hill. When she had been riding, Elizabeth had often stopped there to rest. From the archaeology students, she had learned that Bignor's peculiar Mediterranean look came from the stones of the villa, which over the millennia, the townspeople had taken to build their houses. The villa itself covered several acres, its outlines now marked by stakes in the ground connected by twine.

They carried the picnic baskets to Elizabeth's favorite spot, a large mosaic tile floor with the figure of a dancer. The students thought it was Terpsichore, the muse of dance.

While Arthur spread the blanket, Elizabeth took in the panoramic view of the golden valley and the ocher autumn hillsides. The silver band of the Arun River glinted in the distance. She could smell the chimney smoke that curled up from the wooded village. It all seemed so gentle and soothing, momentarily easing the pain she felt in her legs from the climb and the persistent ache that seemed to come from her soul. Despite her trials, Elizabeth realized that she had come to love this English landscape. She had the strange feeling that something here had protected her and her baby. Perhaps the power of Hermes, who once guarded wayfarers on the Roman road to Londinium, still safe-guarded fools like her who were merely passing through.

She looked down at the mosaic of the young girl in her long pink gown, turning with her arms upraised in a classic arabesque. The pain in Elizabeth's legs had returned and now spread to her belly and her back. Was the dancer Terp-sichore or a favorite slave girl in the service of the Roman viceroy? Elizabeth began to feel light-headed and feverish. She imagined being a slave at the villa in the court of the King Cogidubnus: free only when she danced, only when her robes flowed around her as she turned ever faster to escape the cruelty of the world, a world that was spinning and spinning and spinning. . . .

Elizabeth collapsed. Rushing to her, Arthur looked down to see the blood staining her skirt and spreading slowly onto the mosaic floor.

Chapter 4

Captain Bertrand adjusted his cap and collar for the tenth time, as he sat waiting outside the second-floor conference room. They should have called him in by now. Senior members of the Army Council were reviewing the budget of the Intelligence Service and in particular his proposals for the exploitation of the Enigma materials. Bertrand's unease was magnified by the knowledge that not one of them, including the head of his own service, knew a damn thing about cryptography. He had even once heard the Army Chief of Staff, General Gamelin, remark that reading the enemy's messages was somehow not *galant*.

The large double doors opened up, and an orderly signaled Bertrand to enter. He tucked his cap under his arm and mentally ran through the key points in his presentation. Modern warfare would involve coordinating aircraft, infantry, and tanks in fast-moving operations. That could only be done by radio and the enormous volume of messages would have to be encrypted by machine. The Germans understood that, hence the Enigma. In response, France should create a specialized Radio Intelligence Service and, with the help of the materials from Asche, make a major effort to break the Enigma.

Bertrand anxiously stepped into the former music salon of the eighteenth-century château that served as Intelligence Headquarters. In deference to its serious current purpose,

38

all the rococo moldings and boiserie had been painted army green. Bertrand found himself confronting Marshal Pétain, and three generals—Weygand, Gamelin, Dufieux—and Colonel Bouffre, who was the chief of intelligence. They sat at separate Louis XV desks arranged in a crescent with a single armchair facing them. After saluting, Bertrand was directed to sit in the chair.

As the officer in charge, General Weygand spoke first.

"We have been discussing your proposal to create a special Radio Intelligence Service to try to break the German Enigma machine"—he shuffled through some papers—"at a cost of thirty million francs annually."

"The two ideas do not necessarily have to go together," added Colonel Bouffre.

Bertrand could feel the ground being carved out from under him by his own chief of service. "With all due respect," Bertrand ventured, "the scale of the effort must be such that a dedicated organization would seem appropriate."

"I was coming to that." Weygand's tone reprimanded Bertrand for speaking without being asked. "Is it so that the materials you have received from this agent are not sufficient to break the Enigma?"

"If we had an actual Enigma machine, yes. But we do not, so we must reconstruct one."

"Can that be done?" General Gamelin asked. He was an artillery officer with a reputation for a mind as subtle as a canister of grapeshot.

"It will require very intense work. We shall need the finest mathematicians, and there will be considerable trial and error."

"But can it be done?" Weygand insisted.

"Some consider the Enigma unbreakable," Bertrand admitted. "I do not. But there are no guarantees. . . ."

"So we could spend thirty million francs for nothing," said General Gamelin, "while my men are short of cannons."

"Why not simply steal one from the Germans?" asked General Dufieux. He pushed a Sobraine into his cigarette holder and lit it.

"Their physical security is formidable," Bertrand noted.

"But not, I trust, beyond the capacity of our secret services." General Dufieux pointed his question at Colonel Bouffre.

"Certainly," he replied stiffly.

Bertrand wondered what his chief had in mind. Asche was their only good German agent, and he had refused further help on the Enigma.

"But there are, of course, risks," the intelligence chief added.

Marshal Pétain nodded his agreement. "We do not need an embarrassing incident with the Germans"—he spoke for the first time—"that could strengthen the hand of Adolf Hitler."

"Hitler is a crackpot," Weygand declared. "The Germans may be a warlike race, but they are too sensible to make him their leader."

"I fail to see the point of this Enigma *folie*," General Gamelin insisted. "The Maginot Line will be impregnable. What do we care what the Germans plan to do? Military science is making intelligence irrelevant!"

"Intelligence insures against the unexpected," Colonel Bouffre declared.

"But do we need another thirty million francs of insurance?" asked General Gamelin.

"It's not even insurance," added General Dufieux, "it's a gamble."

General Weygand nodded his head. "If you wish to start a special Radio Service within your existing budget, fine. But no more monies."

"We cannot exploit the Enigma without additional resources," Bertrand protested. He could not believe that they could be so foolish. "Perhaps you would permit me to work out joint funding with the British?"

A series of frowns swept across the faces of his superiors.

"What do we know of their efforts in this field?" asked Weygand.

Colonel Bouffre replied, "They assume the Enigma is unbreakable."

"It doesn't sound like they'd make much of a contribution," Weygand said.

"If I know the English," remarked General Dufieux, "they'll be going through our pockets before they're done."

Bertrand found this discussion incredible. His great coup was going to come to nothing!

"Gentlemen!" he risked speaking out again. "Perhaps I could at least share the Enigma material with the Poles. They must be concerned with the Germans."

"With the Poles?" Weygand sniffed.

"Why not," said Marshal Pétain. "They might be stupid enough to give us something in return!"

And they all laughed heartily at the marshal's joke.

Wellbeck Maternity Hospital, London— October 2, 1935

Wellbeck Street housed the offices and clinics of the second tier of the London medical profession. Number 27, where Arthur rushed Elizabeth on October 2, was a narrow four-story town house with a crisp white plaster facade that had been converted into the Wellbeck Maternity Hospital.

After her collapse, Elizabeth had awakened in her own bed in the cottage with Mrs. Willet hovering over her.

"Have I . . . Did I . . . ?" Elizabeth could not bear to say it.

"I don't think so," the older woman had said. "I've had a few miscarriages myself."

The next morning, her fever had increased, and Arthur brought Elizabeth with him on the train to London. When they arrived at Wellbeck Street, she was bleeding intermittently and could barely climb the three stairs to the front door. A battery of doctors took turns examining her as she lay with her feet stuck up in stirrups. The pains were so great that she felt no embarrassment.

Afterward, the head of the clinic talked to Elizabeth alone in his office. Dr. MacCall was a fine-featured, sandy-haired man of fifty with a soft Scots voice. She was resting on a sofa next to the fireplace.

"Before I talk to your husband," he said coming out from behind his desk, "I wanted to hear from you what's been going on with this pregnancy."

Slowly, the tears formed in Elizabeth's eyes. He gently put his hand on her shoulder. That was all it took for Elizabeth to confess everything.

Dr. MacCall invited Arthur to join them. Elizabeth could not look at him. She focused instead on the electric fire in the grate.

"You've got to stop it," the doctor said without bothering to explain what he was talking about. "If you don't, you'll have a death on your conscience."

"There's a danger of losing the baby?" Arthur asked coolly.

"Aye," Dr. MacCall replied, "and your wife too."

"Surely you exaggerate."

"If you're such a fool then, I'm keeping her here until, God grant, the baby comes. You'd do well to light a candle, or whatever you people do, to pray for the both of them." He fixed Arthur with an angry stare. "And light one for your own soul while you're at it!"

In later years, Elizabeth would often think that this time was the happiest of her life. She felt safe and secure, well taken care of by the nurses and protected by Dr. MacCall. Even as she was on the verge of becoming a woman in the fullest sense, she allowed herself the luxury of being a child again.

Not that she failed to worry about the health of the baby and the risk to herself. Dr. MacCall had told her frankly that the baby could be born dead. If the baby lived, it could be deformed. And she could die in labor. Still, she often felt inexplicably serene. She would hug her stomach at the mystery of another life growing inside her body. As a girl, in Sunday school, she could never comprehend the concept of duality—that God was both spirit and flesh, that Jesus was man and God. But now she instinctively understood: She was one; she was two.

The unborn child had become her friend. No matter how pointless and cruel life might seem, the struggling life inside her stomach gave her days a purpose and drove away the sense of isolation that had haunted her as long as she could remember. Once when she was a child, Elizabeth had told her mother about those feelings. Her response had shut off all discussion. "It's natural," Cora declared. "We're a military family and we move a lot." But when the baby was born, Elizabeth would never be lonely again.

She spent much of her time poring over newspapers and magazines. Elizabeth loved the fact that *The Times*, the most prestigious paper in the world, devoted its entire front page to classified ads. She clipped out several gems:

Unwanted false teeth urgently needed. . . .

Nervous horsewoman wanted for magnificent mare. . . .

She also collected recipes for the latest fads in cooking such as tournedos Rossini and beef Wellington, and kept advertisements for household equipment and baby paraphernalia. One extolled the benefits of Bengers Food, a nursing supplement that could be mixed with milk—and as the ad said, "give the breast a rest." Another was for "Caradium." Her mother had told her stories about women who went gray overnight from childbirth. This product offered an answer:

RADIUM VS. GREY HAIR

Regrows the original color straight from the roots quickly and safely. Prepared with wonderful Radioactive water, Caradium gives a new lease on life.

Arthur's dismay and obvious unhappiness that her pregnancy might come to term cast a cloud on the future. He continued to insist, for example, on keeping the baby a secret. "What if something should happen to it," he would say. "I don't want anyone's pity."

As a result, Elizabeth had few visitors. Mrs. Willet came only once, just before Christmas, armed with a homemade fruitcake made not only from unrecognizable nuts and berries, but seemingly the twigs and branches they had grown upon. To Elizabeth's delight she stayed the whole afternoon describing all the events that had befallen the horses, dogs, cats, plants, and only incidentally the people of Bignor.

She finally met Arthur's parents. Arriving by bus from London's southern suburbs, they proved to be anything but the sophisticated people who might look down on her that she had feared. Arthur's father was a wraithlike man who had retired from the postal service and spent his time building model train layouts. He was particularly keen that the baby should have one of the new Lionel sets with locomotives that puffed smoke. Arthur's mother called on her twice a week. Short and stocky like Arthur, she spent most of her time talking about her work with the Amphibian Society, a group devoted to persuading the highway authorities to bury pipes under the roads so that frogs could cross them safely. Her visits invariably climaxed with a plea to have the baby immediately baptized Catholic so that if it died, it would not have to spend eternity in limbo.

Elizabeth's mother proved to be a poor correspondent. She said she was pleased for Elizabeth, but her true feelings came out in one of her infrequent letters: "Rather than call me grandmother," she wrote only half in jest, "perhaps the child could be trained to address me as 'Countess.'"

George Thorpe sent two letters: The first worried that the child might grow up a stateless "Foreign Service brat" with no sense of patriotism. His second letter addressed the "boy's" education. "I fear that you might send him to one of those English schools where they beat them with a cane so often that they get to like it. A lot of other unspeakable things go on at such places too," he warned.

Elizabeth was not too impressed with British education herself, particularly when she read the pledge by students at Oxford and Cambridge never to fight in any war, even if England were to be attacked. She read Churchill's columns in the *Evening Standard* religiously, as well as the *Daily Mail,* which blasted Churchill for criticizing the Nazi rearmament program in terms that "unnecessarily irritate the Führer."

Elizabeth found the news from Germany appalling. Hitler, in power for two years, had recently reinstituted beheadings, and two women accused of being communists were the first victims. Alfred Rosenberg, the Nazi ideologist, had proclaimed Easter a day to worship the Teutonic gods Thor and Woden. Catholic priests, Protestant ministers, Jews, and socialists were being rounded up and placed in "concentration camps" for their own "safety."

She discovered it was no use trying to talk to Arthur about these things. "The Bolsheviks are the problem, not the Nazis," Arthur insisted, echoing the prime minister. "Hitler's helping to keep the Reds in line."

Arthur had moved from Bignor into the Union Jack Club near Waterloo Station, and came by every evening after work. Mostly he sat in silence, as if his duty was simply to put in a specific amount of time at her bedside. Once, Elizabeth asked Arthur to put his hand on her stomach so that he could feel the baby kicking. He seemed so uncomfortable and reluctant that she never asked him to do it again.

Although she spent most of her time in bed, Elizabeth was not really bedridden. The bleeding had stopped after a few weeks, and for a couple of hours in the afternoon she would be allowed to take the tiny elevator to the solarium on the top floor. There she worked on a scrapbook of pictures cut out of the *London Illustrated News:* photos of faraway and romantic places; the Tonga Islands; the Indian Raj; Tanganyika and British East Africa. She had a special section on Spain, and as she glued in the pictures of bullfights and the boulevards of Madrid she could not help thinking of Antonio de Zaragoza.

They had met only briefly in Washington shortly before her engagement to Arthur. He was an assistant air attaché at the Spanish embassy, tall with straight dark hair and a fine mustache under an aquiline nose and bright hazel eyes. She had noticed Antonio at several gatherings of the Young Diplomats Circle but they had never spoken until the night of the Junior Bachelors' Cotillion at the Willard Hotel.

The evening had grown hot and muggy, and someone had opened the French doors onto the balconies that overlooked Fourteenth Street. Most of the chaperons were sitting in a line of gilded chairs as far from the bandstand as possible. Without the music as a solvent, the boys and girls had again divided into clusters according to gender. Arthur, her escort, was at the bar where he seemed to be fortifying himself with another Scotch.

Elizabeth took a cup of punch and drifted out onto one

of the balconies. The night had a stillness that anticipated a spring thunderstorm. The streets were dark and largely empty except for an occasional automobile or pushcart. Elizabeth remembered feeling a strange sense of anticipation. She had attended dozens of dances since her debut, why should this one be different? I'm on the brink, she recalled thinking to herself, waiting for something to happen to my life. I want someone to give it shape and form. Like Fioretta, the heroine she had invented in a novel that she had written and that had been published when she was only eleven years old. A motherless waif, Fioretta supported her poor father by singing for coins in the streets of Naples. One day in the Piazza de Martiri, she was discovered by the great Scarlatti, who made her an opera star!

"O Cessate di piagarmi!" Elizabeth had sung softly to herself like Fioretta bidding good-bye to Naples in the final scene of her story. "O will you cease to love me!"

I had more gumption then than I do now, Elizabeth thought helplessly. It's ridiculous. I can do whatever I want. But what? I've been bred to wait. To be ready, never to act. She always had thought herself different from the other girls, but was she? Weren't we all waiting for a man to come along and change our lives?

The music had started up again and Elizabeth watched the other girls gliding happily onto the dance floor. No, she *was* different. Most of them were waiting for someone to come along who wouldn't change their lives.

"Please continue. I enjoyed your singing."

Her chest had contracted. Antonio de Zaragoza stood on the next balcony smoking a cigarette.

"That was Scarlatti, no?" he tried again, exhaling blue smoke.

"Yes." In the ensuing silence she desperately searched for something else to say. "It's so close tonight."

He nodded as if he too found speaking difficult. The music drifted out from the ballroom, and she could feel him looking at her.

"Could I have a cigarette?" she finally managed, glancing over her shoulder to make sure her mother could not see her.

"But of course." He quickly opened a gold case and

held it out to her. She leaned across the space between the two balconies but could not reach it. "So sorry, señorita. I will come around."

"No! I'll lose you to one of the others," she said impulsively, then sensed herself growing red. Even in the shadows, she could see his eyes brighten.

"Then I will fly to your side," and he leapt up onto the stone railing.

"No, it's too far!"

He stood poised for a moment, then holding his arms out for balance, vaulted across the gap that separated them, landing gently on the two-foot-wide balustrade.

Before he could jump down, Elizabeth cried, "Wait!" She hoisted herself onto it, swung her feet around and held out her arms. He swept her up. To the refrain of "Night and Day," they twirled along the balustrade, her dress billowing, his tails flying. Down below, a fruit peddler pushing his cart home, stopped and let out a whistle. A passing car honked its horn. Elizabeth was lost in a dream as Antonio whirled her around. He told her of flying by night across the Spanish Sahara, and with her eyes closed, the glinting motes of light reflected from the ballroom's crystal chandeliers became stars in a desert sky. His voice vibrated through her body like the hum of an engine. She felt transported, lifted by the power of his arms, his strength guiding her toward an unknown destination. . . .

"You are intoxicating me," he whispered in her ear. "I cannot fly in this condition." Seizing her by the waist he leaped to the floor of the balcony, holding her aloft then slowly drawing her down. He pulled her close, and she let herself brush against his body in a way never allowed at cotillions.

His medals pressed against her breasts. His smile gleamed in the light from the ballroom. She felt ready to be kidnapped, to be bundled into a carriage and taken through the night to his castle. Touching the floor, she arched her back, stretching onto her toes, her heels coming out of her pumps. As their lips came together, she opened her mouth so she could taste him, devour him as she wanted to be devoured.

Abruptly, he stepped back.

"We must not do that, Miss Thorpe."

She turned away, mortified. "You must think I'm a tramp."

"No, I am the one who is wrong. I let my feelings get the better of me."

She raised her hand to his cheek to comfort him, but he seized hold of it.

"You must understand, I am married."

Everything seemed to stop, the music, the dancing, the chatter, her heart. She pulled her hand back and dashed into the ballroom.

That was also the night that Arthur had first asked her to marry him.

On Christmas Day, Arthur joined Elizabeth in her room for a hospital dinner of goose and bread pudding. The next afternoon, Boxing Day, his parents came for an exchange of gifts. The Packs, looking more stiff than usual, surprised Elizabeth by giving nothing but a sterling silver rattle for the baby. She had hoped for baby clothes, a bassinet, and a bottle sterilizer. Arthur gave her an utterly peculiar present—a swimsuit. New Year's Eve, he arrived with a bottle of champagne. The nurse said she could have one glass. Arthur finished the bottle and went back to his club before midnight.

As the time for the birth approached, Elizabeth's condition turned ominous. Her spotting started up again, and she was stabbed by occasional contractions. Dr. MacCall's professional demeanor could not mask his concern. He moved Elizabeth to a ward near the delivery room so that the nurses could keep a closer watch over her.

After the isolation of her own room, she enjoyed the company of the other women. They joked about what was happening to their bodies. Those who had given birth before urged Elizabeth to rub her breasts and belly with cocoa butter to avoid stretch marks. "You've got a beautiful pair now, dear," one of them warned, "but you could wind up lookin' like me. I've got a couple of fried eggs that I have to roll up to put in me brassiere."

Strangely, the women who had given birth before seemed quite vague about the pain involved. Either they could not remember or did not want to talk about it. Elizabeth thought that there must be some mechanism of the mind that made them forget. Only one patient in the ward was candid. "Dearie," she said, "it's like passing a watermelon, and it hurts like hell!"

On the afternoon of January 19, the spasms began in earnest. At first they seemed like severe menstrual cramps. Soon, they proceeded to a feeling of hot needles piercing her insides and from there to medieval torture. If she closed her eyes, Elizabeth envisioned some hideous iron apparatus gripping her about the stomach and bolted to a hot metal probe thrust up her vagina, the two parts alternately crushing and stabbing her insides. Between bouts of pain, she desperately wondered how the baby could survive it.

Then came humiliation. Two nurses arrived at her bedside with a pan of water. With everyone in the ward looking on, and the nurses chatting about their boyfriends, one spread her legs, while the other shaved her. Presently, her water broke, sending the nurses scurrying for more towels, which she had to hold between her legs as she was hoisted onto a gurney. As she was wheeled toward the delivery room, she saw Arthur, ashen-faced but trying to smile. She thought she heard him say, "Cheerio!"

Then everything became more fragmented and frightening. Waves of contractions piled one upon the other in a storm of pain. Her feet were pulled up into stirrups. Huge lights blinded her eyes. Dr. MacCall loomed over her.

"What's wrong?" she gasped. She couldn't understand his answer. Was the baby stuck? Was it coming out backward or sideways? Would they have to operate? She felt delirious with the pain. "Help me," she groaned as the anesthetist's mask closed over her face.

She did not know what had happened. She did not know where she was. The pain was gone. After a while, Elizabeth was aware of being in a room with others, some moving about, some lying on cots as she was.

"Nurse," she called out weakly. "Nurse."

"How are you feeling, Mrs. Pack?" A ruddy-faced woman bent over her.

"The baby . . ." She struggled with the words.

"It's a boy. Seven pounds, two ounces."

She reached down and touched her stomach. It was gone!

"Is it all right?" she murmured, already drifting back into sleep.

Elizabeth woke up a few hours later. She was back in her room.

"My baby! My baby!" she cried.

A nurse took a little bundle out of a canvas basket attached to the foot of her bed and gave it to her. Elizabeth immediately began to unwrap him, counting his fingers and toes, inspecting every part. She found an ugly red mark on the back of his head.

"What's this?"

"The little fella did na' want to leave. They had to drag him out with forceps. It's only a bruise," the nurse assured her. "He's a fine baby!"

Tears came to her eyes. He wasn't deformed or damaged! He was all right! It seemed miraculous!

Looking at him, Elizabeth had the amazing sensation that she had divided into two parts. But she had not merely replicated herself like the protozoa in the science films at school. The great mystery was that it was a boy! Elizabeth inspected his tiny penis and testicles. She, a woman, had brought forth a little man from between her legs.

Exhausted and feeling extremely satisfied, Elizabeth wanted to sleep, but her breasts were swollen and throbbing. And the baby had started to cry.

"It's very simple," the nurse said. "You put his wee mouth up to your breast and he knows the rest."

"Does he get them both?"

"It'd be terrible painful for you if he didn't. Don't worry about when to switch. You'll feel it."

What she felt was the most sensuous experience in her life. The pressure eased and pleasure flooded through her as she sensed life flowing from her breast and into her child. She marveled that her body not only could produce this new being, but also provide its food! For the first time ever, she felt love for her own body, and then was overwhelmed by love for the small creature in her arms. Is this, she wondered, what it means to be complete?

The next time she woke up, Arthur was sitting beside her. He looked tense and concerned.

"How are you?" he asked.

"Wonderful. And tired. Tired and wonderful. And sore. Have you seen our son?"

"Yes, in the nursery."

"Isn't he beautiful?" She rang for the nurse.

"Well, they all look rather ugly at this stage. I'm told he'll improve."

The nurse brought the baby in and gave him to Elizabeth.

"How can you say that? Here, have you held him?"

"No! No!" Arthur backed away. "He's too tiny. I might drop him or something."

"Take your son," Elizabeth said angrily. "Hold his head so it doesn't fall over."

Reluctantly, Arthur took the infant and held him awkwardly away from his body. In that moment, Elizabeth realized that she secretly had been hoping that a child would bring them together. Instead, she saw the baby driving them further apart.

"He looks like you," Elizabeth said, desperate to encourage him.

"Actually," said Arthur, peering at his son, "like most infants he looks like Winston Churchill."

The nurses called it "postpartum." Depression, they said, was natural three or four days after childbirth. Elizabeth knew it was Arthur. He hadn't allowed his parents to see the baby. He had refused to have the baby named after himself or his father. From his reaction, Elizabeth thought bitterly, you'd have thought I'd borne him a freak! Well, she wasn't going to put up with his attitude. She'd had enough.

"If you won't name the baby," she said on his next visit, "we'll just call him Master Pack until you get used to the idea that you have a son."

Arthur looked more grim than usual.

"Are you all right?" she asked in a gesture of conciliation.

"Sick of that club, but otherwise all right."

"Everything okay at work?"

"Swimmingly, actually."

"So let's decide on the baby's name." Elizabeth rang for the nurse. Her breasts hurt. She was overdue to nurse the baby.

"I have something I must tell you," said Arthur.

"Don't change the subject, please! How about Antony?"

The nurse came in and handed her a strange device. It was a suction cup with a bulb attached.

"What's this?" Elizabeth asked.

"You use it on your breasts to relieve the pressure," the nurse explained.

"Why do I need this? I'm still nursing my baby."

The nurse looked uncertain, then glanced at Arthur.

"Where is my baby?"

The nurse, embarrassed, started backing out of the room.

"Where's my baby?" Elizabeth shouted. "I want my baby!" She started to climb out of bed.

Arthur took hold of her. "You must calm down. It's all for the best."

"What have you done with my baby?" she screamed.

"I told you it was impossible! It would destroy me!"

"You can't take away my baby!" She started beating on his chest.

"The baby will be fine," he said sternly, grabbing her wrists. "I've found a very decent foster family."

"You can't! You can't! You son of a bitch!"

"Pull yourself together! Nurse! Get her a sedative." He pushed her back onto the bed. "You'd better get some rest. You're going to need it. I've a new assignment. We leave in a fortnight for Spain."

PART TWO

July 18, 1936
I remember the intense colors of the
new day and also the stillness. The
sky was Murillo blue and cloudless;
its only inhabitants seemed to be
magpies that harvested here and
there in scattered groups within the
fields; and the fields themselves
spread endlessly beneath the gold of
their grain where great crimson
splashes of red poppies looked as if
the bright blood of fallen Spaniards
was already spilling over the land.

—Notes of Elizabeth Pack, traveling
from Madrid to France on the
first day of the Spanish Civil War

Chapter 5

B.S.-4, Polish Cipher Bureau, the Saxon Palace, Warsaw— December 15, 1932

Captain Gustave Bertrand smiled nervously. Were the Poles interested in the Enigma materials? He couldn't tell.

Major Gwido Langer sighed. "Perhaps this could help us," he said diffidently. "We have been studying the Enigma since 1927, but in five years . . . " He let the phrase trail off with a shrug. The heavyset chief of the Polish Cipher Bureau was dark-complexioned with a friendly and pleasant face. Bertrand liked working with Langer. He felt that despite his Germanic name there was something Latin about him.

"I am authorized to suggest a division of responsibility," Bertrand said, venturing to the heart of his mission.

They were seated in Langer's baroquely ornamented office, where they had been joined by Langer's deputy Maksymilian Ciezki. Outside, the snow that was falling into Staski Square quieted the noise of the city.

"We would provide intelligence," Bertrand continued, "from our agents in Germany that might be helpful in breaking the Enigma."

"And our responsibilities?" Ciezki inquired.

Bertrand pulled down the corners of his mouth and raised his eyebrows in a typically Gallic way. "Presumably, you would continue your study of the Enigma, sharing the results with us, of course."

Langer pursed his lips in uncertainty.

"We could also provide intercepts of the coded German messages," Bertrand hastened to add.

The Pole glanced at his deputy, who nodded slightly.

"France's offer is more than generous," Langer finally replied. "I hope that we can adequately repay you."

The Frenchman felt a surge of relief. This was more than he had dared to hope for; not only would the Poles do all the work, they already had five years' experience. He realized that it might take many more years before they achieved success, but if and when they did, France would have earned a historic return on a small investment.

"I will give you the code name 'Bolek' in our joint efforts," Langer was saying.

"And I will call you 'Luc.'" Bertrand stood up and embraced his Polish counterpart.

"*D'accord!*" they said to one another.

Three weeks later, Langer and Ciezki hurried down the third-floor corridor of the Saxon Palace toward the tiny offices of Marian Rejewski, a brilliant twenty-seven-year-old mathematician who had only joined the cipher bureau the previous September.

"He's broken an Enigma message?" Langer asked.

"I think it's more than that."

They climbed a flight of steps and went through a set of locked double doors into a wing that in the eighteenth century had contained the maids' rooms. Instead of paintings or frescoes, the walls were covered with blackboards so that when the cryptographers met in the halls and talked about their problems they would have a convenient place to write their equations.

To enter Rejewski's office, they had to push aside the heavy curtain that afforded privacy when the door stood open to glean heat from the hallway. Rejewski was a short, stocky, professorial-looking man with wire-rim glasses and thick, sandy-colored hair. He stood distressed and expectant in the middle of his bare office. The walls were covered with more slate blackboards full of diagrams.

"I wanted to make a proper presentation. . . . "

"And you shall," Langer assured him, "but I wanted to come and see for myself what you had accomplished."

"Well, this is it." He gestured at the walls. "This is how the Enigma is built, how all the wires and keys and rotors are connected."

"And you learned all this just from the messages?"

"We had a general idea of the machine from the commercial Scherbius, but knew nothing of how the Germans had changed it. Fortunately, they always transmit the message key twice. That tells how to set up the machine. And they encrypt it both times. With enough messages we were able to use permutation theory to tease out the connections in the rotors and ultimately the schema of the entire machine." His face beamed behind his thick glasses.

"The material from the French that I gave you, it was useful?"

"In a manner of speaking. It confirmed our theory that the Germans had added a plugboard to further scramble the letters, and the list of keys allowed us to immediately begin breaking messages. We can now break the keys ourselves. I was also having difficulty figuring out how the keyboard was connected to the rotors. I thought we would have to collect a year and a half of messages to crack that problem."

"So the French material was crucial?" Langer pressed.

"I found the answer to that the day before you gave me the French material."

"How?" Ciezki wondered.

"By guessing."

Langer gave a short laugh. "Good. We did it on our own."

"It is a Polish triumph!" declared Ciezki.

"Certainly," Langer agreed, "but just as important, we are not obligated to say a thing about it to the French."

Biarritz, France—
July 23, 1936

If they go on about their servants for one more minute, Elizabeth thought, I'll scream. The dinner was over and according to diplomatic protocol the women had gathered in the salon while the men retired to the library for brandy and cigars. Elizabeth had been looking forward to the summer in France as a break from the stiff formality of diplomatic functions in Madrid. But this was just as bad, if not worse.

Each June, for three months, the Spanish government moved its capital to the northern coastal city of San Sebastián on the Atlantic, and the foreign embassies moved with them. Most of the British embassy staff, including Arthur, had rented villas across the border in France for the summer months. Now it appeared that they might remain a good deal longer. Civil war had broken out in Spain. Fierce fighting raged around Madrid between the legally elected Republican government and the insurgents led by Generalissimo Francisco Franco. Democrats, Socialists, Communists, and Anarchists sided with the Republic while Franco had the support of most of the military, the Fascist Falange, the Monarchists and the Church. Hitler and Mussolini were backing Franco and Stalin the Republic. Many people thought the conflict might be the start of a new world war. But at polite British dinner parties in Biarritz, it was considered tiresome to mention the subject.

The conversation among the ladies had turned to children. Elizabeth could not bear it. Arthur had refused her any information about her son, nothing concerning his whereabouts, not even the name of the foster family. She fought, she argued, she pleaded, she cried. Nothing moved him. His only concession had been to accept her suggestion for the boy's name—Antony.

Elizabeth had thought of divorce, but discovered that she needed legal grounds, and she had none. She could simply leave him and go back to America, but that would bring her no closer to her son. She could try to remain in England, but she had no money, and as a married woman, Elizabeth could not even open a bank account without Arthur's consent. She telephoned her mother, who said she was sympathetic but told her she would have to settle her problems with Arthur herself. When she called her father, he counseled patience. There was no practical alternative but to go to Spain and try to put her baby out of mind.

So from the moment Elizabeth had arrived in Madrid, she had behaved like a mad debutante, filling up her dance card to prevent even a moment's reflection. She accepted invitations to every cocktail party, dinner, ball, and theatrical event, soon falling in with a crowd that often ended the night at a club, Jimmy's Place, dancing until dawn. Arthur only accompanied her if he thought it would bring him new contacts, and even then would usually go home halfway through the evening. The love and tenderness and wonder that she experienced giving birth to her son had been walled off, consigned to the deepest dungeon of memory. But every once in a while, when she saw a woman in the park with a baby in her arms, or a governess pushing a toddler in a pram, or like tonight, overheard women exchanging intimacies about their children, she would struggle to keep from bursting into tears.

Shouts and laughter from the library saved her. The women all rushed to see what was going on. They found the men standing in a semicircle around two others who were down on their stomachs on the carpet. They had been blindfolded and lay head to head with their left hands clasped together, gripping rolled up newspapers in their right. One of the men was the host. The other was Arthur.

"Oh, God," her hostess sighed. "They're playing 'Moriarity, where are you?'"

"From Sherlock Holmes?" asked Elizabeth.

"Not exactly. Watch."

Arthur called out, "Moriarity, where are you?"

"Here," his host responded, and tried to twist away as Arthur reached out timidly with the roll of paper to tap him on the head.

"No! No!" cried the men surrounding them, laughing and puffing on their cigars. "Strike him a proper thwack!" shouted one. "Hear, hear!" called out the others.

"Moriarity, where are you?" the host now demanded.

"Here," Arthur replied, and his host smashed him on the head with his newspaper.

"One point!" someone noted.

"Moriarity, where are you?" Arthur responded angrily, flailing around blindly with his paper before his adversary could even answer.

Elizabeth stood open-mouthed. Here were some of the most prominent members of the British community, drunk as lords—some of them *were* lords—rolling around on the floor in their tuxedoes hitting one another on the head with rolled-up newspapers.

Her hostess saw her surprise. "It's really very simple, my dear," she explained. "Englishmen will go to inordinate lengths for an excuse to touch one another."

"Arthur, there has to be more to life than these airless dinner parties." Elizabeth was behind the wheel of the Talbot as they drove down the coast road back to their villa in St.-Jean-de-Luz. The tires slapped rhythmically on the asphalt joins in the concrete highway.

"I suppose you'd rather have been dancing at the casino." Arthur was slumped unhappily against the door. He had scored the least points, and had the most scored against him. He had also drunk too much brandy.

"I'm talking about real life," she said earnestly. "Isn't it time we became serious about having a family?"

"Oh, don't start up again!" He was becoming cross. "We can't suddenly have a six-month-old child appear in our midst."

"I'm not talking about the baby. I'm talking about starting again. We could have another child. You promised!"

Arthur could not understand why she was not content with things the way they were. He had found Madrid disconcerting, the Spaniards always standing too close and touching you when they talked, their conversation full of passionate intensity on the most trivial matters. But he had felt immediately comfortable and happy in St.-Jean-de-Luz. For almost a hundred years, the sleepy and picturesque Basque fishing village, and the area bordered by Biarritz on the north and Pau to the east had been a playground for British aristocrats fleeing the English damp. Queen Victoria had made the place fashionable by summering in Biarritz in the middle of the nineteenth century, and not long after, the first steeplechase on the Continent was built at Pau and the second golf course in Europe laid out near St.-Jean-de-Luz. After the turn of the century, the port town became a haven for pensioners from the British Army and the Colonial Service who took up permanent residence along the strand in sober residential hotels that boasted appropriate names like Britannia and Angleterre.

Arthur took pleasure in rubbing elbows with the retired admirals at Lloyd's insurance office down in the port and loved the fact that he could read the *Times* and the *Daily Mail* at the tea shops along the Rue Gainetta. Since the embassy was cut off from the rest of Spain by territory held by Franco's insurgents, Arthur's job was not very taxing. It mainly consisted of driving across the border thirty minutes each way to San Sebastián where he spent most of his time arranging lunch at one of the city's celebrated dining clubs, followed by eating lunch, and then trying to recover from lunch. Everything was as he wanted, except for the delay in his admission to the English Club in Biarritz, and he thought he knew the reason for that.

"Do you really think," he finally replied to Elizabeth, "that you're ready to settle down?" Arthur did not try to hide the snide tone in his voice.

"I'm sick of the madcap, and I'd give it all up if you're willing to be a real father."

"And you'll give up Antonio de Zaragoza as well?"

Elizabeth was stunned. "What are you saying? I haven't seen him since we left Madrid."

"But you've been trying to contact him. You've been asking everyone about him. Don't think I don't know!"

She could not deny that she was worried about Antonio. He had promised to write, but she had heard nothing for weeks, and phone calls to Madrid had been cut off. "He's been a good friend to both of us," she insisted defensively.

"But people are talking about the two of you! Why do you think that my admission to the English Club has been delayed?"

"I can't believe you're serious!" But she could see from his sullen silence that he was. Patches of fog drifting in from the sea were now glaring brightly in the headlights, forcing her to slow down.

Ironically, it was Arthur who had brought her and Antonio together again. Arriving late as usual for a reception at Puerta de Hierro Country Club, she had been surprised by the sight of Arthur having drinks with Antonio on the terrace. The scene was still vivid in her mind. It was late afternoon, and the moon hung like a bright paper lantern over the purple wall of the Guadarrama Mountains.

Arthur had called out to her. "Elizabeth, you remember the Marqués de Zaragoza." He waved her toward them. "He was one of the carefree young lads at the Spanish embassy when you were a debutante."

She held out her hand feeling strangely shy as he kissed it. "It seems awfully long ago," she managed to say.

"I remember you were a beautiful dancer," Antonio said gravely.

He looked exactly as she had remembered in her daydreams. The fine high-born features, the penetrating hazel-blue eyes, the strong jaw framing a tender mouth. And yes, the magnetism had been there too, undiminished.

Arthur went to get her a stinger. Antonio had smiled oddly, almost reluctantly. "Señora, what can I say? You arrive here a married woman. What is more, a married woman with a certain, shall I say, reputation."

Elizabeth had felt a flash of embarrassment that left her speechless.

"I'm sure," he continued stiffly, "that you feel you are merely experiencing all that my country has to offer. But it is not the Spanish way, and you are sure to be deprived of the essence of this culture if you continue to lead a life that is frivolous, and to respectable Spaniards, bordering on the shameful."

"Antonio," she said slowly, her shock turning to anger, "at least I do not go around encouraging young men to fall in love with me . . . "

Antonio's eyes flickered.

". . . and then crush them by revealing that I'm married!"

It was Antonio's turn to blush. "What in honor can I say?" He had no excuse; he was being a boor. "You know what is said of Spaniards—everything in the extreme—everything to the death. We are passionate; we are prudes. And here I am forced into the prosaic role of husband and scold. Forgive me."

All she had wanted to do was kiss him.

Arthur came back with the drinks. "Well, what are we talking about?"

"Your Spanish education," Antonio had replied. "I shall get my wife, Maria, and we will drink to the old days and new ones too, and then you both must join us for dinner. You'll find Spain an interesting classroom, and Arthur, perhaps with your permission, I could fulfill the requirements as a teacher?"

Arthur had gotten a canny look on his face. "Very well. Could you start"—Arthur pointed toward a distinguished gentleman on the other side of the terrace—"by introducing me to Viscount Terragona? I've been trying to make his acquaintance for months."

So for Arthur's "education," Antonio invited the Packs to shooting parties, bridge parties, and dinner parties where they met the titled families of Spain. Pleased and grateful for the professional access, Arthur seemed unconcerned with how Antonio was conducting Elizabeth's "Spanish education."

Her "school day" usually began with lunch at a traditional restaurant such as Lhardy, where at their first meeting, Antonio had demonstrated how to draw the celebrated consommé from its silver samovar. Elizabeth wanted to set the ground rules at the outset.

"Antonio, it's wonderful to see you again." She picked at her fried artichoke. "But if we're going to see each other, it has to be strictly as friends."

"That's not possible with a Spaniard. *No sea macho.*"

"You're the one who said I have to protect my honor."

"How can I refuse you?" He looked distressed but tried to smile. "This is in the nature of our culture. Order and control on the surface, seething emotions below. It will be part of your education."

"And we'll not talk about ourselves, our personal lives."

"Arthur is turning you into an Englishwoman," he sighed.

After lunch, while most of Madrid took its siesta, they would walk along the hot and empty streets glowing with wine, trying not to touch one another while Antonio told the city's history through its Moorish, baroque, and neoclassical buildings and squares. One day, he took her to the cliff above the Manzanares River where Madrid had begun in the ninth century as a fort built by the Moors from North

Africa. On another, they made an excursion to El Escorial, the severe monastery palace of Philip II, who made Madrid the capital of a worldwide empire in 1561. Often they merely wandered down the narrow streets, staircases, and vaulted alleys of Madrid's old town, lingering at the permanent open-air book fair at Cuesta Moyana. Occasionally, Elizabeth brought a picnic basket and they lunched in a boat on the lake in Retro Park with its formal gardens, colonnades, temples, and avenues lined with statuary. Through it all, they managed to keep a discreet distance despite the powerful attraction between them.

They had found it easier to maintain their distance during the late afternoon *tertulia,* Madrid's ritual exchange of gossip about the day's political outrages. They spent hours in one of the café terraces on the Paseo de Recoletos, Antonio sipping a *café cortado,* Elizabeth spooning a *blanco y negro,* iced black coffee with ice cream, while Antonio's friends would stop by to tell of the latest shooting of a Republican by the Anarchists, or the murder of a Socialist by the Falange. Elizabeth wondered how any work ever got done in the city.

At night, when Arthur was busy and Maria de Zaragoza was away at the ranch as she often was, they frequented bars like Gijon, Lion, and El Espejo near the Plaza de Cibeles, which catered to aristocrats and their reactionary political opinions. One night on the way home, Elizabeth said that she loved the fervor that Spaniards brought to politics. "But it's mad the way you're shooting each other over utterly ridiculous *theories*!"

"I'm afraid that most Spaniards only agree on one thing," he said sadly, "that your idea of democracy is a dreary, boring, middle-class, Anglo-Saxon idea that must be stamped out."

"And what do you believe?" she had asked him.

His reply was to take her the next day to see Goya's etchings at the Prado Museum. His *Disasters of War* filled room after room with pictures of soldiers with their genitals mutilated, farmers with their arms and heads cut off; men, women, and children eviscerated, burned, hacked to pieces; guerrilla partisans impaled on the stumps of trees.

"Our passion for life is exceeded only by our passion

for death," Antonio observed. "I am afraid this is where my country is headed once again."

She had taken his hand and leaned against him as if she could shield him from the coming tragedy. Their meetings, which had started out at twice a week, had become daily events, making their vow of not touching almost impossible to bear. If war was coming, she had thought, Antonio might be killed. What would be the point of their fidelity then? After a strained moment, Antonio had stepped away, honoring his pledge to her.

Damn it all, Elizabeth thought, she was not going accept Arthur's accusations!

"You didn't seem to mind Antonio"—she momentarily took her eyes off the road to look over at her bibulous husband—"when he invited you to shoot pheasants with the aristocracy and entertained us at dinner with industrialists you wanted to meet."

"Don't be crass!" he answered angrily. "That's what diplomatic life is all about. We don't make friends. We make contacts."

Up ahead the headlights picked out a sign indicating that St.-Jean-de-Luz was only two kilometers ahead. "You're right of course," she said to be conciliatory. "I've flirted, and gone out, and danced with other men and spent time, lots of time, alone with Antonio."

"Spare me the gruesome details." Arthur turned away to look out the window at the inky emptiness of the night.

"But I've always been faithful to you! Doesn't that mean anything?"

"Your self-restraint is admirable," he said dryly. "However, appearances also count. And on that score you're hardly an ideal wife, let alone mother." He had turned bitter. "You'll simply have to prove beyond question that you can be a responsible diplomat's wife before I'd even consider starting a family."

Chapter 6

Warsaw, Poland—
June 19, 1937

"We were so obsessed with radio," Leonard Danilewicz was explaining to William Stephenson, "that the other students in Warsaw Polytechnic called us Radiots."

Their car was making its way south out of the city toward the suburb of Mocotow. Danilewicz was describing the origin of the AVA Radio Manufacturing Company. "Later, my brother and I made crystal sets and two tube receivers which we would take to science fairs and sell to the unwary."

Stephenson's visit to Warsaw had two purposes: to look for business and collect intelligence. He was extraordinarily impressed with Poland's industrial and scientific dynamism. Stephenson saw little sign of the Great Depression that had decimated the economies of the rest of Europe. Commercial opportunities, however, were limited. Construction cranes dotted the skyline, but the language barrier put his engineering firm at a disadvantage. Automobile factories were turning out cars at maximum capacity, but the business was dominated by Chevrolet and Fiat. Poles flocked to the movies, but English language film distribution was controlled by MGM.

So far, Stephenson had also learned little that would be of interest to His Majesty's Secret Service. That could change, he told himself, now that he had persuaded Dr. Danilewicz to allow him to visit AVA's new factory south of the city.

Initially, his interest in AVA Radio had been to work out a possible licensing arrangement for General Radio. AVA had surprised him with the sophistication of its transmitting and receiving equipment. But as he became more familiar with the company, he began to wonder how the small Polish commercial market could sustain AVA's sizable research laboratories. The company did not export, so the Polish government had to be subsidizing them on a lavish scale. But why?

Stephenson found that the new AVA production facility located near the Warsaw airport consisted of a modern two-story office building that had already been completed, a four-story windowless manufacturing plant next door and a third, and much bigger, structure under construction in the rear. In the lobby of the office complex, Danilewicz proudly showed Stephenson a display of some of their newest products. One in particular caught his eye, a tall cabinet containing a powerful radio receiver capable of picking up signals across the full spectrum of frequencies. He also noted that it was painted army green.

Danilewicz then took him on a tour of the plant that was under construction. Inside, his host described the layout of the production lines of the various equipment Stephenson had seen in the lobby. But he failed to mention the big olive drab radio receiver.

Over lunch in the conference room of the office building, Stephenson asked where that particular piece of equipment was being manufactured.

"That's a very profitable item," Danilewicz boasted. "The production line is in the plant next door."

"Could I see it?"

"I would like to accommodate you, but that building is off limits, I'm afraid. It is where we do our work for the Polish general staff."

Stephenson then changed the discussion to the subject of mass production of home radio receivers. Dr. Danilewicz did not seem particularly interested. As a business proposition, Stephenson's visit to Warsaw had been a washout. But from the standpoint of intelligence, he believed he now had convincing evidence that the Enigma could be broken.

St.-Jean-de-Luz, France—
August 1936

Elizabeth took up Arthur's challenge to become a model embassy wife. She faithfully attended teas with the other diplomats' wives and volunteered at the local Anglican library. For a reception given by the chargé's wife, to which she was pointedly not invited, Elizabeth nonetheless supervised the wrapping of five hundred prunes in bacon and their delivery to the chargé's back door. She participated in the diplomatic ladies' afternoon bridge parties, which began with pitchers of martinis at each table and ended with the ladies stumbling home tipsy before the cocktail hour had even started. At the mindless round of balls in Biarritz and suffocating dinners hosted by expatriate Englishmen, Elizabeth obediently hovered at Arthur's side, hanging on his every word.

She stayed fit by riding and playing tennis and golf with others in the diplomatic circle. Her most frequent partner was Barbara Brasswell, who, though eight years older, was the next youngest wife in the embassy. She was married to Arthur's deputy and worked part-time in the Passport Control Office.

As the summer waned, Elizabeth increasingly took to long walks on the beaches that lay beneath the grassy cliffs guarding the town. Barefoot and dressed in fisherman's pants and a rough sweater, she would trudge along the shore for miles, feeling the wind on her face and the waves washing against her legs.

She had given up seeking news of Antonio. She stopped frequenting the cafés in the port, where the spies, journalists, adventurers, smugglers, prostitutes, gun runners, and refugees who had flooded St.-Jean-de-Luz gathered to trade rumors about what was going on in Spain. Elizabeth wanted to avoid being seen in such company and also could not bear hearing about any more atrocities; such as the slaughter of the soldiers in Madrid's Montana Barracks by the Anarchists, or the extermination of whole villages—down to the pigs, chickens, dogs, and cats—by Franco's Moorish mercenaries. Such tales only made her fear all the more for Antonio's safety.

She could not forget him. In the late afternoon, while waiting dutifully for Arthur to come home, Elizabeth often stood on the terrace of her villa watching the lights wink on, outlining the coast as it turned west away from France toward the glow of San Sebastián on the horizon. She would stay there until the moon came out, illuminating the mountainous wall of the Pyrenees that cut off Spain from the rest of Europe. And she would wonder if she'd ever see Antonio again.

One evening late in August, Arthur did not return from San Sebastián. When Elizabeth tried to telephone him, she was informed that the lines were down. By midnight, she was worried. By two A.M. she was frantic. What had happened to him? Rumor had it that General Mola's Nationalist insurgents had been sighted in the hills between the border and San Sebastián.

Checking with Barbara Brasswell and the wives of other embassy officers in St.-Jean-de-Luz, she learned that they too had heard nothing from their husbands. When none of them had any suggestions on what to do, she decided to call the Foreign Office in London to see if they had direct contact with the embassy. The night duty officer answered. His voice, tinny and laconic, was barely audible.

"No contact . . . " he was saying. "No telephone . . . no cable traffic."

"What's happening?" Elizabeth shouted.

"No idea . . . " And then whoops and howls on the line punctuated by static.

"I'll send my driver over the border tomorrow."

Static and then a faint "Do call us . . . "

At nine the next morning, Elizabeth's driver set out for San Sebastián. By ten he was back. His diplomatic plates were not sufficient to get him past the Spanish border police.

"They said that there was fighting along the road to San Sebastián," her driver explained, "Mola's making a major push. His Moors are shooting everyone in sight. No one is allowed through."

By noon, the embassy wives had gathered on Elizabeth's terrace. "It's simply outrageous," said the blimpish wife of the second secretary, "treating a British embassy car like that!"

"So our poor dears are trapped in San Sebastián," whimpered a waif of a woman who was married to a vice-consul. "Maybe we should notify the Red Cross."

"I know what I'm going to do," announced the formidable spouse of the chargé. As the most senior woman there, they were supposed to look to her for leadership. "I'm going to lodge a protest with the Spanish consul in Biarritz!"

"But it's the Fascists, not the government, who've cut communications," Elizabeth pointed out.

"It's no good taking sides," the chargé's wife admonished her. "We must hold the responsible authorities responsible." It was unclear whether she was more upset about her husband's fate or the fact that the wives had naturally gravitated to Elizabeth's house.

The ringing phone saved Elizabeth from an intemperate reply. The connection was poor to nonexistent.

". . . get through?" the duty officer asked.

"San Sebastián is surrounded, cut off."

". . . call back if we're cut off."

"No, you don't understand. San Sebastián. Terrible. Cut off." She began to speak as if the phone did not understand English. "People being executed. Killed. Atrocities."

". . . quite agree, atrocious. Any message?"

"Do something!"

"Recommendations . . . War Office."

Elizabeth thought furiously. What should be done? If she asked the women in the other room for advice, they'd probably recommend bombarding the rebels with tea and crumpets.

"Are you there?" the Foreign Office voice demanded.

"Yes. Yes."

". . . need the ambassador's recommendations or the cabinet won't act."

Elizabeth took a deep breath. "Tell them to send the navy."

"You're sure . . . ambassador wants that?"

She looked at the women in the room. They were now debating whether to take their concerns to the local bishop.

Barbara looked at her helplessly and shrugged.

"Absolutely," Elizabeth said.

The Foreign Office called at four in the morning. A destroyer was on its way. If at all possible, she should get that message to the ambassador so he could prepare to evacuate.

The other wives thought she was mad, but by ten, Elizabeth was on the road to the Spanish border. Her chauffeur, who had earned a Croix de Guerre in the Great War, had stacked the trunk with cans of gasoline in case there was none in San Sebastián. He had also attached a British flag across the hood of the car. In twenty minutes she was crossing the two-lane iron bridge over a wash that formed the mouth of the Río Bidassoa and marked the frontier. The border guards on both sides urged her to turn back. The Spanish officials at Irún confirmed fighting along the highway to San Sebastián and warned that she would need a special pass to even try to get through.

Elizabeth ordered her driver to go on. Irún seemed quiet, too quiet her driver said. It was a substantial town with tall and narrow balconied apartment buildings set tight against one another stepping up and down the hilly streets. The few people out of doors hurried along as if they were afraid to be caught in the open.

Outside of Irún, they passed Basque farmhouses with their characteristic thick white stucco walls, solid stone casement windows, and timbered roofs. Elizabeth thought they had a quaint Swiss alpine quality, but she could not help imagining that they also would make good fortifications. Near Ventas, a crossroads flanked by a scattering of such houses, her car was stopped by a roadblock.

An old man with a hunting rifle asked her for her pass. She showed her British passport. He shook his head and ordered her out of the car. She refused. He said, "*Bueno*, I won't hurt you, señora. But you will force me to put a bullet in your driver's head."

Elizabeth got out. She found that despite her defiant feelings, her legs were trembling.

"Where can I get a pass?" she demanded.

He pointed his gun toward one of the farmhouses set into the hillside. "From the *jefe*."

The old man turned her over to a boy no more than twelve who had a revolver stuck in his belt that looked like it weighed more than he did. The boy led her up a flight of log steps dug into the hill to a door on the second floor of the farmhouse. Inside, a fat man with a greasy week's growth of beard sat at a kitchen table eating a chicken, drinking brandy, and cursing two subordinates. Elizabeth noticed that he was wearing the black-and-red handkerchief of the Anarchists.

"What's this?" he said in Basque, then again in Spanish.

"I am from the British embassy," Elizabeth began.

He slammed his hand down on the table. "You see!" he shouted at his cowering troops. "Another spy!"

"I'm not!" she said angrily. "I'm a diplomat's wife, trying to reach my husband in San Sebastián . . . "

"Spies everywhere!" he continued, heaving himself out of his chair. "That, my stupid comrades, is why we are here! To stop these spies! How do you think Mola's Fascist pigs are winning? Spies!" He hit the table again and the plate jumped into the air.

"If you'd just listen," Elizabeth started again, trying to be calm, "all I want—"

"You don't make demands here!" He put his face into hers. "You English think you rule the world! Our Republic fights for its life and England cuts off arms while Mussolini and Hitler pour men and machines into the lap of that bastard Franco . . . !" He was swaggering around the room and Elizabeth realized that, although it was not yet ten-thirty in the morning, the *jefe* was quite drunk.

"You're being ridiculous," she said firmly.

"Look and learn, comrades." He pointed at her. "This is the attitude of a spy. All full of arrogance. If she were not, she would be cringing in fear like the rest. Her papers are forgeries!"

He smiled and his teeth were the color of his gums. "Put her down with the others," he ordered. "I will interrogate her later. Personally!"

"Down" turned out to be a barn under the kitchen. The "others" proved to be a sad assortment of unsuspecting travelers. The atmosphere reeked of sweat, urine, excrement, and fear. One man tried to comfort another who bled from his nose and kept sticking his fingers in his mouth sobbing, "My teeth, my teeth." Elizabeth's mind found it difficult to absorb what was happening to her. It was a beautiful cloudless day. Her home was only twenty minutes away. The other embassy wives were having coffee at that very moment. Her body began to tremble uncontrollably. In the gloom, she saw another man in a good suit who seemed to be sleeping carelessly in a pile of cow dung. Then Elizabeth realized he was unconscious. Deeper in the shadows, several men chained to the stalls had bloodstained shirts torn where they had been whipped. They moaned as they breathed. She was the only woman. She knew what to expect in the interrogation.

To avoid sitting on the floor, she took a bucket off the wall and used it as a stool. The place looked like something from Goya's etchings. The well-dressed man in the pile of dung was hauled out and then she heard a gunshot. Her driver was dragged in. She could see that he had soiled himself. As she wiped the blood from his swollen lips with his handkerchief, he lisped, "Forgive me, madam, but they took the car." Then he passed out.

Fear and despair washed over her. She remembered one evening when, for a lark, she and Antonio had dressed in blue overalls to visit the Café Comercial in the Glorieta de Bilbao in search of Anarchists. Elizabeth wanted to know if they really believed in "free love."

In the noisy, smoky room, they had found two chairs at a table already occupied by a young tram driver and a fresh-faced young girl who said she was a teacher. They acknowledged being Anarchists and lovers, but insisted there was nothing immoral about "free love."

"We have a greater obligation to be faithful to each other," he said solemnly, "precisely because we do not allow the Church or the government to enforce morality."

The tram driver had been very serious about the revolution too. When it came, his task would be to take over the central telephone office and destroy it.

"There will be no telephones or telegraph. We will tear up the railroads and burn the trams. Automobiles will be forbidden. People will live and work only within the distance that they can walk."

"If complete freedom is the basic principle of anarchism," Elizabeth had asked, "what will happen to those who disagree with you—the businessmen, the civil servants, the military, the landowners, the nuns and priests?"

The answer had come from the young woman who had been studying Elizabeth's fine haircut and manicured fingernails. "They will be liquidated."

As Elizabeth sat in the stench and the dark of the barn, more people were brought "down," including a woman and two children, one of them an infant. She looked like a simple farmer's wife. A concerned-looking young man in a military hat with a red star came and gave them water. The red star meant that he was not an Anarchist but a Communist. From time to time, others would be taken away and there would be gunshots.

Elizabeth realized that she could not sit there passively. She would be shot after being raped. Her driver would be killed too, because of her . . . her what? Restlessness? Bad judgment? Foolishness? But what could she do? When she tried to speak to the others, the boy with the pistol waved it at her. She had to look for an opportunity. Only the young man with the red star seemed to have a streak of decency, at least regarding the children. The third time he came to check on them she called out to him.

"Sí, señora?"

"This is all a mistake!" she said in her most intense voice, summoning all her energy to drive her message of innocence into his mind. "I am with the British embassy in San Sebastián."

"I can do nothing." The young man's face was blank with the pain of having seen too much.

"But I live just across the border. I have to go back and forth. I'm accredited to the Republic, don't you understand? The side you're fighting on!" She almost broke down. She had to remember his concern for children. "I just want to go back to France. I have a baby there. He needs me!" She grabbed his hand and put it to her breast. "He'll starve!"

Her eyes seized his with a passion burning from a determination not to be polluted by *el jefe.* The young man appeared to think for a moment, then shook his head.

"You must excuse me, señora." He pulled back and hurried out.

Her hope drained away. She could hear *el jefe* shouting and stamping on the floorboards above her head. She tried to keep from imagining how his fat, fetid body would feel on top of her. Her driver was taken away. She dreaded to think what would happen to him.

Elizabeth found herself remembering Madrid on a warm evening in June when Arthur was busy and Maria at the ranch. She and Antonio had attended a performance of *La Bohème* at the opera, and on the way home had been stopped at a roadblock. An Assault Guard stuck his face in the chauffeur's window.

Antonio knocked on the glass separating them. "What's going on?"

"The big strike, señor. Someone killed the leader of the Union."

"And now they're out for revenge," Antonio muttered. Elizabeth grabbed his arm.

A flashlight probed into the backseat and glinted off the medals on Antonio's uniform.

"Out of the car!" The door flew open and Elizabeth could see a man holding a rifle with others crowded behind him.

Antonio stepped out. "You stay inside," he had said to Elizabeth.

"Papers!" someone ordered.

"Ah! A marqués!" came another voice.

In the glow from the flashlight Elizabeth had seen them break into menacing smiles. Two men grabed Antonio's arms and a third began to tie his thumbs together behind his back with twine.

Elizabeth jumped out of the car. "What are you doing? Who is in command here?" she demanded.

A half-shaven man in overalls, an officer's cap, and a black-and-red Anarchist bandana around his neck stepped forward.

"Don't make trouble, rich and beautiful, or you'll wind up in jail too."

"I'm from the British embassy and this man is my military escort!" She dug her passport out of her purse and threw it at him. "If you don't let him go, you'll be creating a major international incident."

"Take it easy, *rubia*. We'll give you some men to protect you." The others had laughed in the dark.

Their leader was holding her passport upside down. He gave it to a young man to read. He nervously nodded his head, confirming her claims. The chief's eyes flashed in anger. He snatched away the passport and handed it back to her. *"Lo siento, señora.* I'm sorry." He did not sound sorry. He began to finger Antonio's medals then yanked them off his chest.

"Some military hero." The Anarchist boss motioned for Antonio to be released. "You are supposed to guard the lady, but she has to protect you!" He laughed at him. "I deserve these," he said and started to pin the decorations on his overalls.

Antonio stepped toward him. The boss poked him with his rifle. Elizabeth caught Antonio's shoulder and pulled him back into the car. As they drove off, they heard one of the guards complain, "Too bad, I wanted to see his blood ruin that fancy uniform."

"Write his name down on our list," the chief ordered.

Antonio was furious. Elizabeth felt shaken. She took hold of his hands.

"Is this what Madrid has come to?" She shuddered. "An evening at the opera and then you're arrested and shot for dressing properly?"

She insisted that the driver take Antonio home first; she would be safe. He urged her to stay at his apartment. No one would be secure on the streets that night. Entering the Barrio Salamanca where they both lived, they saw a vehicle stopped on a side street by another armed band with black-and-red scarves. Hesitantly, she agreed to stay with him.

A tiny elevator, barely big enough for the two of them, rose slowly through the middle of a circular staircase toward his apartment on the sixth floor. She could smell the cologne, Chicote, that she had given him for his saint's day. It mixed with a deeper aroma, the musk of a man ready to fight. He stood so close that she had to breathe lightly or her breasts would brush against his chest.

The elevator opened onto a landing in front of his door.

The parquet floors creaked as they stepped inside the dark and empty apartment. The servants were in the country with his wife. Antonio turned on a light in the salon. The curtains were drawn. Elizabeth pulled one aside and looked out while Antonio disappeared into the recesses of the flat. The streets were vacant, now. Word of the reprisals must have spread. Normally, the *calles* would be full of people and cars until at least three in the morning. Antonio came up behind her with two brandies.

"I think we both could use this."

"I hope that incident didn't hurt your pride." She could see from his face that it had. "If you'd done anything else, you'd have put me in danger."

"I know." He took a sip of the Fundador. "But you showed such courage, it made me ashamed."

"Don't." She put her hand on his chest to sooth him. He took it, and she could feel his heat. She was drawn to him. In an instant, their mouths were almost touching.

Elizabeth dropped her glass.

"Don't," she said again, not knowing if she meant it.

He stopped. She tasted his breath on her lips.

"If we go any further, I will only dishonor you," she whispered.

"Everyone in Madrid already talks about us. We belong together."

"I knew that from the first moment I saw you in Washington. But you've said it's hopeless."

"I can't stand being honorable anymore. It's cowardly! We talk politics instead of exchanging love. We worry about violence when what we fear is our own passion. I'm sick of art and culture and the dead past. When I see a Rubens at the Prado, I imagine how your body would feel in my hands. When I look at the peasants in Flemish paintings foolishly running about with their erect codpieces, I see myself."

Elizabeth could feel the truth of his words grow against her. She had wanted to reach down and take hold of him, caress him, envelop him. But she stepped away.

"If I stay a moment longer, it will change our lives forever."

"Forgive me. I've been shameless." He dropped his head to his chest.

"I can't control my feelings any longer, Antonio. Maybe we should stop seeing each other, at least alone, at least for a while. Otherwise"—she tried to make a joke—"my Spanish education will go too far."

"That will be a walking death!" he had protested.

"Give me the keys to your car, I beg you. I must go."

"I'll take you."

"No. Please. I'll be safe. But if something happened to you . . . " Elizabeth had wanted to say that she would kill herself, but that was wrong. Antonio was right. Walking out the door that night, she had felt she was already dying.

Looking around the barn, Elizabeth wondered how she could have rejected his love. There were fewer prisoners now after all the gunshots. Was this the sum of her life? A lonely childhood, a vacant marriage, absent motherhood, a love denied and then rape, and oblivion beside a road in northern Spain? At least she wouldn't have to explain to the ambassador about the Royal Navy destroyer. The effort to tell herself a small joke only brought forth tears of despair.

One of the *jefe*'s subordinates came for her. He led her around the house to the other side where the ground was flat and two poles had been stuck into the ground. She averted her eyes from the man who hung lifelessly on one of the poles with a sack over his head. Fresh graves had been dug near a vegetable garden. Several men with old rifles stood in front of her smoking. *El jefe* was not one of them. Just shoot me, she prayed stepping toward the vacant pole.

"Stop, señora!"

It was the young man with the red star. He held her passport in his hand. "I have given you safe-conduct pass." Her driver was waiting beside the car.

"My God, how can I thank you?" she said, surprised and exhilarated.

"By returning to France immediately."

"But my husband's trapped in San Sebastián!"

"That pass won't keep you from being blown to bits by

an eighty-eight. I did not save your life to have Mola's Fascists kill you."

"I'm acting under the orders of the British government. I absolve you of all responsibility."

"So you *are* a spy." He turned serious.

"If you believe that, then shoot me!" She impulsively turned toward the waiting pole.

He grabbed her arm. "We have many women like you fighting on our side," he said with admiration. "All right, I will give you an escort. And I suggest you take this too." He handed her a homemade red flag.

Elizabeth gave him a half smile of appreciation. "What happened to *el jefe*?" she asked casually. She did not want to run into him at the next roadblock.

"He has murdered his last innocent."

The young man pointed at the other pole where a lifeless body slumped to one side with its arms twisted behind it. The boy yanked off the bag on its head. It was *el jefe*.

Chapter 7

San Sebastián Road—
August 31, 1936

There were no other vehicles on the road over the pass to San Sebastián. Black-and-white Merino sheep with their thick, braided coats grazed contentedly in the golden hills to the left while Mount Jaizkibel climbed steeply on the right. Everything seemed quiet, and Elizabeth began to relax enough to start worrying about what she would say to the ambassador. The aroma of burning grass filled the air, a common smell in late summer as farmers cleared their fields. But this odor had a peculiar acrid edge. Just as Elizabeth also began to wonder about the little white clouds that seemed to grow out of the hillsides, her chauffeur drove the car into a ditch.

"Out! Señora, out!"

The militiamen escorting her scrambled out of the car. She managed to get her door open and put one foot on the ground when the concussion hit. It hurled her forward into the grass in a shower of glass. She lay clinging to the earth until her hearing came back. The first sound was that of rifles and a machine gun, and they were very close. As she started to lift her head, she heard her driver cry out.

"Keep your head down. Try to move away from the car. The gasoline!"

"I can't do both, damn it!"

"Be quiet."

Elizabeth ran her hands over her face; blood trickled down her forehead from a cut on her scalp. She was covered with shards of glass. In time, the firing died down. She raised her head enough to see her driver and the militiamen crawling farther down the ditch. Slowly, painfully, with burrs, thistles, and glass sticking to her hands and knees, she followed them, grateful that she had worn slacks and a jacket.

Suddenly, up ahead she saw a half-dozen men with rifles cross the road. One of them seemed to stumble and fall, but he did not get up. Then she heard the clatter of a machine gun. By rolling on her side, she could watch the attacking group work its way up the hillside against the machine gun. They moved forward in short rushes, but each time they advanced, there seemed to be one less, until the attack petered out. A few moments later, two survivors fled back across the road.

Elizabeth lay in the ditch with her head pressed against the ground for more than an hour as the intermittent battle continued. She did not think her heart could beat so fast for so long without bursting. Trying to erase one fear with another, she forced herself to imagine what the ambassador would do to her when he found out that, in his name, she had mobilized the British Navy and proclaimed the evacuation of the British embassy. She might be better off if a shell landed on the car.

Three times, artillery bombardments hit the road and exploded on the hillside in a blind search for the machine-gun nest. Minutes later, a squad of men would cross the road and assault the hill. Within a quarter of an hour, the remnants were fleeing back to the other side. Elizabeth felt sick at the boys and men who lay dead and dying on the pavement and in the tall grass.

Finally, there was a long lull in the fighting. Her chauffeur crawled toward her.

"Let's go for the car."

"They'll shoot us!" Elizabeth could feel the hysteria in her chest.

"No, it's over for now."

"How do you know?"

He tapped his watch. "It's lunchtime."

Elizabeth felt relieved by the healing sight of San Sebastián. Tucked between three mountains and the scalloped curves of two crescent beaches, the city's ocher and ornate Belle Epoch buildings, wide boulevards, and oceanfront esplanades had made San Sebastián the favorite of Spanish kings for almost a century. Once past the last roadblock, the war suddenly seemed far away. The streets were full of traffic, and the sidewalks thronged with commerce. On the beaches, families picnicked beside the gaily striped tents on wheels that were moved back and forth on the sand according to the tide in the bay. The only suggestion of the war in the surrounding hills were the flags that draped the public buildings and the patriotic Basque banners that hung across the major thoroughfares.

And the lobby of the Hotel Continental. It was a madhouse. The British embassy had installed its summer chancellery on the second floor of the famed and richly decorated hotel that overlooked the Bahía de la Concha. Normally, the palm-lined lobby was as sedate as an English drawing room, gentlemen reading their ironed newspapers, ladies sipping tea. But Elizabeth found it packed with men in white suits, shouting and waving little pieces of paper at hotel employees while distraught women fanned themselves as they perched on all the available wicker furniture and on their stacks of luggage.

Pushing through the crowd, she headed toward the staircase to the embassy offices, but it too was clogged with people evidently desperate to get visas. The foyer in front of the elevator was equally jammed. Frustrated, tired, and perspiring from the heat, she decided to try to get something cold to drink in the bar. Despite the leaded glass windows looking out on the sea, it was dark, so Arthur saw her first.

"My God! Elizabeth! You're here!" he said in wonder. He awkwardly threw his arms around her, spilling his sidecar down her back.

"So sorry." He backed off.

"It was refreshing. Could I drink the rest of it?"

"I'll get you another."

"No, I've got to see the ambassador right away. I've got a message from Whitehall."

Arthur blinked and tried to pull himself together. He was not drunk, but he was not sober either.

Gesturing for her to follow, he made for a pair of doors at the end of the bar that took them into the kitchen. "The hotel's mobbed with these Frog vacationers who can't get home. This is a secret access route." Arthur began climbing a narrow circular staircase usually reserved for room service. "How on earth did you get here? We heard there's a raging battle on the road to Irún!"

"Let's put it this way. You said you wanted a convertible."

"What's happened to my car?" he asked anxiously.

"Nothing drastic, but all your windows are gone."

Ambassador Sir Henry Chilton had one of the hotel's Royal apartments. Three of the rooms were used for embassy business and the rest served as his residence. The walls and ceilings of his office, a converted dining room, were covered in ornate moldings and florid frescoes. Elizabeth suddenly felt a mess. Her slacks were covered with grass stains and she had blood clotting her disheveled hair. She was certain that her face must be as dirty as her hands, which she wiped on her jacket before holding them out to greet the ambassador.

Large and calm, Sir Henry smiled quite graciously as he rose from his escritoire. "My dear Elizabeth, what a surprise. You look like you've had quite a time of it." He placed her in the chair next to him. Then he simply waited.

Everything she planned to say went out of her head. She couldn't just blurt out that she told the cabinet office that he wanted to be rescued.

"The Foreign Office asked me to contact you," she finally managed to say.

"We are rather out of touch, what with the telephone and cable interrupted. I hope they're not blaming me for that." He chuckled.

"No, they're just worried."

"Well, you can tell them we're quite all right. Isn't that so, Arthur?"

"Quite." He nodded obediently.

Elizabeth's heart sank. What could she tell the Foreign Office now? That the ambassador had changed his mind? He'd find out and be even more furious for making him look like a dithering fool. But damn it, he was a fool! She had to find a way to make him appreciate the danger.

"Would you mind if I also told them about the situation between here and Irún?"

"I'd be fascinated to hear myself."

So Elizabeth recounted her efforts to get to San Sebastián, leaving out nothing except the way it felt when the young man with the red star in his cap had his hand on her breast. As she described the executions, the shelling, and the firefight, the ambassador grew more and more pale.

"And so I think General Mola's strategy will be to take Irún so as to cut off any supplies from, or escape to, France. Then he'll go after San Sebastián," she concluded. "As far as I can see, neither side is taking prisoners."

The ambassador sat in silence for several minutes, then picked up the phone. She glanced at Arthur. He wore a mask of concern, but about what, it was impossible to read. A moment later, a military attaché unknown to Elizabeth came in and she had to repeat her story. As she did so, Arthur appeared increasingly irritated.

"I think she's right," the attaché said when she finished. Arthur frowned. "Except for one thing," the officer said. Arthur brightened.

Sir Henry raised an eyebrow, signaling the attaché to go on.

"Two Nationalist warships have been sighted on the horizon." He went to the window and pointed out to sea. "If they follow the pattern at Santander and Bilbao, they'll blockade the port and begin shelling us at night."

"Good Lord, we're trapped!" The ambassador displayed emotion for the first time. "What on earth should we do?"

"From what Mrs. Pack reports," the attaché noted, "a land convoy to Irún is out of the question. Too tempting a target."

"I quite agree." The ambassador turned to Arthur. "Any thoughts?"

"A bit out of my line, sir." He shot an angry look at Elizabeth for having put him on the spot.

They all sat in silence. The sounds of hawkers on the esplanade and cries of children playing on the beach drifted in on the ocean breeze. Even if Arthur didn't like it, Elizabeth knew she had to speak.

"Well, I'm going to try to get back to St.-Jean-de-Luz this evening."

"Isn't that rather risky?" the ambassador objected.

"I know everyone at the roadblocks, and I've an escort."

"I do admire your courage. If you arrive safely, please phone the Foreign Office and tell them of the fix we're in."

This was her chance. She had to take it. "Do you think they should send a destroyer?"

Sir Henry's eyes widened. Arthur looked aghast at his wife. Clearly, she had gone too far.

"Yes indeed!" the ambassador exclaimed. His glance chastised the others. "What a splendid idea! Tell them to send one." He tapped the table for emphasis. "Most urgently!"

Just before Elizabeth and her escorts pulled away from the hotel, the military attaché arrived with two more passengers: himself and a personal friend of the ambassador. The attaché explained that the other man, a known Franco sympathizer, would be executed in retaliation when the Nationalists began to bombard the town. Elizabeth agreed to take him along despite the fact that her militia escort would shoot them all if they discovered the man's political leanings. Her only condition was a bottle of brandy to keep the militiamen content.

Everything went smoothly. They saw no more fighting. She dropped the ambassador's Fascist friend at a hotel in Fuenterrabía and the Communist militiamen at the commissariat in Irún. Elizabeth took the military attaché across the border and left him off at the Lloyd's office in St.-Jean-de-Luz. He thanked her for the ride, then noted that they really hadn't been properly introduced.

"I'm Captain Lance." He held out his hand. "I'm sorry you've gotten dragged into all of this. It must have been quite an ordeal."

"Actually," said Elizabeth, shaking his hand and smiling, "I had the most wonderful time."

Three days later, a destroyer brought Ambassador Chilton, Arthur, and the entire embassy staff into the harbor at St.-Jean-de-Luz. Elizabeth and the other wives were there

to greet them at the dock. Everyone was in a holiday mood
except Arthur. She finally confronted him when they arrived home.

"Aren't you the least proud of me, Arthur?"

"Do you think the embassy staff doesn't know what you
did?" He poured himself a whiskey.

"The ambassador seemed very happy about it."

"Did you think for even one moment of the position you
might put me in, not to mention how the other wives would
regard you? You've made an enemy of the chargé's wife."

"Well, the hell with her," Elizabeth exploded. "It was
no time to play the demure diplomatic spouse. If it wasn't
for me, you all could have been captured or killed."

"I realize it's been an effort for you to behave yourself
for the last month," said Arthur, unmoved, "but I'm afraid
that this escapade simply proves that you're an irredeem-
able adventuress." He drained his glass. "You'd have
taken those same irresponsible risks if you had children,
wouldn't you?"

Arthur stomped off to take a nap before she could reply.
But she knew it didn't matter what she might say or that
she had saved him. He had made up his mind against children.

The following morning, Arthur rented quarters for the
new embassy-in-exile above a grocery store in the French
border town of Hendaye. From there, on September 5, Elizabeth along with thousands of other spectators stood on a
hill overlooking the international bridge and watched Mola's Fascists assault Irún. A torrent of refugees poured
across the bridge as the French customs guards fled in
panic. Then the fires started. The local Republican committee, believing that defense of the town was futile, decided to burn it down.

As Elizabeth watched the city go up in flames, she could
not help wondering and worrying about Antonio. Below,
on the international bridge Republican machine gunners
were holding out to the last. Someone in the crowd said
they were not even Spaniards, but French Communists eager to have a chance to kill Fascists.

For the first time, Elizabeth began to appreciate the depth

of the hatreds fueling the civil war and spreading across the face of Europe. The Left and Right would rather destroy their homeland than see it controlled by their enemies.

Elizabeth returned to the villa that night feeling sad and depressed. Now, the British embassy was completely out of Spain. Arthur was dead set against starting a family. And Antonio, wherever he might be, was beyond the mountains, beyond the line of Franco's bayonets that now ruled the frontier.

She was met at the gate by her housekeeper. She looked worried and upset.

"There is someone here for you."

"Who?" Elizabeth asked.

"She claims to be a noblewoman but you can't trust these refugees. I didn't know what to do with her."

"Where is she?"

"I took her in the back way. She's in the kitchen."

Her curiosity aroused, Elizabeth hurried in the front door and straight down the hall. The woman had her head on the table. Her sweater was torn as were her stockings and the hem of her dress. A battered suitcase sat at her feet.

"She claimed to be a friend of yours . . . " the housekeeper explained.

The woman raised her head. Through the dirt and exhaustion on her face, Elizabeth recognized her. It was Maria, Antonio's wife.

"I didn't know where else to come. They took Antonio away in the night. Please, I beg you, help me find him."

White's, London—
June 29, 1937

The captain expertly filleted the steamed turbot, peeling back the spine and serving one half of the fish to William Stephenson and the other to Stewart Menzies. Stephenson was proceeding obliquely; telling him about his experiences in Poland, but approaching the subject of the Enigma with caution.

Menzies had an intimidating reputation. It was not merely that he was "C" 's deputy, or that he was rumored

to be the illegitimate son of Edward VI, closely resembling
the late monarch down to his sandy brown hair and bright
blue Windsor eyes. It was rather that he epitomized the
casual ruthlessness of the English ruling elite, egotistical
and utterly unfettered by middle-class notions of fair play.
Stephenson knew he must lead him to his own conclusions
rather than sell him.

"The science of radio is as advanced as anything I've
seen in America or here," Stephenson was saying. "And
curiously, their army is heavily engaged in supporting it."

"Why 'curiously'?" Menzies ventured.

"Well, the air force and the navy have a natural interest
in radio for communication. But the Polish Army is unique
for its stubborn dependence on horse cavalry."

"Then what's the explanation?"

Stephenson refused to be hurried. "I was particularly impressed with their radio receivers. They're sensitive enough
to pick up every signal transmitted in Germany. And
they've built a number of stations along the border."

"That seems logical. Germany is certainly a potential
danger to them." Menzies signaled the waiter for more
wine. He appeared to be growing bored with the subject.

"But why, I wondered, would they make such an extensive effort to intercept signals that they couldn't read?"

"What do you mean?" His interest quickened.

"As we know, German signals are encrypted by the
Enigma machine. So why would they work so hard to intercept them, unless . . . " Stephenson let his voice fade.

Menzies finished the sentence for him. ". . . unless the
Poles had cracked the Enigma."

Later that afternoon, Dilly Knox was throwing cold water
on the idea. "Maybe they're doing what we do, listening
to a lot of gibberish in hopes of finding a few messages in
the clear." He limped about Menzies's office while Alistair
Denniston and Captain Lance from the operations section
sat on the sofa.

"Still, it's an outsize effort for such a small country as
Poland to make," Denniston remarked, "and for such little
gain. We can hardly afford it ourselves."

"We're not in imminent danger of being invaded by the Huns either," Knox responded peevishly.

"I can't just ignore the possibility," said Menzies. "Stephenson will simply go to Churchill and we'll have a row. What does our man in Warsaw say?" He directed the question at Captain Lance.

"That he hasn't the time, resources, or agents in place to penetrate the security around the Poles' cryptological program."

"So he wants another body?"

"Yes. And took pains to remind us that Warsaw is a very dangerous place. They've got the Gestapo, the Abwehr, the Soviet NKVD operating there along with the Polish Defa, and they're no slouch either."

"Well, we have to send someone." Menzies frowned.

"One of our best men then?" asked Captain Lance.

"Not exactly." He tapped his teeth with a pencil. "I should think we'd be better off with somebody expendable."

Chapter 8

"So Arthur Pack has let you come here on a fool's errand, and without consulting me," the British chargé angrily said to Elizabeth. "You'll take the first airplane out of here. I'll have nothing to do with you!"

She was sitting in the office of John Leche, the senior British official accredited to the Spanish Republican government, which had moved to Valencia when Madrid came under siege. Antonio was reported to be still in Madrid, and Elizabeth was seeking help to get there.

"You're quite wrong, Mr. Leche." Elizabeth pronounced his name in the Spanish style—*leche* meant "milk."

"It's pronounced 'Leech,'" he responded.

"Would 'Your Excellency' do?" She kept her voice low and sincere.

He regarded her sternly, rejecting the joke. In his late forties, tall, rugged, with a lined face and thick dark hair graying at the temples, he had the air of a gentleman-adventurer about him. Elizabeth imagined that he would be most handsome in a military uniform. Unlike most of the British diplomats she had met, John Leche looked like he had done something in his life, taken risks and paid the price.

"Arthur has nothing to do with this." Elizabeth used her warmest and most soothing voice. "No doubt he is even more furious with me than you are! I ran away to go to Madrid. And I'm going to Madrid.''

Leche looked skeptical. So had Arthur when she insisted that she must go back to Madrid. Ever since Maria de Zaragoza had arrived in St.-Jean-de-Luz, she and Elizabeth had been seeking information on Antonio. Maria's devotion to her husband had surprised Elizabeth, for the proud and taciturn marquesa had left Antonio alone in Madrid much of the time, apparently preferring to stay at the family ranch with the children. Arthur surprised Elizabeth even more by inviting Maria to stay with them as long as she liked. As it turned out, he was merely trying to give the lie to rumors about Antonio and Elizabeth, and as soon as he was admitted to the English Club, he began hinting that Maria should leave.

By the time that the marquesa moved back to Spain in early 1937, they still had heard nothing about Antonio. As she departed by car, Maria had embraced Elizabeth.

"He was a pilot and a soldier. I always knew that someday I would lose him." She had begun to weep. "Was I wrong to keep my distance, to hold back my love?''

"You were only trying to protect yourself." Elizabeth had tried to be sympathetic.

Maria had pulled away and drawn herself up. "*Bueno,* I must go on with my life.''

Elizabeth, however, had refused to give up on Antonio. In late spring, while working with the Red Cross across the border in Spain, she heard from Franco's foreign minister that Antonio was held in Madrid. She could no longer deny her unthinkable thoughts. She and Arthur were merely roommates; not even that, since Arthur had taken a separate bedroom. The world was being turned upside down by war and revolution. Right and wrong were changing places. Why couldn't she and Antonio break the bonds that held them apart? If she could find him, save him, why couldn't they find a way to build a life together?

So Elizabeth came up with the idea of going to Madrid to collect the furniture and household effects she and Arthur had left behind when they thought they were just leaving for the summer.

"Don't be ridiculous," Arthur had responded as he

dressed for one of his black-tie dinners at the English Club.
"Madrid is virtually surrounded."

"You're always complaining about money," Elizabeth
argued. "Everything we own is in Madrid. A bomb could
wipe us out tomorrow!"

That gave him pause. "No. You've become quite notorious for delivering medicines to the Fascists. Red Cross or
no, if the Republicans realize who you are, you could be
shot. I absolutely forbid it!"

Two weeks later she was aboard an Iberian Airlines Ford
Tri-motor bumping through the air over the snowcapped
Pyrenees on her way from Toulouse to Valencia. Since Arthur was formally accredited to the Republican government,
its consulate gave her a visa with no difficulty. On the day
of her flight, she left a note on Arthur's breakfast tray and
sneaked outside to a waiting car and her loyal chauffeur.
Once in Valencia, however, she realized she had no contacts other than the British consulate general. But her reception was turning out to be anything but cordial.

"Do you have any idea," Leche demanded, "what's going on in this part of Spain? Up in Barcelona we've just
had a civil war inside a civil war! Stalin's stooges have
slaughtered thousands of their Anarchist allies. People are
shot for subscribing to the wrong newspapers! These so-
called Republicans are more intent on killing each other
than on killing Fascists. I spend half my time saving the
lives of hare-brained English schoolboys who think it's a
lark to come down here and pot Gerries and Mussolini's
I-ties. They're the ones who end up getting potted, up
against a wall by their chums."

He paused to take a breath. "And Madrid's even worse.
It's being bombed and shelled every day and night. There's
no one at the embassy. If you go and are killed I shall be
responsible and there'll be one bloody row. No, back you
go to where you came from!"

"I saw Ernest Hemingway at the airport with a group of
other writers," said Elizabeth. "They're going up to Madrid by road."

"Ernest Hemingway's traveling under the sponsorship of
the Kremlin Communists to distract the world's attention
from the fact that the Reds are slaughtering their former

friends. Ernest Hemingway's going to have an escort of bloody Russian tanks!''

Elizabeth opened her green eyes wider and softly said, "Then perhaps I should go with him." From the way Leche had been inspecting her face and figure, Elizabeth had no doubt that the chargé believed she could arrange it.

"You place me in an intolerable position!" he raged. "You're traveling with British diplomatic papers. You can't take part in a wretched propaganda show!''

"I'm sorry." She picked up her luggage and turned to leave his office. "Mr. Leche, I'm going to Madrid whether you help me or not. Since you'll be held responsible either way, I merely thought you'd prefer to help."

The taxi carrying Elizabeth entered Madrid at daybreak. Since the early months of the war, the city had been surrounded on three sides by the Nationalists and driving the road from Valencia was like running a gauntlet. To provide maximum safety, Leche had arranged for her to leave Valencia in a nighttime military convoy. But outside of Tarancon, as she lay in a ditch trying to escape the strafing "Blackbirds" of the Condor Legion, while flares lit the sky and vehicles burned around her, Elizabeth thought perhaps the whole idea was a big mistake. Antonio would blame himself and curse her if she got herself blown to bits. And she was so scared her bones ached. She decided that traveling in a caravan of targets at forty miles per hour without lights and with the drivers looking more at the sky than the road was not safer than traveling solo.

With the dawn, the familiar streets of Madrid came as an immense relief. Still her feelings were in turmoil: excitement and apprehension at the thought of drawing ever closer to Antonio; shock at what the war had wrought in the city she loved. Above all, Madrid was a city of life. People filled the boulevards at all hours, including *la madrugada*—the early morning—when the partying often continued from the night before. Now, Elizabeth saw no cafés open. The few people on the sidewalks were not revelers but women in rags lining up outside of the *almacenes* for food. Whole blocks of the city were bombed and burnt out. Fires still raged from the night before, and rubble

blocked several streets. La Telefónica, the forty-story telephone exchange that was Madrid's only skyscraper, had
always been lit like a wedding cake. It now loomed dark
and brooding.

In Elizabeth's beloved Plaza del Sol the flower beds were
planted with something that looked like potatoes, and the
beautiful rococo and neoclassical buildings were defaced
with huge portraits of Marx, Lenin, Stalin, and La Pasionara, a miner's wife who had become a celebrity by exhort-
ing the masses on the radio. The history of the civil war
was recorded on the torn banners that hung from the lamp-
posts and the slogans that covered the walls.

LONG LIVE MADRID WITHOUT A GOVERNMENT, the faded
Anarchist slogan was partly covered by NO PASARÁN!—
THEY SHALL NOT PASS—La Pasionara's famous call to halt
Franco's advancing troops. That now seemed superseded
by a newer banner with a far less confident declaration from
La Pasionara: BETTER TO DIE ON YOUR FEET THAN LIVE ON
YOUR KNEES.

Elizabeth reached her flat at Castellana 63, just as the air
raid sirens started up again. She felt grateful that the building was still standing and that her keys still worked in the
gate. Entering the courtyard, she was surprised to find it
full of refugees, some living in boxes and shanties, others
out in the open surrounded by ragged bundles. A dozen
families appeared to live there along with an assortment of
pigs, chickens, and even a cow crammed into an area no
more than seventy-five feet on a side. As the air raid sirens
wailed, they simply looked skyward with resignation, the
older ones crossing themselves and praying.

"Señora Pack!" An old man waved from across the
courtyard. He was gaunt, and as he moved toward her, she
could see he had a terrible limp. His face looked like battered plaster. Elizabeth was shocked to realize that it was
Enrique, the guardian of the building.

"What happened to you?"

"*Una ochenta y ocho al frente.*" He shrugged. An
eighty-eight shell at the front. "Come quickly to the basement. You will be safer."

"What about these people, all the children?"

"There isn't room."

Once in the basement, she saw why. It was jammed with refugees too. "The families take turns," Enrique explained. Elizabeth sat on a box near the furnace.

Soon she heard the bombs thudding far away, then nearer and nearer. Dust danced out of the bricks and the earth shuddered beneath her feet. With the whistle of each approaching bomb, the people around her moaned louder and louder. Only the children were strangely silent.

Elizabeth was silent too, gripped by the fear she had felt during the drive from Valencia. Closing her eyes, she tried to concentrate on Antonio and the happiness they would find when he was free.

In time, the sounds of explosions moved off, and a siren sounded an all-clear. Still trembling, Elizabeth, accompanied by Enrique, climbed the three flights to her second-floor apartment. He apologized that the elevator was no longer working.

"There is no electricity. Also no water."

The seal that the embassy had placed on the door when closing the apartment had been broken.

"We had some troubles with the Anarchists at first," Enrique explained, "but I think almost everything is safe."

The air in the apartment had the familiar closed-off smell of an attic. Morning peeked through the shudders of the darkened flat, sending shafts of light stabbing through motes of dust shaken to life by the recent bombardment. As she wandered through the rooms, Elizabeth marveled at how long ago it seemed that she had lived there, almost as if it were in another life.

"Why has the señora come back to Madrid?" Enrique interrupted her thoughts.

"The furniture. I need to move it to France."

"So you abandon us for good?"

"I'm sorry."

"I will help the señora as much as I can."

"We'll need to make a lot of crates." She began to range through the apartment, imagining what would be required to pack it all.

"That will be very difficult," Enrique said apologetically. "Everything must go for the war and for necessities.

You need someone who is authorized to have wood. If I try to make crates, I would be shot."

"Then what can I do?" She stopped pacing.

He thought for a moment and then brightened. "I know one person who has such a priority."

"Who?"

"The coffin maker."

As soon as she had made arrangements for packing her household effects, Elizabeth headed directly to the Montana Barracks, located in the center of the city. During the initial uprising, it had offered a refuge for insurgent troops and Fascist sympathizers. Besieged by the populace, the barracks became the scene of the first bloodbath of the civil war. Now it was a maximum security military prison.

Elizabeth was full of anticipation, hoping to see Antonio soon, yet fearing that she might fail. Approaching the fortress on foot, she could see the hundreds of pockmarks scaring every window and door and the gaping hole in the wall where the Asturian miners dynamited the gates. The entrance was guarded by a squad of women, none more than twenty years old, with Mausers slung around their necks. They would not let her pass.

"You must have permission," one of them said eyeing her linen slacks and silk blouse. They wore blue overalls, boots, and red stars on their caps.

"Where do I get permission?" Elizabeth asked, trying not to sound impatient.

They shrugged and turned away from her.

"I want to speak to someone in charge!"

They raised their weapons.

"I must find a way to get in!" Elizabeth insisted.

"We could let you in," said the one who had done the talking. "But then maybe we wouldn't let you out."

Elizabeth resigned herself to a long siege of the Republican prison authorities. John Leche had arranged for her to live with the Scottish Ambulance Corps, run by a flush-faced little Scotswoman by the name of Miss Robertson. Elizabeth made clear that she would not be a guest and would carry the same burdens as the other volunteers. So instead of sleeping, she spent each night ferrying wounded soldiers back from the front or pulling people from collapsed buildings while dodging bombs and the antiaircraft shrapnel that rained back to earth during air raids. In the smoking early-morning hours, she would return to one of the bombed-out buildings where she would persuade the survivors to help her load wood scraps into the ambulance so she could take them to the coffin maker. Every morning she would ask him about her crates, and each time he would admonish her with the same reply: "The dead cannot wait."

During the day, the nightmare of bombing was replaced by the nightmare of bureaucracy as Elizabeth pressed her inquiries about Antonio. She devoted a full week to waiting in line and being shuffled from one office to another at the Gobernación in the Plaza del Sol. When she was finally able to tell her story to the allegedly responsible official, she was told to go to the Ministry of War.

There lay chaos. After days of fruitless pleading with underlings, she learned that she had to have a "priority" merely to talk with someone with authority over Antonio's case—not that anyone admitted to having heard of him. And it was several more days before she learned that only SIM, the secret police of the Spanish Communist party, could grant access to the Montana Barracks.

When Miss Robertson heard that Elizabeth was trying to get in touch with SIM, she made her sit down for a talk. They faced each other over an oil drum in the middle of the garage that served as the Ambulance Corps headquarters and dormitory. A bare bulb hung over her head as if she were in an interrogation room. The look on Miss Robertson's face made clear she wasn't buying her explanation of why she was searching for Antonio de Zaragoza.

"I admire your spunk, dear," she said in her burred Scots brogue, "but nobody tries to see the SIM. They find you! They're thugs controlled by the Russian NKVD. Asking them to help you locate some high-born flyboy who's under arrest is a sure way to be getting yourself in jail. That fine diplomatic passport of yours won't mean tuppence."

"What can I do then?" She was frustrated and tired and near to tears.

"Have you no friends or acquaintances who can intercede on your behalf?"

"I've been through my address book. I've called and tried to visit people. Not a single one of them is still in Madrid."

"You traveled in a smart set."

"I even asked the *guardián* of my building. He told me he could find out about Antonio right away. His friends are guards at the barracks."

"What did he learn?"

"I don't know." Elizabeth shook her head. "He's disappeared."

"See what I mean?" said Miss Robertson.

After several weeks, all of Elizabeth's household effects were packed up and Miss Robertson had arranged for everything to be shipped in an empty Scottish Ambulance Corps truck that had to go down to Valencia for supplies. As the day of departure approached, Elizabeth felt increasingly desperate. She still had no information on Antonio and Enrique had not reappeared. All of the horror she had seen had washed over her as she kept herself tightly focused on finding Antonio. But now, as it seemed she might fail, Elizabeth began to react to the brutality she had witnessed—the mangled women, the crushed children, the old people decapitated by flying glass, the families huddled under staircases and burnt beyond recognition, men sitting in bathtubs looking perfectly normal except for the gray matter leaking out of their noses and ears from the effect of concussion. She began to have uncontrollable tremors at odd moments. Loud noises filled her with panic. She had virtually stopped sleeping, because her dreams were even worse than the nightly bombardments. Miss Robertson told her that it was time that she left Madrid.

A few days before the convoy to Valencia was to depart, Elizabeth learned from one of the refugees at Castellana 63 that Enrique had been arrested for showing his POUM identification papers at a Communist checkpoint. He was being held at the Iglesia San Pedro, one of the churches in the old town that had been turned into a jail for minor offend-

ers. Miss Robertson managed to arrange for Elizabeth to
see him.

"I will do all I can to get you out," she assured him
through a chicken wire fence strung across the nave of the
church. "Have you heard anything about Antonio?" His
expression changed, but Elizabeth could not read it. "Have
you?" she insisted.

"He was taken to the Montana Barracks as you
thought."

"How is he?" Her voice rose with excitement. "Can I
get word to him?"

"Months ago, all the military prisoners were taken to
Valencia."

"That's wonderful!" Elizabeth shouted. The guards
looked at her sharply.

"Wait, señora, I must explain."

Elizabeth went silent.

"When they reached Paracuellos de Jarama, something
happened. No one knows why."

Elizabeth watched him struggle to speak with growing
terror in her heart.

"It was a massacre. The Anarchists killed their prisoners."

"No!" she said in a whisper. "No, it's not possible.
No." But as she heard herself repeating "No" over and
over, Elizabeth remembered one of the rumors that had
swept St.-Jean-de-Luz. Anarchist guards escorting detain-
ees to Valencia had gone on a drunken rampage, shooting
their prisoners at point-blank range as they sat in the trucks.
And when their bullets ran low, they made the survivors
run, bent over, head down, with hands tied behind their
backs, while the guards battered the prisoners brains out
with the butts of their Mausers like cattle hammered down
in a chute to a slaughterhouse.

"No!" Elizabeth screamed. She ran out the door and into
the blinding sun of the square. Dazed, she wandered the
winding tortured streets for hours. At the entrance to a
small square, a dead horse killed in the morning bombardment was sprawled on the stones still attached to its wagon.
A half-dozen women in black shrouds were hacking pieces
of meat from the emaciated carcass. In a narrow, rubble-

strewn alley, children with homemade red cross armbands and a stretcher of sticks and blankets played at being rescue workers. Had she really cursed them and thrown stones at them?

By the time Elizabeth returned to the Scottish Ambulance Corps that afternoon, she felt spent, empty of all feeling. Miss Robertson asked her whether Enrique had been of help, and she shook her head.

"Is there any way you could help him get out of jail?" Elizabeth asked. "Could you say he worked for the corps?"

"I'll do what I can, dear," Miss Robertson assured her.

At dinner she was uncharacteristically quiet, eating her beans and rice in silence.

"You don't look well, Elizabeth," Miss Robertson observed. "I think you should stay in tonight and try for a good sleep."

"No!" she said sharply, then apologized. "I'm sorry, but I'll feel better if I go out with the rest."

When the air raid sirens began, Elizabeth pulled on her tin hat and climbed aboard one of the ambulances as she always did. At their first stop, a three-hundred-pound bomb had landed in the street creating a huge crater, blowing out all the windows up and down the block, and collapsing a small building. While the others concentrated on first aid for the scores of people slashed by flying glass, Elizabeth was drawn toward the fallen apartment house where several women and children were climbing out of the cellar.

From a part of the building that was still standing she heard a voice.

"Ayuda! Dios mío, ayúdame!"

She climbed a shaky staircase that was still partly attached to a wall and made her way down a second-floor hallway that ended in the open air. The voice came again from a nearby room. Finding the door stuck, Elizabeth had to kick it open. Half the room was gone, fallen into the street. At the edge of the precipice, she could see someone pinned under an armoire and a ceiling beam. Only an arm and a leg in overalls were visible. The voice had sunk to a strangled whisper.

"Hold on!" Elizabeth tested the floor to see if it would

hold her. Near a window, a heavy wrought-iron curtain rod hung from the wall. Using her weight and pulling with all her might, she broke it free. In a moment she had it jammed under the armoire and began levering the massive wardrobe off of the prostrate and twisted body.

That was when she saw it. The telltale red-and-black cloth. The ubiquitous handkerchief that identified a person as an Anarchist. The people who murdered her Antonio.

She stopped lifting. Elizabeth knew she could simply set the armoire back down and walk away. Or she could yank out the rod and let the huge piece of furniture fall back and crush the figure lying there. As the fury rose inside her, Elizabeth could imagine the sound of bones breaking. . . .

"Here, let us help. . . . "

Miss Robertson and one of the young corpsmen rushed to her side. Elizabeth staggered away. They leaned on the rod, and the armoire went tumbling down to the first floor. Miss Robertson rolled the body over. It was a woman. She was still alive. And she was pregnant.

Reaching for the door frame, Elizabeth collapsed.

She had a fever that lasted for three days. Miss Robertson fed her lentil and barley soup between bouts of delirium. Once when she awoke, Elizabeth sobbed, "The dreams, the killings, I can't take it. . . . "

"You've seen too much, lass." Miss Robertson took her hand.

"I'm doing it!"

When the fever subsided, Miss Robertson told her that the truck could wait no longer. She and her crates must leave for Valencia the next day.

"I'm sorry I've been such a trial. . . . "

"You've been nothing less than a heroine, lass. But this is not your calling, and we've got to be getting on with ours."

Elizabeth turned away to hide her tears.

"You must love this Antonio very much."

"He's dead."

Miss Robertson took Elizabeth into her arms. "It's good to mourn." She rocked her almost like a child.

Elizabeth could feel the strength in the tiny Scotswom-

an's sinewy body. "You've had the rare privilege to see
how precious human life is," she went on. "Now you're
obliged to live it fully."

The next afternoon, Elizabeth watched as the young men
from the Scottish Ambulance Corps and several of the refugees loaded her crates onto the truck. As the last pieces
were being stacked in the back, she saw the shutters to her
apartment being opened. The refugees in the courtyard of
Castellana 63 had found a better home.

The sun was setting as they moved off down the street.
Elizabeth turned for one last look and saw a figure waving
his arms and limping after them.

"Enrique!" she cried out. She told the driver to back up.

Gasping for breath, Enrique climbed onto the running
board. *"Gracias a Dios, señora!* I found you in time!"

"You're out of jail! I'm so glad!"

"How will you ever forgive me?"

"Don't worry about the apartment. I'm happy for them
to use it."

"No, señora. I'm talking of Antonio."

"It wasn't your fault." The pain was still in her voice.

"You don't understand. I was wrong!"

Elizabeth's heart contracted. She was not sure she could
bear what he might say next.

"Antonio is alive!"

Chapter 9

"A woman?" Menzies asked. "An American?"

"She's married to a British diplomat," Captain Lance said to be reassuring. "That would give her excellent cover."

"Hundreds of women are married to British diplomats. That's hardly a recommendation."

They were sitting in Menzies's office at SIS headquarters. The brown walls needed paint. His wooden desk was battle-scarred, the rug frayed, the leather sofa cracked and worn. It looked like a typical English club.

"I saw her in action myself," Captain Lance responded, "when our embassy in Spain was evacuated from San Sebastián." Menzies always seemed quite casual in laying down requirements, but in the event, he was maddeningly hard to satisfy. "She engineered the whole thing," Lance added, "worked her way back and forth across the front lines. She was almost killed."

"We want someone brave, not reckless. She may be expendable, but we don't want a blowup."

"Miss Robertson with the Scottish Ambulance Corps in Madrid gives her high marks for composure. They were shelled and bombed every night."

"What was she doing back in Madrid?"

"Ostensibly packing up her household effects to get them out of harm's way. But in point of fact, she seems to have been searching for Antonio de Zaragoza."

"Do we know him?"

103

"His dossier is right there."

Menzies flipped through the files impatiently. "Well, I can't put a rank amateur on Stephenson's Enigma project. She'll have to go through some sort of operational testing. I want to know if she's loyal and can take direction. Without her knowing, of course."

"That shouldn't be too hard." The relief was plain in Captain Lance's voice. "It took a bit of digging, but I've finally located her. She's on her way to Valencia. I'm sure our man there, John Leche, will be happy to put her through her paces."

"She's stopping there?"

"I think so. She's still looking for the Marqués de Zaragoza."

Menzies was looking through his dossier again. "Are they lovers?"

"Only rumors. But she's very beautiful."

"Then I want that aspect tested too," Menzies ordered. "If it's to be a woman, she can't be an American prude."

"John Leche is divorced," Captain Lance said confidently. "I should think he'd be only too happy to oblige."

British Consulate General, Valencia, Spain— August 15, 1937

"You look exhausted," John Leche said, putting down his pencil and pad. "Let me fix you a gin and tonic."

"It's hardly three in the afternoon," Elizabeth replied. Since she hadn't slept for twenty-four hours, she wondered why she was being so particular.

"Think of the tonic as medicine," Leche replied, "and the gin as concentrated juniper juice." He handed her a drink and took one for himself. "It's a pleasure to see you."

Elizabeth enjoyed the sweet tingle of the drink going down. She was struck by the change in his attitude: the warmth of his greeting and his interest in her activities in Madrid. She liked the way he sat on the edge of his desk while he listened to her. It reminded Elizabeth of her father.

For his part, John Leche was surprised to have received a cable from SIS that morning about Elizabeth Pack. She seemed a bit wild for the sober tastes of the secret service. Still she was an eyeful. Like most people who had spent a month under constant bombardment in Madrid, she looked haunted and war-weary. Yet sitting on his sofa with her legs crossed, she remained remarkably attractive, somehow seeming to fill the room with her intensity. He felt an old and familiar tug that had always meant trouble.

"Don't worry about your household effects," he was saying. "I'll get them transshipped on a British destroyer. It may be a while before you see them, but at least you'll not have the lot end up on the bottom of the Med courtesy of an I-tie torpedo."

She smiled wearily. Too tired to relax, the gin was at least taking the edge off her nerves. "Thank you. I'm so grateful to you." She finished the rest of her drink in one swallow.

Leche's eyebrows raised slightly. "Well, I suppose I ought to think of getting you home now."

This was just what Elizabeth had feared. She felt suddenly depressed, then became furious. "Your Excellency"—she handed back her glass—"I wish I knew why you are trying to chuck me out again. I need three or four more days in Valencia before I can even think of going home!"

He took the glass from her hand and drew her to her feet. "I haven't any intention of chucking you out." He smiled. "When I said home, I didn't mean France, but home with me!"

"The entire staff stays in Las Palmeras," Leche explained to Elizabeth as his car made its way south out of the city, "to avoid the nightly bombings by the Condor Legion."

"I appreciate your putting me up," she said, hoping it meant he was softening toward her.

Leche smiled back. Being a diplomat, he was not, strictly speaking, a member of the secret service. Rather, he was a "cooptee," someone who from time to time did the odd job for "Broadway," as the headquarters of SIS was known. But with Spain in the midst of a civil war that involved Hitler, Mussolini, and Stalin, working for Broadway had almost become his full-time occupation.

As they drove along toward Las Palmeras, he pointed out the strange Chinese-looking houses with peaked tile roofs that sat in the middle of vast rice fields that stretched to the distant hills. On the other side of the road, miles of orange groves ran down to the sea.

"Notice something odd about the trees?" he asked.

They were not at all like those Elizabeth had seen as a girl visiting southern California. The Valencian orange trees were short, no taller than a man.

"They've been bred and pruned to be picked without ladders."

They passed over several single-file sluice bridges that crossed canals linking the sea with a vast freshwater lagoon on their right.

"That's the Albufera," Leche explained. "It makes the rice fields and *paella Valenciana* possible."

Elizabeth was enjoying the tour. She stole a glance at Leche as he steered the big Humber down the highway. He was quite handsome in a raffish sort of way. In another time or another life she might even have fallen in love with him. Instantly, she felt exasperated with herself. How could she even have such a thought? She must be exhausted.

He had caught her look. It caused a small involuntary smile that she took as a certain shyness. He took a hand off the wheel and put it on hers.

"Tell me what's on your mind, Elizabeth."

She wasn't certain what he meant. "I may need a little help in locating an old friend," she replied, "the Marqués de Zaragoza."

Leche looked at her skeptically. "What makes you think he's in Valencia?"

"In Madrid, I was told he had been transferred here from the Montana Barracks."

"You're looking for someone under arrest?"

She had simply smiled back without explanation.

Leche didn't need one. He knew something about Antonio de Zaragoza and the cable from Broadway had mentioned her interest in him. That's what Arthur gets, he thought, for marrying a girl half his age. You keep that in mind too, Leche admonished himself. That might not be easy, now that he had orders from Broadway to "test" her. Of course, he had broken the Seventh Commandment before, but this would be his first for king and country.

"Will you help me find him?" she pressed. "I would be ever so grateful."

He let the question hang without a response. She looked disappointed. He was toying with the idea that her quest for Antonio de Zaragoza gave him leverage to get her help with another important problem—if he could set her and the situation up properly. He turned the possibilities over in his mind.

Where the orange groves gave way to sand dunes covered with Spanish pines and tall grasses, Leche said, "That's Palmeras."

In the distance, Elizabeth could see a stand of thick and sturdy date palms rising on the horizon like a mirage. They turned down a sandy road lined with palm trees and whitewashed walls surrounding houses with railings on their flat roofs like widow's walks. The car stopped at a large compound of bungalows scattered among the dunes near the sea.

In ten minutes, Elizabeth was splashing through the soothing clear water of the Mediterranean, washing away her worries about failing Antonio along with the grime of travel. She had not bathed in such warm soft seas since she was a little girl in Hawaii and her father took her to Waikiki Beach. As Elizabeth floated on her back beyond the gentle shore break, she felt a sense of being alive that she had not known in years. The war seemed far away.

John Leche suddenly burst to the surface next to her. The droplets standing on his skin glistened in the afternoon sunlight. He was deeply tanned and surprisingly well muscled in an opulent sort of way, not at all like the hard crisp contours of Antonio's body. It had been a long time since Elizabeth had felt herself respond to a man's presence. Even in the coolness of the water, she grew flushed and ashamed of her wayward thoughts.

"I could let you stay here for a few days to rest up," he said, treading water, "before sending you home."

"I'm not looking for a vacation, Mr. Leche," she said brusquely and struck out for the shore.

The mission staff dined under a grape arbor attached to the minister's house. Leche had changed into a loose-fitting pair of pants, an open shirt, and rope-soled fisherman's shoes. He could not help staring at Elizabeth, who wore only a halter top and slacks.

As he worked his way through a first course of shrimp and garlic, Leche kept trying to assess her. He had heard that Arthur Pack's wife was something of an adventuress, but who wouldn't be looking for a little excitement if they were married to Colonel Pack. Whenever Leche looked at her, she met his gaze frankly and boldly. He told himself to be careful. Of course, if he'd ever been able to take that advice, he'd be luxuriating as ambassador in Paris instead of dodging bombs in Valencia.

Elizabeth complimented him on the meal.

"You won't find such seafood in Madrid," she said, dipping her bread into the earthenware bowl of olive oil in which the shrimps and garlic had been cooked. "The shells there are full of cordite."

After dinner, Leche invited her for a walk by the sea. The dunes were covered in iceplant with purple and yellow flowers that had started to close as the sun began to set.

"Here, let's take a seat." Leche took her elbow for a moment as she sat on the sand. "This is the best view for the evening fireworks."

In the distance Valencia was strung along the northern horizon under a line of mountains. The sea was calm. All looked peaceful. Soon a dozen little dots forming a string of four triangles appeared against the evening sky.

"Those will be either Henkels or Italian Savoia bombers," Leche noted.

"They don't care what they hit, do they?"

"Franco simply wants to demoralize the populace while the Gerries and I-ties are practicing up for future attacks on London and Paris."

In a few minutes, clouds of smoke began to rise above the city. The line of bombers moved out to sea, then broke apart as each little triangle turned on a different course to come back over Valencia in search of new targets. In the growing darkness, they could see the antiaircraft shells rising upward and exploding like skyrockets illuminating the nearby hills. In time, the bombing stopped and the fires began giving the city and the surrounding mountains an unearthly glow. Sitting far away in Las Palmeras cooled by the onshore breeze from the Mediterranean, they had never heard a sound.

"How can death and destruction be so beautiful?" Her voice was soft and melancholy.

Leche had been attracted to many women in his life, and always it had been a matter of tension, a brittle sense of electricity that had crackled between them. Elizabeth was completely different. He felt her presence like gravity. She engendered in him a deep tidal calm. Leche could hold in check the familiar rise provoked by the curve of her leg against her slacks or the way her halter top cupped her breasts, or the soft sheen on her bare shoulders. But her warm voice and her deep green eyes that flickered with sadness gave him the helpless sensation that he was actually falling toward her. He reached out and put his hand on her shoulder.

The expression on her face told him she had expected it. "You have been very kind in inviting me here, Mr. Leche." He heard her take a deep breath. "But that is as far as my gratitude goes," she said with resignation. "Not so very far, is it?"

Leche withdrew his hand as if it had been slapped. "It's Antonio, isn't it? Is he the only man you have cared for deeply in your whole life so far?"

"Yes," she said with sudden intensity. "Oh yes, I can say that with all my soul."

John Leche managed to obtain Red Cross papers for Elizabeth that enabled her to make direct visits to the local jails. They proved to be more chaotic than in Madrid. The struggle for power between the Communists and everyone else had filled the jails to overflowing and new ones were being created overnight in schools, office buildings, apartment houses, and sports halls. There were so many new political crimes and so many arrests, one guard had explained, that the prisoners had to be constantly sorted, moved, and re-sorted.

And she had heard about the Checkas, the clandestine jails run by Stalin's secret police, the NKVD, where prom-inent political figures like the Anarchist Andrés Nin were detained, tried, and then murdered. If Antonio was in one of those . . . She refused to think about it.

Some of the places Elizabeth visited did not seem like jails at all. In one apartment house, the prisoners mixed with the guards in well-appointed rooms and went outside to run errands and go shopping. She found that this partic-ular jail was for common thieves and robbers who were considered victims of capitalist society.

Most of the places, however, looked like various forms of hell. The office buildings and factories were among the worst, because they had no kitchens, no bathrooms, and inadequate toilets. Prisoners often lay on loose straw hand-cuffed to radiators or chained to pieces of machinery. Every morning Elizabeth would walk through the seemingly end-less corridors, rooms, basements, and dungeons full of sick and desperate people, hoping yet fearing to see Antonio's face among the wretched.

At lunchtime, she emerged into the bright sunshine and headed for the port to join John Leche. In a sidewalk café across from the lime-green rococo merchant marine build-ing, she would pick guiltily at her lobster or paella and pour out her disgust at the ghastly way the Republic treated its prisoners. Leche listened patiently for several days, then pointed out why Franco's Nationalists had so few prisoners; they shot them all.

As the days wore on, Elizabeth talked more and more about her marriage. John Leche proved to be a sympathetic listener. She found that he was never condescending or cen-sorious, but a good friend and companion. Sometimes they would talk about politics and the civil war. John Leche was clearly more on top of things than Arthur and his colleagues at the embassy in Hendaye. Other days, a whole lunch would pass when they would eat quietly together. He was peaceful to be with when she wanted peace.

But underneath, Elizabeth was becoming increasingly worried and depressed. Perhaps it was also the fever and backache that she had picked up in Madrid and could not shake, but after almost two discouraging weeks in Valencia with no sign of Antonio, Elizabeth had a deepening fear that he might have been killed after all, that God had taken Antonio's life as punishment for their illicit love.

One afternoon, when Elizabeth reached her third glass of tinto, it finally came out. "John, can I ask you a favor?"

"Certainly. I was about to ask one of you."

"Would you arrange for me to go back to France?"

"You're joking!" He suddenly looked panicked. "What about Antonio?"

"My search is hopeless. I've been to every prison twice and I've seen every prisoner at least three times! I'm beginning to think it's just a charade, an excuse to avoid Arthur. I sent him a letter, and he hasn't replied. That concerns me too."

"Well, this Antonio business isn't a bust yet." He looked like a man whose horse was refusing to run in the Derby. "If you'll help, we might just learn his whereabouts."

"How?" she asked doubtfully.

"Can you lie? You're so damn honest that I doubt it. Still it would be useful if you could."

"You really know how to build a girl's confidence."

"Hear me out. You know Luis Villada, the Marqués de Arueza?"

"We used to dance together at Jimmy's."

"He's been caught in a roundup of suspected Franco supporters. I'm hoping to get a message tomorrow that will give the go-ahead to try to get him out."

"Out of where?"

"One of the Checkas," he admitted. "But he might know where to find Antonio."

She hesitated. "What am I supposed to do?"

"You'll play the part of his sister. As you're both fair-haired it should work. I'm going to pretend to be your father. With luck, we'll persuade them that it's all a case of mistaken identity."

The next morning the message Leche had been hoping for awaited them at the consulate. His plan was designed to take advantage of three Spanish obsessions: dignity, the siesta, and papers covered with official stamps and illegible signatures. At two o'clock, he ordered the consulate car to be fitted with British flags and switched into his morning coat. "These olive eaters won't know it's not appropriate dress for this time of day," he explained to Elizabeth, "but it adds a dash of class, what?"

In the car on the way to the prison, Leche gave her his final instructions. "Try to relax. As soon as you get to Luis, tell him to speak English."

"He's not very good at it."

"Believe me, the guards won't be able to tell. If there are any questions, his name is 'James.' I shall be busy distracting the guards, so you look after your brother and yourself."

"What will happen if this fails? Will we be arrested?"

"Stand close to 'James' and pray that the guards won't shoot a woman."

The jail was unfamiliar to Elizabeth, another anonymous office building converted to hold political offenders. As they approached it, Leche told the driver to slow down but not to stop as they neared the wooden barrier across the entrance to the courtyard.

He took a deep breath, pulled himself erect, and smiled at Elizabeth. "In for a penny, in for a pound!"

As the car turned into the driveway, the guards raised their guns. But then seeing the flags, the diplomatic license plates, and the speed of the car, the guards leaped to raise the barrier, and they rolled smartly into the courtyard unmolested.

"So far so good." Leche waited for the driver to open the door, then stepped out and grandly surveyed the area. "Follow me," he whispered as the driver helped Elizabeth out of the car. She felt so keyed up that the chronic ache in her back had vanished. John Leche offered his arm and they proceeded across the cobblestones at what she found to be an excruciatingly slow pace.

"I haven't dawdled like this," she whispered, "since I came down the aisle at my wedding."

"Dignity, my dear. And if that fails you, try arrogance."

When they reached a cluster of militiamen half napping

as they guarded the entrance, Leche drew himself up and brandished his diplomatic *salvo conducto* along with a variety of other elaborate documents. The guards merely shrugged in response. Grandly, he led Elizabeth through the door. As they made their way down the ground-floor corridor, they paused occasionally for Leche to wave his papers at guards. Each time, Elizabeth thought her heart might stop, but the guards seemed too busy digesting their noon meal to pay them much attention. Watching Leche's performance, Elizabeth thought, What a superb figure of a man he is, and her own confidence increased.

But as they began climbing the stairs, they encountered a thickset man with a crew cut and a bull neck who could only have been a Russian adviser.

"*Alto,*" he cried in bad Spanish. "Who are you? Let me see your papers!"

"I'm sorry, but I don't speak Spanish," Leche said amiably but at the same time lifting his shoulders to give himself a more commanding presence. Elizabeth wanted to run.

"Papers! Papers!" He swore in Russian and to explain himself pulled some dogeared documents from his jacket that he waved in Leche's face.

To the Russian's surprise, Leche grabbed them away and peered at them. "Sorry, old boy. Can't read a word."

At that moment, a scuffle broke out downstairs as the militia brought in a new gang of prisoners. The Russian snatched back his precious documents. "You wait!" He ordered. "I'll be back!"

Leche waved and nodded, then turned and continued up to the third floor.

They moved more swiftly now. Leche seemed to know exactly the room in which Luis was being held. The guard saluted and opened the door. Elizabeth rushed inside. There, sprawled on the floor with several others was a pale, thin, bruised shadow of a man who used to sweep her around the dance floor.

"Dearest brother James." She knelt beside him wiping his face with her handkerchief. "Papa and I have come for you. Just come along quickly and calmly. And stay close if there's any shooting."

If anything, Leche's exit from the prison was even slower

and more grand than his entrance. "James" was so weak that Elizabeth had to half carry him down the stairs, all the time keeping an eye out for the return of the Russian. With each step along the hall the muzzles of the guards' guns loomed larger. Meanwhile, Leche was nodding and greeting every officer he encountered. As they approached the door, "James" began to cry.

"For God's sake, James, dry up!" said Elizabeth with the sweetest smile on her face.

"We'll never make it," he sobbed. "They'll kill us all."

Elizabeth opened the door and felt a wave of relief. They were outside! Then she saw the Russian was standing by the car with several more armed men and a senior officer of the Asaltos, the dreaded Assault Guards.

"Head for the car and get in," Leche quietly ordered. "Don't react to anything they say."

"Stand up straight!" Elizabeth whispered fiercely to the Marqués de Arueza.

As they neared the car, Leche broke into a broad smile and threw his arms wide.

"Colonel Toledano!" He embraced the officer. "I haven't seen you," he said in Spanish, "since we stole those pigs from the Italians at Guadalajara!"

"The women were a little *gorda*"—he laughed squeezing the fat around his own waist—"but I wouldn't call them pigs!"

Elizabeth and James had reached the car.

"This man speaks Spanish!" the Russian boomed. "When I demanded his papers, he claimed he couldn't understand me!" He put his hand on his pistol.

The colonel frowned at the Russian, then at Leche. Elizabeth yanked open the car door and pushed James inside.

"Oh that was *Spanish* you were speaking." Leche laughed. "A thousand pardons!" The colonel broke into a fit of laughter.

"What are you doing here?" the Russian demanded.

The brother/sister ploy was not going to work. Leche had to improvise. "Every day you inadvertently gather up a handful of innocent Englishmen. My two friends in the car thought you might be holding an acquaintance of theirs here. They were wrong. But you really should be more careful. You're going to end up arresting the Soviet ambassador!''

More laughter from Colonel Toledano.

"He has already been arrested," said the Russian, "and is on his way to Moscow where I expect he will get a fair trial before being liquidated!''

Leche looked taken aback. "Well, I would love to swap stories about the show trials, comrade, but I really must be on to the next jailhouse." He turned to the Asalto commander, who was recovering his breath. "Colonel, do join us this weekend at Palmeras. We still have the most delectable crayfish.''

"And the pigs?" He laughed again.

"We refer to the English girls as lambs.''

The colonel rolled his eyes. Leche opened the door to the car and started to get in.

"We'll leave the pigs for the Russians.''

The colonel doubled over.

"Step on it," Leche ordered. The car shot out of the courtyard and into the street. Elizabeth looked back and could see the Russian railing at the colonel.

They raced down Puerto de Aragon and down the Avenida del Puerto, Leche constantly looking back to see if they were being followed. James appeared to have fainted.

"Pier twelve," Leche instructed the driver. Elizabeth was trying to slap James awake. "Wake up! What do you know about Antonio de Zaragoza? Wake up!''

"Take it easy," Leche said.

They were waved through the naval sentries and pulled up next to a British destroyer at the end of the dock.

"Give me a hand." Leche began dragging the half-conscious marqués out of the car.

"No! I want him to tell me about Antonio!''

Two Royal Navy ensigns took hold of James and helped him toward the gangway. The sailors were already untying the lines, preparing to cast off.

"What about Antonio de Zaragoza?" Elizabeth cried, running along behind them. James stirred. Another ensign barred Elizabeth from the gangplank. She turned back toward Leche. "John, help me!''

James stopped at the top of the ramp and turned to her. "De Zaragoza?"

"Yes!" Elizabeth shouted. "What have you heard of him?"

He shook his head and sagged into the sailors' arms. "*Nada,*" he called back. "Nothing in years."

Chapter 10

6/7/37/19:23GMT
MOST SECRET
VALENCIA STATION SENDS
FOR BROADWAY—00063
1. SOURCE 26/3 EXFILTRATED THIS
DATE VIA HMS GALLWAY BOUND
MARSEILLE.
2. ELIZABETH PACK PARTICIPATED
OPERATION. PASSED EVERY TEST.
PROCEEDING TO PHASE TWO.
LECHE
ENDIT

Las Palmeras, Spain—
July 6, 1937

That night, Elizabeth lay on her cot staring at the bright stars through her window. She could hear the wind rustling in the palms and smell the salt and the scent of oranges carried on the sea breeze. This was no place to be alone. It made her disappointment so much harder to bear.

Elizabeth had not felt love from anyone for over a year. Not a word. Not a gesture. Not one reassuring caress of skin against skin. Turning away John Leche's advances had not been easy. How long could she live on dreams of Antonio's embrace?

As she tossed and turned restlessly, it dawned on her that if John Leche could find the Marqués de Arueza he could also locate the Marqués de Zaragoza. But he hadn't done

it. Why? Because he wanted her. So he had every reason
to refuse. Except one. Again, because he wanted her.
Would she now have to betray Antonio in order to save
him?

She had finally fallen asleep when Elizabeth suddenly
awoke to see someone silhouetted against the open door. It
was John. He knelt by her bed.

"Elizabeth, don't send me away," he whispered.

She felt his firm hand on her thigh. Her mind filled with
confusion. One part of her wanted to give in, take him in
her arms and lose herself. Another wanted to push him off,
slap his face, tell him to get lost. And in her turmoil, she
could hear a voice tell her to stay calm, to suppress her
emotions, to remember what she was trying to do. "I won't
send you away," she said softly, "if you don't fight me."

"I'm not fighting you." He moved onto the bed.
"You're fighting your own feelings."

"John, I like you." She could see that was not an adequate response. "And I'm physically attracted to you." For
her, that might be a major admission, but it seemed to do
nothing for him. She *was* fighting herself. "If you want to
make love to me, you can." She tried to make it sound
very matter-of-fact. "But don't think it means I love you."

"I'll bring you around to that." His sudden smile
gleamed mischievously in the starlight. "Show me your
breasts."

Their eyes locked together as she sat up and defiantly
pushed down the front of her nightgown. She expected him
to seize her, ravish her. But he did neither.

"You are a wonder," he said quietly. "Your shoulders
are so delicate and graceful"—it was as if he were ap-
praising a work of art—"and your breasts so full and
bold." Reaching out, he began to caress them thoughtfully,
slowly, kneading gently with his strong fingers until she
became engorged with feeling.

"You may think you're staying aloof, but your body says
something else."

As he patiently kept drawing and tugging, she felt that
she might burst. She wanted him to squeeze harder, to kiss
them. And when he finally did, she could hardly keep her-

self from grabbing his head in her hands and forcing herself deeper into his mouth and crying for more.

When he pulled away, she could no longer look into his eyes. She cast a glance downward to see her breasts wet and glistening in the dark. The smell of her arousal wafted up to her. She had never felt like this with Arthur!

"Take off your nightgown," he ordered.

She lifted it over her head, and he threw it in the corner. He remained dressed in his silk robe.

"Open your legs."

She could not believe him. She wanted to be romanced, kissed, hugged, maneuvered seamlessly into a position where making love was inevitable, not a stark deliberate act. But when she failed to respond to his command, she watched him spreading her legs apart as if he owned her.

Then he slipped his robe from his shoulders. He was naked. She could not keep from staring. It was thick and heavy and dangerous looking. He lifted her hips, and as she felt him at her threshold, she tightened to resist.

But he did not plunge forward. Instead, he moved himself gently, teasingly, over her most intimate places. As he tormented her, she felt a powerful void of desire begin to grow inside, a vacuum of need rapidly expanding beyond her control.

"Please," she moaned.

"You want me now?" Without waiting for an answer, he breached her.

Her eyes flashed open. She tried to expel him, but inexorably, he pushed in deeper, filling her with his strength, driving away the fear, the guilt, and the loneliness. And then he was drawing out, abandoning her. She tried to hold him, grip him inside, not let him go. But he was slipping away, leaving her yearning, desperate for his return. Then at the moment of dreaded emptiness, he reentered, swelling her with desire, forcing her to begin that hesitant dance where her undulating body anticipated his thrusts and parried every withdrawal.

She lost all sense of time, place, and even self. She tried to urge him on, but he resisted, slowly, rhythmically, with infuriating deliberation. She found herself crying and sweating. Her teeth bit his shoulder. Her nails dug into his back. Still he was so excruciatingly slow!

"Faster," she whispered.

"What?"

"Faster," she said.

"Like this?"

"Oh, yes. And harder."

"Louder."

"Harder!" she cried out shamelessly. "Harder, faster!"

He lifted her up, rolled her back, and plunged in deeper. She began to twist and writhe beneath him. Sweat dripped off his face and onto her breasts. She felt herself trying to engulf him. Each time they slammed together, she convulsed. Her body no longer obeyed. It bucked and heaved.

What's this? she thought. Deep within, a spasm had begun. Oh God, what's happening to me? And as her climax grew in force, she sensed him struggle to stop, to thwart her, to control her. But she held him hostage, clenching him fiercely until she felt him start to quiver, driving her over the edge. Then his string of detonations started, and she panicked.

"No, no!"

She slipped away and seized hold of him. He cried out, and she grasped him tightly until he was completely spent. When she caught her breath, all Elizabeth could manage to say was, "You bastard," and she pulled John Leche's head down onto her damp and heaving breast.

She awoke in a fog of remorse. Leche was gone. It was barely dawn, but she didn't know what the time was and didn't care. Her behavior made no sense to her. She had betrayed everything and everyone. And what was worse, it was wonderful.

Elizabeth found her bathing suit, hung on a nail by the outside shower and faded from days in the sun. In moments she was alone in the cool and soothing Mediterranean. Her thoughts and feelings were a jumble. Treading water, she stripped off her swimsuit. She wanted to feel the water coursing between her legs. She wanted the sea to wash away her sin.

As a deb in Washington she had enjoyed petting with

some of her dates. At Dana Hall she had had some stimulating daydreams about boys, but she soon learned to shut up about them. After marrying Arthur, however, she had begun to accept her mother's notion that sex was only an overrated marital duty. But last night, Elizabeth had been overwhelmed. Leche had introduced her to sensations she had never known. Could Antonio do that? Or could she only feel that way by being bad?

Holding her suit in one hand, she turned over and began a sidestroke that carried her farther out. Then she rolled onto her back to float. Her breasts rose to the surface, the nipples stiff and pointed. She wanted to offer them to Antonio. But they were the nipples that Arthur and John Leche had pulled into their mouths. And her son. She began to cry. If they belonged to anyone, it was her son.

Pulling her suit on again in the water, she swam back to the beach. She sat on the dunes until the sun rose into the sky, trying not to remember or think of anything. But she failed. Over and over, a voice in her mind told her, you are who you are, needing what you need, doing what you must.

And John Leche had to be held to his end of the bargain.

In the Humber on their way into Valencia later that morning, they both rode along in a strained silence. Finally, Elizabeth spoke.

"I've been a fool."

"Are you talking about last night?"

"I'm talking about every night, and every day. This is a farce. You're just using me."

"I'm mad for you," he protested. "I want you to stay with me here in Valencia, at Las Palmeras, and wherever else I might be in the future. You must be mine alone."

"Yours alone? You *are* mad. What have you done for me? Absolutely nothing!"

"I've been protecting you!"

"From what?"

John Leche clenched his teeth like a child refusing to speak.

"From what?" she demanded.

"From Antonio," he finally said.

"What on earth do you mean?"

"I mean your precious Antonio was a spy. He was spying against the British government and the Americans too, if that matters to you."

"You've completely lost your mind!"

"He was trying to recruit you! How else do you think he found so much time to romance you?"

That gave her pause. "You're making this up! You're jealous!" she said, going on the attack.

"I have proof!"

"What is it?" she demanded.

"I can't show it to you."

"Well, you can keep your Most Secret dossier. I don't care what he was doing a year ago! That was another world. I just want him back!"

"What do you expect me to do?" He was growing angry.

"You found the Marqués de Arueza. Find the Marqués de Zaragoza."

"It's not that simple!"

"It is as simple as this," Elizabeth declared. "You can come back to my bed when you find me the man I love!"

It took two days. Leche called Elizabeth into his office at the consulate to give her the news.

"He's being held in a big military prison north of the city on the old Barcelona road."

"How is it that I've never heard of this place?" she responded coolly, keeping him on the defensive.

"It's an old and famous monastery that's been seized by the government, San Miguel de los Reyes." He wasn't about to apologize for holding out on her.

She sat back on his divan and clasped her hands around her knee. "So, how do we get him out?"

She was upping the ante. Well, he had bad news for her. "The Scarlet Pimpernel routine won't work at this jail, I'm afraid. No one can get you in short of the war minister."

"Indalecio Prieto? Isn't he here in Valencia?"

Leche nodded.

"Then it's simple." She smiled again. "You just get me an appointment to see him. I assume His Majesty's government has that much influence."

"Yes," he said irritably. Damn the woman! Was there no end to her cheek? "But what have you to offer Mr. Prieto?"

Her smile turned even more sweet. "Whatever he wants."

The war minister's office was located in a fourteenth-century palace on the Plaza de Manises in the oldest part of the city. As the British consulate car entered the narrow winding streets, Leche gave Elizabeth her final instructions.

"You must make it clear that you come in a purely private capacity and are not acting for the British government in any way. I don't want this to seem official."

"No. It won't be official, John," Elizabeth assured him. "There'll be nothing official about it."

Leche grimaced. Did she insist on being a smart aleck just to see if she could provoke him? He reached into his breast pocket. Perhaps something could be salvaged from this misadventure; he had been authorized to use her and he would. "This envelope contains the names of seventeen others who are in the same prison as your"—he hesitated—"friend. If Prieto seems favorable about Antonio, you might mention these people too. Otherwise forget about them. I trust your judgment. But by all means, let's do all we can."

"Do all we can," she repeated with a sigh, and pulled down the net veil on her hat. The driver had opened the door, but she made no effort to get out.

"Something wrong?" Leche asked.

"The truth is that I'd rather face a firing squad than go in there." She suddenly looked very young and vulnerable.

Leche softened. He squeezed her gloved hand. "Prieto's a pretty tough character, but nothing like the Reds."

"I'm only afraid of making a hash of the situation and getting Antonio into even greater trouble after all the time and effort I've made to avoid just that!"

"Everything will be all right. You'll see."

Elizabeth anxiously handed her identification to the guard who stood behind a sandbagged barricade at the entrance. To avoid his gaze, she stared up at the building. It was very plain except for the medieval stonework around the square leaded-glass windows on the first floor and the sharp Gothic columns trisecting the windows on the second.

The guard passed back her papers then handed her over to a well-uniformed Asalto who led her through the entrance and up a winding stone staircase. They made their way along a balcony thronged with people carrying various rolled-up parchment petitions. When they came to a pair of massive carved wooden doors, her escort opened them and Elizabeth stepped into a large spare room with a ceiling of heavy ornate rafters covered in gold. On the opposite wall, French doors led out to a balcony that overlooked a small garden with several orange trees. To her surprise, the room itself was empty except for a broad desk, two stiff-backed upholstered chairs, and a short, balding, round-bodied man with tired eyes. She had asked for a private audience and she had gotten it.

"Prieto," he introduced himself and offered her a chair.

Hesitantly, she began to describe why she had come to see him. It was a personal matter, not a diplomatic *démarche*. Then, gathering her courage, as she told of her search for Antonio and her earnest hope that the minister would be able to help her. She concluded with a little memorized speech: "I love this man, Señor el Ministro, and through loving him I know all about him. I know that he has never done anything against the Spanish government and so does not deserve to be in prison."

Prieto's baleful eyes had grown wider. He drew his chair over next to her.

"As minister of war, I deal often with life and death, but I must admit, seldom with matters of love."

He put his hand on her knee and continued. "Aren't you an American? And you are married to a British diplomat, no?"

This had been Elizabeth's principal worry. To many Spaniards, an American woman on her own was tantamount to a prostitute. That she was married and in love with another man elevated her status to that of courtesan.

"Possibly, we could work something out." He smiled. His hand had tightened on her leg to explain what he meant. "Where are you staying in Valencia?"

Her next move would be critical. She tried to gauge him. As a Socialist, he had the reputation for being moderate and level-headed. But what did that mean in a situation like this? Was he making a serious pass or merely the obligatory Spanish gesture so as to maintain his self-respect? She would soon find out.

"Mr. Minister"—Elizabeth lifted the veil on her hat—"with all the violence and tragedy you face every day, you deserve the warmth and respite of a woman's love." She leaned closer. "I could go over to that door right now and lock it. I could come back to you, take off my clothes, and you could have me, here on your desk."

Prieto's eyes widened again, and his jowls began to tremble.

"I would do that to save the man I love," Elizabeth continued, her voice dropping an octave. She was operating on instinct now. "But I also know something of your struggle. I've just come from driving an ambulance in Madrid. I saw children, women, infants, old people sacrifice their lives. And what are they dying for?"

She snatched up his hand and pressed it against her breast. Prieto's breath was coming harder.

"Are they not laying down their lives for the future of Spain? So that one day, genuine love can flourish in the ruins of bourgeois morality? So that a woman of honor can seek a favor from the mighty without trading her body and her soul?"

Prieto remained speechless. She could see that his decision hung in the balance. Was she a fool to appeal to the idealism of a man whose portfolio was bloodshed? A bell began to toll in the odd eight-sided tower of the cathedral across the square. She knew her fifteen minutes were up.

He withdrew his hand from her breast and retreated behind his desk. "Can I take it"—he wiped his brow—"that the British minister knows about this visit and the reason for it?"

What was she to reply? Her instructions were explicit: to emphasize that this was purely personal, that it did not involve His Majesty's government. And yet, Leche had given her the names of others to get released.

"He knows," she said firmly, "and he heartily approves."

"Good. Good." Prieto's faint smile suggested he now had a debt he could collect. "I am very grateful to you for coming to see me. There are many things that are not brought to my attention. Is there anything else?"

Did this mean she had succeeded? Or was he putting her off? She would only know by pressing him. Elizabeth opened her purse. "These are also victims of injustice."

He looked at the length of the list, and his eyes widened yet again. He put it down with the mound of papers on his desk. "Señora"—he emphasized her married title—"you will understand that I can do nothing arbitrary. But I promise that I will examine these cases carefully. It would be good to give attention to something other than war. I think I can tell you to have *buena esperanza,* good hope of their release."

"And Antonio?" she insisted.

"When I say 'good hope,' you can count on it."

Elizabeth reached over his desk and joyously threw her arms around the minister, kissing him on his forehead. He staggered back a step and smiled warily. "Are you sure there is nothing else, now?"

"Yes there is," Elizabeth said excitedly. "May I see the man I love and give him some hope too?"

"You may. Indeed you should." And he wrote out a slip of paper. "You will need this to enter the prison. You can go this afternoon."

"You'll never know how grateful I am!"

"I'm afraid," Prieto sighed, "you've made that very clear, my dear."

"He's going to let them go! All of them!" she exulted as she came through the door of John Leche's office.

He seemed utterly uninterested. Something was wrong.

"Look at this," he said and handed over a cablegram. It was from the embassy in Hendaye and marked "Most Urgent":

FOLLOWING FOR LECHE PERSONAL FROM AMBASSADOR STOP REPORT ON WHEREABOUTS OF MRS PACK WIFE OF

COMMERCIAL SECRETARY BELIEVED TO BE VISITING MADRID AND VALENCIA STOP ARRANGE FOR HER IMMEDIATE REPEAT IMMEDIATE RETURN NEXT AVAILABLE DESTROYER STOP

"We'll have to send off a reply," Leche said gravely, coming toward her, "so you must decide about your feelings for me."

What were they, she wondered. Gratitude certainly. Warmth. An intimacy that she had never known. He wrapped his arms around her and drew her down to the sofa. But his kiss felt wrong. He had introduced her to her own body, but was he really a lover or just a friend?

He whispered in her ear. "There's only one answer and it's quite simple." Leche sat back and looked into her eyes. "You are staying with me and that's all there is to it."

Should she tell him that she was not returning to Arthur? That she was running away. That she planned to start a new life. But not with him, with Antonio.

"Stall," Elizabeth said instead. "Send a temporizing reply. Say I'm in no danger and my return is delayed on account of destroyer space." She got up to leave.

"Where are you going? Aren't we having lunch?"

"I have a pass to see Antonio." She could not contain her happiness.

The expression on his face was inscrutable. He might be angry, calculating, or hurt. Thinking about it as she left the consulate general, Elizabeth concluded it was probably all three.

Her driver picked up the Barcelona road across from the squat Gothic battlements of the Torres del Serrans. Proceeding north through the dwindling outskirts of the city, Elizabeth tried to control her soaring excitement. Soon she would see him, hear his voice, possibly even embrace him! Finding Antonio had often seemed a futile dream, and now as the moment approached, it felt unreal. The thought that he would be set free was hard to accept.

For what would happen then? Leche, in urging her to break with Arthur, had helped legitimize her dreams about

Antonio. They would go away together. To France, or even
South America. Antonio could earn a good living as a pilot.
They would both get divorces somehow. And what about
his children? Maria would never give them up. Elizabeth
would give him more children. Maybe she could even find
a way to get back her own child.

But what of Leche's accusations, she wondered uneasily.
Could Antonio have been a spy? Did that explain the knowing looks from Antonio's friends? No! She was letting her
fears get the best of her. It was all absurd. Whatever
Leche's so-called proof, she could see the truth in Antonio's eyes.

Where the city gave way to farmland and scattered
houses, a massive red-brick structure rose up out of the
fields of rice. It might have been a monastery, she thought,
but it was built like a fortress. The iron-studded gate was
flanked by two short stone towers complete with loopholes
and crenellations.

She shoved her pass through the barred window on the
left, and the doors promptly swung open. Elizabeth entered
a gravel courtyard where several ancient date palms stood
guard in front of a large chapel with a bright golden dome.
Her escort led her to a five-story building on the right. Its
tiny barred windows ran all the way up to the eaves under
a tiled roof. Once inside, she was handed over to a pair of
guards who took her to a long medieval gallery on the
second floor that looked out over the rice fields. The stone
floor and walls were bare but the ceiling was of elaborately
painted wood. Two chairs had been provided at the far end
of the room, and as she sat down, the guards retreated to a
position by the door.

The afternoon heat drifted in the windows with the hu-
mid smell of rice paddies. Elizabeth felt relieved to have
seen no pictures of bewhiskered Bolsheviks or lunatic slogans. There were no red flags of revolution or black flags
of anarchy. She prayed that Antonio had been in decent
hands. Would she recognize him? Would he recognize her?
Then she had a sudden fear. Of all the people he might be
desperate to see, was she even one of them?

The door creaked open. A man in loose gray prison pa-
jamas appeared, blinking as if he were either unaccustomed

to the light or unable to believe his eyes. He took a few hesitant steps forward then glanced back at the guards. They nodded. Stiffly, he began to walk faster. Elizabeth stood up. He broke into a run. She held out her arms. Antonio swept her into a wordless embrace burying his head in her shoulder.

Her joy made her start to weep. Through her arms she could feel his heart racing in his frail body. She thought hers might stop beating altogether.

Catching her breath, she pulled back. "Let me see how you look."

"You are like a dream," Antonio responded, touching his fingers to her tear-stained cheek. He was not as greatly changed as she had feared. His skin was gray. He was very thin and he had a long beard, which with his gaunt face, made him look something like a Sunday school rendering of Jesus Christ. As their eyes silently spoke to one another, she could feel the old magic begin to glow deep inside.

"How are they treating you?" She searched for something to say.

"Well enough since I've been here. But in the Montana Barracks . . . " He suddenly grew distant. "Beatings. Shootings every day." He shook his head to banish the memories. "These are not things for your delicate ears. You are so beautiful!" He kissed her hands, and she trembled. "How did you find me? How did you get here?"

"Antonio, you're going to be free!" In a rush, Elizabeth told him how she had searched for him ever since his wife had come to her in St.-Jean-de-Luz. She described Madrid and going to all the prisons in Valencia. Finally she explained about Prieto and what he had said. She never mentioned Leche.

As she rattled on, he sat staring at her, smiling, looking slightly bewildered. Elizabeth had the sense that it was difficult for him to envision all that she had been through, all that she wanted to share.

"And how goes the war?" he asked when she paused for a breath.

"Very bad for the Republic, I think. As I mentioned, I was recently in Madrid, and it was terrible."

"Oh yes," he responded as if trying to remember what

she had just said. "And my family." He became more focused. "Did you say you'd seen my wife? How is she?"
Tears suddenly came into his eyes. "How are my children?"

Elizabeth explained that Maria had lived with them and
had moved back to Spain after the fall of San Sebastián to
the Nationalists. She was safe with his children at his parents' ranch near Zaragoza.

"Can you get them a message? They won't let me
write."

"Of course. I'll memorize it."

"Tell them I'm all right. Tell them that I love them and
I never forget them for a moment. I dream of them every
night. Tell the little ones to be brave."

"I'll tell them," Elizabeth said. Inside, she was growing
cold.

"I dream of you too," he added quickly. "I thought I'd
never see you again. The only thing that keeps you going
in a place like this is the hope that someday you'll see your
family. And your loved ones."

"You'll be free soon, I know it."

"But you'll tell them."

"Naturally."

He looked relieved. Elizabeth felt empty. And the emptiness freed her to ask the question that would not go away.

"Antonio, when we were in Madrid, did you care for
me, or was it merely your duty?"

Surprise, and something furtive, flashed in his eyes. "I
don't understand." He frowned.

"Were you a spy? Was I your 'target'?"

He looked sharply over his shoulder toward the guards.
"Of course not!" he whispered. "Don't be ridiculous!"

She let her face say that she didn't believe him.

"I had to tell my superiors something in order to get to
see you." He put on his charming smile. "I'm not proud
of deceiving them, but to be with you, it was worth it."

Elizabeth was unmoved. In truth, she was afraid to even
speak.

"I never asked you for information." He was pleading
now. "I never asked you to do anything for me, did I?"

She shook her head.

"So, put it out of your mind. It had nothing to do with us. You'll stay here in Valencia and wait for me. We will make love at last. We'll go back to France together. I'll move my family to Biarritz to be near you. Everything will be as before."

"Of course," Elizabeth said. How could she explain that nothing was as before. Even before was no longer like before.

One of the guards clanked his keys. Their time was drawing to an end.

"I believe fate is with us"—Antonio crossed himself—"and that it won't be long before I am free and we can be together again like Madrid."

He took her in his arms. She felt his lips on hers. Part of Elizabeth was begining to withdraw, but another part, the one that had been searching for Antonio for more than a year, the one that had turned him into an obsession, wanted to swallow him, merge with him. Their mouths pressed together so urgently their teeth clashed, their lips bled. She could taste him on her tongue.

Then she felt him being pulled away, slipping out of her grasp. The guards were leading him off.

"Adiós," he called to her. "Adiós! We shall meet soon."

Elizabeth arrived back at Palmeras at nightfall. After leaving the prison, she had asked the driver to go north along the Mediterranean. She stopped at Sagunto and for an hour watched the sea washing the shore with endless indifference. Had the ordeal of her quest for Antonio transformed him into a vision that had never existed? Giving each wave a name, Antonio, John, Arthur, she played a version of loves-me-loves-me-not, wondering whether her destiny would lie with the one that came up highest on the beach. Then she realized the tide was going out.

Returning south, she detoured inland around the city. At a crossroads on the eastern edge of Valencia, the car was stopped by a convoy of trucks laden with men in loincloths and women naked to the waist, their bodies painted with primitive signs and symbols. It had to be Colonel Mangada's battalion of nudists and vegetarians heading for the front. Was there anything so meaningless, she wondered, than losing one's life in a lost cause?

Further on, she passed the Albufera. Through the windows of the car, the strange vast lake looked dark and still. She had felt the need to think, and on the long circuitous journey back to Palmeras, Elizabeth discovered she really had nothing at all to think about.

The smell of fish stew was in the air as she pulled up to the British compound. The staff, as usual, were sitting at the long tables under the grape arbor. Elizabeth had no appetite, and to avoid them she went around the other side of the villa and down to the sea. The fireworks over Valencia had begun, the bombs and shells shattering in the sky, etching the mountains with light.

Soon she was joined by John Leche.

"Why did you sneak out here? I've received another rocket from Hendaye responding to our cable." He dropped beside her and unfolded a paper. "It says, 'RETURN MRS. PACK TO FRANCE WITHOUT DELAY.' "

"I saw a destroyer lying off the harbor today," said Elizabeth, her voice sad. "When does it leave?"

"The day after tomorrow, I think." He looked taken aback. "But I don't know if there would be room for you on board."

"Then I'll stay on the deck with the refugees."

"My God, Elizabeth! What the hell happened at the prison? Why are you talking like this?"

"Antonio's fine," she said, not looking at him. "He's excited about being released, naturally. He looks forward to getting back together."

"That's what you wanted, isn't it?" Leche did not try to conceal his bitterness.

She turned to him. "I love him too much to be the other woman. Just as I don't love you enough to be your wife."

"Goddammit, girl! You don't love your husband at all!"

She reached out to him. "Don't be angry. Just love me. Here. Now."

He glanced toward the villa. "But what about the others?"

"Tonight there are no others," Elizabeth said as she

pulled him down onto the sand. She needed from him the tenderness and excitement that she feared she would never find again.

She felt strange wobbling up the gangplank of a destroyer all dressed up in white open-toed shoes, a hat with a veil, and gloves. Elizabeth had asked Leche to remain on the dock. A lieutenant showed her to a tiny room on the starboard side.

"You might want to come back on deck," the young naval officer said as he stowed her valise. "It will be a few minutes before we weigh anchor."

She thanked him but said she preferred to remain below. Elizabeth needed no more memories of Valencia, or of Spain. It had been a great adventure. She had known love and passion and they had come to naught. Now she was determined to secure the more enduring satisfactions of adulthood. It was time to settle down. She took an exchange of cables with Arthur out of her purse.

TO ARTHUR PACK VILLA TTIRRITTA STJEANLUZ
FROM ITT VALENCIA 7/7/37 08:30
WILL RETURN ONLY IF YOU PROMISE WE WILL START
FAMILY
STOP ELIZABETH

TO ELIZABETH PACK % ITT VALENCIA
FROM ITT STJEANLUZ 7/7/37 10:47
AGREED STOP ARTHUR

TO ARTHUR PACK VILLA TTIRRITTA STJEANLUZ
FROM ITT VALENCIA 7/7/37 11:07
AND I WANT ADDRESS OF SON STOP ELIZABETH

TO ELIZABETH PACK % ITT VALENCIA
FROM ITT STJEANLUZ 7/7/37 16:24
ALL AGREED STOP PLEASE COME HOME STOP ARTHUR

Looking over the cables gave her a sense that at last she might be gaining some control over her future. She would have another child with Arthur, and make a home. That way, in time, it might be possible to get her son back.

The vibrations under her feet increased, signaling that the ship was ready to depart. In spite of herself, she took a last look out the porthole. John Leche stood in the front row, his eyes searching for her. She heard the scrape and groan of the gangplank being hoisted aboard. Suddenly, she saw pushing and shoving on the pier. A thin young man in a suit that was far too big for him squeezed his way through. It was Antonio!

She raced out of her cabin and up the stairs. By the time she emerged on deck and worked her way to the rail the ship was moving away. Antonio and John Leche were standing side by side shouting her name.

She waved back, then took off her hat and sailed it through the air toward the dock. A shout went up. Antonio grabbed it. Leche snatched it away, and struggling with one another they both were swallowed up in the crowd.

Elizabeth had no regrets. She knew that if she wanted to hold on to what she had had with Antonio de Zaragoza or John Leche, she must never see either of them again.

8/7/37/16:42GMT
MOST SECRET
VALENCIA STATION SENDS
FOR BROADWAY—00075
EYES ONLY LANCE

1. ELIZABETH PACK PASSED ALL TESTS.
2. AS RESULT OF HER EFFORTS EXPECT QUOTE LIST OF SEVENTEEN UNQUOTE TO BE RELEASED SHORTLY.
3. RECOMMEND MRS PACK FOR SIS DUTY MOST HIGHLY. YOUR GAIN IS MY LOSS.
LECHE
ENDIT

PART THREE

I had been "in love" or had loved various people for different reasons and in varying degrees, but although I was in my twenties, it still remained for me to find the one man who would have me completely. "Completely" was a very big and awesome word in the meaning it had for me.

—Elizabeth Pack's *Memoirs*
 Churchill Library, Churchill
 College, Cambridge University

Chapter 11

Wehrmacht Staff School, Potsdam, Germany— September 7, 1937

"Do you think your father would have come to his commanding officer with such a complaint, Lieutenant von Aufenaker?"

The commander of the school, Colonel Leber, rubbed his monocle on his sleeve and popped it into his right eye so that he could inspect the young man more carefully. He appeared to be a fine specimen of Prussian manhood: tall, with a correct military bearing, intelligent bright blue eyes, closely cropped blond hair. He had sympathy for the lad but his request was out of the question.

"If I may be allowed to explain?" asked the young man.

"Certainly."

"My first choice was of course the cavalry."

Colonel Leber nodded and leaned back in his chair. His office like the rest of the staff school was located in the former stables of a Hohenzollern prince, and the pungent aroma of horses still permeated the air. The officer corps and students seemed to thrive on it.

"Because I speak English and Polish and French, I was persuaded to enter into intelligence instead," Lieutenant von Aufenaker continued, "but now I find that I am assigned to a communications detachment."

"That is correct. It is one of our highest-priority assignments."

"But I'll be nothing but a glorified stenographer!" he protested.

"I see." Colonel Leber swiveled in his chair and stood up. "You imagined yourself charging enemy cannons on horseback with your saber drawn?"

Von Aufenaker turned red.

"That is not modern warfare." He began to pace. "You were chosen carefully to perform the most critical function in the Wehrmacht. Look around at our enemies: France, Britain, Poland, Czechoslovakia, Russia. We are vastly outnumbered, outgunned. How can we prevail? As we have always done, through order and discipline! In modern warfare that means utterly reliable and secure communications."

"But I want to lead men in battle, like my father, not cower in some van, safe in the rear!"

"Where did you learn that the hand that wields the sword can be contemptuous of the brain? Of all our secret weapons the most powerful and important is being entrusted to you."

"The Enigma machine?" He tried to maintain a tone of respect but failed.

Colonel Leber turned on him. "Our *Blitzkrieg* requires the closest coordination of infantry, armor, and aircraft. Surprise is vital. Mobility crucial. The Enigma makes this possible. It is a triumph of German ingenuity. With trillions of combinations, it produces a code that is impregnable."

"Then I fail to see how that makes my command important," von Aufenaker insisted. "I shall merely supervise typists!"

"It is your job to protect the Enigma! You must ensure that it is used correctly. Mistakes can compromise its security. You will be trained not only in the machine's use but also its demolition. The case is made of wood so that it can be burned if it is in danger of capture. If it falls into enemy hands, it could be used to reveal our strength, strategy, war plans, secret weapons, everything. You and your men are being entrusted with the secret of secrets of the German Reich."

"But this is not—"

"Lieutenant, you are dismissed. And do not look so dejected. Before this coming war is over, I'm sure you will have plenty of opportunity to die in battle like your father."

Southwest England—
September 8, 1937

Elizabeth had forgotten how green the English countryside could be. Spain had its greens, but always colored with more somber hues, the misty green of the olive trees, the twilight green of cypress, the parched green of mountain grasses. England seemed to be the home of green itself, uncomplicated, straightforward, as mother nature originally intended, a fecund, comforting color that covered the passing fields and hills, and conveyed to Elizabeth a sense of serenity.

She welcomed the calming influence of the verdant landscape and the gentle rocking of the railway carriage. It eased her apprehension. She was on her way from London to Bath to do something she had been dreaming about for a year and a half. Yet she was uneasy and more than a little afraid. Elizabeth was going to pay a visit to see Antony, her son.

After Arthur finally gave her the name and address of the child's foster parents, a Mr. and Mrs. George Porter who lived in Bath, she had sent toys and written letters and postcards. But the Porters had given only a single unresponsive reply: The baby was healthy; the baby was happy.

Elizabeth had tried to see him a month earlier when she had initially come to London for a checkup with Dr. MacCall. She had postponed efforts to conceive another child with Arthur because of what her mother would call "female trouble." Ever since her illness in Madrid, she had felt a dull ache in her lower back along with an intermittent fever. When she returned to St.-Jean-de-Luz, she began to experience an unpleasant discharge as well. While Elizabeth had realized that her condition was not conducive to getting pregnant, she had no idea of the shock awaiting her in Dr. MacCall's familiar office when she had gone to see him on that warm afternoon early in August.

The doctor had scowled as he read through the reports of her tests.

"I'm sorry to inform you, Mrs. Pack, that you've a pelvic infection."

"How did I get that?" she had asked in embarrassment, immediately wondering if she had "caught something" from John Leche.

"In all likelihood, it stems from a case of childbirth fever." He went to the window to let in more air. "Your body took a great deal of abuse during pregnancy, and you were undoubtedly vulnerable to infection. Do you remember being sick after you left the hospital?"

She shook her head, but with uncertainty.

"Did you have relations with your husband right away?"

The memory came back in a rush. At the Oddfellows Arms in Pulborough where they had spent the first night after leaving the hospital, she wanted to rest after dinner, and Arthur had stayed behind in the bar. A few hours later, full of whiskey, he had come upstairs and pounced on her like a jackal on carrion, forcing himself between her legs with his usual desperation. Elizabeth had been too tired and weak to resist.

"Yes, the first night. Arthur insisted, and he *had* been lonely . . . " She stopped in mid-sentence, mortified. "I didn't feel well for several days afterward, but I didn't think it was"—she paused—"serious."

"I'm afraid it is." His hard Scots features softened with concern. "You need an operation. We have to remove the source of infection."

"What kind of operation?" Her voice suddenly filled with anxiety. "You mean a hysterectomy?"

"No, most likely we would only take the fallopian tubes."

Elizabeth sighed, relieved.

"But you must realize," Dr. MacCall continued, "you won't be having children anymore."

She had sat for a few moments without reacting. Then she began to shake her head as if to say, that's impossible. "No," she said quietly. It was inconceivable. "No, no," she repeated. It was unacceptable. "I'm only twenty-two years old!" She was pleading for a different sentence. "I can't have such an operation! I want more children, I need them. . . . "

"Elizabeth, understand me, dear. You can't have any children now."

Oh God! This was her punishment! For the sin of loving Antonio. For her adultery with John Leche. For abandoning her baby. For fornicating with Arthur before they had married. She had begun to weep.

The doctor had come and put his arm around her shoulder. "The tubes are blocked," he said gently. "You've an infection. If it gets out of hand, it could well kill you."

"But I feel perfectly fine!" She had protested through her tears, "Can't you do anything else? What about sulfa?"

"I'm prescribing that, but it's no wonder drug for something like this." He shook his head. "There is one possibility." He returned to his desk. "I have a colleague, a surgeon, who's been trying to repair the tubes so they can still function. He's had some successes."

"Why can't we try that?"

"We'd have to open you up first and see what the problem looks like. Then we would remove as little as possible and make a decision on the spot whether the tubes can be restored. You'll run the risk of worse infection and possibly a hysterectomy. Are you prepared for that?"

"What other choice have I?" Elizabeth had said in a voice so small that, with the noise of Wellbeck Street coming through the window, she could hardly even hear herself.

The train was descending from the open fields of Wiltshire into the steep river valley of the Avon toward the ancient Roman city of Bath. In her mind, Elizabeth conjured a picture of its ruins from a fragment of a ninth-century English poem that she had memorized as a schoolgirl:

Wonderful is this wall of stone wreaked by fate.
The city buildings crumble, the bold works of giants
   decay.
Roofs have caved in, towers collapsed . . .
Ceilings save nothing from the fury of storms . . .
. . . A hundred generations of men
Have passed away since then. This wall, grey with
   lichen
And red of hue, outlived kingdom after kingdom.

As she had waited on a gurney outside the operating room, Elizabeth had thought about her father. When she had returned to St.-Jean-de-Luz from Spain, a telegram was waiting from her mother reporting that her father had died. She immediately telephoned Washington. Despite holding the handset against one ear and the extra little earpiece against the other, Elizabeth could barely hear her mother.

"It's been terrible, dear." Cora's voice came through thin and wispy. "The doctors couldn't do anything. He just wasted away in a matter of weeks."

"Why didn't you tell me!" Elizabeth shouted through the phone.

"You're doing such important things over there. And I didn't want to upset you. There's nothing you could have done."

"I could have seen him! We could have talked!" But that, she said to herself bitterly, is exactly what her mother didn't want. Finally she had gotten him all to herself. Elizabeth felt sick with guilt at such thoughts.

"I'll take a plane. I'll fly from Portugal to the Azores, then to Newfoundland. . . . "

"I'd love to see you, of course," said Cora, "but the funeral was a week ago."

"I don't want him to be dead!"

"I'm sorry," her mother said, "but this is very hard for me too. . . . "

For her surgery, the doctors gave Elizabeth gas. She remembered nothing but a dream in which her father appeared. He was in his office on Twelfth Street in Washington. It must have been summer, because the windows were open and the electric fans were ruffling the papers on his desk. He was leaning against it with his arms crossed, saying, "Loyalty makes civilization possible. . . . The individual makes sacrifices for principle, for the greater good of the many. . . . It's the greatest test of character. . . . "

Awakening from her operation in the recovery room at Wellbeck, Elizabeth found that all the other women patients had their newborn infants. She didn't even have her husband. Arthur had cabled to say that embassy business prevented him from joining her. Dr. MacCall had come in looking pleased and told her that the first step had been a success.

"But you have to come back in a month for tests to see if the tubes stay open."

After ten days of lonely convalescence, Elizabeth, still in pain, had gone back to St.-Jean-de-Luz. There was no chance to see her son. Now, having returned to England for her follow-up examination, she had carefully allowed time to go shopping, take in the theater, look up friends. When she had arrived at the Savoy, she had been surprised and pleased to find an invitation to lunch from the mysterious Captain Lance, whom she had not seen since the evacuation of San Sebastián. She planned to visit Arthur's parents, and had arranged to lunch with Vita Sackville-West. She was determined to enjoy herself, to remain optimistic about the tests, and above all to spend at least one day with her son. Her desire to have another child with Arthur only strengthened Elizabeth's commitment to establish contact with her son; she was not going to forget her firstborn.

As her railway car emerged from a long tunnel, the modern city of Bath sparkled in the sunlight, all white marble and polished stone. Its town houses were built in terraces and crescents, gathered together behind common Palladian facades to make them look like palaces. Elizabeth's excitement grew as her taxi climbed from the railway station at the foot of the town; past the ruins of the Roman baths; around a grand circus; and across the imposing front of the Royal Crescent, a quarter-mile arc of homes set in a vast green park.

The Porters lived outside the historic part of town. At 148 Cavendish Road, Elizabeth found a modest and pleasant detached house with a small front yard not unlike any suburb in England.

The driver helped her to the door with her packages. Elizabeth hesitated before ringing the bell. She felt anxious and flustered. Ridiculous, she thought. You have to maintain your dignity in front of these people. As she stood talking to herself, the door opened.

"I heard the taxi," the woman said.

"I was just about to ring the bell," Elizabeth explained.

"I'm Mrs. Porter." She eyed the packages.

"I'm Elizabeth Pack." She held out her hand.

Mrs. Porter shook it with an uncomfortable little jerk. "Please come in, my husband wanted to be here, but he was called to the waterworks. He's the engineer and whenever there's a problem . . ."

As they moved the packages into the house, Elizabeth appraised her. Mrs. Porter was plump, seemingly middle-aged, but perhaps only in her early thirties. Her print dress and sensible shoes made Elizabeth feel overdressed in a linen traveling suit and two-toned spectator pumps.

The parlor was clean and spare. It held a sofa, two easy chairs, and a radio. There was no sign of books or records. There wasn't even a magazine on the coffee table. The crucifix over the coal-burning fireplace indicated that the Porters were Roman Catholic. Elizabeth had often wondered who had arranged everything for Arthur. Now she knew: the Catholic Church.

"The little one's still at his nap. Would you like some tea?"

"No thank you. I had gallons on the train."

They both fell silent. Elizabeth's mind had been filled with a thousand questions, but now she could not remember one of them. Mrs. Porter stood in the middle of the room like a stranger in her own home.

"Perhaps I could see Antony?" Elizabeth finally managed.

A resigned look crossed Mrs. Porter's face. "Well, if you don't mind waking him. He can be cranky."

"I've not all that much time."

"The six o'clock train, is it? You should leave here by half past five."

A cry from the second floor sent them both rushing up the stairs. The baby was standing in his crib, gripping the sides, bouncing and shaking it with all his might. Elizabeth's heart leaped. He was so big! She'd already missed so much of his life! Mrs. Porter scooped him up, and he clung to her, eyeing the stranger with suspicion.

"This is Elizabeth," said Mrs. Porter.

"I'm your mother," Elizabeth said.

With a grin, the toddler reached out and grabbed the brim

of her hat and tossed it to the floor. She held her hands out to take him.

"Uhhh!" He started to cry and held on to his foster mother even tighter.

"He has to be changed," Mrs. Porter announced. "Do you want to do it?"

Mrs. Porter put him on the changing table near the window. Gingerly, Elizabeth started fumbling with the pins. The baby immediately began to climb off the table.

"You have to hold him down with one hand," Mrs. Porter explained impatiently.

Elizabeth had seen it done dozens of times by friends and relatives. But how to unclasp the pins with the baby squirming and wiggling?

"Hold him fast. He won't break."

After finally working the pins out, Elizabeth opened the diaper to find a rancid mess. The smell pushed her back, and she stepped on her hat.

"Don't let go of him! Put the dirty didy here." Mrs. Porter held up a pail.

"Shouldn't he get a bath?"

"Just wipe him. He gets one bath a day. In the evening."

"Well, he needs one now." Elizabeth's voice took on a firm edge. "Please draw some water."

In a few minutes he was in the tub surrounded by an armada of toy boats that Elizabeth had brought with her in one of the packages. She knelt on the floor next to the claw-footed tub and tried to wash him while he slapped the water, happily squealing and soaking her linen suit. But whenever Mrs. Porter stepped out of the bathroom, his smiles turned into anxious cries. She had to hover in the doorway where he could constantly see her.

Elizabeth had also brought him a new wardrobe. As she dried him off, Mrs. Porter inspected them.

"This is too small. That's too big. Have you no idea of the size of an eighteen-month-old child?"

Finally she approved a pair of dark wool shorts and a striped turtleneck that Elizabeth struggled to pull over his head. Her main problem, however, proved to be his new white shoes. They seemed big enough, but she could not fit his foot into them.

"He keeps bunching up his toes!" Her exasperation was beginning to show.

"You do this." Mrs. Porter took over and tickled the bottom of his foot. He giggled, straightened out his foot, and she quickly slipped on the shoe.

They all went out to the backyard. It was a narrow stretch of grass bordered with rose bushes and divided by a clothesline that ran from the house to the garage near the alley in the back. Elizabeth, still wet from the bath, sat on the ground with her son and opened his other presents: a duck that rolled and quacked, a wooden train with four cars and little bells, a set of colored blocks carved with numbers and letters, and a toy telephone. Every gift went immediately into his mouth and then into the rose bushes.

"And finally, I got you this!" Elizabeth produced a red tin racing car with a wind-up key. As her son reached for it, Mrs. Porter snatched it away.

"The little one could cut himself on these edges," she admonished Elizabeth. "And he could swallow the key!"

The rest of the afternoon was spent with Elizabeth trying to find ways to amuse her son while Mrs. Porter watched over them both. The boy soon tired of his new toys and returned to his old favorites—a spoon and a metal pot. Elizabeth realized she didn't know how to play with him. When she picked him up, he wanted to be let down. When she offered him one of the toys, he turned to another. He was happy and smiling and cuddly, but whenever she hugged him he would pull away, often to run to Mrs. Porter. By the end of the afternoon, she sat exhausted in a steel lawn chair and watched him dig with his spoon in the rose beds.

Suddenly, he started screaming. Elizabeth lifted him up and Mrs. Porter came running from the house.

"What happened?" she demanded.

"I don't know!"

The baby was pushing her away and reaching out for his foster mother. "Mama! Mama!"

Elizabeth was dying.

Mrs. Porter took him in her arms. "Poor little one. You have a thorn! There, there." She kissed it.

"Dare, dare," he repeated, and snuggled his head to her

breast. With Elizabeth trailing along behind, she carried him into the house and gave him a bottle.

They sat in the parlor while Mrs. Porter held her foster child in her lap and fed him mashed peas and potatoes. It was growing late.

"Has he been healthy?" Elizabeth was reduced to asking questions.

"Of course! Well, the tyke had a bout of roseola, but the doctors said that's typical."

"And he eats well?"

"Of course. Usually the little fella gets a bottle earlier," Mrs. Porter said with forced patience. "But your visit's changed his routine all round."

The tone of accusation was the last straw. "He has a name, you know." Elizabeth's frustration broke through. "Do you always call him little one, tyke, fella? How about Antony?"

The two women glared at each other. Elizabeth looked away first. "Do you need any more money for his care?" She felt ashamed of her anger.

"No," Mrs. Porter said curtly.

"Are you planning to take in more foster children?"

"Mrs. Pack, I'm not running a business! I took in the little one, Antony, because"—she was growing flushed, agitated—"because I can't have children of my own. Do you know how long we'd have to wait to adopt an infant of our own faith? So I accepted the baby at Father Scallon's urging, and he's become like my own! And now you're going to take him away!" She started to cry.

"Take him away?" Elizabeth was stunned. "I'm not going to do that."

"Then why'd you come? All this way from France?"

"I just wanted to see him!"

"And you don't want him? What kind of woman are you?"

"My husband won't let me!" She started to cry too. "I just wanted to look at him, know that he really exists and let him know I love him. But I'll never be able to change his diapers or take care of him or protect him . . . " Elizabeth was sobbing now.

Mrs. Porter set Antony on the floor. Through large and frightened eyes, the baby watched the two weeping women embrace—the barren comforting the bereft.

Elizabeth looked back at Alice Porter and her son waving good-bye from the platform of the Bath railway station. She had found him, but could not escape the sensation that she was also losing him. More than ever, she felt determined to have a family all her own. As the train plunged into the darkness of a tunnel, she remembered a line from Chaucer's "Wife of Bath's Tale":

> *"I mean to give the last years of my life*
> *To the acts and satisfactions of a wife."*

Chapter 12

"Her code name will be Cynthia and we will be using that name for the project as a whole," Captain Lance explained. He stood in Admiral Sinclair's study while the rest— Menzies, Denniston, and Knox—sat in armchairs, and C relaxed behind his desk smoking a pipe.

"You talk as if it were all decided," said Knox. "I thought this meeting was to take the decision whether to proceed."

"Quite," C agreed.

Menzies could see the meeting getting off the track. "What has your research developed on Mrs. Pack's background?" he intervened.

"Yes, what is she?" C asked. "An adventuress? A romantic? A libertine? Political? What's her motivation?"

"She's an uninhibited American girl with a certain zest for excitement," Captain Lance responded. "She rides the hunt extremely well, for example."

"That's to her credit," C observed.

"Has a bit of a romantic streak, I'd say," Denniston remarked.

"That's a dangerous combination," Knox argued. "The right man comes along and she's doubled!"

"That's a mite simplistic," Captain Lance replied. "She comes from a good family. Her late father was a distinguished Marine Corps officer and her mother is a socially prominent Republican. Mrs. Pack worked with the Red Cross in the Spanish Civil War."

149

"On which side?" Dilly probed.

"Franco."

"Is she pro-Fascist?"

"She worked with the Scottish Ambulance Corps helping the Republican side in Madrid," Captain Lance added. "I don't think her politics are clear."

"That's my point," Knox insisted. "We're taking a risk that's entirely unnecessary."

"Unnecessary?" C looked at him quizzically.

"We've recently broken the Enigma," Knox declared.

"Wait a minute, Dilly," Denniston said. "The most you can say is that we've peeked into the machine used by Franco, but only sporadically when the Spanish operators foul up. And that device is little more than the old Scherbius machine. It's primitive compared to the Enigma used by the German high command."

"But she could alert the Germans to our effort to penetrate the Enigma. As of now, we've given the impression that we believe it can't be done."

"Yes, we have been effective at that," Denniston noted dryly.

"Are you saying she's a German plant?" Lance challenged Knox.

"No," he backed down, "only that by bumbling around with the Poles she might show our hand."

"Well there's damn all in our hand at this point," Denniston complained.

"We'd run the same risk with any agent," Menzies noted. "And I don't see how we can simply ignore Bill Stephenson's recommendations."

"When are you seeing her?" C directed his question at Captain Lance.

"Tomorrow for lunch at Wilton's," he replied. "Stephenson has asked to be included."

C frowned. "He'll be asking to move into my house next."

"Including him might be a good idea," Menzies observed. "Share the responsibility and all that."

"I take your point. All right." C banged out the cinders of his pipe, which had been dead for some time. "You can go ahead and recruit Mrs. Pack, but only as a cooptee, and only after satisfying yourself that she's not pro-German. I don't want you saying anything to her about the Enigma, until we've seen how she works out."

"What then shall I tell her she's to do?"

"Oh, I'm sure you and Bill Stephenson will think of something." And he waved his pipe in a gesture that meant that the problem was now theirs.

Wellbeck Maternity Hospital, London— September 10, 1937

"Positive thinking, the power of positive thinking," Elizabeth repeated to herself as she approached the narrow white-faced house on Wellbeck Street. The nurses took her to an examination room where she disrobed and put on a long gown. She sat on the table praying silently until the doctor came in.

"Mrs. Pack," Dr. MacCall greeted her warmly. "How have you been feeling?"

"Fine. No more pain. I even had a period."

"That's a good sign. Now we've two choices, but I thought we'd start with the Rubin test. Lie yourself back and put your feet in the stirrups. We're going to place some air, nitrogen to be precise, into your uterus to see if it passes through your fallopian tubes."

The nurse came in wheeling a cylinder of gas. Dr. MacCall adjusted the knobs and then attached a hose to the tank and bent over to insert the other end into her.

"Try to relax and this shouldn't hurt. At least not too much."

It felt like making love to Arthur, painful and abrupt.

"That's good."

The doctor turned the valve and she could feel cold gas rushing inside her. Amazed, she watched her abdomen swell as if she were pregnant. Her stomach began to ache and then cramp.

"It's starting to hurt."

"That's enough, then. Hold in the gas and stand yourself up."

Elizabeth felt ridiculous, embarrassed. She tensed the

muscles she hadn't discovered until she met John Leche.

"All right," Dr. MacCall said, "does it hurt in your shoulders?"

She looked at him like he was joking. "No. But shoulders aren't usually considered reproductive organs, are they, Doctor?"

He did not laugh. "Try taking a deep breath. Still no pain?"

She shook her head.

He checked her stomach; it remained distended. "Try bobbing up and down a bit."

She bounced on her toes.

"Still no pain?"

"No. But that's good, isn't it?"

"All right, you can sit back on the table."

The nurse extracted the tube and the gas escaped. Elizabeth felt increasingly nervous. Dr. MacCall explained the next test.

"It's called a uterosalpingogram. Really, that's just a fancy name for an X ray. It should tell us everything we need to know."

The nurse reappeared with the largest syringe Elizabeth had ever seen. The needle was over a foot long.

"I'll not stab you," she said reassuringly. "I'll thread it through the opening in your cervix to put dye into the uterus."

"It'll help the X ray take clearer pictures," added Dr. MacCall.

Elizabeth had to lie on the table for some time while the dye spread into her tissues. She tried to continue her positive thoughts, but worries were taking over. Had she failed the Rubin test? She must have, or she wouldn't need an X ray. Or maybe the test was inconclusive. Stop it, stop it, she told herself. You're just borrowing trouble. You're going to be fine. You're going to have babies! But why didn't the doctor say anything? Maybe there wasn't anything yet to say. The questions and answers chased each other around and around until the nurse came to wheel her away.

She had never had an X ray. The nurse rolled her into a lead-lined chamber with a huge spidery apparatus that looked like something out of the Frankenstein movie. Elizabeth was moved onto a table directly under a large bulb shrouded by metal baffles. Except for her abdomen, she was covered chin to foot with a lead cape.

"Be still! Hold your breath." The nurse fled the room.

Everything was silent except the whirring of a fan somewhere in the X-ray machine. Then she heard a buzz, saw the bulb glow dully and quickly go out.

"That's it." Dr. MacCall came through the door. "You can get dressed now."

"When will you know?"

"It'll take a bit of time to develop." He pulled a large metal plate from under the table. "I suggest you go off for a fine lunch and not worry. I'll leave a message for you at the hotel as soon as I've got the results."

As she got dressed again in her wool gabardine Chanel suit with white piping, Elizabeth wanted to sing. The doctor had said not to worry! He'd call with the results! If he expected bad news, he would *never* use the telephone. That was not the English way. She tried to contain her joy; it still had to be confirmed. But the sense of relief allowed Elizabeth to follow the doctor's orders and look forward to her lunch with Captain Lance at Wilton's. She was extremely curious about him. What a welcome change it was going to be to focus her attention on someone other than herself.

Wilton's was a small, dark, wood-paneled restaurant just off Jermyn Street in St. James. A lovely leaded-glass skylight illuminated a display of game and autumn flowers. Elizabeth was shown to a comfortable nook on the right of the narrow room. She was surprised to find that Captain Lance was not alone.

"Elizabeth, I'd like you to meet William Stephenson." Captain Lance introduced her to a small wiry man with bright intense eyes.

"How do you do." He stood up and offered his hand. The accent was American, but his suit said Savile Row. "Please call me Bill."

Elizabeth did not let her surprise show. She took her place and joined them in a sherry and a cigarette.

"Do forgive me for getting you here under false pretenses," Captain Lance continued, "but I wanted the two of you to meet."

"I'm delighted"—Elizabeth smiled sweetly—"but why?"

Lance looked uncomfortable and Bill Stephenson laughed. "I like your directness."

"Mr. Stephenson is the owner of Sheperton Studios."

"Don't tell me I'm about to be 'discovered' for the movies?"

"We've been very impressed by your activities in Spain," Stephenson explained.

Elizabeth looked sharply at Captain Lance. "You can't be referring to San Sebastián, and if you're talking about Madrid, the ambulance corps people were far braver than I. Any film should be about them. They're still there. I'm here."

"We're also interested in your work in Valencia," Stephenson added.

What was he talking about? She didn't know whether to blush or . . .

"You helped get many of our friends out of jail," Captain Lance prompted her.

"Did I?" Elizabeth leaned back and drained her glass. This was not about movies. It was time to turn the table. She summoned a smile and lowered her voice. "Why don't you tell me more about yourself, Bill."

As they ordered lunch, Bill Stephenson explained how he had been raised in Vancouver, British Columbia, and had been a flier in the Great War.

"Bloody ace, he was," Captain Lance interjected.

Elizabeth remembered reading his name in connection with several air races while following Amelia Earhart's exploits.

"Yes," he confirmed, "I won the Linzer Cup a few years back, or at least one of my airplanes did."

By the time they had worked through Stephenson's curriculum vitae, they were well into their main course. Elizabeth set aside her venison and asked, "So how did I come to your attention?" She was impressed with Stephenson, but still mystified about what he wanted.

He took a bite of his turbot. "I travel a great deal on the

Continent. It's plain to see that Hitler and Mussolini are on the road to war, yet our countries remain fast asleep. I know Prime Minister Chamberlain, knew him when he was in business. He admires the dictators' efficiency, I'm afraid. And hates bolshevism, which is fair enough. But he's deadly mistaken to think he can use Hitler against Russia or achieve peace through appeasement.''

He hadn't come close to answering her question. Then Captain Lance spoke up. "What are your views, Mrs. Pack?''

"Wives of diplomats are not allowed to have 'views,' '' she demurred.

"You've something of a reputation for being sympathetic to the Fascists,'' he persisted.

What on earth was this all about, Elizabeth wondered, some kind of security interview? If she were English, she'd be insulted by so blatant an invasion of her privacy. But, in fact, she was too curious to take offense.

"I can't imagine how anyone got that impression,'' she replied. "I saw nothing to recommend either side in Spain. Franco's bombing is barbaric. The so-called Republicans are equally capable of atrocities, especially against each other. I certainly never understood British policy. London recognizes the Republic, but plays footsie under the table with Franco.''

Stephenson wore a wry smile. "It's been a muddle like everything else. I think Whitehall's policy in Spain is to encourage both sides to kill each other off.''

"That's a high moral position, particularly when women and children are caught in the cross-fire.'' She drew out a cigarette. The waiter hurried over to light it.

"Look''—she exhaled—"I don't know much about the Reds except that one once saved my life and another probably would have killed me. As for the Fascists, they're despicable and ridiculous, pretending to be the wave of the future by taking their countries back to the Dark Ages. They march around with phony pomp and circumstance, wearing comic opera uniforms, addressing one another with made up titles like *Sturmbandführer*. The Nazis claim their gods are Thor and Woden, and Mussolini tells his black-shirt rabble they're Romans. It's a burlesque!''

"If only Hitler were Charlie Chaplin," Stephenson sighed. "And Mussolini Harpo Marx. It's a worldwide epidemic. Here in Britain, it's not just Oswald Mosley, fascism's infected half the royal family. And there's Action Française in France, the Iron Cross in Romania, Tōjō's militarists in Japan. I was just in Warsaw, where I heard that Jews, can you imagine, are joining the Polish Silver Shirts! In the United States, Father Coughlin claims over seven million members!"

Elizabeth had once listened to the "radio priest" broadcasting from the Shrine of the Little Flower in Royal Oak, Michigan. He talked like a lunatic. She was unaware that his influence had grown so great. "It's a dire picture, I agree," she responded, "but what does it have to do with me?"

Stephenson and Captain Lance looked at each other. Something in their glance indicated that she was graduating to the next form.

"What Mr. Stephenson is about to tell you is extremely confidential," Captain Lance warned.

"Should we be discussing it here," Elizabeth teased, "in a public place?"

Captain Lance stiffened. "My dear, the Queen Mother dines here!"

"Captain," Stephenson intervened, "perhaps you could give us some privacy?"

Lance nodded and departed so promptly his spoon remained sticking out of his pudding. The waiter cleared their plates.

"I'm not in government," Stephenson began gravely, "so, what I'm about to say does not involve 'official' secrets. But the unofficial story is harrowing enough. You know British defenses are in a muddle—insufficient men and paltry equipment, mostly out of date."

He paused as the waiter poured coffee, then lowered his voice. "The secret services are in a similar mess."

Elizabeth's eyes widened at the mention of the unmentionable. She had once shocked Arthur by asking if there were any spies at the British embassy in Madrid. "Don't raise such questions," he had replied. "Don't even think of them. Do you want to ruin me?"

"SIS has been starved for resources," Stephenson continued. "They're staffed by second-rate navy officers who were sacked by the admiralty in the budget cuts of 1933. The chief of service can't decide if Germany or Russia is the enemy. Not that it matters; we've no assets in either country that are worth a damn. And when the SIS does happen upon important information about Hitler's plans, Mr. Chamberlain doesn't want to hear about it."

"I'm not being obstinate"—Elizabeth shook her head—"but I don't see where I come in."

"Are you aware of the Walrus Club in New York?"

Elizabeth looked baffled.

"No matter," he continued, "they're a group of private citizens who see the coming danger and are trying to wake up the American government. Many of us here are trying to do the same."

"You mean like Winston Churchill?"

"He's a good friend, and very important to our cause."

"But he's not even in the cabinet."

Stephenson looked around. No one was in earshot. "He has a special relationship with the king, who has placed him on the Imperial Defense Committee."

"From what you say, that doesn't seem to have done much good."

"But we're making a start. Winston's developed his own sources of information, his own networks. We collaborate with like-minded chaps in the SIS and Whitehall. We've even come to be called the Baker Street Irregulars."

He allowed himself a chuckle, then turned serious again. "Poland's the key. It's caught between sworn enemies, Nazi Germany and Red Russia. Hitler can't attack France or England without first securing his eastern front, and that means dealing with Poland. And he can't invade Russia without going through Poland. Our ambassador in Warsaw's hopeless. The SIS has virtually no resources there except one man. We'd like you to keep your eyes and ears open and pass on anything of significance."

Elizabeth felt completely confused. "Mr. Stephenson, I don't know where to begin! First of all, I live in France, not Poland!"

"Hasn't your husband told you?"

"Told me what?"

"He's put in for a new posting. It's being arranged for him to go to Poland."

"Why Poland? He speaks Spanish!"

"Because we want *you* there."

Elizabeth was outraged. "How dare you?"

"Your husband took the initiative. We merely made the choice in the hope that you'd cooperate."

"We? I really don't know who you represent! You say you're not working with the government! You say you're working against it! The Baker Street Irregulars could all be a bunch of Fascists or Communists for all I know!"

"It'd all be on the up and up. We'd arrange your introduction to the SIS station chief in Warsaw. You'd pass your information to the government through him."

"I'm perplexed." She took out another cigarette. The anger was dissipating, but her suspicion remained. "You say you're not *in* secret service but you're asking me to work *for* them?"

"Not exactly, merely cooperate, like I do myself. It would be of enormous value to the service and to the crown."

Elizabeth could not believe what she was hearing. Was this how the vaunted British secret service recruited its agents? If so, they *were* hard up. She looked at Stephenson. He was deadly earnest. She knew she could do what Bill was asking. A grin broke over her face. "I can't think of anything more thrilling . . . "

Stephenson allowed himself to smile as well.

" . . . except starting a family. And that's what I've promised myself I would do."

"Please, don't be hasty." It was Stephenson's turn to look surprised. "Think on it. Here's my card."

"Bill, I simply can't picture myself skulking around dark alleys with a baby at my breast."

"It wouldn't have to be that way, I assure you."

"Sorry"—she stuffed out her cigarette—"I'm flattered, but my mind's made up."

Elizabeth returned to the Savoy feeling excited and pleased. It was an honor to be asked to serve the crown, and she was even more proud of herself for saying no. Opening the door to her room, she found an envelope on the threshold. It had to be from Dr. MacCall. She tossed her hat on the bed and stepped out on the terrace. The trees on the embankment of the Thames were turning their autumn hues. Up river, the houses of Parliament and Big Ben stood outlined against the afternoon sky. Taking a deep breath she slit the envelope open with her nail. All of her hopes were contained on the little slip of paper inside. She read the message:

For Mrs. Pack:

Have results of your tests. Best to discuss them in person. Rest assured, you are all right. Call for an appointment at Bloomsbury 4691.

Dr. MacCall

She looked up. Little had changed. A barge continued its stately struggle against the current. The traffic on the Victoria Embankment proceeded to flow endlessly onto Blackfriars Bridge. Big Ben began to chime three o'clock.

But her whole life was different. If Dr. MacCall had good news, why would he need to see her? She caught a reflection of herself in the door to the terrace. Her body looked trim, healthy, and yes, beautiful. And inside? Hollow. Empty. Worthless. She hated herself. Her feelings imploded. She turned toward the edge of the terrace. What was the point of anything now?

It was a long way down to the river. A fresh breeze came up, tossing her hair and snatching at the paper in her hand. If you can't give life, she thought, weren't you already dead? Who would care, really? Arthur? Her mother? Her son didn't even know who she was. A moment of pain could stop a lifetime of heartache. Yet as she stood there, deadened by shock, feeling lost and hopeless, a corner of her mind said no. Don't. Make the call.

Elizabeth read the message again. The doctor had left his number. She went inside her room and picked up the telephone. What could he possibly tell her that she didn't already know? Fate had settled her future. When the operator came on the line, Elizabeth asked to be put through to the number of William Stephenson.

Chapter 13

Central Railway Station, Warsaw—
October 14, 1937

Wrapped in a fur coat and enveloped in a cloud of steam from the Nord Express, Elizabeth descended onto the platform at the Warsaw Central station. Arthur had stayed in London for briefings and a routine medical checkup, while she came ahead to prepare the flat that she had rented sight-unseen through a friend. She was grateful that the passport control officer from the embassy was there to meet her. He was a large, avuncular Irishman with a florid face by the name of Jack Shelly. His easy manner helped move her quickly through customs formalities.

Elizabeth felt tired, not so much from the journey, but from her effort to absorb everything she saw and read on the trip. Even through the narrow perspective of the train window, she had begun to understand the dynamics of the crisis looming in Europe. France had seemed typically sunny and self-satisfied until the train approached the German border. There, the enormous damage of the Great War was still visible: ruined villages, abandoned farms, and vast cemeteries that carpeted the hillsides with a million white crosses—one for each Frenchman who had died in the slaughter. No wonder the French were not anxious to fight again; the wounds of the last war had not yet healed.

Part of Elizabeth's voyage through Germany had taken place in the dark, but from the glimpses she had caught of the towns and cities, the Third Reich teemed with activity. And the military was in style everywhere: conductors, trainmen, customs officials, passport officers, border police, traf-

fic police, postmen, waiters, not to mention the vast
majority of male passengers, were all resplendent in uniforms of every color and hue. Blue, green, olive, gray, tan,
ocher, black, and white. Elizabeth wished that she owned
the German concession on jackboots, or failing that, brass
buttons.

She had been struck by the irony that twenty years after
the Great War, among the victors, Britain and France, the
military was utterly out of fashion. But in Germany, where
militarism had brought humiliation and defeat, it was all
the rage. Among the Allies, the war was widely seen as not
having been worth it. For the Germans, it obviously was
not yet over.

With the dawn had come the Polish frontier. As she
looked out at the broad and surprisingly empty landscape,
Elizabeth understood why the Poles felt so vulnerable.
From her reading, she had learned that this featureless
plain, which stretched from the dikes of Holland to the Ural
Mountains of Russia, had been the bane and glory of Polish
history. Armies of invaders—Celts, Goths, Vandals, Slavs,
Saxons, Rus, Teutons, Tatars, Balts, Swedes, Austrians, and
French—had swept through the territory, shaping the Polish
character and creating a legacy of heroism, misery, and de-
struction.

Over the last thousand years, Poland had from time to
time been a vast nation. In 1018 it reached farther west
than Berlin and as far south as the gates of Vienna. By
1634 it extended from the shores of the Black Sea to the
Gulf of Finland. Its eastern border lay well beyond Smo-
lensk, on the banks of the Donets only a few hundred miles
from Moscow. But for the three hundred years before 1918,
Poland had ceased to exist. Its lands were divided among
Austria, Germany, and Russia. Poland was a new-old country, rising out of the ashes of the Great War and the Bol-
shevik Revolution. It had been reborn a democracy, under
the charismatic leadership of the statesman and musical
genius Paderewski, but now he was gone and Poland had
fallen into the grip of a military government.

From the train window, the broad and open Polish countryside might have reminded Elizabeth of the American
Middle West, except that it lacked the feeling of elbow

room, despite the distant horizons. Perhaps it was because the earth was not the fresh black loam of Minnesota or Iowa, but instead had the tired gray look of centuries of cultivation.

Warsaw, however, came as a surprise. She had expected a city dark and somber, discounting remarks by friends that the Polish capital was "the Paris of the north." After all, no one ever called Paris "the Warsaw of the south." But the wide, tree-lined avenues did resemble the Boulevard Haussmann and the nineteenth century neobaroque and neoclassical buildings draped with brightly colored awnings did remind her of the City of Light—with one important exception. From the moment she had emerged from the wedding cake railway station and climbed into a Chevrolet taxi, she sensed an energy that made Warsaw feel more like Chicago or New York.

"No one knows why, but Poland's in the middle of an economic boom," Jack Shelly confirmed as he joined Elizabeth in the rear seat. With the back of the cabriolet top lowered, they set off down Jerusalem Street. The massive afternoon crowds did not stroll leisurely as they might in Madrid or Paris, but bustled along the sidewalks with urgency and determination. Apart from the old men in military caps who lined up to shine shoes at the corner of Marszałkowska Street, there was little sign of the Great Depression.

The new buildings going up all over town looked very *moderne.* The huge Prudential Insurance building that towered over the city reminded Elizabeth of Fritz Lang's *Metropolis.* Happy and excited to be away from the carnage of Spain and the somnambulance of England, Elizabeth felt she had arrived in a place where, for good or ill, the future was being created.

Soon they came to Nowy Świat, the New Street, which, Jack Shelly explained, was actually the oldest major thoroughfare in the city. Lined with restaurants, nightclubs, and fashionable shops with bright orange awnings, it connected the medieval heart of Warsaw to the stretch of eighteenth- and nineteenth-century palaces that had become Embassy Row.

The taxi turned right on Nowy Świat, then after a few

blocks, veered left on Wiejska until it reached Ulica Frascati, a gated street not far from the Polish parliament. Turning left again toward the river Vistula, the taxi stopped in front of the Villa Frascati, a brand-new eight-story apartment house across from a small park. Built of red brick and glass with terraces and doors of varnished teak, the building appeared to Elizabeth like a collaboration between Frank Lloyd Wright and Walter Gropius. When she stepped inside her fourth-floor apartment and saw the crimson wall-to-wall carpet and the shimmering silver walls, she decided her Spanish and French Provincial furniture had to stay in St.-Jean-de-Luz.

The shocking color scheme excited her. She was in a new country and a new city with a new, if secret, job to do. She would surround herself with only the new. The flat would be decorated with the most modern furnishings. She would dress in the latest French styles. Her life was off to a fresh start. The Nazis had better look out. She would be the best spy ever! But what, Elizabeth wondered, as she looked around the vacant rooms, did a freshly minted secret agent do first?

"You must make your calls before the end of the week," the passport control officer said, handing her a list. "Lady Kennard has placed you on her schedule for Thursday at three-thirty."

Armed with her engraved calling cards and wearing regulation white gloves, a veiled hat, and solid-color dresses that demurely covered her knees when she sat down, Elizabeth Pack set out to introduce herself to the wives of all the other officers in the embassy. By the time she arrived at the ambassador's residence on Thursday afternoon, she felt like her kidneys were floating in a sea of Earl Grey tea. The embassy wives seemed to be a decent lot, but extremely circumspect if not altogether cowed. The political counselor's wife, Mrs. Norton, who sipped whiskey while Elizabeth had her tea, made clear that the social tone of the embassy was set by the ambassador's wife, Lady Kennard.

"As you're both Americans," Mrs. Norton allowed sullenly, "you shall undoubtedly become her pet."

The British ambassador's residence was formerly the palace of a Russian nobleman who fled Warsaw in 1919 during the Polish war of independence. The marble foyer, with its twin circular staircases and grand chandelier, looked like it had been designed to intimidate bumpkins from the provinces and certainly achieved that effect on Elizabeth. She was shown to a sitting room off the garden where she nervously waited for a quarter of an hour for Lady Kennard to appear. Elizabeth dared to hope that since they both were Americans who had married into British diplomatic service, the ambassador's wife might be a kindred spirit. When she finally made her entrance, Elizabeth steeled herself. Lady Kennard looked like a Biedermeier sofa with pearls.

As they began their chat, the butler wheeled in a giant silver samovar. It had been polished so brightly that the reflection of the light slanting in from the garden made Elizabeth squint.

"And what do you think of the Poles, my dear?" Lady Kennard was asking.

"I haven't actually met any yet, except my housekeeper. She seems nice, but I can't really communicate with her. After living so long in Spain and France where I speak the language, it comes as a shock not to be able to count, or say please and thank you."

"I quite agree. I can't imagine why anyone would want to learn a word of such a barbaric language." Lady Kennard seemed to deliberately miss her point. "Rest assured, anyone worth talking to in this godforsaken place speaks English or French."

The ambassador's wife slowly sipped her tea, all the while giving Elizabeth close inspection. "You should be warned about the Poles. They consider themselves very romantic, but in point of fact they're merely frivolous and light-headed."

This was not the polite small talk Elizabeth had expected.

"And don't let their courtliness and formality fool you," Lady Kennard continued. "They're wild as Cossacks, madly rushing around having affairs with one another's spouses, then dueling in Lazienki Park or throwing themselves off the Poniatowski Bridge. As representatives of the British Empire, it's essential that we not be drawn into this unseemly maelstrom. Our task is to maintain standards of dignity and decorum even if it makes us rather unpopular.''

She set down her teacup and fastened her gaze intently on Elizabeth. ''Is it true that in Spain you participated in a bullfight?''

''I was a *rejonadora*.'' She flushed with embarrassment. ''It was an honor. . . . ''

''There'll be no such foolishness here. And no dancing on tables at nightclubs either. As Americans serving the crown, you and I bear an especially weighty responsibility, particularly with the other members of this embassy, to demonstrate the highest standards of comportment. I may have the title of 'Lady' Kennard, but others in our tight little circle only wait for the day that I commit some egregious American gaffe. I shall not tolerate any behavior on your part that reflects badly on me merely because we're countrymen.''

Elizabeth felt her anger rising. ''You can be assured, Lady Kennard''

''I certainly hope so.'' The ambassador's wife stood up. Their ''chat'' was over.

His Excellency, the ambassador, Lord Kennard was not an improvement. When Elizabeth met him at an embassy reception under the huge chandelier in the foyer, he shook her hand perfunctorily and said something like, ''Well humbard. Izt ohh ohh rye?'' He was trying to say ''Welcome aboard. Is everything all right?'' She understood why the embassy staff called him Mumbles. It was not an affectionate term.

The reception was like all the other embassy functions she attended in the first few weeks; there were few if any Poles in attendance. It was as if British embassy officials believed their primary mission was to entertain themselves and occasionally diplomats from other foreign embassies. Being absent, the Poles were always the butt of jokes. At her first embassy dinner at the home of Clifford Norton, the political counselor, he asked his guests if they'd heard the one about the Poles and the elephant. Even those who had were obliged to say no.

''Well, the League of Nations commissioned a series of studies on the elephant,'' he began. ''The English promptly submitted a short work on the subject of 'Hunting the Elephant.' "

The guests, mostly subordinates from the Embassy, tapped the table and said, "Hear, hear."

"The Germans," Norton continued, "wrote a ten-volume work on the physiology of elephants."

Everyone laughed dutifully.

"And the Poles submitted a manifesto entitled, 'Elephants and the Polish Question.' "

Elizabeth found the ladies of the embassy very considerate. They invited her to all their social events, mostly teas and bridge parties. But she also sensed a wariness that only wives can generate toward unattached females. The one friend she made in the first weeks was Jack Shelly, the passport control officer, who had met her at the train station and seemed as far from the center of influence in the embassy as one could get. A bachelor, whose girlfriend Sonia lived in Vienna, Shelly soon became her regular escort to diplomatic occasions and even took her to the movies to see *The Good Earth* and *Camille*. He was charming and amusing, and to her relief their relationship remained entirely circumspect.

Most of the time, Elizabeth concentrated on furnishing her apartment. She discovered that she could find virtually anything she wanted in Warsaw, and if they didn't have it, they would gladly make it. And the prices were incredibly cheap! She bought a stainless steel and leather sofa created by Le Corbusier, and a pair of so-called Barcelona chairs by Mies Van der Rohe. She found Polish copies of a dining room suite allegedly designed by Marcel Breuer. Her bedroom was rebuilt to accommodate a platform for a half-round bed backed by a half-round headboard and flanked by half-round light sconces. It made her feel romantic and slightly naughty like Jean Harlow.

When she was done, the apartment was a splendor of white wool and silk, black lacquered wood, silver walls and drapes, crimson carpets, and black and red geometric accents for the doors and ceilings. Elizabeth was very proud of herself until Mrs. Norton, visiting for tea, inquired as to whether she had intentionally adopted the color scheme of the Nazi party.

Once the apartment was complete, Elizabeth lapsed into frustration. Arthur had been delayed in London. She still had met no Poles, apart from decorators and furniture salesmen. Moreover, she had heard nothing whatsoever from the British secret service. She'd made a commitment to Bill Stephenson, persuaded Arthur, with some difficulty, that Warsaw was his best assignment, and girded herself for whatever ordeals lay ahead. Then nothing. Only a feckless round of dinner parties cut off from the real life of Warsaw.

She knew that a splendid life was out there. On her way to some stultifying embassy event, she would see horse-drawn carriages pulled up in front of marble palaces. Footmen would be helping ladies in sable cloaks and full-length ball gowns descend onto red carpets that stretched across the snow. Their escorts were often uniformed in colorful tunics and capes of bright blue and scarlet, or green and gold, with white sashes and swords sheathed in silver scabbards. Through her car window, Elizabeth glimpsed the gaiety and romance of Warsaw society, but night after night she was stuck with the secondhand life of diplomats. And while the embassy people were pleasant to her, she felt like an outsider in a clique of outsiders.

On a snowy night in early December, Elizabeth was invited to a dinner dance at the home of the American ambassador, Anthony Biddle, where she was seated next to a young Polish official.

"Count Lubienski *à votre service*." He bowed and brushed her gloved hand with his lips as a footman drew back her chair. With an approving glance he took in her long clinging gown with its plunging neckline and full skirt. The count was tall and spare with bright blue eyes, long sandy hair, and prominent Slavic cheekbones. His uniform glittered with decorations, which Lubienski explained he had earned in the horse cavalry. Elizabeth felt a surge of excitement. This man is madly attractive, she thought. Learn something about him, even if it's only the name of his horse!

"And your unit is stationed near Warsaw?" she asked as they descended from the dining salon to a small ballroom for the first dance. It was impolite, she knew, to ask a count what he did. In Spain, at least, counts often couldn't understand the question, since they generally did nothing at all.

He smiled easily. "My unit is near Brest, but I am here in the Foreign Ministry."

"That must be terribly dreary after dashing all over the countryside on horseback!" she exclaimed.

"Not at all!" Count Lubienski responded. The music drifted down from a chamber group playing above them in an alcoved balcony. "I have the honor to serve as the personal assistant of the foreign minister, Colonel Beck."

"What luck!"

"Not really, we were in the cavalry together." He began to move with familiarity to one of Chopin's waltzes.

"So you're terribly important, then." She smiled her most dazzling smile and leaned her head back to let her eyes catch the light from the chandeliers.

"No, not exactly." The count tried to appear modest, but looked very pleased. "But I must deal with matters of great delicacy," he admitted.

"I don't doubt you do." Other dancers had crowded onto the floor and were beginning to collide with them. "Poland is in such a dangerous predicament," she added earnestly, "caught between Stalin and Hitler."

"The Bolsheviks are a menace, yes, but we don't worry about Hitler."

"You're the only ones in Europe who don't!"

"Well, we understand him," he said reassuringly.

"You sympathize with the Nazis?" Elizabeth made herself look scandalized. She spun away and sat on one of the chairs to the side of the dance floor. The count followed her.

"Some do, of course," the count hastened to explain. "But that's not what I meant. We feel we can"—he paused—"anticipate his actions."

"Then you must be mind readers," she said, accepting a cigarette.

"Something like that." He lit it, and in the flame, his eyes gleamed as brightly as the medals on his chest. She could feel his glance burrowing into the cleavage between her breasts.

"And what," she exhaled, "is the great Reichsführer thinking that's so reassuring?"

"Reassuring to Poland," the count qualified her question. Then he paused as if he wondered whether to continue.

Elizabeth gazed at him warmly, expectantly, insistently.

"He's told his top aides"—his voice became more confidential— "that Germany's need for living space, *Lebensraum*, can only be achieved by force. But his target is not Poland. It's Austria and Czechoslovakia."

To Elizabeth, the rest of the evening was a blur. She danced and made witty conversation and flirted shamelessly with Count Lubienski, but all the time, her mind was going over every word, every nuance of what he had said. She had gleaned her first bit of intelligence, and she was determined to report it, in detail, to the British government the very next day.

Chapter 14

The British Embassy, Warsaw—
November, 29 1937

Lord Kennard's normally glazed eyes appeared to widen as Elizabeth related the story of her conversation with Count Lubienski.

"I thought I should get this information into official channels as quickly as possible," she proudly concluded.

The ambassador sat like a lump behind his massive Edwardian desk. He was so silent that, while his office overlooked the garden in the rear of the embassy, she could still hear the traffic on Nowy Świat.

"Madeh," he finally spoke. "I thochou game begause zovezome dif gully sed lingin," which Elizabeth translated as "My dear, I thought you came because you've had some difficulty settling in."

"You shouldn't trouble your pretty head about such things," she understood him to say. "If you want to be active, time on your hands and all that, take up charity work, That's my advice." Which sounded more like "Thasmy device."

The next thing she knew, Elizabeth was standing outside his door in the hall. Undaunted, she marched down the corridor to the other end where Clifford Norton, the political counselor, had his office. He listened respectfully as she again described her exchange with Lubienski.

"Elizabeth"—he smiled—"that bit about using force to gain *Lebensraum* is in *Mein Kampf*. It's hardly a bulletin."

"But what about Hitler aiming at Austria and Czechoslovakia?"

"That's been in the rumor mill for ages. Hitler's an Austrian! Most of the border area of Czechoslovakia is full of ethnic Germans. There's really nothing new in what he said, I'm afraid." His voice suggested he was trying to be kind.

Elizabeth felt her cheeks growing flushed. "I've been a complete ass."

"Not complete." Norton tried to make it a joke. "But the ambassador's given you sound advice. My wife would help, I'm sure, should you want to do charity work with unfortunates."

"Pull!" she commanded.

The clay pigeon rose no more than six feet before Elizabeth blew it to powder. She shattered the second skeet, crossing from right to left, directly in front of her.

She stood with Jack Shelly on the banks of the Vistula firing out over the water. After her morning of humiliation, he was treating her to skeet shooting and lunch at the embassy's lodge, which was located on the river south of the city.

Elizabeth cracked open her Purdy 12-gauge, popped out the smoking shells, and quickly pushed in two new ones. A biting wind was beginning to stir the leafless trees.

"Pull!" she shouted again.

This time the skeet came at her from the left. She took it down in one shot, then burst the next one almost the moment it was launched.

"You're really something today," Jack Shelly marveled. "That's sixteen in a row!"

"The secret is to point, not aim." She shook the spent shells onto the ground. "It also helps to want to kill."

He raised his eyebrows. "Let's go in to lunch and you can tell Uncle Jack all about it."

Over a hot, thick borscht, she repeated Lubienski's remarks and the mortifying response of Clifford Norton and the ambassador.

Shelly listened carefully. "I think the information's fascinating," he said when she had finished.

"No offense, Jack," Elizabeth sighed, "but you stamp passports for a living. The professionals say it's old hat."

He smiled calmly. "Those particular professionals couldn't find their hats if they were nailed onto their heads. I think your story should get back to London immediately."

She peered at him to see if he was teasing. He wasn't. "But what about *Mein Kampf* and all that?"

"Elizabeth, the important thing was that bit about 'reading minds.' "

"But those were my words. I said it as a joke." He had to be pulling her leg.

"But then Lubienski replied, 'Something like that,' am I correct?"

Elizabeth nodded.

"That suggests that the Poles are reading something else."

"Like what?"

"Like the Germans' mail. How else would he know what Hitler's told his top aides? Think about it."

She was taken aback by his intensity. Normally, Jack Shelly was a teddy bear. "These are figures of speech," she protested. "You've licked too much glue off your visas."

"Elizabeth"—his eyes gripped hers—"I don't dole out visas, not really."

She looked confused.

"I'm your contact."

What did he mean? Suddenly she understood. "SIS?" she exclaimed, then slapped her hand over her mouth. She stared anxiously around the room. The clubhouse was empty except for two military attachés in the corner who were on their second brandies.

"Your information's going straight to Queen Anne's Gate." Shelly quietly continued.

"Why didn't you tell me who you were before?" Elizabeth whispered angrily.

"I wanted to observe you. See what you were made of. When I heard that C had sent me a woman, I couldn't believe my ears. I waited to see if you were worth it."

"Well, am I?" she asked with a touch of defiance.

"To me, you're worth precisely twenty pounds a month—for expenses, no salary, otherwise we'd have to report you to Treasury, and they won't give us the billets."

Elizabeth realized this was her induction into the secret service. She could not suppress a smile.

"Your code name will be Cynthia," he continued.

"Do I get a last name?"

"No. You don't actually use Cynthia. We use it in our files and communications to protect your identity."

"Well, what do I do?" She tried not to sound too excited. "What's my first assignment?"

"Continue working on Count Lubienski. We believe he handles all intelligence matters for the foreign minister."

"Do you have any advice? Are there special techniques for getting people to talk?"

"Not really. I'm afraid you're on your own there. The main thing is not to scare him off." Shelly poked a fork into his chicken breast and watched the butter squirt out. "First you want to cultivate him as a source. Later you can try to enlist him as an agent."

Elizabeth looked troubled.

"What is it?" Shelly asked.

She took a deep breath and sighed. "I'm beginning to realize that this could be much more complicated than I thought."

"Because Lubienski's so attractive?"

She nodded. He *was* observant. "And because Arthur arrives at the end of the week."

"I should caution you that all of your activities must remain entirely secret from everyone, including your husband."

"Of course," Elizabeth reassured him, but she still wore a frown.

"Is there something else?" he asked.

"Where would we be if I hadn't sat next to Lubienski last night? My God, none of this would have happened!"

"Dear girl"—Shelly's expression suggested she had a lot to learn—"do you think that was an accident?"

Over a fresh carpet of snow, Elizabeth gently coaxed her new Polish-built Chevrolet through the city toward the Central Railway station. She had devoted the last several days to preparing for Arthur's homecoming. Her dressmaker had copied a green taffeta cocktail dress that Elizabeth had clipped from *Vogue*. From the large arcaded halls of Mirowski Market, she laid in a supply of meats, poultry, game, and fresh vegetables. At the wine merchants', Simon and Stecki, she had selected Arthur's favorite clarets, ports, and champagne. In the Place Zelaznej Bramy, she found a shop where she bought bouquets of dried flowers and a table setting of pyracantha. The dark green leaves and red berries made a cheerful contrast to the stark white damask tablecloth, which she had set for Arthur's welcome-home dinner. Elizabeth had even personally supervised the preparation of the loin of pork that was, at that moment, roasting in the oven at the apartment.

The Chevrolet slid to a stop against the curb in the diplomatic parking area. Filled with a mixture of anticipation and apprehension, Elizabeth hurried to the gate, where she joined an embassy clerk who would shepherd Arthur's luggage through customs. On the horizon, the train was already visible as a funnel of steam rising into the sky. In a few minutes, it lumbered into the station and Arthur, wearing a heavy chesterfield coat and fedora, stepped down to the platform.

Elizabeth was surprised at how old and tired he looked. She gave him a hug and a kiss on the cheek, which he reciprocated. On the drive to Villa Frascati, he remained silent while she kept up a nervous travelogue about the passing city landmarks.

"Yes, yes," he finally said impatiently. "I know all about these places, I've been studying my Baedeker."

But when he stepped into the apartment, she could see the surprise and pleasure on his face.

"Everything is charming," he allowed. "I give you full marks!"

"Dinner will be ready shortly, but you've time for a quick bath."

"I would enjoy that."

Elizabeth fixed him a martini and set it on the edge of the tub. "Would you like me to wash your back?"

"No, I can manage."

She could feel the old distance reasserting itself.

Over dinner, they sat across from each other at one end of the long dining room table. He told her about his trip (uneventful), the gossip at the Foreign Office (uninteresting), and the health of his parents (growing feeble).

"And how did your tests come out?" she asked.

He grimaced. "The doctors say my blood pressure's sky-high."

"Is it dangerous?"

He nodded reluctantly.

"I shouldn't have bought all this wine and rich food!"

"That's only the half of it. I've been under an enormous strain."

"What then? Something I don't know?" She put her hand on his arm.

"Yes," he said slowly; then abruptly he lost control. "And something you think *I* don't know!" The words burst out of him.

Elizabeth felt like she had been slapped. She withdrew her hand. "What do you mean?" she said stolidly, like a defiant child.

"The Marqués de Zaragoza I could write off as youthful indiscretion. Your American morality. But not John Leche!" he said bitterly. "Don't look surprised. The bastard had the cheek to send you dozens of letters that were forwarded to me. He even sought permission from the ambassador to come to St.-Jean-de-Luz!"

She tried to reach out to him again, but he pushed her away.

"Oh God!" He put his hands over his face and began to weep. The rage had gone out of him.

She sat there helpless, swamped by guilt.

"There's something more," he finally managed.

What else had she done to him, she wondered.

"I've been having an affair, too," he said.

Elizabeth looked at him. She didn't know whether to laugh or cry. Her sudden feelings of anger and humiliation came as a shock. "Do you love her?" she demanded.

"I don't know. I thought so, sometimes. But it's finished. I took this post to cure me of this damnable infatuation."

"Who is she?" That Elizabeth hadn't a leg to stand on only made her more furious.

"It doesn't matter! It's over, I tell you." His eyes closed and his head rolled back. "I didn't mean to do it"—he was like a small boy—"but you were gone so long in Spain and then England. . . . " His skin had turned a waxy gray.

Elizabeth felt waves of shame and sympathy wash away her anger. She got up and cradled his head against her body. "Arthur, I understand." She stood like that for what seemed a long time. "Thank you for telling me. I'm terribly sorry that you feel so bad."

"You don't despise me?"

She shook her head, and he did not resist when she put her arms around his shoulders to help him rise from the table.

"You need some rest," she said gently. "It's been a long journey."

He sat on the edge of the bed as Elizabeth helped him off with his clothes. Pulling up the covers, she gave him a kiss on the lips. "We can try to be good to one another."

"I want that very much," he said.

When she undressed, she left the bathroom door open. She could feel his eyes upon her as she stripped off her clothes and put on her nightgown. When she got into bed he reached over and put his hand on her breast. It was Arthur's signal that he wanted to make love.

"I thought that Warsaw might give us a new start," he said.

"I've felt the same way."

"And I've been thinking that maybe it would bring us together if . . . " He hesitated.

"Yes?" she encouraged him.

"If we went ahead now and started a family."

Elizabeth did not respond. She could sense him growing uneasy at her silence but did not know what to say. "It's too late," she whispered at last.

"Whatever do you mean?"

"Why do you think I was in hospital in London?"

"Some sort of female trouble, I supposed."

"Yes, exactly. The kind that means I can never have another child." The pain and anger came back again, but she could no longer find her tears.

It was Arthur's turn for silence. He stared at the ceiling.

"Was it because of what happened . . . before?"

"Yes." She did not want to punish him with specifics.

They lay there without speaking. "But we still have each other," she murmured.

"Yes, of course," he replied.

She reached out and put her arm across his chest. He took hold of her hand. They stayed that way for several minutes before he turned and rolled away from her.

The icy wind came slanting off the Vistula, whistling through the balustrade and slicing across the broad terrace that overlooked the old castle and the Kierbedz Bridge. Elizabeth huddled in the lee of the fifteenth-century bell tower that was part of the convent of St. Ann. Each time one of the red-and-cream-colored trams stopped in the street, she strained to distinguish among the passengers who, bundled up against the cold in their dark wool overcoats, all looked much alike.

A number three tram came gliding to a halt. Elizabeth easily recognized the man stepping down from the second car by his blue-and-yellow Guards scarf. Quickly, she crossed the terrace and descended a staircase into a bare and wintry park. With the dry snow under her feet crunching with every step, she slowed her pace to a stroll so that Jack Shelly could catch up with her. Together they entered a tiny teahouse that sat on the edge of the bluff above the river.

"I was worried that this place might have closed for the winter," Shelly said, taking off his hat.

The walls were all glass, to maximize the view of the castle, bridge, and river. But with the cold outside and the teapots brewing on the counter, the inside of the windows were opaque with stalagmites of hoarfrost. To Elizabeth, it seemed that they had found refuge in an ice cave. She slipped out of her fur coat.

The fleshy waitress came over and Shelly ordered a Haberbusch.

"How can you drink beer on a day like this?" Elizabeth ordered tea.

"I never drink whiskey when I'm working," Shelly replied.

"You don't look happy."

"London's all over me. Do you have anything new?"

"Our friend says the Germans have moved the Fifth Armored Corps south toward the Austrian border. No details."

"Christ, Elizabeth, Radio Berlin announced that two days ago! You've go to do better!"

She felt stung by his criticism. "I tell you everything he says!"

"Well, get him to say more."

She held her tongue while the waitress set down a glass of beer and a glass of tea.

"And how do I do that?"

"Stop collecting crumbs of gossip. Make him answer questions."

"I don't think so."

"Dammit, why not?"

"He's a patriot," Elizabeth explained defensively. "He's dissatisfied, but that's because he's living in the wrong century. Lubienski was too young to fight against the Russians in the last war, and he knows that his horse cavalry will be up against German tanks in the next one. That makes him melancholy, but I don't think it means he'd tell us everything he knows."

"My bosses have no interest in 'don't,' 'can't,' 'won't'!" he said flatly. "I went out on a limb for you. I set you up with our number one target and you're not performing. Your latest reports are being dismissed as pillow talk without the pillow. Everyone wonders if you're cut out for this line of work."

"It's not easy, Jack," she protested angrily. "Not with Arthur demanding that I account for every moment of my day. And Lubienski's spooked too. We only meet in cafés that are so far out of town the streetlamps run on gas!"

"I could get you an apartment. . . . "

She shook her head determinedly. "I told you, Arthur and I are trying to make things work. We've been through hell. . . . "

Shelly stopped her with a wave of his hand. "You're in secret service, not a sewing circle. SIS has a bias against women for this very reason. They want to know whether you're serious, or just another pretty girl who's playing the tease. If so, our deal is off!"

Elizabeth felt herself grow flushed. "And I joined up to fight Hitler, not sleep around. Do you think I don't know your game? You want me to hook Lubienski by betraying my husband!"

"Let's be frank, girl." Shelly drained his beer and wiped his upper lip. "You've done it before, for less good reasons."

Elizabeth wanted to slap him. She wanted to throw her tea in his face. But before she could react, Shelly had tossed a few coins on the table, put on his hat, and left her alone to think about it.

Most Secret/CYNTHIA
By Pouch

December 6, 1937

Dear Jack,

This will authorize you to terminate Cynthia. From the start the Code and Cipher School chaps regarded it as another one of Bill Stephenson's harebrained schemes.

However, we do believe Lubienski should be pursued with the highest priority as a possible source. C is anxious to move Cynthia out of the way before she does some real damage to that prospect. Send your recommendations by cable.

As ever,
Menzies

10/12/37/11:25GMT
MOST SECRET/CYNTHIA
WARSAW STATION SENDS
FOR BROADWAY—1257

CYNTHIA NOT REPEAT NOT TERMINATED. HAS ONE MORE CONTACT WITH TARGET. IF FRUITLESS WILL THEN CUT HER OFF.
SHELLY.
ENDIT

Chapter 15

Eastern Poland—
December 15, 1937

"There's nothing like it in all of Europe," Count Lubienski said to Elizabeth as the train lurched and rattled through the still-dark countryside. "The land is part of a great estate that belonged to the czar. The woods covered thousands of square kilometers. Actually, they once covered all of northern Europe. This is the last piece of primeval forest left on the Continent."

They were riding in a mahogany-paneled club car belonging to the Polish Army. A long narrow table that stretched the length of the coach was laden with a hunt breakfast: hams and sausages and wursts; cheeses and breads and preserves; pickled vegetables and marinated herrings and salted fish, all presided over by a large copper samovar dispensing strong dark tea.

"We'll be riding trails that date back to prehistoric times," Lubienski continued. "The forest is a refuge for boar, stag, elk, all sorts of game. And in the deep meadows, one can find the great ancient bison."

"It seems a pity to hunt them," said Elizabeth.

"It would be a pity not to. In the winter they die of starvation."

Like most of the men in the car, Count Lubienski was in uniform. In his cavalry tunic and tall boots, he looked more dashing and handsome than ever. Arthur, who was busy with the pastries, had squeezed into his English riding habit complaining bitterly that it had been shrunk by the servants. Elizabeth was the only woman, and she was not happy to be there.

Ever since her blowup with Shelly, she had been avoiding Lubienski, and the last thing she wanted was to go on an outing with him and Arthur. But when she had stopped calling Lubienski, he had started calling her. And when she made excuses not to see him, he approached Arthur to invite them both on the prestigious Bailowieza Hunt—an event usually reserved for much more senior diplomats. As in Spain, Arthur could not say no.

Shelly had also been a boor and a pest. Without once apologizing for his rude behavior at the tearoom, he had been pressing her to introduce him to Lubienski. "If you won't exploit him properly," he insisted, "you can at least hand him off to someone who will." When he had learned that she was going on the Bailowieza Hunt, he declared that it was her last chance to prove herself to the SIS.

Why should it matter if she proved herself to a shadowy group of people she didn't even know? Elizabeth had no ready answer, but somehow it did. She did not want to be a shirker in the great collision between good and evil that Churchill and Stephenson said was coming. But what Shelly wanted seemed far from that struggle. And to be practical, what could she do on horseback in the middle of the woods?

The train slowed as it passed through a dour little town called Białystok, then resumed its journey through an endlessly vacant plain that at that time of year was only beginning to fill with first light at ten o'clock. To Elizabeth, the sad snow-covered landscape seemed to ache for the vanished forest. It was as if the earth, stripped naked of trees, was frozen in shame and had cloaked itself in apathy.

Twenty minutes later, the train jerked to a stop in the middle of an open field. When Lubienski helped her down from the car, she could see a thin slice of dawn glowing in the east, and under it, a dark and forbidding wood stretching across the horizon. From the direction of the locomotive came the sound of yelping and barking as the hounds poured out of the train, swirling and jumping around their handlers. Soldiers were dropping down the sides of the stable cars to free the horses. Wild and agitated after their bumpy confinement, they clambered down the planks neighing and snorting, their iron shoes striking sparks on the stony roadbed. In the cold, steam rose from their flanks and exploded through their nostrils. The animals were big; Elizabeth guessed fourteen to fifteen hands high, and had long hairy winter coats. They wore heavy blankets under their saddles and wool leggings around their fetlocks to keep warm.

Elizabeth staggered under the weight of an enormous fur coat and hat provided by the army. She found that she could barely walk in the clumsy felt boots that Count Lubienski insisted she wear. When she saw Arthur struggling in a greatcoat, unable to pull himself up on a huge gray stallion, she began to laugh. Two soldiers were finally required to push him into the saddle.

She needed their help too. But soon she was mounted on a sturdy brown gelding, her felt boots secured by leather-covered stirrups. In a few minutes, everyone was on horse-back, the dogs had been divided into three groups, and like a small army, the hunting party set off across the frozen fields.

The sun had disappeared into the overcast, and if it were not for the dark line of forest ahead, it would have been difficult to distinguish earth from sky. Elizabeth rode beside Arthur. She could not help remembering the last time they rode together—the autumn days in England when he sought vainly to get rid of her baby. After she explained to him how she became infertile, Arthur had seemed to go numb. Elizabeth had tried to reassure him by offering to make love, but a couple of fumbling attempts had come to nothing. Each day she felt him retreat further. Arthur, Shelly, Lubienski, they all added up to failure on her part.

The edge of the wood was marked by a wooden fence of rough unpainted sticks topped with barbed wire to discourage poachers. They rode next to it for about a mile, before finding an opening. They then had to line up single file in order to follow the narrow track that led inside. Arthur wound up several horses ahead of Elizabeth and Count Lubienski right behind her.

At first, the Bailowieza Forest looked much like any other—filled with elm and chestnut with an occasional yew and a variety of pines. Soon, however, the pines disappeared and Elizabeth began to notice the huge oaks, some of them as big around as California redwoods. Everywhere she could see fallen trees, the huge tangled root systems sticking into the air like masses of frozen snakes. It surprised her to realize that the forest primeval was as full of death as it was of life. She had expected a dense undergrowth, but the thick canopy of trees kept the floor of the woods surprisingly clear.

Riding up beside her, Count Lubienski said, "Our poets write that the trees of Baiłowieza are like the Polish people,

> *'stubbornly clinging to the land,*
> *too deep to be uprooted,*
> *too thick to be cut down.'* "

Elizabeth wondered if the poem had lost something in translation, but she appreciated Lubienski's effort to be charming.

At a fork in the trail, the hunting party turned off to the right. Although they hoped to find bison, they would be satisfied with wild boar, elk, or a stag. No one in the group carried firearms except the huntmaster. In the ritual of the hunt, the dogs would locate the quarry and then the riders would chase the animal to exhaustion. The huntmaster administered the *coup de grâce*.

The cold was relentless. Despite the heavy coat, hat, thick boots, lap blanket, and the heat from the horse beneath her, Elizabeth was freezing by the time she heard the barking of the dogs intensify and saw the line of horses shift to a canter. A shout of *"Jelen'! Jelen'!"* echoed through the forest.

"It's a stag," Lubienski cried. "A big one." He pointed to the left. All she could see was the hounds leaping over fallen trees like spawning salmon. The horses started to gallop. Abruptly, the riders in front of her began to veer off the trail, attempting to cut off the stag's escape. She saw Arthur plunge into a stand of dense woods and almost get swept from his saddle by a low branch. On a horse, he became an entirely different person, brash, aggressive, a taker of risks.

"Follow me!" Lubienski shouted. Elizabeth dived into the forest after him.

Where Arthur and a horse always made for an uneasy alliance, Count Lubienski and his mount seemed to form one sleek creature that was able to find an imperceptible path through the tangle of trees, logs, and bushes. Ahead, where the forest cleared again, Elizabeth suddenly spotted the stag. It had doubled back and was heading toward her. The magnificent buck carried huge antlers bearing more than a dozen points. With a shake of its head the animal vanished into a thicket of bushes and vines. Crashing headlong after it, Elizabeth found herself pulled and grabbed by branches from all sides. She marveled at how the stag, racing ahead of her, escaped being caught up by its own antlers.

For forty minutes they chased the animal through the woods. Sweat lathered her horse's flanks and foam flecked off the bridle. It was the most arduous riding Elizabeth had ever done. She felt exhilarated and exhausted when, at last, they brought the stag to bay in a patch of frozen swamp. The big buck was kicking at the hounds with red-stained hooves and tossing them over its back with crimson antlers. Still, the dogs had done their work. Blood ran from a score of wounds in the animal's flanks. As it finally sank to its knees, the huntmaster fired a single shot into the stag's heart to spare it further pain and indignity.

Elizabeth had only hunted foxes. She always had been fascinated at the ritual of "blooding," the spectacle of the cream of civilized society taking the severed paws of a fox and marking their faces with streaks of its blood. If this was the pagan rite of hunting in England and Virginia, what did they do with a stag on the steppes of Poland?

Shooing away the dogs, the huntmaster dismounted. He took a knife and a silver goblet out of a leather pouch. Bending over the carcass, he drove the knife into the stag's neck, holding the cup so as to catch the spurting blood. With the dogs howling and baying, each member of the hunt took a sip. When the goblet came to Arthur, he shook his head and quickly passed it to Elizabeth. She looked at the men now staring solemnly at her.

"You need not do this. . . . ." Count Lubienski murmured.

She brought the cup to her lips, surprised at how warm it felt. Then, tilting back her head she took a swallow, the blood tasting sticky sweet and metallic in her mouth. A cheer went up from the others. Arthur snatched it back and also gulped down a mouthful. In an instant, he looked like he would be sick. Everyone cheered, but many were laughing too.

Once the antlers, hooves, and tail had been cut from the stag and distributed as trophies, the hunters were ready to move out again. As they formed into a line, Arthur shied away from Elizabeth, but not before hissing, "Don't you ever embarrass me like that again!"

She let him go forward and allowed her horse to fall to the back with Count Lubienski.

"We're going after more game?" Elizabeth asked wearily.

"There's still boar and buffalo."

"I don't think I want any boar's blood, thank you," and she snapped the reins to encourage her horse forward.

"Stay back with me," he urged. "I've a surprise for you."

After trotting along uneventfully for several minutes, he pulled up and raised his glove to indicate that she should quietly follow him. They turned into a difficult and virtually invisible track.

"Where are we going?" Elizabeth asked anxiously.

"You'll see."

"They'll miss us."

"We'll say we got lost."

"That's what I'm worried about," Elizabeth said.

"I spent my youth in these woods," Lubienski reassured her. "You look cold. I want to make you warm."

That's the other thing I'm worried about, she thought to herself, but let her horse go ahead. Isn't this exactly what Shelly had been hoping for? The question made her angry. His strategy had the subtlety of a hydraulic engine: Take Lubienski to bed and then pump him for information. The first might be easy. But getting Lubienski to reveal state secrets? What was she supposed to say? Michael darling, just what are your sources at the German Reich Chancellery? Or maybe she was supposed to bargain with him. One touch above the waist for each diplomatic secret; but to go below the waist, Michael dear, you have to give me military secrets. It was absurd! And Shelly was no help. All he knew how to do was threaten to terminate her with SIS.

She rode along behind Lubienski as he picked his way through a dense part of the forest. Garlands of frozen green moss hung from the trees and mistletoe festooned the oaks. Small birds swarmed through the bare branches feeding on winter berries and luminous red pyracantha.

What would it matter if she were dropped by the secret service? In many ways it would be a relief. Stephenson's offer to work with SIS had filled a yawning void in her life, and she never wanted to stare into that suicidal chasm of meaninglessness again. Yet what Shelly wanted was exactly the opposite of what Arthur demanded from her. Didn't her husband have to take first priority? They had, after all, decided to make a new start. Unfortunately, nothing seemed to have changed between them, nothing except his intense concern about how she spent her days—not whether she enjoyed them or found them productive and satisfying. He only wanted to know where she was and with whom.

Why, Elizabeth wondered sadly, did Arthur care if she slept with other men? Pride? Probably. Power? Possibly. If he could keep her on the reservation without offering her a love life, it certainly was a testament to his control over her. No, she had to admit, nothing had changed. Arthur was still completely absorbed with his work and utterly oblivious to her desires.

But could she blame him? Did she know what she wanted herself? Yes, she did actually. She wanted to get into the fight, the one that was threatening to tear Europe apart, and not just for the thrills. Hitler was on a rampage. Sooner or later, America would be dragged in too, just like in 1917. It might sound corny, but she knew she could help, not just Britain, but her own country as well, if only Shelly and Arthur would give her half a chance.

The cold was making Elizabeth's bones ache. The air was so frigid it felt like breathing a vacuum. Where were they heading? The hunt was to end with a grand luncheon at the Castle Gródek. If Lubienski wanted time alone with her, that must be his destination. The castle would be full of servants, but that wouldn't deter him. Noblemen had a way of treating servants like furniture.

The number of pines and birch trees were increasing while the hardwoods became smaller and fewer. Quite abruptly they came to the edge of the forest. Lubienski spurred his horse over the barbed wire. Elizabeth followed.

"Where to?" she called out.

He pointed to a column of smoke climbing above a low hill.

She raced after him to the top, eager for her first glimpse of the castle. What she found was a scattering of thatch-roofed peasant houses, barns, and chicken coops, some with strange antennas sticking out of them. Smoke rose from the stone chimney of a wood plank cottage painted sky blue with yellow and green shutters. To her surprise, that was where Count Michael Lubienski was dismounting from his horse.

What was it going to be, she asked herself as she hesitated at the top of the rise, Shelly's way or Arthur's way? The hell with both of them; she spurred her horse down the slope. Whatever she decided, it would be her own way.

Chapter 16

Baiłowieza Forest, Poland—
December 15, 1937

As Count Michael Lubienski had led Mrs. Arthur Pack through the woods, he could hardly believe she was going along with his plan! He was filled with the kind of excitement he imagined he would feel if ever faced with battle. He had never done anything like this before.

His friends had often chided him for being so circumspect with the ladies, for never joining them in the brothels on the Praha side of the Vistula. Lubienski was no prude, but he had married the daughter of a minor magnate near Cracow while still a cadet, and he behaved as his family and the Church required. He had thought that he loved his wife even though his marriage had had its disappointments, as all do. But he and his wife had made the best of it, for by bringing together the Lubienskis' social position with his father-in-law's financial strength, it had been good for both families. Like most men, he had a wandering eye, but nothing had ever come of it, for he regarded himself as honest, dutiful, constant, and loyal. Suddenly, Elizabeth Pack had changed all that.

She ignited a passion in him that he found quite baffling. The woman was beautiful to be sure, and with a strange mixture of innocence and voluptuousness that provoked and confused him. But it was far more than simple allure. If he tried to analyze Elizabeth dispassionately, he would have to say he was drawn to her because of her fantastic energy. She listened so intently that he felt forced to talk. She was like alum on the tongue, drawing out all of his pain and

189

confusion. Her silences formed a powerful vacuum that he felt compelled to fill. When she focused her attention on him, the experience was nearly overwhelming. Lubienski felt safe and secure and like quite the most singular man in the world. This did not strike him as flattery, for it did not inflate him with self-importance. To the contrary, he needed her all the more. A conversation with her, even on the telephone, could change a dispiriting and melancholy day into one in which he felt he could accomplish anything. And her rich, warm voice seemed to resonate in his innards, arousing him even when she was talking about ridiculous things like German rearmament.

Lubienski looked over his shoulder at her. That morning he had been startled and pleased to see that she was such an expert rider. He admired the way she now worked her horse skillfully through the dense wood, even though she appeared lost in thought. Hopefully she wasn't having doubts about their little detour!

He wanted her from the moment he had taken her into his arms at the American ambassador's dinner dance. At first, she had seemed to be simple quarry. She was responsive to his every suggestion, even to meeting him in the most out-of-the-way places. But if Elizabeth was easy to approach, she had proven difficult to catch. He would tell her about himself, his trials, his dreams, and, as he worked around to his feelings for her, his need for her, he would inexplicably find himself discussing the character and background of Joachim von Ribbentrop, the new German foreign minister.

However, from the outset of his campaign to win her, he had made up his mind never to tell her any real secrets. He supposed that some of the things he said got back to the British embassy, but that was probably all to the good. The British had the mistaken impression that his boss, Foreign Minister Beck, was pro-Nazi. In fact, he was pro-Poland. So it was important for the British to realize that they had a sympathetic person close to Colonel Beck, even if Lubienski had to admit that he hadn't exactly been charged with that responsibility.

His formal position, secretary to the foreign minister, was a great honor but hardly ever a pleasure. His principal responsibility was vitally important: to provide Colonel Beck with the latest intelligence available to the Polish government. He had a modest office in the foreign minister's suite at the Brühl Palace. It had a high window overlooking Staski Park and a fireplace, which he mainly used to burn sensitive documents. Lubienski had expected that his role would put him in the center of things, but in reality, it was quite alienating.

He found that he was an observer of fateful events with no influence over them. Even on good days, he felt like a mere bureaucratic factotum. On bad days, he yearned to be back with his cavalry unit preparing for the coming war— a war that would be all the more terrible because of mistakes he witnessed but could do nothing to stop. His work was futile, yet all-consuming. He lived at the foreign minister's whim. He had to be on hand from early morning to late at night. Life was passing him by. While he was increasingly praised for his maturity, to Lubienski that only meant he was growing old. Dear God, he was not yet thirty! He was not made for bureaucratic caution, he was made for action! He was made for sacrifice!

Lubienski's horse spotted the fence that marked the end of the forest and began to pick up speed, eager for the jump. Looking back, Lubienski saw that Elizabeth was not far behind. He cleared the barbed wire and raced ahead of her pointing toward a low rise in response to her call.

He loved how she made him audacious again. She even made him bold enough to take advantage of the few perquisites offered by his work. One was that the intelligence services would do his bidding without explanation. Colonel Beck might be feared and hated, but using his name got results.

Like this little cottage on the edge of the Bailowieza Forest. Only the antennas and the fact that it was better maintained than any other peasant house in eastern Poland revealed that the farm was actually a military intelligence listening post. He reined in his horse, dismounted, and pushed open the door.

Everything was as he had ordered. A fire roared in the wall-sized fireplace. Facing it, a large sofa with twin ottomans covered by a goose down comforter offered respite from the cold. Against the far wall, a table beckoned with caviar, champagne, and vodka. And no one else was there.

Lubienski returned outside to help Elizabeth down from her horse. As she looked around, she wore an expression of suspicion and amusement.

"So," she said in her husky voice, "is this where you plan to seduce me?"

"No! No! Don't misunderstand. It's just a place to get warm!" He took her hat and heavy coat as he showed her into the room.

"And cozy." Laughing, she dropped onto the sofa, kicked off her felt boots and pulled up the comforter.

Her laugh struck him in a vital spot. "Would you like caviar?" He blushed. "Something to drink?"

"Vodka would be wonderful. I don't plan to work any more today, do you?"

He shook his head stupidly. "I'll toast the bread for the caviar." She seemed to be in a receptive mood!

He cut a large brown loaf into thin slices and put them into metal baskets attached to a long pole which he placed above the fire. Pouring out two vodkas, Lubienski worried that Elizabeth could see his hands trembling. Facing cannons had to be easier than this!

"Nazdrovia!" he said bravely.

They clicked glasses, drank, and he poured another.

"Your toast is smoking."

He dashed to the fire. Extracting the toast, he burned his fingers.

"Let me see your hand."

"It's not serious."

She kissed it. "Now it'll be better."

Count Lubienski felt paralyzed. He wanted to leap into the air, sweep her into his arms, crush her lips with his. But how would she react? He had to be sure or he might ruin his chance. "My God, you're so wonderful!" he exclaimed and rushed away to bring the caviar and more vodka.

Soon they were side by side facing the fire under the coverlet, eating piles of caviar and sipping ice-cold vodka. Lubienski could not keep himself from talking.

"I'm so fortunate. You're so beautiful. I bless the day I

met you. On the dance floor you were like a dream in my arms, and now with you beside me, I feel transported to Eden . . . to heaven!"

In the glow of the fire, her eyes had turned sea green and her hair gleamed red and gold. He saw a crimson blush on her cheek.

"Michael," she said softly but earnestly, "you're quite the most gallant and dashing man I've ever met. I feel your strength, and your courage. Your intelligence is inspiring. It makes me realize how lucky I am to know you. . . . "

This blizzard of praise embarrassed and excited him. He meant something to her!

" . . . How fortunate Poland is that you serve her," she continued, "and how grateful your wife must be to have you as a husband."

What could he say to that? He felt mocked, but she seemed totally sincere. Should he talk about his wife? No, he was betraying her. He would not dishonor her by talking about their marriage.

Elizabeth reached out to him. "You have my friendship. . . . "

"No! I want more than friendship! It's been agony these past weeks, meeting you in public places, unable to take you in my arms. I need you Elizabeth. I want you. . . . "

"Michael, I'm married!"

"Arthur? I've seen this man." He shook his head. "God forgives us such mistakes. The important thing is to go on living!"

"What about your reputation? People would know." She drew away and turned toward the fire. "And, what of your position in the government? You'd be vulnerable to criticism. . . . "

"I don't care about all that! None of it matters!"

"We can't be foolish!" she admonished him.

A moment ago, she was almost his. Now, suddenly, he was back in school. "No one will be outraged," he said haplessly, and with the sinking feeling that argument had never bedded a woman. "This is not England, or America," he persevered. "There are no Puritans here. The Polish people understand the human heart." He was getting back in stride. "We respect love that comes from the soul.

Most men, respectable men, have wives and families, but they also have a true love to fulfill them!''

"So that's what you want? One wife? One mistress? How bourgeois!'' She turned her back on him again.

"No! I was just trying to explain . . . '' He'd made a mess of it! He began to feel frantic. He had to get through to her! "I must have you. Don't you see I'm desperate for you?'' And with that he leaped up. "Look at me!''

She turned and her eyes widened. He knew she could not miss the bulge in his pants. "I'm in agony,'' he pleaded. "You cannot leave me like this!''

She laughed.

What was wrong with her? Polish women acted coquettish and demure, yet his friends claimed that the moment always came when they abandoned themselves. They knew when to surrender. Why wasn't Elizabeth like that? He fell on his knees, and seized her wrists.

"Elizabeth, Elizabeth! Don't laugh at me! Love me!'' Swept by humiliation, he buried his head in her hands. "I'll do anything you say! I'll be your slave!''

The room filled with the crackling of the fire. He could hear her breathing. It was fast and deep.

"Anything?'' she murmured.

"Anything!'' He looked up. A change had come over her.

"Stand up again, Michael. I want to see you.''

He did as he was told. He sensed himself growing even harder.

"I want to see all of you,'' she insisted softly. For a moment he did not understand. "All of you, Michael,'' she repeated.

He began tearing off his uniform, feeling awkward and clumsy, struggling with his pants and boots. Finally, he stood before her naked and erect.

"Take your hands away.''

He obeyed.

She looked at him without a trace of false modesty. "You're beautiful,'' she whispered. Her voice was a caress that almost caused him to explode. He stepped toward her.

She held up her hands to keep him away. "You say you

want me?'' she said solemnly. "You'd better see if I'm worthwhile.''

Elizabeth got up from the couch and began to undress. What could she be talking about, he wondered. Why did she sound so sad? The figure that slowly emerged from her cocoon of clothes astonished him. Her smooth skin seemed burnished by the firelight. The contours of her body were voluptuous and sensuous, yet strong and lithe. She reached behind her back in a butterfly motion to release her bra, and he gasped to see her breasts swing free. When she slipped off her panties then stood to reveal the dark and forbidden triangle, her aroma enveloped him, triggering a blind need to lose himself within her.

"You're the one who is beautiful.'' He could hardly speak. Elizabeth was beyond his imaginings, a different species from his hard, bony, angular wife. And with the thought of the Countess Lubienski, he began to droop.

As if she could sense his sudden rush of guilt, Elizabeth stepped closer and gathered him up. Looking frankly into his eyes, she caressed him slowly, comfortingly, her soft hands teasing his desire back from hiding, filling him up again, making his need for her exquisite and urgent. He attempted to kiss her, but she gently pushed him back onto the sofa. Then, still holding him tight, she straddled his body.

Oh, the warmth! He reveled in the sweet agony! She rode him smoothly, more fluidly than he had ever ridden a horse. Still she had not kissed him, but continued to stare, as if to absorb him through her eyes. Her breasts swept across his face like a saber slash of pleasure. He strained to reach them, to capture them with his mouth. Below, she squeezed him, pulled on him, her body sliding back and forth. With blurred vision, he saw she was no longer looking at him. Her head had rolled back. She was biting her lip, her eyes opening and closing sightlessly. Moving very slowly now, she rose up, hesitated, then pushed down to engulf him. Up, so that he strained to rise with her, down, so that he thrust deeper inside. Suddenly, she stopped still. Seizing his hair, she crushed his lips with their first kiss and began a long, tumultuous shudder. Then groaning so that he felt her voice echoing in the back of his throat, Elizabeth collapsed.

They lay entwined, Lubienski still within her, still hard, acute, anxiously needing release. With her eyes closed as if she were dreaming, she began to move her hips slowly, languorously. Almost casually she drove him past the point of explosion and onto a plateau of desperation. Like a tender torturer, she pleasured him until his mind was gone, until his loins wanted to spill open and confess. Soon, he felt the aching power gathering in his calves and thighs: in his shoulders and chest, in his stomach and back. This time he knew he had the strength, the force to break through, to end the gorgeous torment, to burst the bonds of ecstasy with which she had enslaved him. But as he trembled on the cusp of victory, Elizabeth slipped away, turned, and enveloped him with a kiss that utterly destroyed him.

How could she have done this? Regret filled Elizabeth as fully as had passion only minutes before. Arthur had been home just a few weeks. She hadn't given it any time! On the other hand, there hadn't been any "it" either.

What about Lubienski then? He lay curled up beside her, sleeping quietly with his head on her breast. Was espionage only an excuse? She had wanted him, she couldn't deny that. But perversely, making love had been a way to retreat from him, a way not to feel the tenderness he invoked in her. The rapture of her body helped obliterate her growing affection for him. What kind of a woman was she, Elizabeth asked herself. A Mata Hari with a useless uterus and the heart of a whore?

For a long time, she stared at the white-washed ceiling with its rude beams covered with bright folkloric designs. Outside, it had begun to snow; inside, the fire had become a pile of glowing embers. The room smelled of ashes and was growing cold.

And lying there in a peasant cottage on the Polish steppe, as far from the world as she had ever been, she felt her sense of remorse fade away. Her body was good for something after all. It had power over men. She could use it for a worthy purpose. Yes, she realized, this would be the day of her first blooding.

Count Lubienski stirred against her. "You're so soft, so sweet," he murmured. "Thank you."

"For what?"

"You make me happy with myself."

"Is that so difficult?"

He sat up and put his arm around her shoulders, speaking as if in confidence. "My life is a charade. I'm nothing but a bit player in an epic tragedy. Oh, I cannot bore you with my sadness."

"And why such sadness?" she asked quietly, sensing that his operatic mood meant that he wanted to say more. "You've a noble title, an important position, and now you have me."

"You, you." He rose to kiss her. "You are wonderful!" Then he sank back to her breast once again.

"A title in Poland is a curse. There are so many 'counts,' it does not make you distinguished. It only imprisons you in a code you cannot break. As for my position," he sighed, "it allows me an orchestra seat to view Poland being ground to pieces between Hitler and Stalin."

"I thought you didn't worry about Hitler."

"That's the official line. We know what he's up to. But it's like standing paralyzed on a railroad track with a train coming at you. Our only chance lies in an alliance with France and England or even America. But we also know that's a hopeless dream. So everyone in Warsaw behaves like they're at a party at the end of the world, forcing themselves to be gay, carrying on at balls and masquerades, drinking and dancing all night, throwing themselves into passionate affairs."

"Is that what we're doing?"

"No, of course not." He seemed shocked at the thought. "Elizabeth, I only mean that when there can be no happiness of the spirit, there is only the happiness of the flesh. . . . " He caught himself. "But you are both," he added anxiously. "You've touched my soul."

Lubienski fell into an uncertain silence. This seemed to be her chance. She had to make the most of the moment.

"Before"—she hesitated—"before, you said you'd do anything for me."

"I would. I will!" He sat up.

"Will you answer a question?"

He turned her shoulders so he could look directly into

her eyes. "I'll lay my life bare. If I don't know the answer, I'll go on a quest. I'll search the world over until I find the answer and bring it back to you!"

"You don't have to do all that." She laughed and put her hand on his chest, winding the blond hair into her fingers. "I simply wondered how you know some of the things you tell me."

He looked blank. "What do you mean?"

"For instance, how do you know what Hitler's up to? How do you read his mind? You also once said you knew in advance about the Night of the Long Knives, when he murdered the Brownshirts. How, Michael?"

She tried her best to make her questions sound casual, interested, innocent, but they fell awkwardly off her tongue. Elizabeth could feel him stiffening, and not in the right place.

Count Lubienski opened his mouth but nothing came out. He looked confused, then uncertain, then appalled, then terrified. "You're a spy!"

"Don't be ridiculous, I'm just curious."

"You planned this!" He leaped up and began to dress hurriedly.

"Michael, *you* brought *me* here!" This was going horribly wrong.

"Put on your clothes! Immediately!" he demanded.

"Why are you acting like this?" she said, reaching for her underwear. Dammit, how else was she to ask such questions? Oh, the hell with the questions! She'd ruined everything! She was losing him! Half dressed, Elizabeth reached out. "Michael, you're making a mistake!"

He pushed her away. "We'll join the others at the castle. We were chasing a boar and got lost." His voice was firm, but his eyes were wild as he backed away toward the door. "Then we must never, ever, see each other again!"

Chapter 17

"You don't look very excited about the party," Elizabeth said aloud, as she stared at her reflection in the dressing table mirror. She and Arthur were ringing in the new year at a costume ball at Łazienki Palace, the former summer home of the last king of Poland. All Elizabeth could feel was ennui.

Jack Shelly and his girlfriend visiting from Austria soon would arrive in a carriage that they had rented for the occasion. When Elizabeth had told him of her catastrophic failure with Count Lubienski, he was deeply disappointed, but to her surprise very kind.

"It's the fortunes of war," he had sighed into a coffee and slivovitz at the Café Gogolewski, near the old town. "I'm not sure I can maintain your stipend," he had explained apologetically.

"Will I be a black mark against you?"

"You've blotted my copybook, but touch wood I'll still get my pension." He smiled. "Of course, if there's any way you can reestablish contact with Lubienski ... "

"If you'd seen his face, you'd know it's hopeless."

"Well, at least it gives the lie to your fear of being a prostitute."

"Whatever do you mean?" Elizabeth had said with a trace of shock. She meant, "However did you know?"

"Professionals always ask for what they want in advance."

Elizabeth knew she should laugh but tears had come into her eyes.

"I'm sorry," Shelly said. "I've been awfully rough on you."

"My regret"—Elizabeth used her napkin—"is that betraying Arthur isn't very difficult for me anymore. And when I'm being faithful, I feel I'm betraying myself."

"Arthur's behaved badly about your little hunting excursion?"

"He insists I humiliated him. Now, whenever I go anywhere, he asks if I'm off to see my 'lover, the Count Lubienski.' I've tried to reassure him, but it's no use. Maybe it's the pressure of the holidays, I don't know, but things are deteriorating. I spent an entire day going up and down Marszalkowska to find him a Boxing Day present, and he pushed it aside like it was an insult."

"What did you get him?"

"A set of Indian clubs."

Shelly had laughed.

"They're very good for exercise," Elizabeth insisted. "And Lord knows he needs it!"

Arthur had bought her a set of silver-backed brushes and combs. They would have made a thoughtful gift except that he had given her the same thing for her birthday the year before.

Elizabeth drew one of the combs through her hair, smoothing it for the Valencian mantilla that she would wear on her head as part of a Spanish costume she had acquired in Madrid. The dress was floor-length black lace with a low-cut bodice that showed her figure to advantage. Looking at herself in the mirror, she sighed. She had to admit it. She deeply missed Count Lubienski's attentions. Would he be at the ball, hidden behind some mask? She had made herself easy to spot, but she knew he would never speak to her. Would she recognize him? Should she try to talk to him? What would she say?

Arthur emerged from his dressing room in a matador's costume, which he also had obtained in Spain. It now appeared several sizes too small. His short arms stuck out to the sides like a child wrapped up to play in the snow. "How is it possible to fight a bull in such an outfit?" he complained.

"I don't think you should worry about that this evening," Elizabeth said, "unless you intend to waltz with Lady Kennard."

"And you plan to spend the night dancing with Count Lubienski?"

"Arthur, don't start. If it will make you happy, I'll dance with no one but you."

A line of torches marked the gravel road that wound through Łazienki Park to the palace.

"King Augustus transformed it from a hunting lodge about the time you Yanks were foolishly declaring your independence from George III," Shelly explained. He had dressed as Pierrot. His date was Pierrette.

"It's now used to host official parties and diplomatic balls. Of course with the Poles," Shelly cautioned, "these are not necessarily staid affairs."

The palace occupied an island in a frozen lake. As their carriage crossed the bridge to the entrance, the rococo facade shimmered in the torchlight. Elizabeth immediately saw what Shelly meant. A satyr carried a nymph over his shoulder out the front door. Couples spilling their champagne glasses could be seen embracing on the second-floor balconies. A knight in shining armor lumbered across the terrace after a Gypsy queen. Off to an early start, thought Elizabeth with a touch of envy.

Trumpets sounded as they alighted from the carriage and proceeded toward the entrance on a carpet of tulip petals. Once inside, they were caught up in a swirling crowd garbed in bizarre and breathtaking costumes. Many men flaunted their most gaudy military uniforms, but covered their faces with elaborate and often realistic animal masks. Elizabeth saw one officer, outfitted in white and gold with a sword and crimson cape, who had the head of a wild boar. Another wore the head of a bull and yet another, a ram. A large man, wearing the head of an elephant, could somehow manipulate the trunk, dipping it into people's champagne glasses and down the front of the ladies' décolletage. If Lubienski was under one of those masks, how could she possibly recognize him?

Shelly led them to a room on the left of the foyer that was completely lined in blue and white Dutch tile. "This was the king's bathroom," he explained. "His Highness evidently did much of his drinking here as well." Shelly pointed to a large painting of the god Bacchus that hung over an ornate porcelain fireplace. In front of it, waiters were pouring champagne out of huge Nebuchadnezzar-sized bottles. Arthur sucked down two glasses quickly and with a third in hand, pushed into the ballroom, leaving Shelly and his date behind. Elizabeth tried to stay close to him.

An orchestra at the opposite end of the room was playing a popular Polish ballad, "This Time It's Real." Elizabeth noticed that she was not the only woman who, forced to cover her face, had resorted to revealing a good deal of something else. A young lady, dressed as Salome, wore such a flimsy gown that her entire body including the shadowy places could be seen through the gauze.

Arthur was sweaty and complaining. "It's so abominably hot in here! How's one supposed to have a conversation, when you can't tell who anyone is?"

"Let's dance," she suggested. The orchestra had started a waltz.

Joining a handful of other couples, they moved in a clockwise direction, turning across the parquet under the glow of a half-dozen candlelit chandeliers. Elizabeth had never danced in a more beautiful ballroom. It rose two stories with floor-to-ceiling windows surrounding three sides and Greek statues and bas-reliefs decorating the fourth. As Arthur rotated her around and around, mechanically counting the steps in his head, she could not help but imagine waltzing in the arms of Count Lubienski. Soon the dance floor became more crowded and collisions more frequent. Each impact made Arthur more angry. "Can't these bloody fools keep to themselves? This isn't the damned polka!"

He stopped and said he wanted to go outside for a cigarette. Elizabeth went with him. In her lace dress, she was freezing.

"Aren't you cold?" she asked. She could see the perspiration on his brow and sweat stains on his silk costume. In the glittering light from the ballroom, his skin looked gray.

"It's a relief!" Arthur exhaled, the smoke mingling with his steamy breath.

"You're going to catch your death out here," she warned.

Staring at her sullenly, he slowly and deliberately smoked his cigarette down to a stub.

As they stepped back inside, Arthur recognized a contact at the Polish Trade Ministry.

"Is that you, Andrzej?" He pulled up his own mask.

A white-faced clown nodded with a small smile and invited them to join his group. The conversation switched from Polish to French. They were speculating on what 1938 might bring.

"Hemlines are going up," a woman dressed as a fairy princess predicted.

"And women's hair will be coming down," a ballerina added.

"Ladies have such trivial interests," Andrzej declared. "What about something important, like who will win the Polish Grand Prix?"

"Do you think Hitler will invade Austria?" Elizabeth asked when she had the chance.

"Elizabeth," Arthur cut her off, "you mustn't abuse people's hospitality with such serious questions!" Then, Arthur steered Andrzej into a discussion of the Polish trade balance for the next fiscal year.

Elizabeth excused herself to go to the powder room, which was located on the second floor of the palace. As she climbed the broad staircase, the man in front of her suddenly stepped across to a woman who was coming down the other side. Without a word or a moment's hesitation, he swept the woman into his arms and kissed her passionately.

"Monsieur," the woman protested in French, "I am a married woman! Do I know you?"

"Tadeusz Brzezinski at your service." He bowed. "You do not know me, but you shall!"

Elizabeth turned away from the scene and hurried up the stairs, her own heart racing with excitement.

King Augustus's palace proved to be short on lavatories, and she had to wait in a long line before crowding into a tiny room hidden behind a bookcase. When she returned downstairs, Arthur was nowhere to be found. She danced a rhumba with Jack Shelly, and then, feeling remote from the gaiety of the party, Elizabeth wandered alone through the portrait gallery and several of the other salons, fending off invitations to dance. None of them, she could tell, was Count Lubienski.

In the rotunda, she found that the cabin of a carriage had been suspended like a swing from the center of the four-story cupola. A line had formed for those wanting a ride. Elizabeth took a place with the others, accepting more champagne from the waiters in an effort to make herself as lighthearted as the rest of the crowd.

When her turn came, she insisted on entering the enclosed cabin alone. As the swing was pulled back to be released, she braced against the seat. Abruptly, the swing stopped, suspended. She could hear an argument going on in Polish. Then the cabin was lowered again. The door opened and a uniformed man wearing a frightening eagle's head jumped inside. She knew at once it was Lubienski.

"Forgive me. I've been watching you all night. Following you like a fool. Afraid to talk to you. I had to see you!"

The swing was released and began its slow arc across the rotunda.

"Take off the mask."

"Do I look ridiculous?" He pulled it over his head, his hair went flying.

"Now, you look ridiculous!" she laughed. He had suddenly made the evening glow.

"Don't tease me!" he pleaded. "I've thought of nothing but you since we parted. I can't work. I don't even want to ride my horses!"

"You must be sick, you poor thing." She stroked his cheek.

He grabbed her hand. "I must see you again! I must have you!"

"But I'm a spy . . . "

"Don't say that!" He grabbed Elizabeth and covered her mouth with a kiss as if to stop her from saying more. Suddenly, the swing jerked to a stop. They both tumbled onto the floor. The door flew open. Arthur stood there enraged.

"I thought so!" he bellowed. "I thought so!"

He slammed the door on them. By the time Elizabeth managed to climb out, he was disappearing into the crowd.

"Stop, Arthur!" she called out, but her voice was swallowed up in the wave of laughter from the onlookers.

She rushed after him, pushing through room after room, past portraits, and statues, and *trompe l'oeil,* and bas-reliefs. Shelly spotted her and joined the chase.

"Arthur's made a terrible scene," she shouted to him. "I'm afraid he might do something crazy!"

Ahead, she saw Arthur yank open a door to the terrace. Then he turned as if to warn her against following him. His face was bright red. He raised his hand and opened his mouth, but nothing came out. He seemed frozen in the moment. His head rolled back. She was almost to him. Elizabeth reached for his hand, but missed it. Pitching backward, Arthur collapsed through the doorway.

"My God!" Elizabeth cried.

Several ladies screamed.

Shelly bent over him as he lay in the snow.

"What's wrong?" Elizabeth pleaded.

Arthur's eyes were open but staring sightlessly. She could see that the pupil of one was very large and the other very small.

"He needs to be gotten to hospital," Shelly declared.

"Take my carriage." Lubienski had arrived at their side.

"What is it? What's happened to him?" Elizabeth was too stunned to cry.

Jack Shelly picked up Arthur's arm, and it fell back limply. "I think he's had a stroke."

In the bare vaulted corridor of St. Tadeusz Hospital, Elizabeth clung to Jack Shelly as they listened to the embassy doctor. Count Lubienski sat with Shelly's date on one of the hard wooden benches along the wall.

"He's stable now," the doctor was saying. "But Poland's not the best place for treatment. They're partial to useless remedies like flushing his system with evil-smelling mineral water, or packing him in mud."

"What can I do?" Elizabeth felt the weight of Arthur's life on her shoulders.

"Get him to London as fast as you can," the doctor advised. "By airplane. I don't think he'd survive a boat or train."

"Will he need a stretcher?" Shelly asked. The doctor nodded. "Then it'll be Monday before LOT flies out with one of its big Junkers or a Lockheed Electra."

"That'll give me time to pull things together." Elizabeth tried to sound in control, and failed. "Oh, Jack." Tears came into her eyes. "What will happen to us?"

"Don't worry," he reassured her. "The Foreign Office has to help. And if they don't, I'm sure our people will." He glanced over at Count Lubienski. The young man looked miserable and utterly in love with Elizabeth. "It's a damn shame all the way around," Shelly sighed.

Count Lubienski took Elizabeth back to the Villa Frascati in his carriage. On the way, they huddled under a heavy bearskin rug, saying little to one another. As they drew up in front of the apartment house, Lubienski took her hand.

"Can I come up for a while?" he asked.

"Michael, my husband's in the hospital close to death! And we put him there!"

"You must not blame yourself. It's all my fault." He fell silent for a moment. "I hope this"—he groped for the right word—"tragedy does not come between us."

What could he be thinking? "You know I must go to London." It was all she could say.

"But you'll come back!"

"I don't know, it depends on Arthur's health."

"But you don't love him! You could not have been with me, in the way that we were. . . ."

"I gave you my love and my body, Michael, I did not give up my honor and sense of duty."

"Forgive me!" he begged. "I didn't mean to insult you." His voice had an edge of panic. "But I'm in a turmoil. I can't lose you now! You must come back to me!"

She could not help feeling concern. He was suffering too. But how could she comfort him? "I don't know what—" she started to say.

He put his hand over her mouth. "I need you! I can't do without you!" He made no effort to hide his desperation.

"Would you come back to me"—he pressed his cheek against hers, dropping his voice to a whisper—"if I told you . . . " He hesitated. Then he blurted, "If I told you everything you want to know?"

The wind had picked up and she could feel the carriage rocking beneath her. How could she refuse Lubienski? How could she abandon Arthur? What would she say to Shelly and Stephenson if she neglected this chance? She drew back and with her fingers brushed the hair from his brow. "At least we have tonight," she murmured. "And tomorrow night, and the night after that. . . . "

Chapter 18

London, January 17, 1938

Dear Mother,

Arthur's much better. Until a few days ago, all he could do was follow me around the room with his eyes. Yesterday he spoke for the first time. It's all mumbles, and the words are confused, but he can say yes and no, even if he can't tell left from right.

I'm spending most of my time at the hospital, trying to get him to talk. The doctor says I'll probably have to teach him the names of everything all over again. He can't walk of course, but his left side's not completely paralyzed, and the doctor says there's hope of recovery, particularly now that they've got his blood pressure down. Thank God the Brasswells are here. They're an embassy couple we knew in St.-Jean-de-Luz, and Barbara's become a stalwart friend, spelling me at Arthur's bedside.

My biggest problem is with the Foreign Office over our allowances. This little wart of a man from the F.O. actually came to Arthur's room to tell him that his medical allowance would only last a few more weeks and then he'd have to move to a veterans' hospital. As for me, there was nothing they could do about my expenses. I could return to Warsaw, leaving Arthur here until he is better, or Arthur could formally transfer back to London, but then of course he would lose his posting in Warsaw along with the housing allowance.

Worse, there are no slots for him at the F.O. He'd

*run the risk that Treasury would force him out of the
Foreign Service altogether, since he's a "B" list not
"A" list (I never knew about it, but apparently "B"
list appointments have limited prospects, which
means Arthur can never make ambassador). Anyway,
this toad tells Arthur all this when he can't even
respond! His blood pressure rose another ten points!
I ordered him out of the hospital.*

*The upshot, Mother, is that this whole exercise
has been a great financial drain, and I was hoping
that you might provide a little help to tide us over. I
hate to ask and know you've your own needs since
Father died, but the situation has become quite tight
and any assistance would be greatly appreciated.*

Love,
Elizabeth

February 5, 1938

Dearest Elizabeth,
   *Glad to hear Arthur's better. Love to help, but
depression still rages here. Have you spoken to
Arthur's family? Or maybe the Brasswells are a
possibility. Keep your spirits up.*

Love,
Cora

54 Broadway, London— February 23, 1938

"I know it must be tiresome," Commander Alistair Denniston said to Elizabeth. "But could you run through your
story once more?"

She had been very proud to get Lubienski to talk. But
for several weeks, between visits to the hospital, she had
been running through the "story" of Lubienski's revela-
tions in a frustrating series of SIS interrogations: first, in
out-of-the-way flats, then, in anonymous town houses, and

now again, in a shabby meeting room in a faceless building on Broadway across from the St. James Park tube station.

It was ostensibly the Passport Office. But after Captain Lance escorted her up a rickety lift to the fourth floor then through a rat's maze of corridors, he had stopped and pointed down a hallway that disappeared into the gloom. "That's the secret passage to C's residence in Queen Anne's Gate." Elizabeth had realized that she was being admitted to the holy of holies—the headquarters of SIS.

The meeting room had a single window with frosted glass that virtually blocked out the weak winter daylight. In addition to Denniston and Lance, she was being asked to repeat her "story" for the benefit of a Mr. Dillwyn Knox.

"Hitler is planning to annex Austria before spring," Elizabeth began. "If the Austrian government calls a plebiscite to show how weak the Nazis really are, he plans to invade—"

"I don't care about all that," Dilly interrupted her, "I want to know about the Enigma."

"The coding machine? It isn't very complicated," she began again. "Count Lubienski said that a team of Polish mathematicians had solved the German cipher system. Actually, he claimed that they had broken the codes even before Hitler came to power. . . ."

"That's preposterous!" Knox declared.

"Please go on," Denniston said.

"That's basically it. The mathematicians' names are Marian Rejewski, Henryk Zygalski, and Jerzy Rozycki. I've given you the spelling. Supposedly, they've set up shop in a hunting lodge in the Pyry Forest south of Warsaw."

"And they read everything?" Knox challenged her.

"I don't know. Count Lubienski said that it's like a duel. The Germans make changes and then the Poles figure them out. But he claimed that they routinely read the signals of the Wehrmacht, the Luftwaffe, along with a few from the German Navy and all the SD messages. SD is the Gestapo," Elizabeth explained.

"I know what the SD is," Knox sniffed. "And did he, perchance, tell you how they manage this feat?"

"He said something about number theory, group theory.

Does that make sense? He didn't understand it and neither did I.''

"Well, I just don't believe it!" Knox insisted. "We've only recently broken the older Enigma, the one being used in Spain. None of our techniques work on the newer models. The Germans obviously believe it can't be broken. And, despite what you say, young lady, I believe they're right!''

Elizabeth felt herself redden. "Then why would Count Lubienski tell me such a thing?"

"In order to send us off on a wild goose chase. Waste our precious resources attempting the impossible. His boss, Colonel Beck, is in the pocket of the Nazis, isn't he?"

"That's rather conspiratorial," she replied.

"Professional disease," Denniston noted.

"We can't go on hearsay," Knox challenged her. "I'll believe the Poles have cracked the Enigma, when I see it.''

"Well"—Elizabeth showed her irritation—"I don't see how I can help you."

"When you go back to Warsaw," Denniston intervened, "we want you to put a series of detailed questions to Lubienski.''

"That won't work, I'm afraid," said Elizabeth flatly.

"Why not?" Dilly Knox asked. "He seems willing."

"Yes, I could get him to respond, but it's still impossible.''

"So what, pray, is the difficulty?"

"The difficulty," she said firmly, "is that I can't go back as long as my husband needs me."

"And how long is that likely to be?" asked Denniston.

"The doctors say recovery could take six months to a year.''

"We can't wait that long," he said in dismay.

"Jack Shelly said you might be able to help us out financially." She hated raising the subject.

Denniston frowned. "We might be able to provide a little something. . . . ''

"But you can hardly expect," Knox added, "that you'd be paid for work that you refuse to do."

* * *

The car came to the Savoy to pick up Elizabeth at nine A.M. William Stephenson had asked her out to Sheperton Studios for lunch, and she had eagerly accepted. It was a welcome relief from helping Arthur distinguish between his bedpan and the bedpost.

Stephenson's Rolls-Royce carried her across the Thames, through south London, and into open country. Scheduled to arrive at ten-thirty, Elizabeth assumed her host planned to give her a tour of the studio. She had not seen a movie lot since she was a child. Returning to the States from Hawaii, her family had stopped in Los Angeles where her father arranged for Elizabeth to spend a magical afternoon watching Theda Bara film *The Cheat*.

As the Rolls-Royce drew up in front of a stately old mansion flanked on one side by a massive greenhouse, Elizabeth thought that it looked nothing like the Spanish-style studios she had seen in California. Excited, she plucked a rose from the vase attached to the door pillar of the car and pushed it through the buttonhole in the lapel of her trim navy-blue suit. When she stepped out of the car, however, a polite young man disappointed her with the news that Mr. Stephenson would not see her before lunch. Apologizing, he showed her through the front door, across a huge foyer paneled in mahogany with a roaring fireplace, then up a sweeping staircase to the second-floor room that proved to be a private movie theater. It had a dozen large and comfortable English club chairs arranged in three rows. Each chair was equipped with a panel of knobs and switches set into the right arm. To the left sat a small table with a telephone.

Elizabeth was asked to take a seat, and the room immediately darkened. For the next three hours she felt plunged into a bizarre and terrifying world. First came a newsreel of Hitler's takeover of Austria and his entrance into Vienna. Vast and adoring throngs, particularly women, cheered and tossed bouquets at the Führer's open car as he made his way down the Ringstrasse. This was juxtaposed with Nazi hooligans beating Jews and various democratic political leaders. The narrator announced that tens of thousands of people were being arrested.

This was followed by a seemingly endless documentary

of a Nazi rally in Nuremburg. Thousands and thousands of uniformed men marched across the screen in lockstep like automatons for the glorification of the *Hakenkreuz,* the "broken cross," the swastika. Hundreds of thousands rallied by torchlight in vast stadiums, their gleaming faces rapt with devotion beyond reason, their voices cheering in unison and ecstasy the most appalling lies of a sweaty little man with a comic mustache who mysteriously held them in his thrall. It was absurd; it was horrifying, and Elizabeth was fascinated with every frame.

"How did you like *Triumph of the Will*?" Stephenson asked when she was shown into his private office. "It's Germany's latest cinema masterpiece."

"It should be called 'Triumph of the Willies,' " Elizabeth replied. "I feel like I need a bath."

"Would you like to dip into a daiquiri instead?" He led her through French doors and onto a balcony that protruded into the greenhouse. "This is where we grow the plants for our jungle movies."

"The weather seems just right." She felt the moist air from the forest of potted palms and banana trees below. The waiter poured her drink as they sat down at a small table.

"Cheers." Stephenson toasted and they each took a sip.

"What is the idea of that movie?" Elizabeth exhaled after he lit her cigarette. "Do the Germans think that it makes them look admirable? It shows them as a nation of maniacs."

"Fear and grandiosity inspire them, I'm afraid."

"And why did you show it to me?" she asked.

"You've been doing a remarkable job in Poland. Have they congratulated you on your reports on Hitler's annexation of Austria?" The first course, baked oysters, arrived.

"No, they haven't said a thing, and they evidently don't believe a word I've reported about the Enigma business, either." She put out her cigarette.

"That's English arrogance and professional pique. But now they can't stop until they prove you right or wrong. Unfortunately, they haven't even one mathematician on their staff."

"Mr. Knox isn't a mathematician?"

"Lord no, he's a classics scholar. Greek, I believe."

"Well, I can't even balance my household accounts. They'll have to do their proving without me."

"And how is your husband?" Stephenson looked genuinely concerned.

"I can understand some of what he says these days, though I'm probably the only one."

"And your son, have you had time to see him?"

Elizabeth stared at Stephenson in shock. "How do you know . . . " She stopped. Of course they'd know.

"If you'd rather not talk about him . . . "

"It's all right. He's fine. But it's difficult. More for me than him, of course. Staying here will allow me to see him more often."

"So that's why you're not going back to Warsaw?"

"So that's why you invited me to lunch?"

"Touché." He looked contrite.

"People have personal lives," she continued solemnly, "and no matter how hateful, they impose the most important obligations. Who would look after Arthur the way I do? I dress him and give him baths. Milbank Hospital treats people like cattle. And as for my son"—she paused—"well, I like to think he needs me too."

"I'm sure he does," Stephenson allowed, "particularly if you consider the future he could well inherit. Do you want him to grow up in a world like the movie, where Hitler's 'will' is triumphant?"

Elizabeth put down her oyster fork. "I've been flattered by a lot of men, Bill, but I've never been told the fate of the world is in my hands. Surely there are minds in Britain as swift as the Poles' who can break the Enigma."

"Yes, but they're closed. You heard Dilly Knox. He can't do it, so he's out to prove it's impossible. Denniston isn't so sure, but he's no expert. You're the only one who can show that it has been done. Even then, it may take years to duplicate the Poles' work. We need everything you can possibly get from Lubienski."

The second course had been served and Elizabeth had eaten very little. The daiquiri had made her suddenly tired. "I'm sorry, Bill." She shook her head. "Maybe I need my head examined, but I can't leave Arthur now."

Stephenson reached out and took her hand. "I know it's been very difficult. Are you all right financially?"

She shook her head and the tears came.

"If you're staying," he relented, "you'll need a job. SIS only pays women a pittance. Take this number." He handed her a card. "I'm sure I can help find something suitable."

She wasn't exactly happy, but for the first time in months, Elizabeth felt that she was getting her life under control. She had a job and a tiny flat in Golders Green. So what if she had to feed shillings into the heater to keep warm? At least she now had the shillings. Hastening up the steps of Milbank Hospital she was eager to see Arthur. He had been moved to a large dingy ward where most of the other stroke victims were in long-term care, alive only in the sense that their bodies continued to produce waste. To his credit, Arthur had not complained, although Elizabeth was not sure he fully understood his circumstances.

He was sitting up, staring into space. Barbara Brasswell sat beside him reading.

"I've got good news," she exclaimed.

He looked at her balefully.

"Everything's arranged. I've got a job at the BBC World Service, writing the news!"

"Wonderful!" Barbara hugged her.

"Isn't that exciting?" Elizabeth said to Arthur. "It pays enough so I can put you back into a private room and get you a therapist. I'll be able to come and see you every morning and evening. Oh, it won't be easy, but you'll get better every day and we'll ... "

Arthur had began to grunt. His eyes were flashing.

"Is something wrong?" she asked.

He wobbled his head and tried harder to form his words.

"Arthur, I can understand you better if you calm down."

He stopped and took several deep breaths. "Nuh!" he managed to say.

"No?" she asked.

He nodded.

"I'll leave you two alone." Barbara discreetly moved away.

"No, what?"

"Nuh, shay. Guh bag."

Elizabeth couldn't believe what he was trying to say. She didn't want to believe it. "Are you saying I shouldn't stay? That I should go back to Warsaw?"

He nodded his head vigorously.

"My God, Arthur, whatever for?"

"Safe pshun! Safe jub!"

"To save your job? You want me to leave you here in London to hold your place at the embassy?"

He nodded again and let his head drop back onto the pillow. Arthur was clearly pleased to be arranging matters the way he wanted. He was smiling with half his face.

Chapter 19

Villa Frascati, Warsaw—
May 5, 1938

Elizabeth lay in bed. The window to the balcony stood open, and petals from the blossoming apple trees drifted in on the morning breeze. Count Lubienski had just left for the Foreign Ministry. Now she would get up, bathe, and dress for her daily contact with Jack Shelly. And she dreaded it.

Not that she had nothing to report. Today, she would pass along the fact that the German general staff had informed Hitler of the completion of "Case Green"—their plans for the invasion of Czechoslovakia. She also had learned that Lubienski had been ordered to go to Berlin on a mission that was so secret even he had not yet been told its purpose.

But Shelly would not be satisfied unless she had information about the Enigma. Inevitably, he'd start in on her about getting Lubienski under "positive control." When would she stop dealing with him as a source and recruit him as an agent? To prove that the Enigma could be broken, SIS wanted Lubienski to find out how the Poles had done it. That meant turning him from a collaborator, who shared what information came across his desk, into a traitor who actively spied on his own intelligence services.

It was the most delicate step in espionage. If Lubienski reacted badly, they could lose an extremely valuable source, as well as provoke a major crisis with Poland. Elizabeth might even find herself under arrest. Not to mention what might happen to Lubienski. So she had been dragging her

217

feet while Shelly became more adamant that she make a move. Easy for him to say, Elizabeth thought angrily, as she slipped into her bath. Neither he nor SIS had been of much help in preparing her to "turn" Lubienski.

Before returning to Warsaw, the "old boys" at the Broadway headquarters had decided reluctantly that she should be given some training. She spent several weeks at a large stone house in Prae Wood near St. Albans learning what her secret service instructors called "tradecraft."

How this related to her assignment was not always clear. She started out learning to pick locks and proved to be a whiz. Next she graduated to opening and resealing letters. Elizabeth hated the steam kettle because it frizzed her hair. Her favorite tool was the bobby pin. Since the bottom flap of envelopes were never glued all the way to the corner, she would insert a bobby pin into this gap, making sure that the prongs gripped either side of the letter paper at the fold. By twisting the bobby pin, she could roll up the letter inside the envelope. Once tightly wrapped around the bobby pin, the letter then could be pulled through the unglued corner. Reinserting the letter was more tricky, and Elizabeth found that the technique worked best on thin airmail paper.

Her instructors also put a good deal of effort into the preparation and use of secret inks. In the end, however, they admitted that lemon juice, which Elizabeth had learned about as a child from the back of a Post Toasties box, worked about as well as anything SIS chemists had concocted. Messages written in lemon juice were invisible until the paper was heated by a candle or a light bulb.

After some insistence on her part, the teachers at Prae Wood finally agreed to give Elizabeth lessons in the use of a camera. She had imagined learning how to use one of the new cigarette-pack-sized Minoxes that she had seen in the movies. Instead, they produced a bulky two-pound British Argus, which needed a special tripod and lens to take pictures of documents.

"This would be a dead giveaway," Elizabeth pointed out. "What about a miniature camera?"

"Forget that," an instructor known as Rob responded.

"We've only got a handful of them. They're all spoken for by real agents."

Elizabeth spent a week practicing surveillance and countersurveillance. On the crowded streets of central London she received pointers in how to spot a normal tail, a decoy tail, and a front tail. She also learned how to ditch them without appearing to have recognized that she was under surveillance. Elizabeth's favorite ploy was to dodge into a clothing store and emerge from another entrance dressed in a different outfit. She sent the bills to Captain Lance at 54 Broadway.

Her final classes dealt with different ways of contacting an agent. She concentrated on the art of the brush pass, a seemingly accidental collision with someone on the street, or in a doorway, or on a train, that enabled one agent to give documents to another. She learned how to set up and service "dead drops"; variations of the proverbial hollow tree where she could leave messages for agents and vice versa. Elizabeth proposed taping notes to the underside of toilet seats in ladies restrooms: The exchange took place in the privacy of a stall, and unlike men's rooms, the seat always remained down. Her instructors pointed out that the technique would restrict her contacts to women and transvestites.

She brought a definitely female perspective to the traditional techniques of tradecraft. On her last evening at Prae Wood, her instructors took her for a congratulatory pint at the Round Pub in St. Albans. Well into her second shandy, she said that she had a new idea about concealing small negatives and messages on her person.

"Do tell," said Rob, faintly amused at her presumption. "We've explored that rather thoroughly, as you might imagine."

"Have you ever thought of putting them in a sanitary napkin?"

Rob spit his lager all over the table.

When she returned to Poland, Elizabeth's extensive training in clandestine contacts proved almost entirely irrelevant. Count Lubienski simply came to her flat in Villa Frascati every morning at five A.M., crawled into her bed and stayed until he had to go to the Foreign Ministry. At five each afternoon he would come back for cocktails, then return to the office about seven to look over the late cable traffic. In the evening, they would go out for dinner at the Bristol, or the Europejska or Gastronomja; perhaps later catching the review at the QPQ or dancing the "tango milonga" at the Aquarium. They seldom went to plays, because Elizabeth did not speak Polish, but she spoke some German and so could follow the Yiddish productions at the Kaminski Theater in the ghetto.

Instead of acting surreptitious or clandestine, Elizabeth adopted a strategy of "utter blatancy" in her liaison with Count Lubienski. Affairs and mistresses were openly accommodated in Warsaw—to the point that Elizabeth often accompanied Lubienski to Colonel Beck's official receptions. In fact, the beady-eyed Colonel Beck always made a point to talk to her in a way that suggested a certain envy of Lubienski's affair with Elizabeth. To have concealed their romantic relationship would only raise suspicions that Elizabeth was doing exactly what she was doing.

This behavior engendered a good deal of disapproval and ostracism from the other wives at the embassy, who could not understand why she was allowed to stay in Warsaw disgracing the British community. Fortunately, Lady Kennard was away in America, which enabled Shelly, with C weighing in strongly from London, to overcome the ambassador's reluctance to permit her continued presence while her husband was on indefinite medical leave.

The Countess Lubienski proved not to be a problem. Elizabeth once asked Michael how his wife tolerated their open liaison. He replied that she only insisted that he come home every night.

Taking a page out of Antonio de Zaragoza's book, Elizabeth arranged to provide Lubienski with confidential information on British policy, which he could pass to Colonel Beck as a way of justifying his close association with her. Jack Shelly gave her "chicken feed," scraps of diplomatic information cleared by SIS that Lubienski could present as an intelligence windfall. He believed that he was doing good for his country—strengthening Poland's ties to Britain—by collaborating with her, and she was constantly trying to find ways to reinforce that conviction.

All of this was part of Elizabeth's carefully designed strategy to bring Lubienski under "positive control." This was the ultimate goal of any recruitment. Theoretically, an agent under positive control would do what he was told, no matter what. According to SIS doctrine, positive control consisted of two elements: first, the personal bond between the agent and the subagent; and second, coercion. Her instructors at Prac Wood were very creative at coercion—suggesting to Elizabeth all sorts of schemes of blackmail and intimidation—but they hadn't a clue how to blend attraction and coercion into an effective program of manipulation. They put that into the category of "talent" or "instinct." Elizabeth concluded she would have been better off discussing this aspect of her mission with her instructors' wives.

That gave her the idea of seeking help from her old friend Vita Sackville-West. A few days before Elizabeth departed for Warsaw, they met for lunch in a lovely suite Stephenson had provided her at Claridge's after her return from Prae Wood. Cocktails and appetizers had been spent commiserating over Arthur and catching up on mutual friends. But with the main course, Elizabeth turned to business. As casually as she could, she asked Vita for advice on how to get someone to do a thing they otherwise wouldn't dream of doing.

"Darling"—Vita put down her lobster fork—"why are you asking me?"

Elizabeth was ready for the question. She would hide behind British understatement.

"Because of your experience."

Vita looked amused. "You mean, because I'm lesbian? Don't tell me you're thinking of . . . "

"No! Nothing like that!"

"Pity." Vita shrugged. "Men are so boring and easy."

"Not this one. I've got to get him to do something that goes against every fiber of his being."

"You're trying to make Arthur laugh?"

"I'm serious," Elizabeth insisted. "But don't ask me what it's all about, because I really can't tell you."

Vita Sackville-West looked suspicious, then mischievous. "All right, your rules." She opened her cigarette case and they both lit up. "First, you must give him a reason for doing it, no matter how implausible."

"I've done that." Elizabeth was thinking of Lubienski's constant rationalization that he was only strengthening relations between Poland and Britain, which was of course true so far as the two of them were concerned.

"And you have to give him a reason for doing it for *you*."

"I've done that too. He claims he loves me. But how do I get him to take the plunge without destroying everything I've established between us so far?"

"Ah, that's the trick." She got up, came around to Elizabeth and put her hand on her shoulder. "What if I asked you to go to bed with me?"

Elizabeth was not ready for that question.

"I'm sorry," she coughed, "but I couldn't possibly . . . "

"What if I said, I wouldn't tell you the secret of how to manipulate this man if you didn't."

Was this part of the lesson, Elizabeth wondered, or was Vita actually making a pass at her? "I'd still refuse," she said categorically.

"Of course you would." Vita gave her shoulder a squeeze then took her hand away. She drew up a chair and sat down close to her. "Now, what if I asked you whether you found me attractive?"

"Well, yes," Elizabeth replied. In fact, Vita looked stunningly handsome and much younger than she was, with wide dark eyes, thick silky hair, and a bold mouth. Her lean supple figure carried her Liberty silk shirtwaist gracefully. "But I don't mean in a physical way, to me," Elizabeth added.

"And if I asked whether you considered me a friend? Whether you cared for me?" She was staring into Elizabeth's eyes.

"Yes." She looked away. "But again, not in a physical way. What has this . . . "

"Give me your hand," she said softly.

Elizabeth obeyed. Her touch was warm and strange.

"Does that disturb you?"

"No," she lied.

"Can I ask you a favor? Would you kiss me?"

Elizabeth withdrew her hand.

"That's all I'm asking," Vita pressed.

"I don't see how this relates . . . "

"It will, I promise."

Elizabeth stood up and gave her a peck on the lips.

"No, I mean, a real kiss." Vita rose and put her arms around her. "Like this."

Elizabeth was disoriented by the sensation of Vita's lips, her tongue flitting around the corners of her mouth. Feelings stirred inside her, confused by a powerful urge to push Vita away. She could not deny the excitement that lay beneath her sense of disgust. Her face felt hot and flushed. Vita pulled back slowly.

"Now you know it's possible, don't you?" She ran her hands over Elizabeth's cashmere sweater and over her hips in an expert way. "Your body is aroused. Only your mind says no," Vita murmured.

Elizabeth felt her breath coming shorter.

"Your mind is fighting what it knows. You're curious. You're surprised that you like my touch." She was caressing her all over now. Vita bent her head to kiss Elizabeth's neck, her hands went up into her hair.

"Don't be angry with me," Vita whispered. She pulled Elizabeth down onto the brocaded sofa. "You have the same feelings yourself." Her hand brushed aside Elizabeth's skirt and her fingers began to trace a line up the inside of her thigh. "You're excited. You want me."

"No!" Elizabeth jumped up. "I'm sorry, Vita. This is not why I asked you here!"

Her guest sat back and smiled easily. "Would it bother you if I told others that we were lovers?"

"That's not true!" Elizabeth reeled with dismay.

"Only technically," Vita suggested. "Of course, if we *were* lovers, I'd protect your reputation."

Elizabeth felt consumed by guilt. How had this happened to her?

"I don't want to hurt you—" Vita got up and came toward her—"but I must have you. I'll have you somehow," she said with growing intensity, "no matter what. You'll be safe with me." She again took Elizabeth in her arms.

Elizabeth was trapped, overwhelmed. She burned with shame at the knowledge of her own forbidden feelings, yet Vita's embrace felt oddly comforting. She was a friend. She couldn't help what she was doing. Why should Elizabeth destroy their friendship, or her own reputation by rejecting sensations that they both shared? What difference did it make if she gave in? Vita was stroking her intimately, and her body was responding. Elizabeth could feel Vita's hard insistent breasts against her own. Surrender seemed inevitable.

"No," she struggled to say. But it sounded like the kind of no she would have said to a groping boy in the back row of a movie house in Washington. "No!" She tried to be more convincing.

"You don't like this?" Vita purred as she caressed Elizabeth intimately.

"No." But she could feel the strength going out of her as the pleasure began to spread. "I mean it." Elizabeth said helplessly.

"I know you do," Vita sighed. She released her, and walked away.

Elizabeth stood there stunned, drowning in embarrassment.

Vita coolly sat down to her lobster and took a sip of wine. "I'm sorry, Elizabeth, but I thought it best to show you how it's done. I wouldn't take advantage. I know you don't live on my side of the street."

"My God, how did this happen?" She covered her face.

"You can't ask them straight out, no matter how much they care for you," Vita continued matter-of-factly. "One emotion is never enough. There must be two, and they must conflict, need and shame, fear and desire, that sort of thing. To produce such conflict you've got to get them to step over whatever line they've drawn in their minds. For you, I would guess the line was the kiss. After crossing it, your prey will be slowly paralyzed by guilt, and you can manipulate him as you will. If you proceed carefully, you'll find it works with the strongest character. In fact," Vita concluded, "I'd say the strongest are the most vulnerable."

Where did Count Lubienski's line lie? Elizabeth wondered as she climbed out of her bath and began to dress.

She didn't know, or maybe she didn't want to know. She had tried hard not to love him. But she found herself incapable of lying in bed with him, listening to his innermost fears and hopes, sharing the sweetness of his body and the passions of their union without experiencing a profound affection and tenderness—feelings that she cherished as much as he did.

So, she held back, and tried to delay the day of reckoning. But Shelly would not be put off indefinitely. What could she do to buy more time or reduce the risk of failure? Give Lubienski an audition? A trial run? A test? Yes! That was it: a test to see how much "positive control" she could exert over him. His mission to Berlin provided the perfect opportunity. She would insist that he tell her what his secret trip was all about. No, she would do more than that. She would demand he take her with him.

Chapter 20

The Wasserspiele, Berlin—
May 25, 1938

"I feel like a kept woman," Elizabeth complained. "No, worse. I feel like a bored housewife. You hide me away at the Hotel Adlon while you disappear all day for your mysterious meetings."

The illuminated fountains in front of the bandstand rose and fell in time to the music. As the orchestra segued from "Blue Skies" to "Red Sails in the Sunset," the lights playing on the water changed from blue to red. Elizabeth found it unbearably corny.

"We never go anywhere nice," she continued petulantly, "and we never meet anyone." Her frustration came from being isolated, her anger from having failed to worm out of him the secret of his mission. "You only sneak me out at night to some seedy corner of Hitler's 'new order.' "

That evening, they were at the Berliner Wasserspiele, a nightclub renowned not only for its fountains and thirty-piece orchestra, but for having a telephone at every table so that the patrons could proposition one another anonymously.

"Have you seen the Imperial Museum?" Lubienski offered. "The Humboldt collection is remarkable."

"I've become an expert on the pre-Columbian artifacts he stole from Ecuador."

"How about sightseeing?"

"What's to see? Monstrous old buildings. Monstrous new buildings that all look like bloated versions of Roosevelt's New Deal post offices. Flags and soldiers everywhere. Everyone looking spic and span, except, of course, the wretches with the yellow stars who clean the sidewalks with their toothbrushes.'' Her eyes flashed with the bright green of her low-cut chiffon dress.

"Anger makes you more beautiful," he tried to compliment her.

She was having none of it. "Maybe you'd like me to go shopping? Pick you up some Hitler memorabilia? Beer steins painted with swastikas and the words to the 'Horst Wessel' song? No, Michael, nightmares are bad enough at night." She lit another cigarette. "And I want to see you in the daylight."

"You know we have to be discreet," Lubienski pleaded.

"Do you think we're fooling anyone? I'm followed every time I leave the hotel! This afternoon I stopped to drink a Berliner Weisse at an outdoor café on the Unter den Linden. My 'escort' looked so bedraggled I sent him one too. I'm sure we've been followed here this evening."

At this remark, Lubienski's glance began to dart around the room.

"And this morning," Elizabeth continued, "I found a microphone in the lamp by our bed. I expect the Gestapo has enjoyed hearing us play 'horsey'!"

Lubienski's eyes widened even more anxiously, not at what she had said but at something over her shoulder.

The phone rang.

Lubienski froze. It rang again.

"Do you want me to answer it?" Elizabeth asked.

"No!" Lubienski said too loud. He snatched up the receiver.

"*Guten Abend, mein lieber Graf,*" a voice said. Elizabeth could not make out the rest but Lubienski began nodding and stuttering. "*Ja, ja. Ja! Jawohl!*" He hung up, "My God, it's Colonel Kruzel! Gestapo! He's here! He wants to meet you!"

"How do you know him?" Elizabeth brightened. The evening might become interesting after all. Before Lubienski could explain, a mousey man in an expensive-looking mauve brown civilian suit with a red swastika armband arrived at the table.

"Heil Hitler." He flapped his right forearm up like a semaphore.

"Heil Hitler," Count Lubienski responded. Elizabeth smiled warmly at Colonel Kruzel. His face was round and smooth with tiny features that included sharp black eyes. Lubienski introduced them. Colonel Kruzel bowed but did not click his heels. His teeth needed work.

"Won't you sit down?" Lubienski said uncomfortably.

"Perhaps the colonel would dance with me?" Elizabeth intervened.

He looked surprised. Lubienski looked appalled.

"Certainly," Colonel Kruzel responded. "If Count Lubienski does not mind."

"Please!"

They moved out onto the dance floor to the tune of "Ghost of a Chance." Elizabeth found Colonel Kruzel to be a half head shorter and a very determined dancer. Maybe he could shed light on Lubienski's mission. But he began the interrogation first.

"So. What brings a lovely American girl to Berlin in such days?"

"Just pleasure. It's exciting."

"You admire National Socialism?"

"Germany's the only nation in the world that's put its house in order. And there's such a sense of energy!"

"And where do you live?"

"Warsaw."

The band had shifted to rumba, and the Gestapo colonel had a difficulty keeping time and carrying on a cross-examination at the same time.

"So that is where you met the count?" he grunted.

She nodded and moved away, shaking her hips at him. "I'm sure I surprised him by showing up here. I leave in a few days for Prague."

"Whom do you know there?"

"The American ambassador. He's an old family friend."

"Ah, so. Then it is coincidence that you are here together in Berlin. . . . "

At that point, Count Lubienski appeared beside them. "This song was my request, Colonel Kruzel. Do you mind?"

The colonel didn't seem to know whether to bow or say *"Heil Hitler,"* but made way for Lubienski to resume the dance with Elizabeth.

"Please join us at our table," she called to him.

"What did he ask you?" Lubienski whispered with a note of desperation. He then had to move away in time to the music.

"About you." She turned. "Me." She turned again. "Everything."

As they approached one another again, he said, "This is a disaster." His face was ashen. "He's my German contact!"

"Why have you kept me from such a lovely man?"

"This is serious." Lubienski seized her by the waist and began to spin. "He will demand to know everything about you!"

"Then tell him the truth," Elizabeth suggested coolly.

"Are you mad?" Lubienski began to sound frantic.

"Don't you pass on to the Germans the information I've been giving you?"

"What do you take me for?" He looked offended as the music separated them again. She also saw that he was thinking through her point. "Of course we do share *some* intelligence with them," he said uncertainly.

"Then tell him I'm your mistress"—She stopped dancing and led him off the dance floor—"and your agent inside the British embassy. Meanwhile"—she paused at the table to smile at Colonel Kruzel—"I think I'll powder my nose."

Elizabeth was operating entirely on instinct. Being portrayed as Lubienski's agent might make her part of their "club," and somehow put her in a better position to uncover the secret of why he was in Berlin. When she got to the ladies' room, she found a line. Once inside she discovered a woman dressed in a tuxedo hogging the mirror as she tried to glue on a mustache. By the time she returned to the table, Colonel Kruzel had gone. Elizabeth felt disappointed. Lubienski seemed morose.

"How did it go?" she asked.

"Fine, he congratulated me."

"Then why do you look so glum?"

"You don't know this man. He's dangerous, twisted."

"Don't worry so. How can this Colonel Kruzel hurt you?"

Count Lubienski struggled. "Through you," he finally said.

Elizabeth could feel his fear. "What do you mean?" she said carefully.

His eyes showed his shame. "He accepted my story about you, but ... " Lubienski clenched his teeth. "Please understand," he pleaded. "My work with him is extremely sensitive. I've never had such responsibility. Oh, God"— he reached out for her hand—"this could be the end of us both."

"Michael, tell me what's going on," she said gently, soothingly.

The orchestra started "Begin the Beguine." "Colonel Kruzel insists you prove that you are no risk to our undertaking with the Third Reich."

"What does he have in mind?" She pulled her hand away.

"He wants you to ... " He shook his head as if to deny the words. "When you go to Prague, he wants you to do a 'favor' for the Gestapo."

Prague, Czechosovakia— May 28, 1938

Elizabeth leaned on the railing to survey the guests. The American minister to Prague, Wilbur Carrs, was holding an afternoon tea dance at Barrandov Terrace, a fashionable restaurant on the city's southern outskirts, which had been designed to looked like a ship: railings of iron pipe following the line of curved concrete walls, porthole windows, tiers of rounded decks, and a tall central structure, displaying the Czech flag, that resembled a forecastle. Terribly *moderne*, Elizabeth had thought when she first saw it.

The day was sunny, and the guests had spilled out on to the terrace that overlooked the river Valtava and the freshly green forested hills beyond. From under her broad-brimmed hat, Elizabeth searched for her targets, two men whom she had persuaded Carrs to invite that afternoon. She needed to take them in the right order.

The thought that she was being set up by the Gestapo had never left her. The assignment seemed simple. She was to carry a sealed envelope into Czechoslovakia and deliver it to a Herr Konrad Henlein.

"Who is he?" she had asked Lubienski as he briefed her in the German staff car that carried them toward Tempelhof airport. He would be departing for Warsaw shortly after her flight to Prague.

"Henlein's the head of the Sudeten Germans in Czechoslovakia."

"The pro-Nazis?"

Lubienski nodded. He looked miserable. Elizabeth had decided it would be better to do nothing to ease his conscience.

"Why can't they send this thing through their diplomatic pouch?"

He reached forward and slid the window to the driver compartment closed. "Kruzel claims that they have to keep their distance from Henlein because all the German diplomats and Gestapo officers in Prague are under intense surveillance by the Czechs. They're trying to provoke an incident to prove that Berlin is behind the Sudeten Germans."

"Perish the thought!" Elizabeth waved the secret message under Lubienski's nose.

At first, she had considered refusing Colonel Kruzel's proposal, but the more she thought about it, the more she liked the idea. It fit Vita's prescription. Lubienski was putting her in a dangerous situation, and he hated himself for it. That could come in handy later on, if there *was* a later on. She had no illusions about the risks. If the operation was bona fide, the Gestapo clearly was not willing to jeopardize one of their own people. If it was not, she could be in even greater danger.

So far, everything had gone smoothly. She had sailed through the formalities at Prague airport. Now, she stood in the spring sunshine wearing a polka-dot linen dress, pretending to enjoy the band, refusing invitations to dance, and looking for Herr Henlein and the British passport control officer, Clive Dunphy—Jack Shelly's counterpart in Prague. If she was going to deliver a secret message on behalf of the Nazis, she damn well was going to find out what it said. But she needed help. The envelope for Henlein was too thick for the bobby pin trick.

"That's Herr Henlein over there." Wilbur Carrs came up to her. "I hope you appreciate the scandal I'm causing among my diplomatic confreres by inviting such a skunk to my garden party. Your mother would never approve."

"You're a darling." She kissed him on the cheek. "But I haven't seen Dunphy."

"He's in the bar getting tight."

When she found His Majesty's passport control officer and local chief of the Secret Intelligence Service Elizabeth wondered why it was called getting "tight." Whiskey seemed to have had the general effect of unraveling him. He was leaning on the bar, tie askew, one hand hanging on to his suspenders, the other holding on to his glass. Her heart sank. Dunphy looked like one of those ex-navy officers Stephenson warned her about. With a ruddy face, reddish hair, and droopy mustache, he bore a slightly dazed expression as if he had just been hit by a yardarm.

"Hello." Elizabeth approached him.

He reacted like she had stepped on his toe. "Oh, how'd you do?"

"I'm a friend of Jack Shelly's in Warsaw."

"Oh, are you now?" He screwed up his face in a semblance of a suspicious look.

"My name is Elizabeth Pack." She held out her hand. "My husband's assigned to the British embassy in Warsaw, but I work for Jack. And not licking visas. I was the one who arranged for you to be invited here this afternoon."

It was too much for him to absorb all at once. He decided first to shake her hand. "I'm Clive, Clive Dunphy."

"We must find a place to speak privately," Elizabeth insisted. "Come with me."

"Slow down, young lady," he complained, following along after her with a sort of seaman's stagger. At the top of a short flight of stairs, she turned into a vestibule. Holding up her hand to keep him back, she opened the door to the ladies restroom. It was empty.

"You can't be serious, miss," Clive protested as she dragged him inside and propped him up against the door.

"I'm in possession of a sealed document from the German SD to Herr Konrad Henlein," she said quickly. "I don't know what it is but I thought we should find out."

"How'd you get such a thing?" he asked skeptically.

"I can't tell you that, right now." She was not about to share her story, let alone Lubienski's identity, with a drunk.

His eyes narrowed. "This is irregular." He shook his head, as much to clear it as to disagree. "Definitely irregular. We should meet in my office." He blinked firmly and looked uneasily around the ladies restroom, tilting his head to see if there were any ladies in the stalls.

"There's no time for that." Elizabeth reached under her dress and pulled out an envelope bearing an elaborate wax seal. He averted his face. "This is the document," she explained. "I'm supposed to deliver it today. Can you help me open it?"

He took the envelope in his knobby hands. "Just pull the bloody thing apart!"

"God no!" She snatched it back. "I've got to hand it over intact. Don't you have equipment for removing and replacing the seal?"

"No! And if I did, I bloody well wouldn't tell you!" He was trying to recover his manhood by getting belligerent. "I don't even know who you are!"

She lifted her skirt and pushed the envelope back into her garter belt. "I'll have to think of something else. Go back to the embassy, and wait for my call."

"See here, young lady . . ."

"Cable Jack Shelly to check on me. But I swear, if you don't do as I say, you'll be back in Broadway cleaning dust bins before the next bank holiday. Now, get going before I start to scream."

When she introduced herself to Herr Konrad Henlein, führer of the Sudeten Germans, Elizabeth found it hard to keep from laughing. Stumpy, dark, swarthy, and pockmarked, he did not exactly fit the Nazis' ideal of a tall blond Teuton. She spotted him standing alone at the edge of the terrace pretending to be interested in the scenery. Not a soul at the party had gone near him.

"Herr Henlein, so good of you to come," Elizabeth greeted him.

He clicked his heels and bowed.

"I bring you greetings from mutual friends in Berlin," Elizabeth continued.

He looked quickly around. "You are an American?"

"Yes, but I have something for you from Colonel Kruzel."

He became agitated. "We cannot speak here," he hissed.

"No one can hear us, but if you wish, we can talk in your car on the way back into the city."

"Who are you?"

"Elizabeth Pack." She took his hand. "And I'm a friend." At that Henlein looked even more wary.

"Look, I can prove it," she said warmly. "I'll even dance with you in front of all these people."

The smell of the oil from the two-cycle engine of Henlein's Tatra coupe filled the interior of the car. Elizabeth lit a cigarette to cover the odor.

"You can hand it over now," Henlein said from behind the wheel.

Elizabeth reached out and touched his arm. "I would, but it's concealed on my body."

"I will take you to your hotel. You can get it then."

She thought she detected a hidden agenda in that suggestion. "Unfortunately I'm staying at Ambassador Carrs's residence. Don't you have some place where we could go?"

Henlein appeared uncertain. "My office. But my apartment is right above it."

Perfect. She put her hand on his arm again. "I think we can be discreet, don't you?"

The afternoon sky was becoming overcast, and Elizabeth found that Prague had taken on a strange menacing quality. Built on a series of hills along the Valtava, it was a baroque city of damp winding streets and brooding Gothic towers. Henlein had headquartered his movement in an undistin-

guished four-story house in a small German neighborhood
tucked under the ramparts of Hradcany Castle near the
Charles Bridge. Through the windows of the ground-floor
storefront, she could see uniformed workers in Sam Brown
belts scurrying around under posters of Adolf Hitler and
Konrad Henlein.

She and the Sudeten führer entered a separate doorway
on the left and climbed a flight of stairs to the first landing.
Elizabeth surmised that this was his private office and that
his apartment occupied the next two floors.

He quickly closed the door behind them. "Would you
like a schnapps?"

The place looked less like an office than a storeroom.
Piles of papers, pamphlets, posters, and books covered most
of the floor. Mysterious wooden crates were stacked in the
back. Ominously, the walls were covered with gun racks
holding a variety of rifles and pistols. Was this armory designed to make Herr Henlein feel secure, she wondered, or
provoke a raid by the Czech police?

"I'll drink, if you're having something. We should
toast," she replied invitingly and perched on a leather sofa
wedged into the mess.

"Yes, yes." He rubbed his hands together eagerly. From
his desk, which was set between two windows that looked
out onto the street, he produced a bottle and two glasses.
Weaving his way through the debris, he sat down beside
her and filled their glasses.

"Now, you give me the documents?"

"Oh, let's have a drink first."

"*Jawohl.*" He tossed his back. "Now, the documents,
please."

She smiled coquettishly. "You must hide your eyes."
Elizabeth thought she could detect a hint of a blush under
his sallow complexion as he turned away. She reached under her skirt and pulled out the envelope. When he took it
in his hands, she knew he could feel that it was still warm.

Henlein examined the seal carefully. "*Sehr gut!*" he declared. He got up and went to his desk where he slit open
the envelope and unfolded the document, spreading it out
across the desktop. He reached into his vest for a pair of
spectacles. "Oh! Oh!" he rhapsodized. "*Fraülein,* you

have made my dreams come true!'' He folded the paper again and put the document into the top drawer, locking it with a key.

He hurried to the sofa, his little eyes red with excitement. "We must toast again!"

Elizabeth shuddered the next one down. She was starting to realize that the plan she had been developing had certain major flaws. To get her hands on the document, she first had to get the key. To do that, she had to put Henlein to sleep. To do that, she would either have to drink him under the table, have sex with him, or both. But then what?

"Prosit!" He had refilled her glass.

She couldn't steal the document. The Gestapo would come after her. And Lubienski. But with her rudimentary German, she might not be able to read it, let alone commit it to memory after her third schnapps. In fact, if she had one more drink, she'd be the one that passed out first. Of course, if she was going to have sex with Herr Henlein, that would be the only condition to be in.

Already his hand was on her knee, his face looming close to hers. What an idiot she'd been to get herself into the situation! Henlein's forehead and cheeks gleamed, not with perspiration exactly; it looked more like the film on the skin of an amphibian.

"Herr Henlein." She firmly pushed him away. "You presume too much! I'm happy for your success, but we must maintain our sense of decorum." She tried to get up, but he roughly pulled her back down. His grip was strong.

"I am the führer here. My will is law." His eyes had turned flat and evil. If he decided to rape her, what could she do?

"If you force your attentions on me"—she thought quickly—"you'll have to answer to my lover."

He laughed. "Who might that be?" he asked scornfully.

"Colonel Kruzel."

That stopped him. But only for a moment. His ugly smile returned. "Colonel Kruzel would never have anything to do with you!"

"Because I'm not an Aryan?" She yanked her hand away.

"No, because you're not a young boy!" And he shook with laughter.

Elizabeth leaped off the sofa and stumbled to the nearest wall where she yanked a Mauser pistol off its peg. "Herr Henlein, I've completed my mission. If you stay out of the way, I'll not report you to my superiors in the Gestapo. If you don't, I'll shoot you."

"Not with that," he moved to block the door, "it has no magazine."

Elizabeth glanced at it. He was right.

He stepped toward her. "I like that you struggle. It excites me. Do you want to see?" He began to unbutton his pants.

She could try to hit him with the gun, or as the saying went, she could relax and enjoy it. The thought made her sick. Maybe she could bite it off, but when he exposed himself, she nixed that idea. His penis was short and fat, like the head of a sledgehammer. She could scream, but in this place, a scream might not be unusual. It would probably keep people away.

So she did the only thing she could; she laughed. Elizabeth laughed as loud and as lustily as possible, throwing in some sharp "oohs" and "aahs" for good measure. Henlein looked baffled. But then his expression turned to panic when he heard the knock on the door.

"*Katzi! Katzi!*"

"*Mein Gott! Meine Frau!*" The color drained out of his face.

"Open up, *Katzi*! Open up!"

"*Ja, Shatzi! Einen Moment!*" He bent over to stuff himself back into his pants. Elizabeth flew to the door and yanked it open.

"Whatever is this foolishness?" Frau Henlein demanded. She was tiny but she carried a large wooden spoon. The führer of the Sudetenland Germans looked as spent and guilty as if he'd had an orgasm.

Elizabeth handed him the Mauser. "*Heil Hitler*." She saluted. His other hand flapped up involuntarily. Smiling, she then reached into his fly and gave his *schwanz* a vicious twist. As she dashed down the stairs, she could hear Frau

Henlein striking him with her spoon, and yelling, *"Schwein! Schwein!"*

Six hours later, Elizabeth was back on Henlein's door-step.

Chapter 21

Malá Strana, Prague—
Sunday, 2:00 A.M., May 29, 1938

Clive Dunphy remained behind the wheel of his Austin while Elizabeth, dressed in a navy-blue turtleneck, pea coat, and wool sailor's cap, all several sizes too large, picked her way past the simple outside locks and into Herr Henlein's stairwell. The risers were the most formidable obstacle. With every step they groaned like the oppressed of Europe, the sound echoing upward into the dark as Elizabeth inhaled the odor of Frau Henlein's rabbit stew, a pungent *Hasenpfeffer*. It took five minutes for her to climb up to Henlein's office door on the second floor, but with the help of Dunphy's burglary kit, less than a minute to get through it.

She paused. Everything was quiet. With a hooded flashlight, she made her way across the room toward Henlein's desk, then tripped over a pile of books. Frozen, she listened for sounds coming from the apartment above. Did she hear the ceiling creak? Footsteps? She waited, breathless and impatient. Clive had given her only fifteen minutes. Otherwise the chance of encountering the police or a patrol of Henlein's Blackshirts became prohibitive.

Straining, Elizabeth could hear nothing. She stepped to the desk and tried the drawer; it was locked.

Immediately, she went to work, using a small hook to snag the lever inside. With a snap, the lock opened and she could pull out the drawer. She found it jammed with papers. Was it the document on top? No! He must have come back and moved it! She clutched. Maybe it wasn't in the drawer at all!

239

She had to calm down and think. Did he put it back in the envelope? She couldn't remember. What did the contents look like? How did it feel when she was carrying it? Not a simple sheet of paper and not a heavy document. And when Herr Henlein looked at it, what had he done? He'd *unfolded* it.

She searched through the drawer. At the bottom, she found the envelope with the seal. It was empty. But under it was a folded paper that felt right. Placing it on the top of the desk, Elizabeth opened up the pages. In the glow of the flashlight, it appeared to be a map.

The contours were of Czechoslovakia, but there were other lines and marks cutting across the country with arrows pointing in different directions. A huge chunk of western Czechoslovakia had an arrow pointing west and the legend *Nach Deutschland:* To Germany. Attached to one corner was a brief memo to Herr Henlein. As far as Elizabeth could make out, it instructed him to demand that the Czechs allow all of the Sudetenland to be unified with Germany. This was Hitler's plan for the dismemberment of Czechoslovakia!

Time was running out. She reached into her tool bag and took out the bulky Argus camera and a short tripod. She set it up, extending the legs as far as they would go. Still, she realized that several pictures would be needed to get the whole map. Measuring the distance from the camera to the desk, she adjusted the focus, shutter speed, and F stop accordingly. Attaching the cable release, she then snapped the first picture.

What an idiot! It was dark! Digging into the camera bag, she came out with the flash attachment and a box of bulbs. Remeasuring the distance between the map and the flashbulb, she had to reset the F stop. Time was speeding by. She could imagine Clive starting to work on the flask of whiskey she knew he kept in his pocket. Finally, after checking the apparatus three times, everything seemed ready. She released the trigger.

Sitting outside in the darkness, Clive thought the building had exploded. My God! he thought, she's forgotten to close the bloody curtains! The flash lit up the entire street. Then another bolt of light bounced off the buildings and then another. He could see lamps being switched on in windows up and down the block. Another flash and the window of Herr Henlein's apartment began to glow. Clive panicked and hit the horn. Lights suddenly appeared everywhere. Windows and shutters were opened. People looked out. He dropped the gearshift into first and stepped on the gas.

The horn stunned her. Wait for me you bastard, she swore silently. Elizabeth was trying to pack away her equipment and get her eyes reaccustomed to the dark at the same time. Overhead, she heard a dull thud. Was that Henlein walking across the floor? Quickly, she refolded the map and stuffed it in the bottom of the drawer. Then she suddenly realized: She had been taught how to pick locks, but not how to lock them again. As she struggled at the keyhole, she thought she could hear steps coming down the stairs. She tried to relax, to concentrate, to visualize how the lock worked. No, the footfalls were unmistakable. A light appeared under the crack in the door to the landing. A hand rattled the doorknob. The latch on the drawer finally slipped back into place.

Elizabeth rushed to the back of the office and ducked behind a stack of crates. She was trapped. Should she call out to Clive? Would he hear her? Would he get to her in time? Would he come at all? As the door opened, she discovered that her back was pressed against a railing. It was a spiral staircase. It lead to the ground floor. She heard Herr Henlein cursing and stumbling over a pile of fallen books as she scampered down the steps. Elizabeth moved swiftly to the front door. It was bolted. While she frantically picked at it, the lights suddenly went on. A portrait of Der Führer glared down at her. Herr Henlein was coming down the spiral staircase.

The lock gave way. She pulled open the door and rushed outside. The street was empty. Where the hell was the car? Where the hell was Clive?

Dropping to the sidewalk, she began to crawl, dragging her tool bag and camera behind her. She prayed Henlein could not see her through the storefront window. Just as Herr Henlein stepped out, Elizabeth made it to the next doorway. Pressed against the wall, she listened helplessly as his footsteps came toward her. Then he paused. Cursing again, he walked back inside, slammed the door, and locked it. She could not breathe until the lights went out.

Now what should she do? Wait for Clive to come back? God no. The American embassy was nearby, but how, at that hour of night and without identification, could she explain herself to the Marine guards, let alone her friend Wilbur Carrs? Going to the British embassy would violate every rule of security. She had to make it to the safe house near the old town square where she had changed clothes and Dunphy had a photo lab. Elizabeth had a vague idea that the square lay across the river and up a hill. In the maze of streets at night she could easily get lost. Still, it was better than standing there paralyzed waiting for a police patrol or a group of Henlein's Nazis to show up.

The cobblestone streets were damp and dark with long shadows cast by the infrequent lamps. A mist was drifting up from the river. All the buildings appeared closed and shuttered. It might have felt menacing, but exhilarated by her escape, Elizabeth's imagination ran toward triumph. She could have been in the eighteenth or seventeenth century, a revolutionary fighting for Jan Hus against the Hapsburgs, or a spy in the service of Napoleon. She'd done it! Stolen the Nazis' secret map. And all on her own! She felt very proud of herself.

Walking under the streetlamps, she played happily with her own shadow, watching it grow to cover complete buildings, an entire side of a street. But as she did, she suddenly thought she detected another shadow, a shadow that seemed to be following her.

The twin towers of the Charles Bridge loomed ahead, the chisel-shaped Gothic roofs floating above the fog that lay on the river. Glancing furtively backward, Elizabeth passed under the towers and hurried out onto the ancient medieval bridge. Mist rose in spindly tendrils to envelop the dozens of religious statues that lined both sides of the span like holy sentinels. She passed St. Wenceslas, pious and heavily armed, and farther on, the figure of St. Vitus arrived out of the night. Why was St. Vitus garbed as a Roman Legionnaire, she wondered, her mind seeking to escape the growing fear that she was being trailed. She began to walk faster.

From the left, St. Augustine with a burning heart in his hand came toward her out of the fog. A tortured St. Francis Borgia materialized from the right. A vacant-eyed St. Wenceslas appeared again, then St. Christopher's staff thrust at her from the mist and John the Baptist, swathed in hides and sheepskin, revealed himself momentarily in the swirling damp. Whenever Elizabeth strained to look behind her into the nebulous night, she found it difficult to distinguish the statues from the apparition that seemed to be stalking her.

If she hurried faster, the figure seemed to keep pace. When she slowed down, it dropped back. Nearing the Old Town Tower at the end of the bridge, the last statue, St. Bernard, appeared to bend toward her in a useless offer of help. Once past the tower, the fog cleared and Elizabeth started running. The street was steep. Her breath came harder, the bag of tools felt heavier and heavier. At the top of a short flight of steps, she looked back. A man had emerged from the mist. He headed straight toward her.

Down the street she saw a high wall and then a church. Hurrying forward again she opened the bag and took out the Argus. By the time she reached the wall, Elizabeth had removed the film. She heaved the camera and the bag over the wall and made for the sanctuary of the church. Only it turned out not to be a church. It was a synagogue, and it was closed. She began to run again. Rounding the corner, she found two more synagogues, and between them a low iron gate that barred the way to a graveyard. It was the only place to hide.

She had never seen a cemetery like it. A jumble of tombstones leaned against each other like dominoes. Thousands and thousands of them, only inches apart, stuck out of huge mounds of earth with narrow footpaths running in between. Elizabeth realized that this must be the ghetto cemetery. For hundreds of years, it was the only place in Prague that Jews could be buried. Generation after generation had been stacked one upon the other in an area no larger than a city block.

She heard the gate crash. He was coming in after her. And he had a flashlight. Lying down, she began to crawl through the thicket of headstones. A misty rain had started to fall.

Elizabeth could not see her pursuer but could follow his movements from the beam of his flashlight. As far as she could tell, he was staying on the paths, not venturing into the wilderness of gravestones. She continued crawling through the mud until she found a spot where she could wedge herself in between a sizeable mausoleum and several very old and tall stones that leaned against it. With her face pressed against the black earth she began to pray. Given her circumstance, she addressed her prayers to Jehovah.

Suddenly, the flashlight lit the stones near her head. Unknowingly, Elizabeth had picked a hiding spot only a few yards from another path. Should she get up and run? Surrender? Craning her neck, she could see his feet coming down the path. Who the hell was he? The police? Why didn't he shout for her to stop? Henlein? Why didn't he curse her? The man had on heavy shoes with thick soles, the kind someone who had to stand around a lot would wear. She felt a chill colder than the ground. Maybe he was Gestapo. As he passed by, Elizabeth could see that the hand not holding the flashlight held a gun.

He continued down the path a few paces and stopped. Then he came back toward her. Sweeping the light in a circle around him, he stood still, listening. Elizabeth's heart beat so loudly in her ears she was certain it would give her away. She could feel the flashlight stabbing at her between the gravestones. Fear erased all thought. She pushed her face against the ground until mud filled her mouth. He was almost on top of her. She heard the metallic rasp of his pistol being cocked. A thunderclap shattered the air.

The skies opened up and the rain poured down. Seconds, minutes, hours all seemed the same. Time remained suspended, paralyzed, until finally, he clicked the safety back into place and slowly moved away. When the dawn came up, Elizabeth was still huddled under the gravestones like one of the dead.

Trans-Carpathian Express—
May 31, 1938

"He was probably from the Czech secret police," Count Lubienski said, "watching Henlein's house." He had flown down to Prague to accompany her back to Warsaw by train. They were sitting in a nearly empty dining car finishing lunch. Elizabeth continued to gaze out the train window at the sharp snow-clad peaks of the High Tatras.

"I don't think he was out to kill you." Lubienski tried to sound reassuring, but succeeded only in belittling her.

"Michael, I want to know all about it."

"What more can I say?" he protested.

"Why you, why me, why the map?"

He remained silent for a minute. The guilt was etched in his face. "You must understand, I've only given you information about the Germans or Russians. I've never told you anything about my country's secret plans."

"You told me about the Enigma."

"Only to help you against our enemies. But if I explained the map, it would be treason."

So this was the line that he had drawn in his mind, the line she had to get him to cross.

The sound of the train against the track turned into a roar as they crossed a bridge that spanned a wide ravine. A waterfall tumbled down the mountainside and disappeared beneath them.

"Michael, I almost lost my life for you. If I had refused to cooperate, what would the Gestapo have done to you? Think about it. I have."

Lubienski rolled his eyes as if he refused to hear what she had to say. "You put me at risk by going to Henlein's!"

"I could have easily handed the envelope over to British intelligence in Prague, but I delivered it as promised. And do you know why? To save you." She could see the shame spread across his face. "What does a gentleman do in response to such a generous gift from a lady?"

"Is that why you have rejected my attentions?"

"Michael, you don't want to make love to me"—she

had kept him at bay for two nights—"you want me to tell you that everything's all right. That you're still a man in my eyes. You are! But only if you've the courage to tell me why you put me in such a position. What if the Czechs had caught me? You know you were risking my life."

He stared out the window at the clean white mountains rising to a bright blue sky. When he looked back his eyes were full of sadness. "I know we are going to part, you and I, and one day I feel we are going to meet as enemies. You must wear a white carnation on that day to show that you won't kill me or denounce me!"

"What are you saying?"

"We're going to take a bite of the apple."

"You're going against Czechoslovakia too?"

"That's what the map shows. When Hitler invades Czechoslovakia, Poland will also take a piece, the province of Teschen. That's what I was arranging in Berlin."

"You'll be Hitler's ally! That could mean war with Britain!"

"Yes, we will be on opposite sides. I'm against it, but I have my government's orders! You must protect me!"

Elizabeth sat quietly for a moment. She could see the worry on Count Lubienski's face.

"Of course I'll protect you. They'll never know this information came from you."

Lubienski sagged with relief.

"But on one condition," Elizabeth continued.

"What more do you want?" he begged her.

She smiled and reached out her hand, placing it on his arm in a gesture of reassurance. "The secret of how you've broken the Enigma."

Chapter 22

"Don't you bloody lie to me, Elizabeth," Shelly whispered fiercely. "You didn't do it all by yourself."

They were sitting in the plush loge seats of the Hollywood cinema on Hoza Street watching *The Lady Vanishes*. Margaret Lockwood had just returned to her train seat to find that her friend, Dame May Whitty, had disappeared and everyone else in the compartment pretending that they had never seen her.

"Of course Clive helped me," Elizabeth whispered back. "He checked with you."

"I mean that cock-and-bull story you fed Dunphy about a stranger on the plane giving you an envelope to deliver to Henlein. Do you take me for a fool?"

"I told you . . ."

"That map is tantamount to a declaration of war!" The whispering frustrated him. "No Nazi agent would just hand that over to some American girl he'd just met on an airplane! And why did you accept it?"

"I'd no inkling what it was about until Wilbur Carrs explained that Henlein was a Nazi.. . ."

He glared at her in disbelief while she pretended to watch the screen: Margaret Lockwood was trying to persuade everyone on the train that her friend had been abducted, but they wouldn't believe her. Elizabeth had to admit that leaving Michael and Colonel Kruzel out of her story made it sound quite lame. But she had promised to protect Lubienski.

"I want you to leave the theater," Shelly growled, "walk over to Marszałkowska, and take the number three tram toward the Place Wilson. Get off at the next stop and take the first one back. We"ve got to talk!"

Elizabeth did as she was told. When the tram hissed to a stop, and Shelly climbed aboard, the car was virtually empty. She assured him that none of the passengers got on with her.

She could see that he was in a rage. "Let me explain something to you, Elizabeth. Downing Street plans to warn Hitler that Britain will side with the Czechs and French— all because of your map! But we don't know if it's a deception, a provocation, or real. We must know how you got it. If you don't come clean, it's back to London with you. And don't think that'll be the end of it. You'll spend weeks, months, even years being interrogated at Prae Wood. Only you won't have that comfy little room overlooking the downs, you'll be living in the cellar."

She could not look at him. Instead her mind had fastened on the women bustling along Marszałkowska Street preoccupied with their daily shopping. What would their kind of life be like? To go to the stores in the afternoon with girlfriends. To go back to a modest apartment and prepare an evening meal and then have your husband come home and share it? To have someone in your bed the entire night. There were children too, in Elizabeth's fantasy.

"Answer me!" Shelly said angrily.

"But I gave my word," she said quietly.

"You also gave your word to me. And to His Majesty's government. If you break it, that's the first step in being turned. Is that what's happening here? Are you being turned by someone? By Lubienski?"

Good God, Elizabeth thought, maybe that was the setup after all. Maybe Michael was trying to get her under "positive control." Maybe that's why she'd been followed ever since returning from Prague.

"Was it Lubienski who got you to carry this map to the Sudeten Germans? The Poles are becoming thick as thieves with the Nazis now. Once you start to lie to me, you can never tell me the truth."

Shelly was right. But how, Elizabeth asked herself, can

I explain having knowingly worked for the Gestapo? That will really send him and the boys in Broadway around the bend.

"Tell me what happened, or I won't ever be able to trust you again!"

He doesn't trust me now, she realized. He won't if I lie, and he won't if I don't. She had been too clever by half. Was her career over just as she was about to suceed? She decided to tell him everything.

His face went blank in amazement. "You'll have to go back to London for a debrief," he gasped.

"I can't do that," Elizabeth said firmly. She had not finished her explanation.

"It's not a question of can or can't!"

"If you force me, I'll have to cancel my dinner party."

"Pity," he said sarcastically. "Should I be crushed?"

"Only if you care about getting your precious Enigma machine."

"Now what are you talking about?"

"Lubienski told me that in breaking the German code, the Polish Cipher Bureau also figured out how to duplicate the Enigma machine."

"No." His mouth hung open in disbelief.

"They've made a dozen copies, and I've a scheme to get the plans."

The Broadway Buildings, London— June 9, 1938

Menzies thumbed through a black folder tied together with crimson ribbon, "Cynthia's" operational plan for getting the schematics for the Enigma machine. The concept looked simple, but he saw that the execution could be quite tricky. Cynthia proposed to invite Edward Fokczynski, founder of the AVA Radio Manufacturing Company, to dinner along with the British assistant commercial attaché and Count Lubienski. Ostensibly, the purpose would be to discuss the export of AVA radios. The real reason was that AVA was the company manufacturing copies of the German Enigma machines. Where there were copies, she reasoned, there had to be diagrams of how to make them. Menzies turned to the key parts of her plan:

MOST SECRET/CYNTHIA page 2 of 2
—Fokczynski usually spends 18 hour days in his office on Nowy Swiat. It is only 10 minutes away from the Villa Frascati.

—The Enigma machines and other secret equipment are produced at a modern factory in the suburb of Mokotow. Unfortunately, surveillance has established that the factory is impossible to penetrate, because of the guards and the 24 hour work shifts. However, Lubienski believes copies of the schematics are also kept at Fokczynski's laboratory in Nowy Świat.

—Fokczynski is usually the last to leave, exiting by the back door and putting the keys in his coat pocket.

—At the dinner party, Lubienski will pretend to be called back to his office. He will take the keys from Fokczynski's coat and enter the AVA laboratory. There is only one guard stationed at the front door.

—Lubienski has visited the laboratory several times and knows where to look for the plans. The drawers have only simple locks, and the keys should be on Fokczynski's ring. If not, I have taught Lubienski how to pick them.

—After photographing the relevant documents, Lubienski will return to the party and replace the keys.

—Cost of the dinner should be about 30 pounds.

A stack of memos followed with various amendments and changes. They added up to a bureaucratic muddle. If the plan succeeded everyone could claim credit; if not, it would be Menzies's mistake. He pushed the button on his intercom.

"Are they all here?" he asked his secretary.

"Everyone but Dilly. . . . No, here he comes."

They all filed in, Lance, Denniston, and Knox bringing

up the rear as usual. Menzies began tapping a pencil on his desk.

"So, how do we all come out on the Cynthia caper? I've read your memos and I'd like your candid opinions."

Captain Lance spoke first. "The chaps in operations think it's damn silly, a dinner party and all, but when I pressed them they had no better ideas."

"Well, I question the whole thing," Knox broke in. "Here's this woman who admittedly did a job for the Nazis, and lied about it at first, coming up with a plan that puts our best source in jeopardy."

"Best source?" Denniston noted. "That's the kindest thing you've ever said about our Cynthia."

"I don't follow you, Dilly," Captain Lance added. "If she's been turned, it would have been Lubienski who did it. He wouldn't be blowing himself."

"Shelly says"—Menzies picked up a cablegram—"that 'if this comes off, we can stop worrying about whether Cynthia or Lubienski have been "doubled" by the Nazis.'"

"And if it doesn't?" Knox insisted. "What if it's all a provocation? An excuse for the Poles to break with Britain and side openly with the Germans?"

That gave them all pause.

"Poland is already siding with Nazi Germany over Czechoslovakia," Denniston observed. "So we must expect that Cynthia's days are numbered as a conduit of Polish intelligence on the Germans. That's all the more reason to spare no effort to get enough information on the Enigma so we can break the code ourselves."

Menzies rubbed his face. "All right then, we'll go with it. But I want each of you to monitor every detail with the utmost care." That meant if something went wrong, he intended to blame down.

Warsaw—
Thursday Evening, June 23, 1938

Elizabeth's plan turned out to be misleading in one respect. Her dinner became an elaborate affair that cost over one hundred pounds, not counting the price of her gossamer gown, a copy of a Jean Patou that revealed more than it concealed.

For the sake of security, Elizabeth decided to invite all four of the founders of AVA—Fokczynski; Antoni Palluth; and the brothers Danilewicz, Ludomir and Leonard. She wanted to make sure that none of them accidentally showed up at the laboratory while Lubienski was rummaging around inside. But to make the event more festive, she had also invited the popular tenor Jan Kiepura and the architect Bohdan Pniewski. Everyone brought his wife or mistress.

This was the first dinner party Elizabeth had hosted since returning to Warsaw. Her American Revere silver, traditional English china, and Spanish table settings looked out of place in her sleekly modern apartment, so Shelly's fiancée kindly lent her Jugenstil flatware and dishes from the Josef Hoffmann studio in Vienna. She reinforced the kitchen with two *sous-chefs,* and for the occasion, hired two waiters as well as a butler from the British embassy who was given instructions to make very large drinks for the cocktail hour.

In Elizabeth's experience, it was easy to get the Poles to drink but not to get them drunk. However, having talked her guests into trying American dry martinis, things were moving right along. By the time they sat down to dinner, everyone was quite merry. Halfway through the quail eggs à la Russe, the butler arrived at the table with the prearranged telephone call for Count Lubienski.

"I've got to go into the office," Count Lubienski apologized when he returned to the dining room.

"Is it war?" Elizabeth asked in mock horror. "Should we pack our bags?"

"No, it's far worse," Lubienski replied. "It's Colonel Beck."

Everyone laughed and raised their eyebrows at his candor.

"Your foreign minister needs a social life," Ludomir said.

"But who would invite to their table," the architect Pniewski asked, "a man that Paderewski describes as 'that little shit'?'' He got up and bowed to Elizabeth. "Forgive me, madam, for my language."

Joining in the laughter, Lubienski also bowed, then kissed Elizabeth's hand. That brought her a surge of relief. The kiss indicated that Lubienski had gotten the keys to the AVA lab out of Fokczynski's overcoat. "Hurry back," she said as he departed.

The issue of the keys had been a major point of dispute with London in planning the party. Broadway wanted a black tie dinner on a weekend in order to minimize the chance of anyone being at the lab. SIS preferred black tie, because Fokczynski was known to be very fastidious about his appearance. They assumed that he would leave his bulky key ring in his overcoat rather than spoil the line of his tuxedo.

Elizabeth overruled them. It would be a weeknight and business dress. She wanted to be able to explain Lubienski's departure more easily, and to ensure that Fokczynski came directly from his laboratory. If he went home to change, he might well leave his keys behind.

She examined Fokczynski as he finished his Baltic salmon. He was the most reserved of the four partners. When Lubienski had balked at becoming a burglar, Elizabeth threatened to introduce herself to Fokczynski and seduce him into giving her the plans. Lubienski had flown into a rage, but in the end, agreed to do what she wanted. He needn't have worried. As far as Elizabeth could tell, the AVA founder would have been completely impervious to her charms. Spare and austere, Fokczynski accurately fit Shelly's profile as a man passionate only about his work, his country, and his church.

She checked her watch. It was nine-ten. Lubienski should have arrived at the lab. She took another sip of Chablis to calm herself. There was a time when she had thought the operation would never get under way. Even when Shelly's surveillance had confirmed that the plan should work, and after they'd gotten a preliminary green light and all the dinner invitations had been sent out and accepted, London still had not given its final approval.

"What's taking them so long!" Elizabeth had demanded one day from Shelly.

"Our superiors are arguing over the cover story."

"If we fail?"

"No, if you succeed."

"They're planning to take out an ad on the front page of *The Times*?"

"Don't be silly. But we'll have to explain to our cryptographers how we got hold of the plans."

"I see. And who's going to get the credit?"

"I'd say that right now, the leading contender's a nameless Polish mechanic who works in a German factory where the Enigma machines are made."

"And who gets the blame if something goes wrong?"

He smiled sympathetically. "It's a man's world, Elizabeth."

"And I'll be odd woman out?" Shelly didn't have to answer.

The butler suddenly arrived at Elizabeth's side. "Sorry to disturb you, madam, but I have a phone call for Count Lubienski."

She was startled. "Who could it be?"

"It's from the Foreign Ministry." Everyone at the table heard him.

Elizabeth felt her heart constrict. They hadn't planned that his office might actually need him! "Say he's on the way." She tried to sound casual as possible.

But her mind raced. It was nine-thirty. If everything went smoothly, Lubienski would be back in a half hour, and he could call his office with some excuse. He'd been busy with Beck and hadn't seen whoever was calling, or something like that. She told herself to relax, and rejoin the conversation.

The assistant commercial attaché and Antoni Palluth were exchanging experiences about crystal sets in high school. As they talked, Elizabeth could not keep from imagining what Lubienski was doing at that moment. She could see him inside the laboratory trying to determine which of the dozens and dozens of thin file drawers held the plans to the Enigma. Lubienski had made several visits to AVA and saw that the lab had no special storage vault for highly classified material. By the same token, there was no way to know which file drawer might contain the Enigma drawings. With growing nervousness, Elizabeth could picture Lubienski frantically unlocking and ransacking every file in the place.

To clear her guests' palate between courses, the waiters arrived with a champagne *sorbet*. Behind them, the butler appeared again to tell Elizabeth that the Foreign Ministry had called once more. "They were very insistent. I took the liberty, madam, to say he had left for the ministry a half hour ago."

She felt helpless. She was helpless. By now Lubienski should have found the drawings and be photographing them. Shelly had warned that it was bad luck when Lubienski had refused his Argus and insisted upon using an eight-millimeter Minox given to him as a gift by Colonel Kruzel. She had to stop being superstitious. She had to calm down. She had to pay more attention to her guests. Lubienski was late, but not overdue. Besides, Shelly was parked outside the lab to cover him. The only person they had to worry about was the guard, an old man who hardly ever left his office. As for the Foreign Ministry, what could they do? Nothing. She and Lubienski would make up a story.

"Sorry, madam. It's the telephone again," the butler whispered. "A Colonel Beck. He asked for Count Lubienski but now insists on talking to you."

Elizabeth excused herself from the table to receive the call.

"What have you done with my aide?" Beck demanded.

"I might well ask you the same thing," she responded coolly, but trembling inside.

"Don't be impertinent. This is a matter of the utmost urgency. Your servant says he was there."

"Was, yes."

"Well, he has not arrived here! Perhaps you're not the only woman in his life, Mrs. Pack."

"I expect him back," she protested.

"When?"

"Soon."

"I'm dispatching a messenger to your home with important documents which he is to read and then phone me at my office." He hung up without saying good-bye.

What was she to do? If her guests saw the Foreign Ministry messenger, they might begin to wonder what was going on. Damn! When she took this job, she knew she was going to need an apartment with two entrances and three exits!

By the time she returned to the table, her guests were well into the roast veal. She made sure that their wine glasses were refilled. Leonard Danilewicz was telling a story.

"This peasant was under his apple tree holding a huge pig in his arms. He was lifting it up to reach one of the apples. Each time the pig ate an apple, the peasant, exhausted, would have to set it down to rest. Then he would pick up the pig again and maneuver it into a position where it could get at another apple. Finally his neighbor came over to him and asked what he was doing.

"'This is my favorite pig,' the peasant replied, 'and he just loves apples.'

"'But why don't you simply shake the apples from the tree? It would save a lot of time.'

"The peasant grunted as he struggled to lift the pig up to another apple. 'But what is time to a pig?'"

Everyone laughed except Elizabeth. Time was everything! Her guests were enjoying themselves enormously, and she was dying inside. Her watch indicated that Lubienski should be out of the lab and on his way back. She prayed that he would arrive before the messenger. That way he could explain to the guests that he forgot something. . . .

"We started AVA with what for you would be one thousand dollars." Fokczynski had finally warmed up and was talking about the origins of AVA. "It was 1925. We all had other jobs. . . ."

The butler appeared again. This time he merely put his fist to his ear and Elizabeth knew she had to take the phone.

Beck was on the line again. "Is he there yet?" he said peremptorily.

"No, I'm sorry, he's not here. Neither is your messenger."

"I didn't send him. I'm coming myself!"

"But I have guests!"

"And would it be a disgrace to have the foreign minister of Poland call on you?"

He was getting on his high horse, and that was when Beck could be most troublesome. Once when he was to go to London to receive a huge amount of economic aid, he postponed the trip until he was assured that a red carpet would be unrolled from the steps of his train, all the way through Waterloo Station, to the door of his Rolls-Royce.

"Of course you're welcome to come," Elizabeth said soothingly. "Would you care for dinner?"

"That won't be necessary. Just produce Count Lubienski." He rang off.

The Foreign Ministry was in the Brühl Palace on the Plac Theatralny, less than fifteen minutes away. When Beck got there, would he recognize her guests? Of course. Everyone knew everyone in Warsaw and AVA was renowned in the government for its secret projects. And, when Beck saw the directors of AVA gathered together at Elizabeth's table while Count Lubienski had mysteriously disappeared . . . Lubienski had to get there first.

Where the hell was he? Maybe Lubienski had already been caught. Maybe Beck's call was designed to keep her there until the security police arrived. Stop it, Elizabeth warned herself.

"Competition is very difficult," Palluth was saying when she rejoined the table. Elizabeth saw that bottles of cold Goldwasser vodka had replaced the wine. Her guests were happily settling in for a real party.

"If only we could handle our competition the way Fuch's handled Wedel," Palluth concluded.

"Do you know our famous candy makers?" Pniewski asked, and Elizabeth nodded.

"Wedel was advertising," Kiepura the tenor inserted himself in the conversation, "that he had 'one hundred flavors and each one different.' He bragged about having a shop in Paris and a private plane to bring in fresh candies every other day. How could Fuch's beat that? To Poles, what could be better than things French? Only the fruits of our own countryside! So Fuch's comes back with signs proclaiming 'Ten tastes and each is *Polish*!' "

There was a murmur of approval around the table.

"Of course it was also a subtle way to remind everyone that Wedel is Jewish," Pniewski noted.

Elizabeth felt a grin frozen on her face. What a nightmare. Beck would arrive momentarily and then what? She could imagine the scene.

"I'm waiting for Count Lubienski," he would explain to her guests.

"But we thought he went to the ministry to see you," one of them would respond. Uncertain and uncomfortable, they would start to thank her and ask for their coats. When Fokczynski put his hand in his pocket and found his keys missing . . .

Cut it out! Elizabeth told herself. She waved to the butler. "Serve the cheese tray and then please go out on the balcony and watch for Colonel Beck. His car will have flags flying from the fenders."

Over the Bleu de Bresse the architect and the singer fell into an argument. Jan Kiepura, the tenor, declared, "I admire what Hitler's done for Germany. Particularly his architecture. It's grand, bold, new, not soulless like the Jew architecture from the Bauhaus."

"How can you like Albert Speer's buildings," Bohdan Pniewski demanded, "and also the design I did for your house?"

"Ha! My house, I could have designed myself," the tenor sniffed, "for half the price."

"And for half the price," the architect retorted, "I could sing you an aria!"

Elizabeth jumped up about to intercede, then saw the sign from the butler. "Excuse me," she said abruptly. She rushed into the foyer, and grabbed her fur cloak. Beck had to be kept out of the apartment at all costs. But what could she say to him? Damn Lubienski! Where was he? Then she felt a stab of guilt. She could imagine him handcuffed on a stool, a bare bulb over his head, being beaten by the Defensywa, the security police.

When Elizabeth opened the front door, Colonel Beck was already getting out of his car. He was small, thin, with a beaked nose and a black stripe of hair down the middle of his bald head. She hurried down the path to meet him. The foreign minister greeted her with a cruel smile as if he were about to make another rude remark about Count Lubienski's liaisons. Of course! That was it! She knew what to say.

"Your wayward count has still not returned?" Beck appeared to be enjoying her discomfort. "You should get another man." He leered.

They stood face-to-face. In the glow from the fluorescent porch light, his skin, like the tulips in the flower boxes, looked gray. "I look forward to meeting your guests."

"I have to ask you not to come in."

Beck was taken aback, but before he could be offended, Elizabeth let her cloak slide open so that he got a view of her breasts rising above her low-cut gown.

"You're right about Michael," she continued in a pleading tone, "there is another woman. He had to go and see her."

"It's a wonder he gets any work done at all."

"He told everyone at the party that he was going to the ministry and would be back. Obviously, she's delayed him. If you go inside, it will be a great embarrassment for me." She managed to bring a tear to her eye.

Beck slowly inspected her from head to toe. She felt like her dress was transparent. Then he clicked his heels and bowed.

"If you hear from him, tell him to call me."

Elizabeth escorted Beck down the path to his car. Getting in, he shot her one last malign look. "And do you know who this other woman is?"

"Of course." She made herself look brave. "His wife."

Beck grinned and the driver closed the door. Elizabeth clutched her cloak tightly in a gesture of pain and to hide her relief.

As the car made a U-turn another pair of headlights appeared at the entrance to Frascati Street. Drawing nearer, Elizabeth could see that it was Lubienski.

The two automobiles stopped in the middle of the street facing in different directions. She saw Lubienski get out to talk to his foreign minister. Then he returned to his car and pulled it to the curb.

Lubienski got out again and joined Beck. Helpless, Elizabeth could only stand there, watching them disappear into the night.

"Well, at least he had the presence of mind to leave Fokczynski's keys on the front seat," Elizabeth said to Jack Shelly. Nervously, she tried to fit another Craven A into her cigarette holder. It broke. "Oh damn!"

Her guests and the help had gone. The party, at least, had been a smashing success. On leaving, a tipsy Edward Fokczynski had confided, "It just goes to show you don't need Count Lubienski to have a good time."

"I think you ought to pack," Shelly said. "He can't know what you said to Beck, and when he invents yet another story, the alarm bells are sure to go off."

"What about the plans?"

"If he doesn't get arrested, he can get them to me."

"Where will I go?"

"A safe house in Danzig for a few days, then a boat to Stockholm or Helsinki."

"I meant, what will happen to me?"

"Back to Arthur, I suppose. I'm sorry, Elizabeth, but it's better than a Polish jail."

"Can't you get Michael out?"

"Would he come?"

"He's talked about us running away together. The more I manipulate him the more devoted he becomes. God, what will happen to him?"

Before Shelly could say anything, the door chimes rang. Elizabeth crushed out her cigarette and started eagerly for the foyer. Shelly stopped her.

"Let it ring again," he mouthed silently and moved toward the balcony. The chimes rang a second time. He stepped outside and motioned for her to follow.

"We can't jump four floors," she whispered. A quiet knock began and rapidly grew more insistent. "You hide out here. I'll answer it," Elizabeth decided.

When she turned the knob, the door was pushed open in her face.

"I did it! I did it!" A flushed and excited Count Lubienski swept her up and carried her into the apartment.

"You got the plans?"

"I told Beck all about us!"

"Michael"—Elizabeth caught her breath—"I think he's known for some time."

"Yes, but not like this." He sat her down.

"What did you say?" She forgot all about the Enigma.

"He brought it up. Whatever did you two talk about? Well, it doesn't matter." Lubienski made straight for the decanter of Scotch. "I was glad he didn't ask me where I'd been! He just wanted to know my intentions toward you."

"What are they?"

"I'm going to divorce my wife so that I can marry you."

Elizabeth was nonplussed. "What about my husband?"

"You're going to get a divorce too!"

What gall! She tried to control her anger. "And how did our dear Colonel Beck react to all this?"

Lubienski took a large gulp of Scotch. "He hit the roof, isn't that how you say it?" He smiled, but the look was a little uncertain. "He said it was 'Unthinkable. International developments rule it out!'" The steam seemed to go out of him as he repeated Beck's words. "If I persisted in what he called 'this folly,' he said I'd have to leave the service. If I changed my mind, he'd allow me to go on seeing you, but only if I were much more discreet. I believe he's actually jealous! He added that I'd have to bring my wife to all official functions. Imagine!" He concluded with a burst of defiance.

Elizabeth turned her back on him and lit another cigarette. "Colonel Beck's right, Michael. I can't be responsible for destroying your career or wrecking your marriage!"

Lubienski's jaw went slack. "But don't you love me?"

"I don't know what I'm capable of." She faced him. "I'm a loner really. I come and I go and no bones broken, and no hearts either, I hope. I don't like broken hearts." She went to the bar and poured herself a Scotch. "I'm not sentimental at all. Does that shock you? Can you understand that, Michael?"

He had dropped onto the sofa. His head was in his hands.

"But I love you," he said miserably.

"I have to be *free*." Elizabeth's tone became softer. "That you *must* accept."

"Do you mind if I intrude on this delicate scene?" Shelly stepped in from the balcony. His clothes looked a mess, as if he had tried to climb down the drainpipe and failed.

"How long have you been listening to us?" Lubienski demanded indignantly.

"Not long enough to find out whether you got the bloody pictures of the bloody plans!"

"That's all either of you care about!" Furious, Lubienski sprang from the sofa and headed for the door. "You want your 'bloody pictures'?" He reached into his pocket. "Well, here they are!" He hurled the little camera down onto the marble foyer floor and shattered it into bits.

Chapter 23

The Broadway Buildings, London—
July 8, 1938

"Stephenson's being a pest, so I've been asked by C to have this little get-together," Menzies began. "He's understandably eager to learn about your progress with the Enigma."

Dilly Knox glanced uncomfortably over at Denniston. "May I be frank?" Knox shifted his anxious gaze to the note taker.

"Please," Menzies commanded gently, but saying nothing to deter his secretary from recording Knox's comments.

"It's been a disaster," Knox sighed.

"But I thought Cynthia got you the plans."

"Not all of them. The camera was broken and some of the pictures ruined. Still we thought we had the drawings for all the vital bits, but somehow . . . " His voice trailed away.

"Cynthia suggests the French could help," Captain Lance offered.

"Bloody Frogs!" Denniston exploded. "It turns out they've been holding out on us for years! Had an agent in the German Chi-Stelle and gave the take to the Poles! That's their gratitude to us for saving their necks in the war!"

"Agree with you there." Menzies lit his second cigar of the morning. "Lost most of my Eton chums at Ypres."

"We built a machine according to Cynthia's plans," Knox explained, "and we've applied everything the French have finally given us to a number of German messages. Still, all we get is nonsense."

"How am I to explain this to C?" Menzies's voice was bored, deadly.

"He has to understand the Poles are five years ahead of us," Denniston complained. "We've much to learn even with the Polish plans to the Enigma."

"If they are the plans to the Enigma," Knox interjected. Denniston shot him a warning look.

"What do you mean?" Menzies seemed genuinely interested in the conversation for the first time.

"Oh, don't start," Denniston protested. "It's Dilly's old song that the whole thing's a deception. A plot between the Germans and Poles to keep us chasing after chimeras."

"Well, the plans don't work, and that's a fact," Knox declared. "The photographs are spoiled just enough so that we think there's something we haven't got right, that something's wrong with our approach."

"Perish the thought," Denniston murmured loud enough for the note taker to record it.

"And I consider it passing strange," Knox continued, "that our agent suddenly has no contact with her Polish source, so we've no ability to follow-up."

"Shelly reports they had a lovers' quarrel," Menzies observed. "He witnessed it."

"Such things can be staged," Knox noted.

"So you think our agent is in league with the Poles and Germans?"

"Look at the facts. A twenty-two-year-old American girl suddenly provides intelligence that Sidney Reilly would envy?"

"Hold on," Lance protested. "We found her, not the other way around."

"So why has Colonel Beck allowed one of his closest aides to carry on openly with Cynthia?"

"The Poles are playing all sides at this point."

Menzies drew long and hard on his cigar. The smoke drifted up to add to the yellow patina of the ceiling and walls of his office. "What would make you a believer, Dilly?"

"Clear text."

"And what does that require?"

"An Enigma machine. Not on paper. A real one."

Saski Park, Warsaw—
July 18, 1938

"You've got to see Lubienski again," Shelly demanded. He was sweating in his white wool suit as they walked along one of the wide paths through the formal gardens.

"Don't be a bully," Elizabeth responded. She stopped at a cart to buy an ice cream.

"It's not just me," he said, exasperated. "And it's not just Broadway. Lady Kennard's on my neck about you. She sees no reason for you to be in Warsaw. I've only held her in check so far by telling the ambassador that your contacts with Lubienski are crucially important. He's hated it, but gone along. Now, with you putting Lubienski off at every turn . . ."

"And how do you know that?" She let her irritation show. "Is it you that's tapping my telephone and following me everywhere?"

"At this point Elizabeth, you've got the secret services of at least three nations keeping track of you."

"Well *our* secret service can relax. I know what I'm doing."

"If you think"—Shelly pursed his lips to measure his words—"that this other young man, Adam, can replace Count Lubienski as a source you're gravely mistaken."

For several weeks, since Lubienski had stormed out of her apartment, Elizabeth had been seeing another young officer at the Foreign Ministry, Adam Kianowski. The two of them were out every night at the same spots she used to go to with Lubienski: the Theatre Ateneum in Czerwonego Krzyza and the Narodowy in Plac Teatralny; the QPQ; dancing at the Adria and the Aquarium; dinner at the Bagatelka and the Gastronomja; oriental food at the Mikado, and even lunch at The Lunch on Nalewki Street. By crossing paths with Lubienski, she was proving that she could have a marvelous time without him. And when he called her, or sent notes or flowers, she consistently refused to respond.

"He's going to give up on you," Shelly complained worriedly.

Elizabeth looked at him and shook her head. "Men can be so stupid, sometimes," she said.

Behind the Warsaw Opera stood the Brühl Palace, a grand eighteenth-century confection that was the home of the Foreign Ministry. As he often had before meeting Elizabeth, Count Lubienski was taking a break in the evening to attend the opera. Afterward, he planned to return to his office to read and summarize the late cables from the Polish embassies in Berlin, Prague, Paris, and London for Colonel Beck's breakfast reading. With each passing week the reports on the crisis over Czechoslovakia had been growing more ominous. The Soviet Union had said it would come to the defense of Czechoslovakia against Nazi Germany. Paris had declared that its commitment to Prague was "indisputable."

If the opera offered Count Lubienski an escape from Europe's agonies, it provided little respite from his own. Almost every time he attended, he would see Elizabeth Pack, looking radiant and beautiful on the arm of Adam Kianowski. In fact, there seemed no place in the city where he could go without running into them. And tonight, there they were again sitting in the first tier, laughing and whispering together throughout the first two acts of Moniuszko's *Halka*. It was maddening! What did she see in the little worm? He was a mere assistant desk officer for the Balkans!

From his box looking down on her through opera glasses, Lubienski could see Elizabeth in her sky-blue dress, its tight bodice pushing up her breasts so that they quivered as she laughed. An ache ran through him. He couldn't bear it! Excusing himself to the others in his box, he went directly to the bar. Two quick vodkas and he felt he was getting control of himself. He still had work to do that evening, so he decided to switch to champagne.

Standing in the still-empty foyer, he could hear the music swelling for the second act finale. *Halka* always moved him deeply, made him feel his Polishness and his pride. But tonight, the tragedy of a squire who traduces a peasant girl made him feel ashamed of himself. He had betrayed his country and his marriage for a woman who now openly humiliated him. What had he done to deserve such treatment? Only declared that he loved her and wanted to marry her! He finished his champagne and ordered another vodka.

A roar of applause signaled the second act curtain, and people began pouring out into the foyer. Lubienski knew that Elizabeth would head for the promenade room. There, under a vaulted ceiling covered by frescoes of battling gods and warriors, the audience stretched its legs by forming two concentric circles, each proceeding in opposite directions around the long narrow room. He could imagine Elizabeth and Adam joining one of the circles, strolling arm and arm, nodding and smiling to the important figures in Warsaw society. Hating himself, Lubienski could not stay away. Downing the vodka, he made his way to the promenade room.

And when he saw them, her hand gripping Adam's arm, their bodies touching as they walked, their eyes flashing with intimacy, Lubienski felt impaled on a pike, like one of the soldiers painted on the ceiling. He no longer cared about shame or humiliation. The whole charade had to stop!

He joined the outside circle. Everyone else seemed to be part of a group, chatting, laughing, enjoying themselves. He never felt so utterly alone. At the far end of the room, Elizabeth, in the inner circle, turned toward him. He saw a flash of recognition on her face and then she averted her eyes. As they approached one another, he realized that she was going to ignore him.

"Elizabeth," he called out.

She turned away as if to whisper into Adam's ear.

"Elizabeth!" he shouted, and reached for her. Heads turned, the promenade stopped, and strollers in both directions started piling up. A thrill went through the crowd. A scene was taking place!

"Take your hands off her!" Adam demanded.

"Shut up," Lubienski ordered, "or I'll have your pig's ass shipped off to Bulgaria."

"Michael," Elizabeth declared, "you're drunk!"

"Drunk? I'm destroyed! Devastated! A dog dragged through the dirt!" Tears started down his face, and he couldn't control them. "My God! What you've done to me!" He grabbed her arm.

Adam raised his fist, but Elizabeth turned on him. "Don't you dare strike him!"

Count Michael Lubienski sank to his knees, clutching the hem of her dress. "I just want to see you. Talk to you."

"Get up, Michael," Elizabeth ordered. "Adam, help him."

They both lifted Lubienski to his feet, and began to walk him through the tittering crowd. There was nothing like scandal to give zest to an evening of opera.

In the corridor near the grand staircase, they sat Lubienski down on a marble bench.

"Adam," Elizabeth said gently, "be a dear and leave us alone for a minute." Looking rejected, the young man headed for the bar.

Lubienski felt consumed by remorse. "I've embarrassed everyone." He could not look at her. "Oh God, I don't care!" He seized her face and kissed her. Elizabeth jerked away and slapped him hard.

That sobered him. "I'm sorry," he pleaded. "I'm coming undone. I don't know what to do!" The tears were pouring down again. "I must talk to you! See you! Please!" He was begging.

"You know my phone's tapped. My letters opened. I'm followed almost everywhere. The only privacy I've got is in public. Are you determined enough to brave that?"

"Anything you say."

"Sunday then. At noon. Take the road on the other side of the river. Go past the embassy's summer lodge."

"But where will we meet?"

Adam had returned. The third act was starting. Elizabeth stood up.

"Just keep driving south. I'll find you."

It was the first warm day of the summer and the British embassy's riverside retreat swarmed with families and children. On the terrace overlooking the beach, Elizabeth found Shelly swimming in a gin and tonic.

"You look like a happy man," she said.

"You're making me so," he admitted. "How do you think it will go?"

"You know I do care for him." She took off her hat and

sat down. "I'm afraid I'm going to ruin him."

"That's my girl!" Shelly toasted her.

She frowned. "Anyway, I think what Broadway wants is quite mad."

He looked at his watch. "The car is the green Opel four-door." He handed her the keys. "When you're done, bring it to my flat and I'll drive you home to the Villa Frascati. We can come back here tomorrow to pick up your car. Were you followed?"

"Right across the road. Obvious as can be."

"Well, wear my hat." He handed her a floppy Panama. "Maybe you'll fool them."

Elizabeth planned to wait inside the driveway to the lodge until she saw Lubienski's Fiat go by. She would then pull out and follow him for several miles making sure that neither of them were being tailed.

It worked smoothly. Lubienski was shocked to see her wave as she passed by him. He raced down the highway after her, finally catching up when she had to slow down behind a fragrant manure wagon. Soon they were again hurtling down the road, past truck gardens and tin-roofed farmhouses, along the crest of levies built to hold back the Vistula and through spare villages of bare unpainted stucco and shoeless children.

Shortly beyond the twenty-kilometer mark, he saw Elizabeth turn off toward the river along a dirt road lined with bushes and aspen. Soon he was following two muddy tracks running beside a split-rail fence that crossed a deep green pasture dotted with black-and-white Holsteins. When the ruts gave out, Lubienski found himself driving upon a carpet of wild flowers, purple clover, and yellow buttercups.

Ahead, Elizabeth's car navigated around a fallen tree and came to a halt under a stand of willows on a grassy bank above the broad, flat river. Before he could reach her, she had leaped from her car and was racing toward the water, progressively shedding her sandals, then her cotton blouse, then her brassiere, pausing only to wiggle out of her peasant skirt. He skidded to a stop, and without hesitating dashed after her. She was already splashing into the sandy shallows, her breasts bare and sparkling in the sunlight. As he sloshed toward her through the water, she stopped on a sandbar, and smiling mischievously, bent to peel off her underpants. Just as he reached out to grab her, Elizabeth laughed and dove into the deep water.

He plunged in after her. The freezing river came as a shock. Lubienski suddenly felt extremely heavy as the water filled his clothes. He could barely lift his arms to take a stroke and kicking was impossible. His legs were dragged down by the weight of his pants and shoes. He stopped trying to swim in order to take off his jacket, but found it difficult to keep his head above water. Then he sensed the current pulling him out from the shore, moving him faster and faster downstream. Water filled his mouth when he tried to breathe. He struggled with his coat, but it was a tangle. He went under. He was drowning! Terrified, he gave a powerful kick and broke the surface, gasping, coughing, and thrashing.

"Elizabeth!" he cried and began to sink again. His jacket had wrapped over his head so that he could no longer see. Desperately he held his breath until his lungs felt like they would explode. In panic, he exhaled and suddenly sank deeper. He fought not to inhale, but his body refused to obey. The water rushed into his lungs strangling, burning, sending a blackness into his brain. And as he slipped over the edge of consciousness, he could sense being lifted up, being transported, as if the angels had already come down from heaven to claim him.

His throat and chest felt on fire but the rest of him trembled with cold. Lubienski opened his eyes. Elizabeth lay next to him on the sand, peacefully absorbing the midday sun. She was completely naked. Beads of water gleamed on her stomach, breasts, and thighs. A flurry of pale freckles were spreading across her chest. And her skin was so smooth. Was he alive, or was this a dream of death? He had to touch.

"Don't." She turned to him, her eyes nearly chartreuse in the sunlight.

He jerked back.

"Are you all right?" Her voice softened.

"I thought I had died. Then I thought I was in heaven."

"You went down twice."

"Thank you."

They lay side by side in silence for a moment. He reached for her again.

She sat up and pushed his hand away.

The movement of her body made his flesh groan. "Why?" he muttered miserably.

"I'm not trying to make you suffer," she said in earnest. "I'm trying to protect you."

"I know what I must do to have you." He shuddered uncontrollably again.

"That's my point, Michael. The things I ask of you, you must not do for me. I don't want you to hate yourself, and I don't want you to come to hate me."

What the hell did she want? Lubienski felt angry and confused. But he said nothing, because she now was kneeling next to him, her hands stroking his face.

"I want you to appreciate what you've been doing for your country." She helped him slip off his jacket and began unbuttoning his shirt. Her lips were warm against his chest. "I want you to be proud of yourself," she murmured. Her hand had reached into his pants. "Future generations will see you as a hero in the struggle against Germany."

"But we're on their side. . . . "

"No, no." She smothered his mouth with kisses, while she caressed him. "Time and again you've told me Poland's future lies with us."

Her words seemed surreal. Lubienski could not argue. His mind was shutting down and his body taking over. "Yes . . . yes." He lay back and she knelt across him, gently, purposefully, reuniting her body with his. He was home. Home, in a sweetness Lubienski had feared he would never feel again.

He forgot the pain in his chest and throat. He forgot his fear and guilt. There was only Elizabeth fondling, touching, moving above him with the sun making a halo of gold in her hair.

And then his strength returned with an urgent need to possess her. He was on his feet, her legs wrapped around him, splashing in circles through the shallows, her back arched as he devoured her breasts, the laughter and crying bursting out of both of them, until finally, he placed her on the grassy bank and slowly lowered himself into her.

They lay still, staring soundlessly into each other's eyes. Her body clutched him. Her breath came faster. As her grip intensified, her eyes focused harder. Still she did not move. He tried to disengage; her body refused. It massaged him, drawing his passion toward a peak. Suspended above her, he felt himself a captive, his desire enmeshed in her internal rhythms that relentlessly provoked him, urged him, goaded him. Lubienski started to cry out. His body yearned for release. Yet he was not quite there. In exquisite agony, he hovered on the brink, and Elizabeth, teasing and tugging, could not pull him over.

So she pushed him off. And with that sudden decompression he exploded.

"I'm sorry," she gasped.

"No, no," he said, desperately pulling her against him as his pleasure surged over and over, at last becoming painful before it would subside.

Lubienski realized he must have slept. For how long, he did not know. The shadows of the willows had moved over him. He saw that his clothes were spread out on the sand bar to dry. Elizabeth stood in the river washing her hair. A barge moved silently along the far shore, ignoring them. Overhead, large white clouds moved majestically across the summer sky. He was suffused with a vast contentment.

She came up the bank, drying herself with a towel. "Are you hungry?" she asked. "I've a picnic."

"Ravenous." But as they lay there naked on the grass, he found himself picking at the wursts and sausages and salads spread out before him. The calm had ebbed away.

"Something wrong?" she asked.

"I can't help wondering what you will want me to do next."

"It's not so formidable," she answered lightly. "We need to get ourselves an Enigma machine."

Lubienski laughed. "That's ridiculous, Elizabeth. You're joking."

"No, I'm deadly serious."

How could she change so suddenly? He felt a tickle of fear in his abdomen. "I can't imagine how it could be done."

"AVA made a dozen of them, or so you said."

"But they're all being used twenty-four hours a day!"

"Well, you'd better find a way."

"Better?" The tickle had grown into a puncture of anxiety. "What if I refuse?"

"My colleagues are quite keen on this, Michael. I'm afraid that if you don't cooperate, they'll reveal how you helped us get Hitler's plans for Czechoslovakia."

Lubienski was stunned. What kind of devil was she? "Colonel Beck would never believe you!" he declared. Then she reached across to him.

"It won't be Colonel Beck," she said, taking him in hand. "They'll tell the Germans."

With that, she once more started stroking him, and despite her threats, her reckless ideas, and her suicidal determination that he feared would be the death of them both, he again began responding to her touch.

MOST SECRET JIC/P/0117/22/38
EYES ONLY FOR PRINCIPALS
To: The Joint Intelligence Committee Operations Working Group
Subject: Operation Encounter
Approval requested for following operation.

1. Purpose is to obtain principal German cipher machine (Enigma) used for radio communications by all armed forces and security services.

2. To this end, special Commando unit consisting of a dozen officers and men will be infiltrated into Poland by SIS. (See Annex A to Operations Plan attached.)

3. Unit will intercept Wehrmacht communications van carrying an Enigma transiting Danzig corridor from East Prussia. (See Annex B attached.)

4. Under Polish German agreements, German army units have the right to cross Polish territory on a periodic basis. Communications vans usually precede the main body by 4–6 hours. By allegedly reading the Wehrmacht Enigma messages, the Poles know the precise schedule of such transits. Our agent in Poland will provide intelligence for proper timing

and coordination of attack on van described in the
attached Operations Plan.

5. Team and Enigma machine will be exfiltrated via
   submarine on Baltic coast. (See Annex C attached.)
6. Target for initiating operation late August.
7. Costs for non-naval expenditures to be covered by
   supplemental Treasury allocation T/S—5487m.

C

MOST SECRET July 26, 1938

Eyes Only for C
From: JIC
Subject: Operation Encounter

1. Foreign Office considers proposed operation too
   high profile, too risky, and potentially extremely
   damaging to British relations with both Poland and
   Germany at a time when the Government is seeking
   to ease tensions over Czechoslovakia.
2. Accordingly, Operation Encounter is disapproved.
3. Whatever substitute plan may be developed must be
   carried out with assets in place, be small in scale and
   utterly deniable.

MOST SECRET/CYNTHIA

FOR BROADWAY
WARSAW SENDS 0853/2/8/38/14:25GMT

CYNTHIA HAS DEVELOPED ALTERNATIVE PLAN FOR
CARRYING OUT VAN INTERCEPT. DETAILS VIA POUCH.
REQUEST PRELIMINARY AUTHORITY TO PROCEED ON
CONTINGENCY BASIS. FINAL APPROVAL NEEDED BY 15
SEPTEMBER.

SHELLY

Queen Anne's Gate, London— September 15, 1938

"The next transit is September 25." Jack Shelly placed the
pointer on a rickety easel as he concluded his presentation.

"I won't deny it's audacious, but it's the best we can do under the circumstances."

This was the first time he had ever been in the residence of the chief of the secret service. In addition to C, the meeting in the library was also attended by Menzies, Denniston, Knox, and Captain Lance. Instead of books, the library walls were covered with drawings, paintings, and engravings of an armada of Royal Navy dreadnoughts.

Captain Lance took advantage of the awed silence. "May I comment? I find Cynthia's plan audacious to the point of being foolhardy. It depends critically on split-second timing. She's under constant surveillance by the Polish secret police and possibly the Gestapo. She and Lubienski are trying to do the work of a dozen commandos!"

"Cynthia anticipated such an objection," Shelly responded. "She wrote a note for me to read." He unfolded a paper from his breast pocket. "May I?"

C nodded.

"'Gentlemen. You have repeatedly impressed upon me the vital importance of obtaining the secret of the Enigma. I have given much in the effort to do so, and now I am prepared to give my all. This is not because I enjoy being reckless. A grave conflict looms in Europe. We are already engaged in the secret skirmishes that precede war. I am volunteering for this mission as would any soldier. I can only pray that my commanders have the courage of their troops.' Signed, 'Cynthia.'"

"As you can see," Shelly continued as if to apologize for the tone of her message, "having gotten the bit in her teeth, Cynthia refuses to give up."

"I'm not criticizing her," Captain Lance insisted. "It's the weak sisters in the JIC who vetoed a sensible operation. It's so typical of frightened bureaucrats to cut back our plans to the point that they'll surely fail. . . . "

"Yes, yes." C cut him off. "It's dangerous, no doubt. But Hitler's deadline on Czechoslovakia's only a week away. That's likely to mean a state of belligerence with Germany and Poland by the end of the month. Today"—his voice became more grave—"the cabinet will put the Royal Navy on full alert."

The others tried to hide their surprise.

"Under the circumstances," he sighed, "it's essential to make the attempt. After all, Cynthia's made clear that if she and Count Lubienski fail, they should be considered casualties of war."

Chapter 24

"We're evacuating!" Mrs. Norton announced. "All women, children, and nonessential personnel. I need your help tomorrow to organize a convoy to Danzig."

Elizabeth stared at the phone. What could she say? "I'm afraid I can't. I'm helping Jack Shelly in the Passport Office. We're quite overwhelmed."

"The ambassador's wife specified that you be in the first group to leave Warsaw," Mrs. Norton insisted.

"Tell her I appreciate her concern," Elizabeth cooed. "But it would smack of favoritism."

She immediately called Shelly. Keeping her voice calm for the benefit of anyone tapping her phone, she relayed Mrs. Norton's message.

"I'll take care of Mrs. Ambassador. How's it going?"

What kind of a question was that with half the intelligence services in Central Europe listening in? "Jack," she responded lightly, "you know I never talk about my private life."

For more than a month, Elizabeth and Count Lubienski had worked to establish a pattern that she hoped would enable her to escape later that morning from the watchful eye of the Defensywa, the Polish counterintelligence police. As the crisis over Czechoslovakia deepened, their surveillance had intensified to the point of harassment. Lubienski claimed he could do nothing about it. He even argued it was to their benefit, since it would show that they were

having a completely innocent affair. However, to gain some
privacy, she and Lubienski spent every Saturday night on
board the *Kościuszko*, a side-wheel steamer that made
weekend excursions down the Vistula. It was the only place
they were not followed. But every Sunday evening when
the boat returned to Warsaw, her watchers were waiting at
the dock in their telltale black Chevrolet sedan.

Elizabeth checked herself in the dressing table mirror.
The days now gave a crisp hint of autumn, and she had
chosen a green tweed suit with a pleated skirt along with
a new felt hat with a bright collection of pheasant feathers
in the brim. Standing back, she decided that her low-heeled
brown alligator pumps gave a suitably sporty panache to
the ensemble. More important, she would be able to run
when she had to. She judged herself ready.

The maid helped carry her two suitcases down to the taxi.
Since she usually took only one bag, Elizabeth prayed that
her watchers would not become suspicious about the second. It contained pieces and parts of the Enigma machine
that Dilly Knox had fabricated according to Polish plans.
Smuggled into Warsaw in the British diplomatic pouch,
they would play a vital part in covering up the operation.

The *Kościuszko* was tied up at Riverside North under the
battlements of the Old Castle. With the black Chevrolet
dutifully following behind, Elizabeth's taxi turned at the
entrance to the Old Town, taking Nowy Zjazd, the New
Descent, under the viaduct Pancer to the steamer dock. Lubienski, waiting at the foot of the gangplank, embraced her
while a cabin boy took her bags. The chase car stopped a
few yards away, but no one got out. As Elizabeth looked
back at them, she could not help wondering if they sat there
all weekend.

A steward showed them to a tiny cabin on the main deck.
It was wide enough for only a small double bed, an armoire
and a sink. Lubienski appeared flushed and tense. Before
he could say a word, Elizabeth put her finger to her lips.
She had become worried that the secret police did not follow them on board because they had an agent among the
crew, a microphone in their cabin, or both. Until they were
off the boat, they would play carefully the role of lovers.

From the anxious look on Lubienski's face, Elizabeth wondered if he would be up to his part.

When she felt the unmistakable sensation of the boat floating free of its moorings, Elizabeth pulled Lubienski outside to the rail. Instead of the usual crowd, there were only a handful of other passengers on deck and well-wishers on the dock. Autumn and the prospect of war over Czechoslovakia was keeping people at home. That made her uneasy. It might be more difficult for their absence to remain unnoticed when they slipped away from the boat at Toruń.

As the surging side wheel pushed the boat away from the shore, Elizabeth took in the spires of the Old Town, peacefully gleaming in the morning sun. She felt excited and apprehensive but, above all, a surprising sense of being free. A glance down on the dock, however, gave her a sudden chill. One of the secret police was out leaning against the side of the car pointing something in her direction. It was a camera. They were taking her picture. They had never done that before. Why now?

The trip down the broad placid river proved uneventful, except for a fight that broke out on the rear deck among members of a wedding party that had consumed too much Goldwasser. In typical Polish fashion, there was more pushing than punching, and the only knockdowns were scored against tables and chairs.

At Toruń, the *Kościuszko* docked for the night. As was their habit, Elizabeth and Count Lubienski dined early and went for a stroll in town. That also gave them a chance to check out the warehouse where their car was waiting. As soon as they returned to the boat, they retired to their cabin.

At four in the morning, Lubienski stole out on deck and down the gangplank. Half an hour later, having changed into slacks and a sweater, Elizabeth followed him. She locked the door behind her, and dropping to her knees, inserted a wire tool to trip the inside bolt. Before slipping away, she hung the PROSZĘ NIE PRZESZKADZAĆ, PLEASE DO NOT DISTURB, sign on the doorknob.

The large bright red Aero Type 50 roadster with silver exhaust manifolds flowing out of the hood gleamed in the dim light of the warehouse. As she thought, the car was perfect for the operation, but getting it had been a three-week battle with the SIS comptroller. While Lubienski busied himself with strapping their luggage to the rear trunk lid, Elizabeth took a nap in the front seat. With the dawn, they were off into the Polish countryside, heading east with Lubienski at the wheel.

The early Sunday morning roads were empty of traffic. Birch trees flashed by on either side, their leaves already turning a bright yellow. In the fields, the harvest appeared well advanced. Peasants had rolled up the hay like giant crullers from Ziemiańska's confectionery. For long stretches, the ground showed dark scars where the potatoes had been ripped up from the earth. Unlike England and France, Poland's farms were organized into large estates, but nowhere did Elizabeth see the huge combines, threshers, and other machinery that would cover Minnesota at that time of year. She took off her hat and let the wind blow through her hair. It was a glorious early fall day, and she found it hard to accept the fact that it would end in violence and death.

From time to time they would come up behind horse-drawn carts that looked like long rowboats on wheels—complete with a pointed prow where the farmers perched to drive the horses. Laden with hay, the wagons sometimes filled the whole road and crept along at two miles an hour.

"I hope we don't run into one of these at the wrong moment," Elizabeth called out to Lubienski over the rushing wind. "It could ruin our timing."

"I hope that's our biggest problem."

"What's wrong?"

He said nothing.

"What is it?" There must be a secret reason he had been so quiet and moody. "Don't keep bad news to yourself."

"It's more like no news," he finally admitted. "We planned on confirming the movement time of the XIX Panzer Corps, but it hasn't been possible."

"Why not?"

"On the fifteenth, the Germans changed their keying procedure for the Enigma. It's part of their preparations for invading Czechoslovakia. We haven't read a single message since then."

"You mean our last information on the van's schedule is ten days old?"

"Yes. And since then, the Germans have been mobilizing, moving units all over the place."

"Why didn't you tell me? This could be a colossal waste of time."

"We can stop right now." He said in a tone of relief and started to pull over to the side of the road.

"No, dammit!" Elizabeth swore. "It's our only chance! What's the likelihood that they'll stick to their schedule?"

Lubienski shrugged. "We'll just have to count on the Germans being Germans."

Their destination was Jabłonowo, a small town at a rail junction in the Lutryna River valley near the East Prussian border. Because Elizabeth had been so closely followed, she had been forced to do all of her planning from photographs, maps, and timetables supplied by Lubienski and Shelly. Now, she wanted to take a look for herself.

It was much as she had expected. Outside of Toruń, the countryside had been dead flat, as it was for hundreds of miles in almost every direction. But now, to the northeast, she could see the land rising into a range of low hills that ran into East Prussia. They followed Route 52 until a turnoff shortly before Brodnica. The secondary road took them over the hills and down into the river valley. As they approached the town, she found that the inn was located precisely two kilometers before the even deeper descent into Jabłonowo. More village than town, it consisted mainly of poor wood houses with a handful of two-story stucco buildings and an old brick church. A thicket of willows separated the town from the Lutryna River, which was crossed by a one-lane high arched bridge better suited to oxcarts than automobiles or trucks. On the other side, the road intersected a railroad track before proceeding across the flat farmland, all the way to the Vistula and the Polish-German border beyond. If everything went according to plan, the Wehrmacht communications van would never reach its destination.

With a stopwatch, they retraced the route several times, then returned over the bridge through the town and past the inn until the odometer counted off a kilometer and a half. At the first left turn, they took a dirt path through a small pasture and into a stand of fir trees. There, as planned, stood the big Ursis dump truck, with the name of the well-known construction firm, K. RUDZKA, lettered on the side. Lubienski got out of the car and tried to start it. They held their breath until the big diesel finally rattled into life.

"So far, so good," he said, returning to the car and offering Elizabeth a cigarette. "Be careful when you get to the bridge"—he exhaled—"too fast, and the car could bounce right over the side into the river."

She nodded and checked her watch. It was 11:40. If their information was still correct, Elizabeth should spot the communications van shortly after noon. Adhering to their usual pattern, the Germans would stop at the inn for a meal lasting about forty-five minutes, leaving no later than one o'clock. Elizabeth had to delay them so that they arrived at the bridge sometime between 1:14 and 1:16. Too early, and the plan would unravel, and she would be in grave jeopardy. Too late, and it would be too late.

"Should something happen"—Lubienski interrupted her thoughts—"I want you to know I love you."

She reached up and gave him a kiss. He responded eagerly. As his hands started to move over her body, she gently pushed him away. "It's time you got moving. We've time for that tonight."

"If we're alive." He let go of her and climbed back into the truck. After a prolonged grinding of gears, he lurched down the dirt path toward the highway.

"Do you know how to drive that thing?" Elizabeth called out. Lubienski merely waved back and crashed another gear change. Elizabeth winced. If he did not arrive at exactly the right time . . . She didn't want to think about it.

*"Die Fahnen hoch! Die Reihen dicht geschlossen.
S.A. marschiert mit ruhigem festem Schritt . . ."*

As von Aufenaker's unit rode through the Polish countryside, Sergeant Hans Beekman was leading them in song—as usual, a rousing chorus of the Nazi anthem, the "Horst Wessel Lied."

"Raise the banners! Stand rank on rank together.
S.A. march on, with a steady, quiet tread . . ."

Sitting in the front seat with the Enigma machine between his feet, Lieutenant von Aufenaker shook his head. The stupid Nazis were always marching around in circles, he thought disparagingly. But at last they were preparing to march forward, and he was thrilled to be part of it.

He had objected to his assignment at the outset, but when he was sent to his home region of East Prussia he felt even worse. Relatives and friends asked why was he not in a combat unit, as if he had made a cowardly choice. Added to this humiliation, Sergeant Beekman had been assigned to his small group. Beekman was a Nazi and an informer. Von Aufenaker complained to his commander, who stiffly informed him that the Gestapo insisted that every Enigma unit have a Party member for security. That made him even more angry, a Prussian officer being watched by a plumber's son from Düsseldorf! But the other two members of his unit were solid fellows. Fritz, his driver, was a veteran of the Great War and took no lip from Beekman, and his radioman, Kurt, was a schoolteacher who kept a diary—giving the little Nazi something to worry about.

The only good thing about his posting was that he could get home to his family estate on weekends to ride his horses. However, that also meant that his social contact with the ladies was confined to Freidle von Papke. She was attractive and charming, and ever since they were children, both families had expected that they would marry. He had no objection to this, but Dietrich wanted to live a little first. Now with his unit on the move, he might at last have the romantic experiences he had been dreaming about.

When the mobilization against Czechoslovakia was begun, it looked like his unit would be left out completely. He felt crushed. But suddenly orders had come through on his Enigma machine that his *Panzergruppe* was to move out and redeploy in the second echelon behind the Sudeten front. He prayed that he might see some action at last. The weather was fair, the ground firm, perfect conditions for battle. As the van rolled down the road toward the inn at Jabłonowo, Lieutenant von Aufenaker was so full of anticipation he wondered if he could even eat.

Chapter 25

Jabłonowo Road, Poland— September 25, 1938

It was eleven fifty-five. The minutes moved slower than the patches of white cloud that floated overhead. Elizabeth focused her attention on the road. She remembered her father talking about ambushing Muslim rebels in the Philippines after the Spanish-American War. "It was generally a life of complete boredom, punctuated by moments of desperate fear," he would say. "But I never felt more alive."

Her mother hated it when her father told her his war stories. "It's nothing for a lady to know about," she would lecture. Ignoring her, he'd continue, "Oh, our boys never got killed unless the plans went wrong. Of course, the plans always went wrong."

As she sat in the car, keyed up, smoking her fifth cigarette, Elizabeth wondered if her mother wasn't right. What was she doing there? She had justified it in her mind a hundred times, but now, on the brink, she couldn't help thinking about the Germans. What would they look like? Monsters? Villains? Or just regular people with families, parents and maybe even children?

And where were they? Had they changed their itinerary in the last ten days? The thought gave her more relief than disappointment. Rummaging in her purse for another pack of cigarettes, she almost missed the van coming down the highway as it vanished behind the trees. Quickly, she fumbled to start the car. When the Aero's engine fired, it sounded like a popcorn machine. Blue smoke poured out of the exhaust from the two-cycle motor.

Stepping hard on the gas, she found that the car moved forward sluggishly. My God, what a gutless wonder! Then, as it gained momentum, she felt the rear end sliding uneasily on the muddy track. Oh, no, don't get bogged down, Elizabeth thought desperately. With one foot on the gas and the other on the brake, she nursed it across the pasture, using sheer willpower to levitate the car over water-filled holes left by Lubienski's truck.

When she finally reached the road, the van was out of sight. But she took her time following it. The sooner she got to the inn, the more time she would have to spend talking to them. That was one of the trickiest parts of the plan. She had carefully scripted what she would say, and had taken special German language instruction for several weeks, but she was still far from fluent.

As she approached the inn, Elizabeth's concern at being too early evaporated; the van was nowhere to be seen. They hadn't stopped! She stepped on the gas again, and the car slowly gained speed. Where did they go? Someplace else? Maybe she could still make the plan work. What if they were not stopping at all! Could she follow them? Extemporize? Extemporize what?

Already she was entering the village, but saw no sign of the van. Driving up and down the few streets she found nothing. Then she headed toward the bridge. In the thicket of willows she turned off to where Lubienski was waiting. He was shocked to see her.

"Have you seen the van?" she called to him.

"No! What's going on?"

"I've lost it. Stay here!"

She turned the car around and headed back through town the way she had come. Where the hell was it? She stopped at a crossroads. Jabłonowo had been picked because it was a shortcut from the Wehrmacht camp at Scharnau to the Pomeranian border of Germany. The van could not have turned off on the other road. And she couldn't have missed it in town.

The inn was coming up again on the left. Two old cars and a truck were parked in front. Wait! What was that in back? The van! Painted in camouflage and discreetly hidden among the trees at the rear of the inn. She swerved across the road and slid the Aero to a stop on the gravel near the front door. Taking a deep breath, she tried to calm herself for her next performance. Her watch said 12:35.

When she walked in the front door, all eyes turned toward her. The inn was a converted farmhouse with two public rooms. To the left was the dining salon with white tablecloths and patrons dressed in their Sunday best—black wool suits, black wool dresses. In the bar on the right, four German soldiers were sitting at a large round table. The bar looked even dirtier and darker than she had anticipated. The only decorations were posters for Egyptskie cigarettes and Haberbusch and Schiele beer.

Following her plan, Elizabeth asked the barman in English, "Where can I find the road to Grudziadz?" She expected that he would respond by shaking his head and otherwise indicating that he could not understand her. Then as a natural alternative she could approach the Germans.

But the barman did not cooperate. "You're American!" he exclaimed. "I'm from Chicago!"

Elizabeth was speechless.

"I live South Side twenty-five years. U.S. citizen! Speak good English, no?" He beamed.

"Extraordinary," she managed.

"Here I retire from stockyards," he added proudly. "I start real American roadhouse. Good steaks! Where you from?"

"Minnesota."

"Burr," he muttered and wrapped his arms around himself. "Colder than Chicago! Cold as Russia!"

The Germans, except for a young officer, had lost interest in their conversation.

"I will direct you." The innkeeper put an arm around her shoulders and led her toward the front door. This was going all wrong!

"No," she said a little too loud. "I'd like something to eat first." She turned to the Germans. "What are they having?"

"Sausages," he replied a little perplexed. "They look maybe different in Minnesota?"

"Sehr gut?" she asked the soldiers in German, trying to keep desperation out of her voice. Her script was in tatters.

The oldest soldier, who had heavy jowls, a gray crew cut, and a bushy mustache, answered with a burst of goose noises that she found completely incomprehensible. She looked for help from the others: the blond, fresh-faced lieutenant; a bookish corporal with wire-rim glasses; and a dark-haired scowling sergeant in his thirties. The old-timer continued grinning at her, waiting for an answer.

"He asks to know if you his sausage want," the young lieutenant said with a slight blush.

"I'll have one of my own, thank you."

When the young man translated, they all burst into laughter, except the dark-haired sergeant.

"Please, you sit down?" The lieutenant pulled over a chair from a nearby table. "Please to introduce, I am Lieutenant von Aufenaker and these are my men—Hans, Fritz, and Kurt."

"And I'm Cynthia." Elizabeth shook his hand. "Cynthia Beresford." She took a seat. "I'll have the sausages too," she said to the innkeeper from Chicago, "and some mineral water."

The Pole could not keep the disapproval from his face, muttering, "I did not know that they so much liked pig in Minnesota," as he went off to the kitchen.

Lieutenant von Aufenaker was smiling eagerly at Elizabeth as if he were trying to think of something to make conversation. "Minnesota is home of Charles Lindbergh, 'the Lone Eagle,' isn't it?"

"He was born there," she explained.

The Germans then began an animated discussion of Lindbergh, his solo flight to Paris, the kidnapping of his baby and the trial of Bruno Hauptmann the kidnapper. Elizabeth could follow only part of it, but she did not mind. The minutes were ticking away.

"Sergeant Beekman"—the lieutenant pointed to his dour companion with black hair—"believes Hauptmann was innocent and that it was all a plot to dirty the Germans."

"Who would do that?" Elizabeth asked. She anticipated the answer.

"*Juden*," the Jews, the dark sergeant said.

As she was served her bratwurst, she peeked at her

watch: 12:52. The soldiers had almost finished. Somehow she had to keep them there another fifteen minutes. "But Lindbergh is of German background. He was the victim." She began to eat slowly.

"That is how they are clever," Beekman said through Lieutenant von Aufenaker. "First the Jews bring misfortune on a great German, then they blame it on a poor one."

The others, Elizabeth noted, appeared uncomfortable, particularly the young lieutenant who was translating. Then she noticed the wooden box with the handle sitting next to his chair. That had to be the Enigma! She could just grab it and dash out the door! But she wouldn't get three steps before she got a bullet in the back.

The old-timer looked at his watch. The corporal with the glasses excused himself to go to the toilet. They were getting ready to leave, and it was not yet one.

"Lindbergh is a great admirer of Germany." Elizabeth tried to change the direction of the conversation. She was slicing her sausage thinner and thinner.

"A great admirer of Der Führer," the dark one corrected her. "Lindbergh knows America would be foolish to side with England against the Reich. We are so powerful and we are the future." Translating, the lieutenant blushed again.

The corporal with the wire-rim glasses returned to the table. It was one o'clock. She had to delay them at least five more minutes.

"Don't worry about me, I can finish eating by myself."

"Not at all," Lieutenant von Aufenaker declared. But the corporal pointed at his watch.

"To Hitler." Elizabeth raised her glass to the soldier who seemed to be a Nazi. They all obediently raised their glasses.

"You favor him?" The Nazi looked suspicious.

"He's made the trains run on time," she said with a straight face.

"In Germany, the trains have always run on time," the bookish corporal declared.

"To trains running on time!" Elizabeth said coquettishly.

"Madam, you must excuse," Lieutenant von Aufenaker

apologized. "We have a schedule." He stood and bowed with a click of his heels. "Possibly, we meet again?"

"That would be charming."

"So, my card, please. Have you one?"

"Of course." She took another minute looking through her purse. The others congregated at the door. "No, sorry, I don't." Von Aufenaker looked crestfallen.

At 1:06, he kissed her hand, picked up the Enigma and departed. A minute later the van pulled out of the drive and onto the highway.

Elizabeth paid quickly and rushed out to her car. By 1:09 she had caught up to the van on the road winding down to the town. She honked and waved. Suddenly the van put on its brakes and slowed to a crawl. Pulling out, Elizabeth could see the way was blocked by a hay wagon. It was 1:10. Only five minutes to go. Slowly they crept along behind the wagon: 1:11, then 1:12. At the entrance to the town square it came completely to a stop.

The lieutenant jumped out of the van and began arguing with the farmer. Finally after an exchange of rude gestures, it moved out of the way at 1:14. They were late!

Elizabeth stayed behind the van as it threaded its way out of the village. But the plan required her car to be in front by the time they reached the bridge. As soon as the road widened, she stepped on the gas to pass. The car responded anemically. She could see the bridge looming ahead. Her car pulled abreast of the van. They were waving at her, having fun, giving her a race. Fritz, the old man at the wheel, blew her a kiss. She moved slowly ahead. Out of the corner of her eye, she saw Lubienski's truck ready on the side road as she flashed by. The car had gathered speed, and the bridge was coming up fast.

She hit the brakes. The nose of the car dipped down, then bounced into the air as the front wheels struck the ramp of the bridge. Next, the rear wheels became airborne. Elizabeth could feel the whole car drift sideways until it slammed against the stone railing and began scraping along the right side.

Luckily, that got her pointed in the right direction as she came off the bridge. The car was under control, but she could feel the fenders rubbing against the tires. The train tracks lay ahead. If she had a blowout before reaching them, everything would be ruined.

Her watch said 1:15. The van was fifty yards behind her, coming over the bridge. As she mounted the railroad crossing, she braked again, this time more carefully. But she stopped too far beyond the tracks. For a panicky moment, she couldn't find reverse. Then she managed to back the car up to the edge of the crossing, just as the van mounted the tracks. She jumped out of the car waving her arms. The van bounced to a halt behind her.

"Something's happened to my car!" she shouted. *"Kaputt!"* In the distance she could see Lubienski approaching in his truck. The young lieutenant opened the door and stood up on the running board. "What is it?" he shouted.

"I don't know! It won't move!" she called back but her voice was lost in the shriek of a whistle from a train hurtling around a bend right toward them.

Elizabeth saw the lieutenant freeze. The van sat squarely on the tracks. The driver was working madly at the gears. But just as he managed to get the van moving backward, Lubienski and his truck slammed into their rear.

The collision hurled von Aufenaker onto the ground. He rolled over and came up with a Luger in his hand. The train was bearing down on him less than a hundred yards away. Confused, he pointed his gun at the truck, then at Elizabeth. The train's whistle screamed again and he whirled around to face it. The sound of broken glass and machine-gun fire came from the back of the van. The train closed in. The lieutenant tried to dive to one side as the locomotive plowed into the van, picking it up, tumbling it over and over down the track before casting it aside like a crushed paper cup.

The Baltic Zephyr roared by without slowing, a few startled passengers curiously peering out the windows. In a few seconds it was gone. The track was clear. The Aero and the Ursis dump truck bracketed the crossing and the space between them stood empty.

Elizabeth forced herself to move. If she did not, she knew she would go into shock.

"Are you all right?" Lubienski called out.

"Yes, and you?"

He nodded and poked two fingers through machine-gun holes in his windshield.

"We've got to get moving!" Elizabeth opened the trunk of the car and took out the bag with the bogus Enigma parts. By the time she got to the crumpled van, Lubienski was using a crowbar to force open the rear door. Inside, they found a horror. Blood was spattered everywhere. The bookish corporal's arms and legs were tangled in knots, his glasses embedded in his face. The dark-haired Nazi seemed to have come apart; his severed head, a leg, and an arm were scattered amidst the trash that had once been radio equipment. Elizabeth threw up.

"We've only got a few minutes," Lubienski said with an edge of hysteria. "The town will be all over us."

"You get the gasoline," she coughed. "I'll find the Enigma."

She feared that it too had been smashed to pieces. A few crates remained intact, but they contained paper. A trunk proved to hold dress uniforms. The Enigma was nowhere in the mass except possibly under the corporal's torso. Steeling herself, she rolled him over. Nothing.

Lubienski returned with the gasoline, and began to pour it all over the inside of the van.

"Wait! I haven't found the machine yet!" Elizabeth yelled at him.

"We can't! We'll be caught!"

"I've looked everywhere!"

"Then let's go!" He pulled her out, and threw in a match. Flames roared up.

"There's one more place!" She pulled away from him.

"It could explode!"

She rushed to the front of the van. The doors were crushed shut, but the windshield had been smashed out. The old-timer hung through one of them staring up at her with a lifeless grin.

Already the flames were surging into the driver's compartment. Elizabeth had to climb onto the body of the driver to look inside. There it was, wedged against the firewall on the passenger side, its wooden case cracked. But there it was!

"Help me, dammit!" she shouted at Lubienski, who

hovered indecisively nearby. The metal body of the van was getting too hot to touch. She reached down and grabbed hold of the handle on the case. Lubienski lifted both of them away from the van.

Stumbling back toward the car, Elizabeth clutched Lubienski's arm. "The phony parts! They have to go into the wreckage!"

"It's too late!"

"We have to, or the Germans will know!"

Lubienski raced back to the van, picked up the bag, and heaved it into the flames.

"Don't leave the gas cans!" she shouted after him. Closing the trunk, Elizabeth went around the side of the car to get in. Suddenly, she stopped. She screamed.

Lieutenant von Aufenaker had crawled halfway into the front seat; his face was a bloody mess. "Help me," he moaned.

Lubienski ran up beside her. "Oh, my God," he said. "What shall we do?"

"Please," the German whimpered.

"Get the crowbar," Elizabeth said.

While Lubienski did what he was told, she sat in the car with her hands over her ears trying to block out the sickening sound of the young man having his life beaten out of him.

Chapter 26

Warsaw—
Sunday Afternoon, September 25, 1938

BRINK OF WAR! The headlines of the *Warsaw Courier* blared from the kiosks. TROOPS ON THE MOVE. TESCHEN IS OURS! In the thirty-one hours since Elizabeth and Count Lubienski left Warsaw on the boat, the city had been put on a war footing. The government had deployed police and soldiers throughout the city. Troops and concertina wire guarded the Co-op Bank and an antiaircraft gun had been installed between the two giant stone eagles on the roof. Armored cars protected the post office and the railway station. And when Elizabeth approached the British embassy to deliver the Enigma, she was shocked to find it completely blocked off. A mob of Silver Shirts numbering in the thousands surrounded the compound, spilling into Nowy Swiat, snarling traffic. The demonstrators carried signs proclaiming TESCHEN IS POLAND, Hitler Our Savior, HANG CHAMBERLAIN. Only the surge of the mounted Horse Guards kept the crowd from tearing down the gates. A column of black smoke could be seen rising from the courtyard.

"Good Lord!" Elizabeth exclaimed. "They're burning the files!" That was the last stage of evacuation. There would be no more diplomatic pouch. How would they get the Enigma out of the country?

"Take me home," she told Lubienski.

They were driving in his Fiat with the Enigma in the trunk. Lubienski had ditched the truck in a barn not far from the "accident," and the roadster in a garage on the outskirts of Warsaw. As they turned into Ulica Frascati, Elizabeth shouted, "Stop!"

Ahead she could see four of the Defa's sinister black Chevrolets blocking the street in front of her apartment house. She pointed to the right and Lubienski quickly turned down Senacka Street, and then into a driveway that cut through the Foreign Trade Ministry. They picked up an alley on the other side that wound through a complex of heavily guarded government buildings. Elizabeth bit her lip. If the troops stopped them, searched them . . . Finally, they emerged next to the Sejm, the Polish parliament. It was surrounded by tanks. An army patrol waved them over.

Elizabeth started shaking. Lubienski arrogantly waved his Foreign Ministry identification. The soldiers saluted but were not intimidated. They wanted to see her papers as well.

"She's my wife," Lubienski protested.

They insisted. She showed her American passport.

"Actually she's my mistress," Lubienski admitted.

The officer in charge raised his eyebrows, smiled knowingly, bowed, and let them pass.

In a few minutes they had managed to get back to the downtown area. Elizabeth directed Lubienski to pull over on Długa in front of the Café Gogolewski. She had an emergency telephone number. The cashier took her time giving her a token for the pay phone. It was in the back near the coat rack.

"*Da?*" a voice answered.

"I need a return call," she said without identifying herself. "Two-four-one-seven-eight." Again she repeated the telephone number of the café and hung up.

Her stomach was empty. She had not eaten anything since the sausages at the roadhouse, but the sight of the huge cheesecakes and the smell of the strong coffee made her nauseated. Forcing herself to take deep, even breaths, Elizabeth waited. A man wanted to use the phone. She smiled and shook her head. He went away. But a few minutes later, a bullet-headed woman would not be denied. Elizabeth stood by anxiously as the woman talked without apparent haste. Outside, she could see Lubienski arguing with a mounted policeman. Michael, she silently screamed in her head, don't pull rank! Do whatever he says! Finally the woman hung up and the phone rang immediately. It was Shelly.

"Don't go home," he said first.

"I know. What's going on?"

"They have orders to arrest you."

"Do they know about—"

"No," he cut her off. "It's a general security sweep. Many of our people have been picked up."

"But I'm a diplomat!" she protested.

"Arthur's the diplomat, and he's not here."

"What should I do?"

"Did you finish your 'shopping'?"

"Yes." She could hear him sigh. When he spoke again, he had less tension in his voice.

"We've got to get you and your new purchases out of the country immediately. Do you have your American passport?"

"Yes, it's in my maiden name, Amy Thorpe." Elizabeth saw that Lubienski's car had disappeared. She felt a stab of concern.

"We'll get you on a flight this afternoon. Can you stay where you are for a few hours?"

Through the front windows of the café, she could see Lubienski pass by. He was circling the block.

"No. I'll go to Michael's. His family's away for the weekend."

"Someone will call with the time of your flight. But don't stay there too long. Once the *Kościuszko* docks, and you're not on it, that's the first place they'll come looking."

In all their days and nights together, Elizabeth had never seen Count Lubienski's home. He lived across the river in Saska Kepa, a new and fashionable residential area, which had been built since the end of the war. Unlike Warsaw with its palaces, flats, and town houses, this was a suburb of single and attached homes set on lots surrounded by grass and trees. It strongly reminded Elizabeth of Minneapolis. Riding through the curving tree-lined streets, with children playing happily in the yards and the precious bloodstained Enigma machine in the rear of their car, she had a sudden, powerful, almost desperate desire to be back in America, to be safe and content, and to be ignorant of the world.

The modesty of Count Lubienski's home surprised her and made her feel closer to him. Like the others in the neighborhood, it stood two stories high, and was made of tan stucco with a peaked roof covered in flat red tiles. The exterior was completely plain, with no shutters, moldings, or other adornments. Inside, it had a small foyer with a narrow stairway that led up to the bedrooms. Lubienski took her to his study, which was behind the living room looking out over a garden.

They stood awkwardly and apart in the center of the book-lined room. In the long drive back to Warsaw, neither had spoken much. Elizabeth's feelings had run the gamut from remorse and fear to a gradual sense of triumph. After Lubienski had killed the young German and gotten back into the car, she had said, "I'm sorry." His reply had been terse and bitter. "It's the destiny of young Germans and Poles to kill each other."

Looking at him now, she wanted so much to comfort him, but there was so little time. She stepped closer and put her arms around him. They kissed and embraced one another silently for several minutes.

"I can't bear to think of the days ahead," he whispered. "I don't know what could be worse, war or losing you."

"Do you want to make love?" She unbuttoned her sweater and unsnapped her brassiere.

The phone rang. He picked it up.

"Five-fifty," a voice said. "Someone will meet you."

Lubienski put down the phone and repeated the message.

"How far is it to the airfield?" she asked.

"Mokotów is twenty minutes."

"We have to leave right away."

"Not yet." Lubienski came to her.

She expected him to sweep her into his arms, but instead, almost shyly he took her hand. "I want you to touch," he said hesitantly, leading her toward the bookshelves.

Half naked, she moved along the walls, caressing the bound leather volumes with her body. He opened a glass vitrine and took out a handful of medals. "Press them against your breasts,'' he whispered. Then he led her to his desk. "Sit in my chair, I want you to touch everything that's mine."

She sat at his desk and passed her hands over his pipe, his pens, his lamp, his diary, the inkwells, the document boxes.

"Michael," she finally said, "I'm sorry, but we have to go."

He lifted her from the chair, placing her on the desk. Then he pulled down her slacks and panties, and she opened her legs to envelop him. In a moment he was inside. A moment later, as they soundlessly stared into one another's eyes, he was spent.

"Now," he said, "there will always be something of you here."

As they drove away from Lubienski's house, Elizabeth pulled over the rearview mirror to check her makeup. She gasped. Two black Chevrolets had just turned the corner behind them.

"Step on it," she ordered. "It's the Defa!"

Lubienski made a hard left and then a quick right.

"They've spotted us!" she cried. "They're gaining!" He hurtled through a stop sign, and crossed into the thickly forested Paderewski Park. Jumping the curb, he drove onto a bridle path. Startled horses reared in the air and bolted for the woods, their riders tossed to the ground or hanging on in panic. Desperately twisting to look through the rear window, Elizabeth could see the Chevrolets sliding around on the dirt trail, but doggedly still in pursuit.

"We're running out of time!" She had barely ten minutes to meet her contact. "Look out!"

The car plunged through a hedge, crashed a fence, tore across a picnic area, and emerged onto a wide boulevard that led to the Poniatowski Bridge.

Picking herself off the floor of the car, Elizabeth glanced back. "I think you finally lost them."

Located near the village of Mokotów, south of the city, the Warsaw airport consisted of two huge hangars, flanking a small three-story building topped by a central control tower. The diminutive terminal looked like a gay summer pavillion with several terraces that the public would visit on Sunday afternoons to watch the planes take off and land. The terminal was fully adequate to handle the dozen flights and the four hundred passengers that passed through it each day. But when Elizabeth and Count Lubienski roared up at 5:51, the building was surrounded by at least five thousand people desperately trying to flee Poland.

Elizabeth could see no way to get through the crowd. She would never find her contact. She wanted to sit down and cry.

"Here we go." Lubienski picked her up by the waist.

"What are you doing?" she protested.

He put her over his shoulder, bent to pick up the Enigma machine and began to shove his way into the building toward British European Airways, shouting, "Emergency! Emergency!"

He set her down next to the BEA desk. A sign indicated that the London flight left at 6:00. Through the large glass windows that faced the runways, Elizabeth caught sight of passengers boarding a large Vickers airplane. "Can I make it?" she asked the attendant. He nodded and asked for her name and passport. As he checked his list, Elizabeth spotted two men at the departure gate in the telltale black leather coats. They were making all female passengers take off their hats and then were checking them against a photograph held next to their faces.

Elizabeth snatched back her passport. She turned to Lubienski and pointed toward the counterintelligence police.

"More trouble." He nodded toward the exit to the street. Two more Defas were pushing their way into the building.

"Oh, God, I know them! They sit in front of my flat all day!" She ducked down and tried to elbow her way toward the restrooms, stumbling over feet, suitcases, dogs, children. Lubienski, lugging the Enigma, struggled to follow her. Just as she reached the door to the ladies room a hand reached out and seized her arm. Elizabeth started to scream.

"Shussh, for Christ sakes!" It was Jack Shelly. "Where's the machine?" She pointed back toward Lubienski, who was squeezing through the crowd. Behind him, one of the Defas was looking in their direction.

"This way," Shelly herded them through a door marked PRIVAT and into a massive hangar. Outside on the tarmac, a Junker trimotor with the markings of Finnish Airways stood warming up.

"What's going on?" Elizabeth cried over the noise of the engines.

"Second prize," Shelly explained. "You'll be met in Helsinki."

Shelly and Lubienski lifted Elizabeth and the Enigma up the steps and into the plane. Before she could turn around, the door was closed and the aircraft had begun to taxi onto the runway. An attendant led her to a seat at the front of the plane. As she looked back toward the hangar, Elizabeth saw a squad of Defensywa seize Shelly and Lubienski. She strapped herself into the wicker seat, and gripped the Enigma between her legs.

The door to the cockpit was latched open with the curtain tied back. She could hear the pilot and the tower talking to one another on the radio in English. The pilot spoke with a British accent and looked like a grizzled Royal Flying Corps veteran.

Finally she heard the magic words from the tower: "Finnair Seventy-seven, you are cleared for takeoff."

The airplane turned and started down the bumpy runway, gathering speed.

Abruptly the tower came on the radio again. "Finnair Seventy-seven, do you have a female passenger on board? Over."

"Roger. Several. Over."

Fear shot through her. She waited for the next message. The plane continued to accelerate.

"Finnair, you're requested to return to the hangar area. Over."

"I'm already behind schedule. It'll be dark when I get to Helsinki. Over."

"Just a second. Over." Then an excited voice came on the air.

"Tower," the pilot said dryly, "I don't speak Polish. Over."

The aircraft was beginning to bounce, signaling a desire

to be airborne. Elizabeth strained forward against the seat-belt to hear her fate.

"You must stop!" the Polish voice demanded.

"Tower, I'm going to file a complaint of interference on takeoff. Over."

And with that, the Junker lumbered into the air.

"Roger Wilco, Finnair Seventy-seven," the tower operator came back. "We'll sort it out on your return. Over."

Elizabeth collapsed back into her seat. She had escaped! But there was no exhilaration, no sense of triumph. As she watched the city of Warsaw turning beneath her, looking all golden and untroubled in the autumn twilight, she felt a tremendous sense of loss, for she had left her whole life behind.

Chapter 27

Palace Hotel, Stockholm— September 30, 1938

Elizabeth stood at the window of her room gazing out at the harbor. Sailing boats drifted lazily by, framed by the medieval town rising on the island across the water. The scene was tranquil; she was not. She hated the waiting.

In Helsinki, a middle-aged Finnish woman from the British Passport Control Office had met her at the plane with a suitcase full of fresh clothes and a case of toiletries. She took Elizabeth directly to the port and put her aboard the ferry to Sweden. In the dark, she had seen little of the Finnish capital except for a remarkable number of extremely modern glass buildings sprouting up between old wooden houses that reminded her of pictures of Russia.

On the boat to Stockholm, she locked herself in her cabin. The Swedes returning from a weekend in Finland drank all night. Several times she could hear them toast in English, "To the next war, may it make us rich!" And later when the party became morose, they turned to French: *"Au fin du monde!"* To the end of the world.

The young Englishman who met her at the dock in Stockholm and whisked her through customs showed no interest in the Enigma machine. When he dropped her at the Palace Hotel, he merely told her to wait and she would be contacted. That was seventy-two hours ago. Why had no one shown up? Had something gone wrong? Didn't they care? Was all the sacrifice in vain? As the hours slowly passed, Elizabeth had stayed in her room with the Enigma machine, ordering from the hotel kitchen, listening to news of the Czech crisis on the BBC.

In a surprise move, Mussolini had asked for a conference among himself, Hitler, Chamberlain, and French Prime Minister Daladier. The Czechs were left out. But as the Big Four powers met in Munich, Hitler remained adamant that he get a third of Czechoslovakia and war still seemed inevitable. Germany and Poland were fully mobilized. Children were being evacuated from London. Gas masks were being distributed to the populace and antiaircraft emplacements dug into Green Park. The news made Elizabeth worry all the more about Lubienski and Shelly. It made her think about death.

The image of the train striking the van, the bodies inside, the driver's last grimace, the young man pleading for his life, would not go away. But it wasn't the violence and horror that obsessed her. It was the finality, the irreversibility, the irrefutable truth that the avalanche of the coming war would destroy everything in its path. Youth, she realized, would offer no protection. The war would be a youth festival of death.

Elizabeth had tasted the irreversible; she herself had not only killed, but she had died a little, perhaps a lot. If life's purpose was to beget more life, she was dead already. Was that what lurked behind her inability to sustain a sense of pride over the operation? The guilt that she had secretly been taking revenge on the living? Killing had always been an essential element of her plan. Was she proving that she too could be violent, competing with men when she could no longer compete with women?

The face of the young German lieutenant came to her again and again with surges of remorse. Why was she obsessed with him? Because he was kind to her? Because in a different time and place they might have fallen in love? Were the others' lives less valuable? Had she any more right to take them? How could she be so indifferent about the soldier with the spectacles or the old-timer? How could she have been so glad about the Nazi sergeant? Because he despised Jews? Arthur, her mother, and plenty of her parents' friends often talked just like he did. So what right had she to take satisfaction in killing him? For that was how she had felt, even as her body made her vomit. Was it her Viking blood, the blood of the Thaarps? Had she something of the berserker in her? Was she becoming a monster, like the Nazis she was so proud of fighting?

The self-flagellating questions circled endlessly through her mind, allowing no rest and little sleep. To distract herself she wrote letters: a short note to the Porters asking about Antony, and a long sprawling one to her mother trying to explain her feelings about the last few days without revealing what she had done. Much of the letter dwelled on how her father must have felt after killing the enemy. Did his patriotism, his love of country, erase the horror of taking human life? Had he ever even met his enemy as she had? The letter closed by asking her mother how she had comforted her father. When Elizabeth was finished, she tore it up.

When you're young, she thought as she sat in the window overlooking Stockholm Harbor, death is a game of cowboys and Indians, cops and robbers, and time is like the air; there's so much you hardly notice it exists. There is always the possibility of new beginnings. What new beginning did she face now? Another assignment from Broadway? They seemed to have forgotten her already. A new lover to replace Lubienski and offset the tedium of life with Arthur? The prospect held no interest. Against great odds, Elizabeth had gambled and won a victory for Britain, but somehow she felt she had lost everything.

She worried helplessly about Lubienski and Shelly. She was afraid to try to call them, both for their sake and for fear of letting Polish intelligence know where she was. Why had she pushed the plan forward even when they were prepared to give it up? She had persevered in the belief that the Enigma in British hands would save untold lives. But where were the British now? All she had done was kill four German soldiers and jeopardize the lives of her friends. If the Poles had any inkling of the operation, Shelly would face a brutal interrogation. She prayed his diplomatic status would save him. Lubienski might be treated as a traitor. He could be shot. The thought made her weep.

Arthur was also on her mind. If he had heard of the embassy evacuation, he might be concerned about her. Not long after her arrival at the hotel she placed a call to him in St.-Jean-de-Luz where he was now recuperating. When she finally got through, Barbara Brasswell was there to answer the phone. Arthur was out taking a walk. Barbara said he would be relieved to hear that she was safe in Stockholm.

As the harbor shimmered in midday sunlight, Elizabeth decided to order lunch from room service. A few minutes later, she heard a knock on the door. That's Swedish efficiency, she thought opening it.

Her surprise was complete. There, with a bouquet of flowers in one hand, and a cart of champagne and caviar behind him, stood William Stephenson.

"What you've done is spectacular," he toasted her. His ostensible reason for coming to Stockholm was business with Svenska Metallverken; his real purpose was to escort both her and her prize back to London. "If the Government Code and Cipher School boys can't break the Enigma now, I say sack the lot of them."

For the first time, Elizabeth allowed herself to feel proud. Still, she choked back her emotions.

"The Enigma's vital," Stephenson assured her. "Parliament is to declare war tomorrow. What you've done will not only save thousands upon thousands of lives, it may well save Britain itself."

"It's a relief to hear you say so," she whispered, then burst into tears, and he held her for a long time like a child.

Unwilling to risk leaving the Enigma in the suite unguarded, they ordered up a party. While Elizabeth happily changed clothes, room service delivered more champagne and a timbale of crayfish. The radio provided music—Lasse Thomassen and the Stockholm Strings.

After lunch, as they stood close together at the window, Elizabeth could sense that he was preparing himself to ask her a question.

"I hope you won't think of me as crass . . . " he began.

"Bill," she said softly, "you can ask me anything you like."

"Well then"—she saw the eagerness growing in his eyes—"could I see the machine?"

"Of course!" Elizabeth laughed, leading him into the

bedroom. She took the Enigma out of the closet and set it up on the writing table near the windows.

Stephenson opened the case. A broad smile took over his face. He pulled a sheet of paper from his inside pocket and began to set the rotors. When he was finished, he pressed the letter "N." Nothing happened. He looked alarmed.

"Is it broken?"

"I don't think we'll know," she said kindly, "unless we turn it on."

"Oh, of course!" He searched around, turning several switches before the machine lit up and began to hum.

"Oh good! Good!" He was like a child at Christmas. "I've got a message fragment that we intercepted some time ago. We know we've got the key right, but we still can't decipher the bloody thing. Can you take down the letters as the bulbs light up?"

Every great man needs a secretary, she thought as she fished in the desk for a pencil.

He began pressing the keys: "KZLTO FQNPY WAEMG SIOUD ROFGH . . . "

Elizabeth wrote the letters that appeared on the bulbs. "HIMML ERKOM MTBAL DNACH KOLNX . . . "

"It still makes no sense," said Elizabeth, dismayed.

"Yes! Yes!" Stephenson was even more excited. "It's German of course. Break it up this way."

He drew slashes through the five letter groups: "H™MML ER/KOM MT/BAL D/NACH /KOLN/X."

"Himmler is soon coming to Cologne!" he shouted triumphantly. Elizabeth hugged him with joy and relief, and then they realized that the phone had been ringing. Elizabeth had to dash into the other room to answer it.

"Hello," she said, wondering who it could be.

"Elizabeth, is that you? It's Hallet Johnson."

"Hal!" He was an old friend she and Arthur had known in Madrid. "Where are you calling from? How did you find me?"

"I'm now the U.S. consul general in Stockholm. I've just got a wire from Arthur asking about you."

Wasn't it just like him to answer her phone call with a cable. "What does he say?"

"He wants to know why you're here."

"Because Britain's about to go to war with Germany and Poland, that's why!"

"You haven't been keeping up. The Big Four powers reached agreement in Munich. There'll be no war. You can probably go back to Warsaw tomorrow."

"That's wonderful!" She put her hand over the phone and turned to Stephenson. "Chamberlain and Hitler worked it out."

"I hope we can see each other before you return," Johnson said.

"By all means. If I've time, I'll come by and send a message to Arthur." She rang off.

Stephenson had already gone to the big Ericsson radio and was tuning in the BBC overseas service. It confirmed that Hitler, Chamberlain, Daladier, and Mussolini had reached an accord. But peace had its price. The British and French had capitulated to Hitler's demands. Czechoslovakia would be dismembered just the way the Nazis outlined it on the map Elizabeth had stolen from Henlein in Prague.

But the people of Britain were joyous. The BBC reported that cheering crowds greeted Chamberlain at Heston Airport and lined the streets into London. While room service set the table for dinner, Elizabeth and Stephenson leaned close to the radio to catch the British prime minister's voice as he stepped to the window of 10 Downing Street and waved the Munich Agreement to the throngs below.

"My good friends, this is the second time in our history that there has come back from Germany to Downing Street peace with honor.

"I believe it is peace for our time!"

Stephenson looked as if he might be ill. "A disgrace, a sham," he muttered.

"Well, maybe Chamberlain's weakness has bought us time to get ready when the war finally does come," Elizabeth said.

The phone rang. The switchboard operator announced that the call was from Warsaw.

"Elizabeth! You're safe!" Count Lubienski shouted over a poor connection.

"And you?" she shouted back, thrilled to hear his voice.

"Everything has come out fine! You have the news from Munich?"

"Yes."

"It changes everything. I've talked to Beck. You can come back."

"I don't know." She looked at Stephenson.

"Don't worry. You'll be perfectly safe now," Lubienski insisted. "You won't even be followed by the Defa."

"That's a break." She felt an uncontainable happiness. "I'll have to contact the embassy, of course."

"Certainly. Call me back. I'll meet your plane, train, boat, however you can get here."

"What about Jack?"

"Expelled, declared *persona non grata*. He can't come back, I'm afraid. But he told me where you were."

"I'll call you as soon as I have plans."

"I miss you. I love you," Lubienski declared through the static.

"I miss you, too," Elizabeth called to him, cradling the phone as if it were his face. "You don't know how much."

As she hung up, she cried, "I can go back!"

"I understand completely," said Stephenson, but there was a touch of regret in his voice. "I was supposed to fetch you to London. C wanted to meet you. I think tea at Buckingham Palace is in the works."

Elizabeth felt overwhelmed. The importance of what she had done was finally sinking in.

"I don't want to disappoint the king!"

"Well, the Queen Mother, actually."

"But isn't Poland even more significant now?"

"It's either going to be Hitler's ally or his next conquest."

"So shouldn't I go back before they change their minds? Beck has cleared it."

Stephenson smiled and shook his head in respect. "You're a marvel," he conceded. "I'll square it with the chaps at Broadway."

While Stephenson packed up the Enigma, Elizabeth booked a telephone call to the British embassy in Warsaw.

"I'll have to hurry to get the last flight out tonight,"

Stephenson apologized for his hasty departure.

"It's been lovely." Elizabeth smiled warmly. He was a man who spoke little, yet she felt they somehow deeply understood one another.

"Don't take too many risks. You're too valuable to the cause," he said at the door.

She gave him a kiss on the cheek and watched him lug the heavy Enigma down the hall to the elevator. The ringing telephone called her back into the room. It was Clifford Norton from the embassy in Warsaw.

"I'm planning to take the first plane or boat that I can," Elizabeth explained.

"No, you mustn't."

"Why not?"

"I've got orders that you're not to return."

"Why not?" Elizabeth was flabbergasted. "You know what I've done for the embassy."

"If it weren't for you," Norton admitted, "we might as well not be here."

"Go to the ambassador, please. Tell him it's all right with the Poles. Tell him my husband ordered me to go back."

"I'll try my best, Elizabeth. But I don't have much hope."

She hung up. This was preposterous! She tried to call London, but all the circuits were booked until well after midnight.

Two hours later, after she had watched the lights come on along Stockholm's waterfront, Norton called back.

"The ambassador says no."

"For God's sake, why?"

"He said that it's in the best interests of the Foreign Service that you not return."

"But my work . . . "

"With the Munich Agreement, he believes that your kind of work will no longer be necessary."

"What an ass! What's really going on, Clifford?"

She could sense his hesitation.

"Promise you won't get angry with me?"

"I promise." She was furious.

"It's Lady Kennard. She's put her foot down. She sent a message refusing to come back to Warsaw if the embassy, and I'm quoting here, 'continues to be disgraced by that tramp.'

"Sorry, Elizabeth."

PART FOUR

*My best and most vivid memories
come from "aloneness." It's not
fantasy or dreaming, but things and
life seem more real to me when I'm
alone, my impressions are sharper
and all of me is focused. I even
associate love with aloneness—and
parting from love. For when parting
comes—and it nearly always does—
then it is the rememberance of it,
in solitude, that sustains one far
more than the company of friends.*

—Elizabeth Pack, interview with
  H. Montgomery Hyde

Chapter 28

Toronto, October 10, 1938

Dear Winston,
   I read your masterful speech in Commons,
denouncing the Munich accords. Historians will
endlessly debate whether it would have been better
for Chamberlain to stand up to the Führer at
Munich. I believe he was right not to do so because
we are so woefully unprepared for war. However, he
is tragically wrong to present this as a victory for
peace. Instead of letting the public go back to sleep,
he should be using Munich to sound the alarm, to
mobilize the Commonwealth and ready ourselves for
the inevitable battle to come.

Yours,
Bill Stephenson

The Other Club, London— December 12, 1938

When Admiral Sinclair arrived, they all abandoned the library and climbed the creaking stairs to the greater privacy of the small paneled dining room on the second floor. Winston Churchill, as a tireless critic of the prime minister, was somewhat surprised to be invited into the company of Chamberlain's men: the minister of war, Thomas Inskip;

Maurice Hankey, secretary of the cabinet and the Imperial Defense Committee; Major Desmond Morton, who headed the Industrial Intelligence Center, and of course, Admiral Sinclair, who as C headed the SIS. Only the slim and elegant Morton, a neighbor of his in Kent and a sometime confidential source, was a friendly face.

Over drinks, they had been arguing about Munich, with Churchill pointing out that Hitler's appetite had only been whetted, and he was now hungry for Poland. After they had sat down to dinner, Admiral Sinclair refueled the debate by stating that all the intelligence prior to Munich underscored that the Germans were thoroughly prepared for war over Czechoslovakia, and that Britain would have been foolhardy to challenge them.

"My sources," Churchill responded, "tell me that the Führer would have backed down if Chamberlain had taken a resolute stand."

"Don't confuse opinion with intelligence," Sinclair responded tartly. He looked up to see if the door was closed. "One reason for this gathering, is to address the intelligence situation."

Inskip, who had the shrewd eyes of one who had advanced in politics by avoiding responsibility, nodded to Morton to pick up the conversation. They were all clearly proceeding from a script, so Churchill waited.

"I know you are aware of the German Enigma machine," Morton began. "What you may not know is that we have at last been able to break it."

Churchill did know. In fact, Morton himself had told him. He had also been the one who reported to Churchill that the Enigma messages indicated that Hitler's generals had warned against provoking a war that could draw in Britain and France.

"We had a storehouse of intercepted signals from our antennas at Bridgewoods and Flowerdown. As we went back through them, it was clear that Hitler had carefully prepared for a Czech invasion. We could have done little to stop them."

Churchill was in no mind to argue over the past. "Well, can I hope that the prime minister has learned from this debacle that the Nazis are not champions of peace?"

"Quite," Maurice Hankey spoke up. Fine-featured and meticulous, he spread his manicured fingers on the table. "I am authorized to tell you that the PM has instructed Admiral Sinclair and his chaps to spare no effort in carrying out a clandestine program to undermine Nazi influence throughout Europe."

"That's gratifying to hear," Churchill said, "but what is he going to do publicly to halt Hitler's march? Covert means cannot substitute for overt means. They can only support them." He directed this last remark to Admiral Sinclair.

"We shall do what we can," C replied. "But we need some help."

"Mine?" Churchill looked surprised.

"Winston"—Inskip spoke again—"we've been trying to persuade you that the government is alert to the dangers ahead and so enlist your cooperation."

"I take it that it's not a position in the cabinet that you've in mind," he responded dryly.

"No," said Hankey carefully, "it has to do with Poland."

Admiral Sinclair continued. "On September fifteenth, not long before we were able to break the Enigma, the Germans changed their keying procedures, making breaking the code all the more difficult. Now it appears that they also have made new and significant modifications to the machine, adding new rotors. The details are not important. The essential thing is that we can read all the old messages we had in our inventory, but we've not been able to read a single new Enigma message since the middle of September last. We need some assistance, and the Poles are the only ones who may be able to provide it."

"The Poles?" To Churchill, this was getting curiouser by the moment.

"My chaps will give you a full briefing on what's been going on," Admiral Sinclair pressed ahead. "We've been trying to approach them through the French who have an intelligence relationship going back several years, but Colonel Beck, the Polish foreign minister, wants to have an 'off the record' chat with us first."

"What do you want from me?"

"You're our choice for interlocutor," Hankey explained. "Since Munich, the Poles are convinced that Britain lacks"—he searched for a word that would not be too embarrassing—"lacks calculability."

"Your opposition to Munich lends credibility to our offer of cooperation," Morton explained.

"Well, I can well imagine what they want from us—arms, and assistance—but what, specifically, do we seek from them?" Churchill asked.

Admiral Sinclair made an unhappy face. "It all has to do with a device they've reportedly invented. Supposedly, it's a sort of electrical brain that helps them solve the Enigma."

"Why 'supposedly'?"

"There's some question among my chaps as to whether this thing actually exists."

"That's one reason we too want an off-the-record talk," Hankey added. "We don't want them to see what's in our hand before we see theirs."

Churchill frowned. "On the remote chance that this is a useful exercise, what is this thing I'm supposed to be asking for?"

They all looked at C.

"It's called the *bombe*."

Villa Ttirritta, St.-Jean-de-Luz— December 26, 1938

The rain battering against the terrace door made Elizabeth shudder. All the heat was on in the house, and still it was cold. She couldn't use the fireplaces; if she opened the flues, the gale would come right down the chimney. For months since she had returned to St.-Jean-de-Luz, the sky had been overcast and dark. When the weather wasn't damp, it was drizzling; and when it wasn't drizzling it was blowing. Often, the windows rattled and whistled so loudly that she had to raise her voice to be heard. No wonder the French saw St.-Jean-de-Luz as fit for year-round habitation only by the English.

Her Boxing Day luncheon that afternoon would be a gloomy affair if it were not for the Brasswells, who were still stationed at the rump British embassy in Hendaye. Barbara had been a tower of strength in London when Elizabeth was trying to get Arthur proper medical treatment. And while she was in Poland, the Brasswells had arranged for him to recuperate back in St.-Jean-de-Luz, where they continued to be extremely attentive. Elizabeth would not have been surprised if they had a poor opinion of her for having abandoned Arthur, but upon her return, Barbara Brasswell had become her first real female friend, apart from Vita, since leaving Washington.

After the excitement and the horror of Poland, her time in St.-Jean-de-Luz seemed like limbo. Unable to return to Warsaw, she had stopped in London to be "debriefed." Stephenson already had gone on to Canada. Denniston and Knox had listened politely to her report until she added that the Poles had developed a machine they called the *bombe* to help them crack the new German ciphers. As usual, Knox was skeptical. He had no faith in what he called "clumsy machinery," and Denniston, typically, saw both sides to the question. C had been indisposed, but she had met with Colonel Menzies who gave her five minutes, and then stood and said, "Well, we're all terribly grateful. Thank you very much. Good-bye." A visit to Buckingham Palace was never mentioned. Since then, she had heard nothing from Broadway.

The only bright spots of her stop in England were a visit to Bath to see her son and high tea with Vita at Claridge's. Vita arrived wearing tweeds and tall boots fit for the country. Elizabeth noticed that she was letting her hair go gray.

"An instinct told me to bring along this," Vita said, handing Elizabeth a copy of her book *Saint Joan of Arc*.

"How dear." She thumbed through the pages. "I've always been fascinated by her. What do you think turned so simple a peasant girl into such a patriot?"

They skipped the scones and pastries, and ordered watercress sandwiches.

"Well, in her case, she heard voices from God," Vita replied.

Elizabeth could feel Vita inspecting her closely.

"You're not hearing voices these days, are you?" she continued.

"Certainly not." Elizabeth laughed a little sharply. "But sometimes I'm mystified by my feelings for this country. Lord knows I've had my share of bad experiences here, yet I find myself more patriotic than most of the English I meet."

"And do you feel that way about America?"

"Even more so. And I believe the fates of the two countries are linked, as Churchill said at dinner that night at your house."

"Oh yes," Vita said vaguely as if the memory was not too clear. She reached out and put her hand on Elizabeth's. "I don't know what you've been doing with yourself in Poland, and I'm not pressing you to tell. But when Joan of Arc lifted the English siege of Orléans, she said she would be happy to go home and feed her goats. Unfortunately, she had come to love war too much. It was her undoing."

"I think I know how she felt," Elizabeth said with a sigh. "But at least she became a saint."

Vita had looked at her sternly. "Five hundred years *after* she was burned at the stake!"

Once back at the Villa Ttirritta, Elizabeth had tried "tending her goats," but found herself incapable of re-entering the vacuous round of dinner parties that constituted the quiet life of Biarritz and St.-Jean-de-Luz. It was too soggy for golf and too miserable to ride. Even walks on the beach were cold and empty and offered no solace. So she holed up in her library, reading and listening to the BBC as it reported the total dismemberment of Czechoslovakia, and, ominously, Hitler's new demands for the return of Danzig and large stretches of Poland to the Third Reich. As she stared at the glowing yellow dial on her radio and heard Hitler blowing hot and cold in his demands on Poland, she was reminded of the opening gambits of his successful campaigns to take over Austria and Czechoslovakia. Only this time she knew there would be war; the

Poles would fight. She desperately wanted to be at Lubienski's side for the battle.

For in those long gray wintry hours she could not help but think of him. Elizabeth did not simply miss Michael Lubienski; she had to admit that she loved him. They corresponded. She wrote noncommittal notes to him at the Polish Foreign Ministry; he wrote passionate letters to a post office box she had set up in Biarritz. But why did she find it so difficult to tell him how much he meant to her? What was so hard about writing "I love you"? When she had last talked to him on the phone from Stockholm, the words stuck in her throat like a forced confession.

Lubienski was gallant, brave, passionate, childish, endearing, brilliant, and often had no sense—an impulsive cavalry officer at heart. Sometimes she felt there was something trivial about him, a strange superficiality that made her uneasy. Was this the kernel of contempt her teacher at Prae Wood had warned that all spies develop toward their agents? Or did she envy the way he had somehow maintained his innocence while she was losing hers?

As a girl, she had always imagined that the man she would love would be so far above her: wiser, stronger, more solidly anchored to the earth. Antonio had seemed to be that man, until she had discovered his attentions were more professional than personal. In contrast, Count Lubienski was in many ways so much more romantic and frivolous than she. So how could she entrust her love to him? All Elizabeth knew for certain was that during her drifting, cheerless days in St.-Jean-de-Luz, she never stopped thinking of him. He had made the world Technicolor, while life with Arthur was barely black and white.

And yet the less Arthur gave to her, the more she felt bound to him. When they married, she had seen him as strong and steady. Now their life together was steadily going nowhere. What she had seen as taciturn strength turned out to be uncaring self-centeredness. She had gotten beyond the point where he could make her feel guilty with a glance, but still she found herself trying to please him when he was in one of his moods. How did he continue to have a hold on her? She knew part of the answer: unfinished business. They had a son. In some inexplicable way, the pain of that fact made her cling even more stubbornly to her marriage.

At least twice a week, she had tea in town with Barbara Brasswell, who listened sympathetically as Elizabeth talked about her longings, her emptiness, her marriage. But never once did Barbara criticize her or Arthur; her only advice and comment was that everyone had a right to their own life.

Physically, Arthur had gotten much better. Over the months, his speech had cleared, and while he occasionally used a wheelchair, he could now walk some distance each day with the aid of a cane. He seemed remarkably incurious about how Elizabeth had spent her time in Warsaw, and his lack of interest only reinforced the glacial atmosphere at the Villa Ttirritta. When she mentioned that she had visited their son, that he was getting big and starting to talk, Arthur's only response was silence.

His stroke had given him a new weapon to use against her. When he did not like what she was saying or doing, he simply did not react. Elizabeth was left to guess whether he disapproved, could not hear her, or was having another small seizure.

His response to her preparations for the Boxing Day luncheon was typical. Was he happy with pressed duck for the entrée? Silence. Did he think she should light the candles on the tree? No answer. Would he like a drink before the Brasswells showed up? Grunt. That meant yes.

But as soon as their guests arrived, he began to talk. Over lunch he held forth quite eloquently on the recent Polish/Soviet trade agreement. "Bloody bad business for us, I'd wager."

He also questioned Tom Brasswell closely on rumors of year-end Foreign Service assignments. Arthur had been brooding about them for weeks, fearful that he would lose his posting. Tom would know, because he was the sort of ambitious middle-grade officer who spent much of his time on Service politics.

"Bit of bum luck, I'm afraid," Tom responded candidly. "Word has it that your replacement's been named for Warsaw."

Elizabeth felt the life go out of her. So that was it. Whatever small hope she'd held that she would somehow return to Poland was now extinguished. She looked over at Arthur. He also looked crushed. She took his hand. It was deathly cold. He didn't speak again until they opened their presents.

They sat around the tree. Outside, the gale had reached the point of driving water from the terrace under the French doors. The maid sought to block it with a levee of bath towels. On the radio, Handel's *Messiah* was syncopated by percussive zaps from lightning far at sea. The atmosphere was funereal.

Elizabeth gave Arthur a new pair of slippers; the old ones were worn through. She also gave him a carved Basque walking stick and heavy wool jacket. He said nothing. Arthur gave her a set of lace napkins and an embroidered tablecloth. Elizabeth thought, How personal, but said, "How sweet." The Packs gave the Brasswells a tea set. The Brasswells gave the Packs an empty box.

"What's the idea?" Arthur's disappointment broke through.

Tom Brasswell smiled easily. "I've got something better than a gift."

Arthur looked at him stony-faced.

"I didn't tell you all the news from the Foreign Office. A new commercial minister is about to be named."

Arthur's eyes became expectant.

"It's a new slot, Arthur, and you're to get it."

"Isn't that wonderful?" Barbara exclaimed.

Elizabeth feared Arthur might have another stroke.

"You're not joking?" he asked.

"No, it's true!"

Arthur smiled for the first time in almost a year.

"What's the post?" Elizabeth asked anxiously.

"Santiago! You'll be the commercial minister in Chile!"

"Isn't that wonderful!" Barbara said again.

Wonderful? It was the far end of the earth! But Elizabeth could see that Arthur was delighted. He and the Brasswells immediately fell to planning the details. Arthur would have six to nine months for further recovery before he had to be en route. Tom would become his commercial attaché. Barbara wouldn't have to work. They all would rent a beach house at Vina del Mar for weekends.

"And what do you think you'll do?" Tom turned to Elizabeth.

"I really have no idea." She tried hard not to sound dismayed.

A few moments later, the maid entered the room. "Telegram for Madame."

The others watched closely as she opened it. Was this another joke present? Dated December 23, it had been sitting at the telegraph office over the Christmas holiday.

SORRY SO LAST MINUTE STOP CAN YOU JOIN ME FOR FEW DAYS AT MAXINE ELLIOT'S IN CANNES DEC. 29 STOP SHOULD BE SMASHING GOOD TIME STOP REPLY SOONEST CHATEAU DE L'HORIZON STOP VITA

She read it again, aloud.

Arthur said nothing.

"Is it an invitation for you alone?" Barbara asked.

"I think so," Elizabeth answered.

Arthur continued to be mute.

"Well, it would be good for all of us if you could bring good weather back with you," Barbara laughed, trying to make light of it. "We'll certainly take good care of Arthur."

He still said nothing. The wind howled outside.

"Go, if you want," he said finally. "I don't care much for New Year's Eve anymore. I'll be in bed early."

Cannes, France— December 29, 1938

The sun! Elizabeth leaned her head back against the seat of the Talbot Lago roadster as it climbed the palm-lined driveway toward a magnificent white château gleaming at the summit of the hill. Red, violet, and orange bougainvillea cascaded over the ramparts of the château's many terraces. The hillsides were covered with cactus and olive trees and dark green cypress. The air smelled of rosemary and sage. Elizabeth could feel life surging back into her body.

The surprise of Vita's invitation was nothing compared to her shock upon arriving at the tiny Cannes railway station. Through a long night of fitful sleep on the Mistral Express, Elizabeth had luxuriated in the anticipation of a holiday with Vita's smart set, a parole from the somber world of diplomats and spies. But it was not to be.

On the train platform, among the passengers, porters, stacks of baggage, flower sellers, and hawkers of fruit and *pan beignat* stood Captain Lance in a white flannel suit and Panama hat.

"I didn't know you were a friend of Vita's," Elizabeth said, offering her hand.

"I'm not, actually. We hope you won't tell Vita about this little subterfuge."

"You mean she's not here at all?"

" 'Fraid not. It was the most discreet way we could think of contacting you."

"Then what's this all about? Is Bill here?"

"You mean Mr. Stephenson?" Captain Lance asked. "No, he's not." He helped her into the open car. "You'll find out what's what when we reach the château."

The streets of Cannes had brought back memories of Spain, the ocher and terra cotta walls, the wrought-iron balconies bursting with bright red geraniums, the green shutters framing every window and the colorful beaded strings that hung in shop doorways like a north African *souk*. She wondered what new scheme the ungrateful wretches at Broadway had in mind for her. But with the sun on her face and the wind tousling her hair, she had found it difficult to hold on to her irritation. Whatever they had cooked up, it had to be better than mildewing away in St.-Jean-de-Luz.

The car was approaching the top of the hill. On one side, the bright blue Mediterranean stretched out to the curve in the earth. On the other, the purple Alpes-Maritimes reached for the sky.

"Who is Maxine Elliot?" Elizabeth asked as they drew up to the front door.

"A stage actress who married well."

"Welcome to Château de l'Horizon." Maxine met them

at the tiled entrance in a flowing silk gown. Though beyond
a *certain âge,* she bore the burden with professional ele-
gance. The jewelry in her blond upswept hair, around her
neck, and on her hands flashed brilliantly in the winter sunlight as she directed her servants to take the luggage. Elizabeth felt like a country mouse.

"You'll be a beautiful addition to our party." She assured Elizabeth as if reading her thoughts. "I'd let you go
up and refresh yourself but he insists on seeing you immediately."

Who was "he"? she wondered. But before she could
ask, Maxine whisked her down a flight of stairs and along
a corridor. "He's in the solarium," she said as if that explained everything.

Full of ferns, orchids, and tropical plants, the solarium
was thick with humidity and ripe with the smell of cigar
smoke. At the window, overlooking a swimming pool and
the Bay of Cannes, sat a large heavyset man reading a stack
of English newspapers. He wore a red bathrobe over his
swimming trunks and was refreshing a goblet of orange
juice with a bottle of Pol Roger champagne. It had been a
long time since Elizabeth first had been introduced to him.

"Winnie," Maxine called out. "She's here."

He put down his newspapers and struggled to his feet.
"I don't believe we've met," said Winston Churchill. She
did not feel the need to correct him.

"So you're a spy," Churchill began ingenuously. Maxine had excused herself and Elizabeth and Captain Lance
were settled in lounge chairs. "Is it difficult for a woman
to be a spy?" he continued, his old child's face full of calm
wonder.

Thrown by his directness, Elizabeth shot a questioning
look toward Captain Lance. Stephenson had said that Churchill was an ally, but how much was she to admit to anyone
outside SIS? This could be some sort of test. "Women
make the best spies, I should imagine."

"And why is that?" He leaned back and drew on an
unlit cigar stub.

"Women have to hide things all their lives," Elizabeth

responded. "They're trained from girlhood to conceal their true selves. To dissimulate. To plot. To get what they want by stealth."

"No wonder I've never understood them." He appraised her carefully. "Friends say you've done first-rate work in Warsaw."

Elizabeth allowed herself to look pleased but remained quiet, hoping to draw him out on why she was there. Her curiosity had her imagination racing a mile a minute.

"We could use your help in settling a question"—Churchill sucked on his lower lip—"and perhaps in handling a tricky bit of diplomacy."

Elizabeth felt out of depth. Diplomacy was not her line of work.

"Captain"—Churchill waved his cigar like a scepter—"fetch Commander Denniston and Mr. Knox."

Elizabeth looked perplexed.

"You're wondering, in your honest American way," Churchill observed, "what this washed-up backbencher is doing cavalierly talking the king's secrets and ordering about the king's officers."

"I've the greatest admiration for you, sir," Elizabeth tried to reassure him.

"Good. I can't abide false modesty. Unfortunately, it's the only kind of which I'm capable. Still, you want to know by whose leave I've gotten you here and for what cause I intend to press you into service."

"That's true."

"Despite my fallen state in Commons, I've been asked to do a bit of work for the government. Of course, it's all deniable." He boyishly put his tiny hands over his eyes. "Me." Then, over his ears. "You."

Commander Denniston and Dilly Knox arrived, the former looking slightly awed by the surroundings and the latter rumpled and irritable as usual. "Mrs. Pack." They each nodded to her, and drawing up chairs, sat down. Churchill indicated that Denniston should begin.

"Mrs. Pack," he said appreciatively, "the Enigma machine you secured for us was invaluable in enabling us to read intercepted German signals."

"Thank you," she said simply.

"However"—he cleared his throat—"that only applies to signals intercepted before the middle of September last, about the time you obtained the machine."

"Is it the keying procedure?" she asked.

"Yes, every operator now makes his own rotor settings each day and transmits this key separately. They also seem to have added additional rotors."

"I explained that when I was in London," Elizabeth said with a note of impatience. "And I told you that the Poles were working on a machine to find the keys."

"This is the electrical brain?" Churchill asked, refilling his glass with champagne.

"In their silly way, the Poles call it a *bombe*." Elizabeth explained, "I suppose either because of the way it ticks, or because it was invented over a dish of ice cream."

"Well," Knox sniffed, "I think it's all a confection."

Elizabeth shook her head. He still could not accept the idea that the Poles were better cryptographers.

Seeing her reaction, Knox grew impatient. "Well, then how does this *bombe* purport to work?"

"I've no idea," she replied. "You wouldn't let me go back to Warsaw!"

"We couldn't overrule the ambassador."

"Don't blame Broadway, my dear," Churchill interjected. "It was Lord Halifax. The Foreign Office is the putative master of the secret service and on occasion feels compelled to exercise some petty bit of authority—invariably with disastrous results."

"Why can't you approach the Poles directly?" Elizabeth suggested. "Hitler's made clear they're next on his list."

"Evidently, Colonel Beck is playing coy," Churchill replied.

"He's no friend of Britain," Knox warned.

They were enveloped in the kind of pregnant silence that gave Elizabeth a sense of opportunity.

"Is there something I can do?" she asked.

"We need you to work on the Poles," Churchill replied. "We need an intermediary. Good offices. As you can see, we're as suspicious of them, as they are of us."

"Am I going back to Warsaw?" She could not conceal her excitement.

"That shan't be necessary." Churchill stood up. "Colonel Beck and his party will be arriving for dinner at eight o'clock tonight."

Chapter 29

Château de l'Horizon, Cannes—
December 29, 1938

The servants wore red livery. A score of guests drifted about Maxine's sparkling gold and white drawing room, a gathering far more glittering than Vita's set. Among them, she recognized Somerset Maugham, looking wan and dyspeptic; Josephine Baker, triumphant in a translucent dress of beaded pearls; and Noël Coward, who surprised Elizabeth by greeting Captain Lance as if they were old chums. Lady Rothermere arrived with a brace of spotted dalmatians trotting along beside her. Furious, Maxine sent them to the kennels. "Daisy," daughter of the Duc de Decacazes, made an entrance on the arms of two young men whom she immediately banished to the servants quarters. The Duke and Duchess of Windsor appeared fashionably late. Elizabeth was startled to see him wearing a white tuxedo jacket over a Balmoral tartan kilt with a dagger and long green knee socks.

They then waited for the Polish guest of honor. Elizabeth felt shy and out of place. After being introduced, she found it difficult to know what to say. Maxine, declaring all of her clothes unacceptable, had loaned her a long clinging velvet gown with a scoop neck that allowed her to say nothing and yet still remain the center of attention.

Maxine also insisted that she try a new drink that was all the rage in Hollywood—a Singapore sling. Elizabeth would have preferred the cold anesthetic of a dry martini.

All afternoon, she had tried to avoid the thought that Count Lubienski might be in Beck's traveling party—particularly after she learned from Captain Lance that it was not Broadway but the Poles who insisted that she attend the meeting. She had gone swimming in Maxine's Olympic-sized pool, had a massage, and lay in her shuttered room trying to sleep. She had smoked a pack of cigarettes and brushed her teeth three times. It was no use. She prayed that he would be coming.

"It looks like your Polish friends are going to stand us up," Maxine whispered into her ear at nine. "We'll have to start dinner soon. Can't keep the duke and duchess waiting."

"Do give them a few more minutes," Elizabeth urged. "They don't operate on Greenwich time." She went out onto the terrace where she could see any car approaching up the long grand drive. In the dark, she could see the necklace of lights from Nice to Cap Ferrat, with Cap d'Antibes gleaming like a jeweled pendant in the evening sea. She felt like a waif with her nose pressed against the window at Tiffany's. Despite Maxine's hospitality, this was not her world. She was there for a reason, like the butler or the chef. And while all of the women and most of the men could not take their eyes off her, there was only one pair of eyes she longed to see.

Down in the valley, she thought she detected a flash of light from an automobile. Soon, three pairs of headlights appeared at the gates at the bottom of the hill. It had to be them!

"They're coming," Elizabeth told Maxine who was hovering around Churchill, competing for his attention with "Daisy."

"The Polish Muhammad has come to the mountain after all," Churchill grumbled. "He's guaranteed a grand reception because we're all famished!"

Elizabeth heard the sound of tires crunching gravel. Two bodyguards appeared at the top of the stairway that descended into the salon. Then she saw Beck's antlike head emerge from under a top hat. He wore a red sash covered with medals as he stepped slowly down the stairs greeting the other guests as if he were royalty.

Holding her breath, Elizabeth searched to see who might be with him, but no one else followed. Unable to wait any longer, she rushed up the stairs to the foyer. There, busy giving instructions to the bodyguards and the chauffeur, she found Count Lubienski.

"Do you think you'll have any time to talk to me?" she inquired softly.

He whirled around. "My God! Elizabeth!" He dropped to one knee to kiss her hand.

"Michael, don't make a scene!" she whispered. "Come, let's get some privacy."

Snatching a Singapore sling from a silver tray and steering him through the party, Elizabeth led him onto the terrace. The smell of the sea and the rosemary from the hillsides textured the night air. A bright early moon was climbing over the mountains. Michael stood awkwardly away from her. "I prayed you'd be here...."

"We'll be going in to dinner in a few moments," Elizabeth told him gravely. "And if you don't kiss me first, I think I shall burst!"

He took her in his arms. Her body remembered how to fit against his. The fire in his kiss ignited her desire. She stepped away gasping. "I missed you so," she stammered.

"I came with Beck to France hoping somehow to find you, but I never really believed..."

"Why is he here?"

"You mean apart from the prostitutes? You can't imagine how depraved the man is. He likes little girls, he likes to watch sex shows, women with women, women with animals. Sick games. And this is the Christmas season!"

"Then why did he want you here?"

"I'm the camouflage. I make it seem that he's come for this so-called private chat with Churchill. But I doubt if he cares about it, really. It's the general staff that's pushing him. They're terribly anxious to establish some contact with the British. We desperately need military aid. We can't even handle the Enigma problem without help."

"I can tell you the British are interested..."

"That's a relief, but I can't figure out Beck..."

The dinner bell had rung and the guests were moving toward the dining salon.

"Will I see you later?" They both asked at once. "Yes!" They simultaneously replied, then laughed.

"I've been invited to go along to the casino tonight," Elizabeth explained. "Churchill plays every evening till dawn. I'll try to slip away."

"And I'll leave Beck to his whores."

The walls of the library were covered in a padded sea-green brocade. Churchill and Beck were seated on separate sofas in a corner. Elizabeth and Count Lubienski sat opposite them in Louis XIV armchairs. Heavy drapes covered the French doors.

". . . he who lies down with dogs, rises with fleas," Churchill was saying.

"Is that an insult to Poland?" Beck stiffened.

The "chat" was going badly.

"We're past the point of playing games, Colonel Beck. Europe needs principled decisions."

"Like Mr. Chamberlain made at Munich?" Beck inquired sarcastically.

"You know how wrong I believed that to be. But at least we British took nothing for ourselves."

Count Lubienski had remained completely quiet. Elizabeth was dying to break into the conversation. Her fear of being inadequate to the situation was fading fast.

"And what," Beck said with a smirk, "would your self-less nation do if Poland were attacked?"

"I would think that the prospect of the British Empire and France, not to mention Soviet Russia, standing shoulder to shoulder with Poland would give even Herr Hitler pause."

Beck looked unconvinced.

"But let me turn your question around." Churchill shifted course. "What would England derive from an alliance with Poland?"

Beck's smile broadened to include Elizabeth. "I suspect you have some concept of our strategic resources."

"More games!" Churchill muttered and rang for another round of brandy. "You'll still be dropping your veils, one by one, when Nazi jackboots are echoing in the streets of Warsaw."

Elizabeth stared hard at Lubienski. Why didn't he speak out?

"May I say something, gentlemen?" She could not hold back. "As an American?"

Beck appeared too surprised to object. Churchill looked like he had wondered why she had taken so long.

"Each of you mistrusts the other because of Munich," she plunged. "Poland fears that open cooperation with Britain would provoke Hitler, maybe Stalin too, and that Chamberlain will let them down as he did the Czechs." Beck nodded in agreement. "Britain on the other hand would assume great risks in backing Poland and stands little to gain, particularly if that support might be used in some devious way to actually help Hitler."

"What do you mean?" Beck replied testily.

Elizabeth knew she was courting an explosion. "Like exploiting an alliance with Britain to forestall a Nazi strike on Poland while also promising Hitler help should he go after Romania or the Soviet Union."

From the look on Beck's face, Elizabeth could see that the idea had occurred to him. He gave her a look of admiration.

"I don't take offense at your analysis," Churchill said affably.

"So what are you suggesting?" said Beck.

"Why not start out with something quiet, but important. Something that will build confidence on both sides?"

"Such as?" Churchill prompted.

"An exchange of intelligence," Elizabeth said.

Colonel Beck broke into a mirthless smile. He looked from Elizabeth to Lubienski. "That's not a self-serving suggestion, is it?"

Elizabeth responded coolly. "It was wise of you to permit my contacts with Count Lubienski. Otherwise I doubt any of us would be meeting here this evening. I'm suggesting a further step, something rather more official, but still secret so as to not complicate our problems with Berlin and Moscow. Still, London would get a meaningful token that the relationship was a serious one."

"And what does Poland get?" asked Beck.

"An ally," Elizabeth said.

"A secret ally? What good is that?"

"I think you'll be impressed with what Britain can

share,'' she said, glancing at Churchill and bidding a no-trump.

"If the alliance is genuine from your side,'' Churchill declared, "I've no doubt we could consider military aid at the opportune moment.''

The waiter came in and poured more brandy for Churchill. Beck put his hand over his glass. For a Pole, it was a signal that the discussion had come to an end.

Beck stood up. "Thank you for your hospitality. We shall give these ideas''—he bent to kiss Elizabeth's hand—"all the attention they deserve.''

She looked worriedly at Lubienski as he escorted Beck out of the room. Churchill gestured for her to stay with him.

"Well,'' she sighed when the door had closed, "that didn't get us very far. We didn't come close to talking about the *bombe*.''

Churchill shrugged and took a long pull on his brandy. "Difficult people, the Poles. They always behave most admirably when they've a boot on their necks.''

The beach was cold. Elizabeth stayed wrapped in her cloak. The stone seawall pressed against her back, but all she could feel was Lubienski around her, urgently consuming her. Music from the casino drifted down as their bodies desperately danced against each other. Elizabeth could hear the words in her head.

I'll remember you.
You're the one who made my dreams come true, a few,
kisses ago . . .

And then the song was obliterated by the strength that was filling her, making her body come alive for the first time in so long. . . .

"We have to . . . '' she said heavily.

"What?'' he gasped.

"Have to talk . . . '' Oh, how she had missed him.

"Yes?''

"About how . . . how we get . . . get the two sides together," she panted. He was wonderful. Glorious.

"Uuh," he responded. His hands were over all over her
body, tearing at her clothes. His hips drove her backward,
lifted her up, suspending her.

"The French . . . " she groaned. She felt his lips on her
neck, his hands pulling her open wider, hoisting her onto
him. ". . . as go-betweens" And between her thighs, his
pounding was making her lose control. She grabbed his hair
and began to thrash and jerk.

He slipped out.

"No!" She reached down. He was coming. She
squeezed with her hand to stop him, but he was convulsing
like a mad snake. And suddenly, as she desperately pressed
him against her, she felt her own climax start, then grow,
then without pity shake her to the core.

They lay on the sand like dead soldiers. Maxine's dress,
she thought, would never be the same. She felt the tears on
her cheeks. There was something terribly final in their love-
making. The song from the casino still hovered in the air.

> *When my life is through,*
> *and the angels ask me to recall,*
> *the thrill of them all,*
> *I will tell them I remember you . . .*

On the promenade above, a man who had been watching
them dropped his cigarette and crushed it out with his foot.
Then, Colonel Beck returned to his limousine and disappeared into the night.

Chapter 30

MOST SECRET

January 4, 1939

To: Menzies
From: Denniston
Subject: Polish/British Intelligence Cooperation

As follow-up to non-meeting between Beck and Churchill, Poles have responded through French (Bertrand, Chief of Radio Intelligence) urging tripartite meeting in Paris early next week.

Request authority to participate on an exploratory basis.

MOST SECRET

January 5, 1939

To: GC&CS Denniston
Request for tripartite meeting approved. However, great care should be taken to avoid exposure of our sources and methods except on a strictly reciprocal basis.

Menzies

10/1/39–23:42GMT
MOST SECRET
FOR BROADWAY 0026
PARIS SENDS
EYES ONLY MENZIES FROM DENNISTON
TRIPARTITE MEETING A FIASCO. POLES REVEALED

335

NOTHING, NOT EVEN WHAT WE KNOW THEY KNOW. PER
INSTRUCTIONS WE TOLD THEM NOTHING IN RETURN.
FORMAL MINUTE STATES THAT WE WILL STAY IN
TOUCH, WITH FURTHER MEETINGS IN LONDON AND
WARSAW AS DEVELOPMENTS WARRANT. NOT TO HOLD
ONES BREATH. DETAILS ON RETURN.

Mme. Elizabeth Thorpe
P.O. Box 247
Biarritz, France

January 27, 1939

My Darling,
    As you may have heard, the party in Paris was a
disaster. It would have been a glory if you and I could
have been there. I long for you every moment I am
awake and see you in all my dreams. . . .

All my love,
Michael

Michael Lubienski
The Ministry of Foreign Affairs
The Brühl Palace
Warsaw, Poland

February 10, 1939

Dearest Michael,
    I have heard nothing from my friends in London,
but I'm sorry they didn't get along with yours. . . .
    It's so awkward trying to put my feelings into
words, all the more so since I can't believe our cor-
respondence is truly private. Could you get a post office box or something. . . .

As ever,
E

Mme. Elizabeth Thorpe
P.O. Box 247
Biarritz, France

February 26, 1939

My Darling,

You can write to me at your old address at the Villa
Frascati. The manager will collect them for me. I want
to know your every thought, wish, feeling and desire. . . .

With undying love,
M

Michael Lubienski
Villa Frascati #4a
Warsaw, Poland

March 4, 1939

My Dearest Darling Michael,

You may have to destroy the envelope to read this
letter. I put on a wax seal and glued the corners. . . .

All so I can tell you what is in my heart, a passion
and a longing that leaves me drained and empty. I
dream of the blond hairs on your thighs tickling my
lips and the sweet musky smell of your secret
places. . . .

Is there no way you can come to me, be with
me. . . .

I love you Michael,
E

March 23, 1939

My Darling,

Your last letter caught fire in my hands. The words
burned into my brain. . . .

But I cannot come to you now. I cannot abandon
my country in its time of ultimate peril. Nothing is
going right. After swallowing up the rest of Czechoslovakia, Hitler has taken Memel away from us without a shot. Your "friends" are no help. We are
abandoned. I miss you so . . .

March 27, 1939

Dearest Darling Michael,

I would come to you, but if I leave Arthur, I will
lose all claim to see my son. Yet I cannot bear the
thought that I may never see you again. . . .

. . . I also have heard nothing from my "friends."
I pray for your safety. . . .

Arthur's much better and looking forward to his
next posting. Life without you is so utterly pointless,
I may just go with him. . . .

March 31, 1939

My Darling,

I will be in London next week with Beck. Fly to
my side. . . .

April 6, 1939

Dearest Michael,

By now you know I could not get to London. I've
no money of my own anymore, and Arthur refuses to
give me any. I can't get a job because the French have
refused me a work permit. . . .

The Broadway Buildings, London—
April 17, 1939

Menzies glanced through a transcript of the meeting with
Lubienski on April 4, during his trip to London with Colonel Beck.

Knox: My dear Count, you're simply not cooperating,
are you? We've been given nothing of value on the
Enigma, isn't that so?

Lubienski: And what have we received? Exactly nothing as well!

Denniston: May I point out that yesterday and today we've been working out mutual aid arrangements with Colonel Beck and your delegation on a wide range of military matters. But intelligence, which is your responsibility, remains a blank.

Lubienski: This subject is best handled in Warsaw. We should have another meeting. . . .

Knox: The last meeting was a farce. You didn't even tell us what we know you know.

Lubienski: And you didn't tell us what I know you know. You must understand how delicate this matter is in my government. Many are persuaded that you are asking for the crown jewels. I'm sure another meeting with all the interested parties would be productive. You can send Mrs. Pack to Warsaw in advance to make sure that it will be so. . . .

At the top of the transcript, Knox had attached a note to Menzies complaining:

Can we do nothing in Poland without this damnable tart?

Menzies wrote back:

Evidently not.

Villa Frascati, Warsaw—Thursday, July 13, 1939

In the summer heat, the humidity rolled up from the Vistula and enveloped the city like an invisible fog. Dressed in slacks and one of Arthur's old shirts, which she wore tied at the waist with the sleeves rolled up, Elizabeth was perspiring through a third day of packing her household effects at the Villa Frascati. She was using the same excuse she had employed in Spain for returning to Warsaw, but her

real task was to find out whether the Poles were finally
serious about intelligence cooperation. If their response thus
far was any sign, they weren't, and Menzies had only given
her ten days to set up a tripartite meeting that would pay
off. While she rummaged through closets and trunks and
basement storage lockers, Lubienski assured her that he was
hard at work arranging the necessary appointments. He insisted that in the current crisis, it took time to coordinate
the schedules of all the important participants. And there
were security problems. German agents were everywhere.
Meanwhile, the days passed.

She had been so excited at the chance to be with Michael
again that her briefing by Denniston in Paris had been a
blur. But from the moment at the railway station when she
stepped down from the Nord Express and saw him waiting
for her, Elizabeth sensed an unfamiliar tension. Was it her?
Was it him? Was it the pressure of her mission? They both
were responsible for making it a success. Or was it that
they had been through too many good-byes? Had time put
distance between them?

"My God, you're beautiful!" he had exclaimed, taking
her one suitcase. "Is this all you have?"

"Traveling light."

Holding her arm, he led her to a side exit onto Jerusalem
Street where his Fiat was parked. She remembered his
touch; it felt good.

"Thank you for meeting me," she said as she got in the
car. "The embassy refused to help. The ambassador says I
can't speak to anyone there."

"Perfect. You're all mine." He started the car.

She could sense Lubienski trying to be as romantic and
eager as ever. But he looked weary; his young and handsome face bore the lines of unremitting tension. His skin
was gray, without his usual summer tan. The endless hours
at the Foreign Ministry dealing with the growing crisis with
Germany were obviously taking a toll on him.

Warsaw also appeared subtly changed. The same pig-
nosed omnibuses still sniffed after one another down Marszałkowska Street. The orange awnings over the shops
flapped lazily in the afternoon breeze. But there were fewer

shoppers and no young men unless they were dressed in uniform.

"The city seems so quiet," Elizabeth had noted.

"Crisis always produces calm. It's the mobilization."

In St.-Jean-de-Luz the threat of war had seemed remote, but here it was palpable. As they passed the British embassy, a line of people wound out of the consular office and onto the sidewalk. Lubienski pointed to it. "You should see the lines outside Cook's and the American embassy."

"Are people trying to flee already?"

"Mostly the Jews," Lubienski sighed. "We spend decades trying to penetrate the Enigma to discover when Hitler plans to attack us, and these people know by instinct."

The tide of refugees explained why her travel orders were so rigid. She only had until July 20, to work out an agreement in principle for an intelligence exchange and set up a visit on the twenty-third by Menzies, Denniston, and Bertrand from the French service. Then she had to return to England by rail with her household effects.

When she arrived at her apartment at the Villa Frascati, she found that it looked exactly the same. The easy days and nights with Lubienski a year ago had come back to her in a rush, followed immediately by panic at what she now had to do.

"Oh Michael, are we making a mistake?" Her anxiety broke through. "Will your generals pay any attention to a woman? Why would they listen to me?"

"Is this what living with Arthur does to you?" he teased.

She reddened. In the months since their meeting in Cannes, she had gone into suspended animation as a defense against the aridity of her daily life. Now, as if she were emerging from hibernation, she could not get her reflexes working properly. She felt hesitant, tentative.

"Michael, I'm sorry, but I'm scared. I'm no diplomat. I've never felt so much responsibility. And"—she paused—"I'm also afraid of being with you again and for so little time."

"That's reason to seize the moment, not hold back." He swept her into his arms and carried her into the bedroom. In a moment they were a tangle of clothes, sheets, blankets, and pillows, as their bodies broke through the barriers built by their minds. Later, as they lay exhausted and close, Michael spoke again. "And don't worry about the general staff." He tried to lift his head but it fell back on her shoulder. "You'll do fine."

In the following week, for the first time, they lived together like man and wife. In the past, she felt she had been living two lives; but now she realized that she had only been living two half-lives. She was sharing an intimacy that she had never known: the luxury and joy of reaching out to Michael in the middle of the night and of having him wordlessly respond. Elizabeth even reached the point that she would moan over and over, "Michael, I love you. I never wanted to," she would confess, "but I love you."

During the days of waiting for the Poles to respond, she worked nonstop. Because space was limited on the train, she had to go through everything she owned to see what could be sold, given, or thrown away. It was like purging life of its memories.

On that hot and muggy Thursday afternoon, all the French doors stood open while Elizabeth worked through a large steamer trunk. Folded on the top, she found her wedding dress. It gave her pause. Should she leave it behind? What use was it? Unable to decide, she put the dress aside, with a decision to mail it to her mother.

The rest of the chest seemed to be full of Arthur's old uniforms. She lifted up a jacket and a pair of pants. Why did he keep them? They certainly would never fit him again. Had she the right to throw them away? Farther down in the pile, she detected a lump, as if something had been secreted among the layers of clothing. Uncovering it, Elizabeth discovered a small rectangular box that somehow looked familiar. She opened the lid. Hidden in the tissue she found a small antique silver rattle. It was the gift Arthur's parents had brought to the hospital for baby Antony.

Her heart contracted. Why had Arthur saved it? Was he hiding it from her? Or did it mean that in some deep recess, he really cared for their child? Could she bear rekindling the hope that someday the three of them could be together as a family? The past and the future collided. Elizabeth sat down amid packing boxes and cried.

The phone rang. It was Lubienski, and he was excited. "A staff car will pick you up in five minutes," he announced.

She stood there disoriented for a moment, tears and sweat dripping down her neck and staining her blouse. "Thank you for the advance notice," she said.

By the time the car arrived, she had managed to get into a cotton dress and stockings. She splashed on My Sin to cover the sweat. For dignity, she grabbed a straw hat with a veil.

An officer she did not know awaited her at the curb. He did not respond when she asked about Lubienski. The car had its windows blacked out. Getting inside, she found that the opening to the driver's compartment had been blocked by a painted metal plate. She could not see where she was going.

Her sense of direction, however, told her that they were heading south, out of the city. After about twenty minutes, the car made several turns, and she then heard the sound of the tires leaving pavement and traveling onto cobblestones. Soon, she felt the car bouncing over a dirt road.

When they came to a stop and the door opened, she found herself in what she guessed was the Kabackie Woods. In front of her stood an old wooden hunting lodge. In the distance through the trees, she could see a fence and guard tower. Rising behind the house was a tall radio antenna. This had to be Station BS–4, the headquarters of the Polish General Staff Cryptological Service.

"Follow me, Mrs. Pack," her escort said.

This was unlike anything she had expected. Lubienski had led her to believe that she would have a series of meetings with Polish officials. In their offices or over lunch or dinner, she would lay out the British proposals and requirements. Now, for all she knew, she was about to be held incommunicado in a camp in the Pyry Forest.

Inside of the lodge, everything was strictly military. The space had been cut up into a series of small offices with metal doors and frosted glass windows. At the back of the building, she was led down a flight of narrow stairs toward a small basement anteroom with a guard and a heavy steel door. When it swung open, Elizabeth realized that she was entering a large underground bunker. Passing along a wide corridor, she estimated that the installation covered an area four to five times larger than the hunting lodge above it. Hallways to the left went off to what seemed to be sleeping quarters and, if the smell of cabbage was an indication, kitchens. To the right, she glimpsed more offices. At the end of the corridor, she arrived at a set of double doors flanked by armed guards. They stood aside, ushering her into a low-ceilinged conference room.

Two dozen military officers seated at a long table rose to their feet. The air was blue with cigarette smoke. Anxiously, Elizabeth searched for Lubienski's face. He was at the far end of the room, against the wall. She was on her own.

Her escort, who had said nothing during the drive, introduced her to the assembled group in Polish. He then turned to her in English. "You may now make your presentation, Mrs. Pack. There will be simultaneous translation." All the officers sat down and put earphones over their heads. She was left standing.

Her mind raced to remember what she was supposed to say. This was not the relaxed, calm, intimate discussion she had been planning. The faces arrayed around the table were polite, but not particularly friendly and certainly not inviting. They had put her at a disadvantage. She decided that they would respect her only if she struck back.

"Gentlemen, let me begin by offering you my condolences." There was a shuffling of feet. "I offer these condolences," she continued, "because in the coming war with Germany, you will surely lose."

That produced an explosion of protests.

"We have a million men under arms!" cried one officer.

"We've the best cavalry in Europe!" shouted another.

Elizabeth held up her hands. "Poland has the bravest and fiercest fighting men in the world. But your horse cavalry will be no match for German tanks."

"We beat the Russians in 1922!" an elderly officer with a monocle stormed.

"A woman knows nothing of such things," declared a beribboned general with a large white mustache.

"How many of you have seen the war in Spain first-hand?" Elizabeth demanded. They quieted down. "I stood on a hill outside of Madrid and watched the German Henkels and their PzKpfw II tanks slaughter the elite Republican assault troops. The Condor Legion's weapons are nothing compared to what Hitler plans to hurl against you."

"But England and France are helping us," her escort remarked.

"Yes, but you know in your hearts that it's too little and too late." There was no argument from her audience. "You're gripped in a tragedy and you must make bold decisions if Poland is ever to emerge from the coming nightmare."

"What are you suggesting?" The question came from a middle-aged man with a colonel's insignia on his epaulets.

"I am only qualified to discuss intelligence cooperation. We and the French are prepared to give your cryptographic team asylum. The French have already prepared facilities where they can work as we carry on the war against Germany. My service has organized escape routes through Romania."

There was silence. No one in the chastened group wanted to respond.

"If you are confident of peace or of victory," Elizabeth added, "you can regard this as contingency planning."

"And what," the colonel asked, "do you want in exchange?"

Elizabeth paused. This was no time to beat around the bush, yet she wasn't supposed to know about the *bombe*. "Everything you've got," she replied.

Chapter 31

Warsaw—
Wednesday, July 19, 1939

"You were wonderful!" Lubienski had assured her over dinner the night of her appearance before the general staff.

But as the days passed with no response from the Poles, Elizabeth began to worry that she had bungled things completely. On Monday, July 17, Lubienski admitted that he had been cut out of the discussion of her proposals, and had no idea what, if anything, was going on. All he knew was that the French were still angling for a tripartite meeting on the twenty-fourth. By the evening of the eighteenth, a discouraged Elizabeth sent a cable to Broadway over ITT lines through a fictitious Professor Sandwich at Oxford.

CANNOT FIND BOOKS YOU SEEK IN LIBRARY HERE STOP
ADVISE YOU PUT YOUR VISIT ON HOLD STOP MUST DE-
PART TWENTIETH STOP REGARDS STOP CYNTHIA

When her household goods were packed and at the train station, Elizabeth took a suite at the Bristol. For her last evening with Lubienski, Elizabeth saved the dress she had worn when she first met him at the American embassy eighteen months earlier. Standing in front of the full-length mirror, she tried to stifle her despair. Why had the Poles refused to cooperate? It was her fault. She had been too harsh, too insensitive to the masculine pride of the officers in that command bunker. Behaving like a man instead of a demure woman had been a fatal miscalculation. She hated failing. She hated losing. And she feared the consequences for Britain.

The looming separation from Count Michael Lubienski deepened her sense of dread. At first, she had been grateful to have had the time for a long good-bye. But they had grown so close in the last ten days that parting would be surgery without anesthesia. They both sensed that after so many leavetakings, this was the final evening they would ever spend together.

Looking in the mirror, the length of her old dress came as a surprise. In the last year, hemlines had been rising rapidly, and evening dresses no longer touched the floor. As she adjusted the top to cover her breasts, Elizabeth decided that her gown might be out of date, but it still showed her to the best advantage.

She heard a knock on the door. He's early, she thought. It was not quite eight o'clock. Quickly, she checked the sitting room. The Veuve Clicquot sat on ice. The mounds of black Beluga caviar waited in the silver goblet. Dammit, she was going to enjoy her last night in Warsaw no matter what! She pulled open the door with a smile.

Count Lubienski stood with a bouquet of long-stemmed red roses in one hand and an envelope in the other. He had not taken off his gloves. The look on his face was of pure pain.

"My God, Michael"—she drew him inside—"what's the matter?"

Wordlessly, he handed her the envelope. It was embossed with the seal of the Foreign Ministry. The card inside said,

The Minister of State for Foreign Affairs, Colonel Joseph Beck, requests the pleasure of your attendance at dinner, 8:30 P.M., July 19, 1939, at his residence.

Stunned, Elizabeth searched Michael's face for an explanation. Tears were running down his cheeks.

"He says," the words choked in his throat, "that it's strictly business."

* * *

The foreign minister's residence was a grand white palace in French rococo style on Belwederska. Beck had sent a car, and as it drew up to the entrance, Elizabeth was met by a half-dozen military footmen in nineteenth-century uniforms. They escorted her across the foyer and up the sweeping marble staircase to a large library on the second floor. A table for two had been set in front of a walk-in fireplace that had been filled with a bouquet of summer flowers. Books covered the walls all the way to the ceiling. Every few feet around the perimeter of the room stood a suit of armor from a different period of Polish history. Elizabeth was left alone to wander among the carcasses of Poland's military past.

She did not feel afraid. Her only concern was for Michael who stayed behind at the Bristol gulping down the champagne. "If the filthy lecher touches you," he swore as she left, "I pledge to God I shall kill him!"

The suits of armor ranged from simple hammered steel of twelfth-century knights to even simpler "wooden armor" wired together from blocks of oak that had been used by peasant soldiers through the centuries. When she came upon a suit of elaborately engraved and enameled armor from the period of Stanislaw Augustus, Elizabeth wished that she had worn that instead of a low-cut dress.

The door opened and the Polish foreign minister came in, accompanied by a waiter with a bucket of champagne.

"Good evening, Mrs. Pack. So nice of you to accept on such short notice." He took her hand and bowed as he kissed it. "I hope I'm not interfering with any plans for your last night in Warsaw."

You oily son of a bitch, Elizabeth thought as she smiled back at him. Colonel Beck looked as appalling as ever. The streak of long black hair that he slicked straight back over his balding head gave him a remarkably skunklike appearance. His pointy face added further to the impression that he was some kind of varmint. But the eyes were his most frightening feature: whites so yellow that they were darker than his light blue irises. The hooded lids and the bags underneath gave Beck an aspect that struck Elizabeth as utterly subhuman.

"It's an honor to be here," she said easily, lifting a glass of champagne.

"Let me show you the view from the balcony." He took her through a set of French doors. The summer twilight glowed in the sky above the trees. "Down below is Łazienki Palace, where your husband had his unfortunate stroke. How is he, by the way?"

"Almost fully recovered, thank you."

A sly glance belied his condolences. But he steered the rest of their conversation away from personal matters. Over champagne and through the first two courses of the meal, he concentrated on history . . . with a point. The point was that Poland had been repeatedly victimized by everyone. With dessert, a bombe of ice cream, praline, schnapps, whipped cream, and wild strawberries, Colonel Beck turned to Elizabeth's agenda.

"I imagine you're wondering about my government's response to your proposals."

"Having heard nothing, I assumed they were rejected, and I've so informed my colleagues."

A momentary alarm crossed Beck's face. "That may have been premature." Then he pursed his wide lips into something resembling a smile. "And then again, maybe it's not," he said, trying to recover his bargaining leverage.

Elizabeth decided to wait him out.

"I assure you, we're not going to haggle like Jews, Mrs. Pack." He took a sip of Château d'Yquem. "It is, as you Americans say, a 'close call.' The Polish government has placed the decision entirely in my hands. You're here tonight to help me make that decision." His eyes took on the aspect of a predator stalking prey.

"How can I clarify our proposal? What would you like to know?"

"About you, Mrs. Pack, or may I call you Elizabeth as Count Lubienski undoubtedly does?"

"As you wish." The drift of the conversation was not unexpected, but she didn't like it. She had hoped Beck's penchant for girls under the age of thirteen would protect her. Evidently, he was omnivorous.

"And what do you want to know about me?"

"How you do it."

"What do you mean?"

"You've proposed an exchange of intelligence. I'm testing that offer. Tell me how you do it. You've seduced and compromised my closest aide. Do you love him, or is it strictly professional?"

"I hardly see how that relates to the Enigma," Elizabeth retorted.

"That's for me to judge, isn't it? I know all that you've done together, you know. Lubienski has confessed everything to me. About the Enigma. That he told you about the *bombe*. I'm owed an explanation. Is it love?"

Elizabeth was shocked. Lubienski had told her nothing about this. Or maybe Beck was guessing, or lying about where he got his information. Whichever, she had to remain composed. "Perhaps I might help you," she replied, "if I understood what you're driving at."

"If you want me to be crude, so be it." He sat back. "Can you separate sex and love? Most women cannot, unless they're prostitutes."

Elizabeth stood up. "I didn't come here to be insulted!" She threw down her napkin.

"Please! Forgive my choice of words. Accept my apology!"

Elizabeth liked him on the defensive. She sat down again. "How dare you ask such questions?"

"Because I myself do not believe that sex and love need have any connection," he persisted. "Sex can be experienced for itself, don't you agree?"

Knowing that this was true gave her a tinge of guilt. "I suppose."

"And sex can be linked to other powerful emotions," Beck continued.

"Like what?" Where was he headed with this line, she wondered. It made her extremely uneasy.

"Sex can be indistinguishable from anger and hatred. Rape for instance. Or fear. Sex can be tied to fear. Hangmen tell how criminals on the gallows get erections as the rope is put around their necks. They even ejaculate as the trap drops out from under them."

Elizabeth had never had such a conversation with anyone, and it filled her with disgust. "I'm sorry, Colonel

Beck, what does this have to do with our proposals?''

"Come with me.'' He stood up abruptly. "I want to show you something.''

He led her downstairs and through a series of utility rooms to another staircase that descended to the basement. All of the footmen and servants seemed to have vanished. She began to feel trapped.

"This palace was built in the mid-seventeen hundreds as a showcase for a mogul from Silesia. Though it served no known purpose at the time, he even included a dungeon!''

Beck pushed open a heavy wooden door. A low stone room glowed with the light of torches burning against the walls. Elizabeth stifled a nervous laugh. It looked like the set of a Lon Chaney movie. The excitement in Beck's eyes, however, told her this was no joke.

"You see, he had an iron maiden!'' He proudly pointed to a trunk in the shape of a human figure standing open to display the spikes that pointed inward. "And a rack. And a torture table. I've restored them all to their original condition.'' He burnished the waxed wood table with the cuff of his coat jacket.

Elizabeth could feel fear creeping up on her. She had to remain calm, aloof.

"This''—he gestured to the room—"is not just a place of cruelty and pain.'' His face shone in the torchlight. "It was lovingly constructed by a man who saw it as a place of passion.''

"You mean perversion, don't you?''

"Oh yes! Perversion.'' He seemed stimulated by her anxiety. "The bizarre! That is sex in its most human form. What people call 'normal' intercourse is merely what animals do. Human beings are more evolved. For the most highly developed, the touch of silk panties or the lash of a whip can bring orgasm.''

Elizabeth saw that he was excited. Yet he had not touched her. She measured her distance to the door. "What do you want from me?''

Triumph flared in his eyes. "The bizarre!''

She took in the strange instruments that hung from the walls. How had she allowed herself to get into this situation? From the moment Beck started talking about sex she had known that she might have to trade her body for the *bombe*, but she was not prepared to lose her life!

"I won't hurt you," he said as if he read her mind.

Perhaps if she played along. . . . what did he mean by "bizarre"? She must not be squeamish. Elizabeth steeled herself.

"You understand that I will approve your proposals," Beck added.

She would be saving lives, striking a blow against the Nazis. This was the payoff for years of work. "We want the *bombe*."

"Yes, yes!" He glowed.

"A high-level delegation"—Elizabeth pressed—"can be here by Sunday to effect the exchange."

"I'll arrange everything." He was rummaging around in a wardrobe. He pulled out a bundle. It was all leather and metal and black mesh. "Put this on," he said excitedly.

Her eyes darted toward a folding screen in the corner.

"Ah!" he exclaimed. "You want privacy. Of course. It is so much better to begin with modesty!"

She ducked behind the screen. Her hands were shaking and she could make no sense of the garments. They had slits and gaps in peculiar places. Finally, she managed to struggle into what turned out to be a short leather tutu with metal breast cups that had holes cut out at the tips. A black garter belt held up a pair of net stockings. As she pulled a masked hood over her head, she began to feel she was making a serious mistake. She was ignoring the most important lesson she had ever learned: to get what you want first.

Stepping out from behind the screen, Elizabeth found Beck in his underwear. His pale white body was thin and flabby at the same time.

"Tell me to undress," he whispered.

"Undress," she said.

"No, more domineering," he said impatiently.

"Undress!" she commanded.

Beck cringed and pushed down his undershorts. He was only half aroused.

"Tell me to lie on the table," he prompted.

"Lie down!" she commanded. The fact was, there was

no way she could be sure that Beck would keep his end of the bargain.

"Threaten me if I don't obey." He was climbing onto the table and putting his wrists and ankles into the restraints.

"Do you want me to fasten them?" Elizabeth asked.

"Don't ask! Order me! Punish me!"

That was a thrilling prospect. "All right! Put your hands and feet in the blocks! Don't move!" She snapped them shut.

"Tell me I'm bad!"

"You terrible man!"

"I'm only a boy!" he hissed.

"You horrible child! I'm going to punish you!" Elizabeth felt herself getting into the spirit of it.

"Oh yes, I deserve it!" He had become rigid.

"I'm going to hurt you! You're going to suffer!"

"You're so cruel! Be cruel to me!" he begged. "Please be cruel!"

Elizabeth did not know what to do next.

"Don't beat me!" He eagerly nodded his head toward a cat-o'-nine-tails hanging behind him on the wall.

She took it down and found that the braids were made of silk. "You disgusting little boy," she said, "you want me to punish you? I'm going to punish you!" She lashed him across his chest. Her fear was turning to anger. "Punish you for all your vile thoughts!" She lashed him across his thighs. "For all the terrible things you've done!" For what he was doing to her! She lashed him across his groin. Beck pressed against his restraints, his eyes wild. His skin was turning red as she beat him harder and harder. A rage had seized hold of her.

"Get that!" he gasped, gesturing with his bulging eyes toward a shelf next to the torture table. On it was a thick curved ebony rod with a head carved on each end. Elizabeth picked it up. It was heavy.

"Me . . . " He panted. ". . . you! Together!"

Oh no. This was far beyond every line she had ever drawn in her mind. Even if she crossed over, her instincts were telling her that he would never give her the *bombe*. So would it really matter what she did?

Elizabeth released his restraints and ordered him to turn over. "On your knees!" His ugly rear end was up in the air. She relocked his wrists and ankles. "You want something bizarre?" Her voice shook and her breath was coming shorter. "I'll give you an experience more bizarre than anything you've ever had!"

"Oh yes, please!" His body trembled with anticipation.

"Are you ready?"

"Yes! Yes!" His voice cracked with lust.

"You're sure?"

"Now! Please, now!"

"All right!"

With that, she stepped backward out of the chamber and slammed the heavy door shut, leaving the Polish foreign minister pinned on his favorite piece of furniture. For good measure, she jammed the ebony rod through the handles of the door. Whatever cry for help Beck may have uttered, it died, trapped inside the stone dungeon with him.

She inhaled Lubienski's aroma. He smelled of musk and sex. How many times had they made love that night? It seemed that they never stopped, one climax leading to another and another. There was a fury to her passion, as if she were trying to exorcise the demons that Beck had let loose inside of her. But the orgasms did little to overcome the twin griefs of failure and loss. In the war to come, the riddle of the Enigma would be buried along with Polish independence. She trembled to think of Count Lubienski in the same grave.

Maybe she had made a terrible mistake with Beck. She was a professional. Her own feelings should not have gotten in the way. She should have paid any price. But how could the Polish government have delegated such a vital decision? How could they have let their security turn on the notorious whims of the degenerate Colonel Beck? No, they must have already made their decision, and it must have been against sharing the *bombe*. Beck was just trying to exploit her.

She sat up on the side of the bed and held her head in her hands. What choice did she have but to leave Lubienski and Poland to their fate? Broadway couldn't help either of

them now. And after the mess she had made of everything
. . . There wouldn't be any more SIS assignments. That part
of her life was over too. Had she any alternative but to go
off with Arthur to South America? She would be so far
from her baby, Antony. At least she'd done one thing right;
Lubienski knew at last how much she cared, even if it
would only hurt both of them more.

Morning was drifting in around the edges of the heavy
velvet drapes. Her train was at nine-thirty. She had to get
up. A knock from the hall made her open the bedroom
door.

"Come in," she called out. "Leave the breakfast in the
sitting room."

Michael stirred. She kissed him. Then she slipped out of
bed and into the shower. The hot water did not lift her
spirits, neither did the cold.

Michael was awake and sitting up when she came back
to the bedroom. "Breakfast?" she asked.

"I suppose so." He shared her gloom. She opened the
door to the sitting room and stopped. "My God!" she
shrieked. "What's going on?"

Lubienski leaped to her side. Standing in the doorway,
the two of them surveyed a sitting room full of roses. Dozens and dozens of vases filled with pink, yellow, and white
roses rested on every available surface. A huge blood-red
bouquet sitting on a small trunk in the middle of the floor
had a white envelope tucked in among the blossoms. Warily, Elizabeth opened it.

"Bizarre indeed!" was all it said.

Then Elizabeth realized that the trunk was not hers. Louis
Vuitton did not make luggage of olive green metal. She
handed Lubienski the vase and carefully lifted the top. Inside she found a bewildering assembly of wheels and wires.

"What's this?" she asked aloud.

"If I'm not mistaken," Lubienski marveled, "that's the
bombe."

"If they get the cable I sent this morning, Professor
Sandwich should arrive on Sunday by air from London
with two companions," Elizabeth explained to Lubienski
as he helped her stow the precious trunk containing the

bombe in her railway compartment. "You can tell Beck that Sandwich is actually Colonel Menzies, the deputy chief of the Secret Intelligence Service."

"Beck can kiss my ass," Lubienski growled as he jumped down to the platform.

"Michael, nothing happened!" She followed him down the steps.

"You call that outfit you were wearing, nothing?"

"I'm going to save it as a memento," Elizabeth laughed.

"Wear it for Arthur. It might give him another stroke."

Elizabeth put her hand on his cheek. "Take care of yourself. I'll worry about you so."

"I'm the one to worry!" he said with exasperation. "Take that damn machine to the British embassy. Let them figure out how to get it out of the country."

"I'm forbidden to have any contact with them."

"You're just being pigheaded!" Lubienski said angrily. "Think for a minute. You're taking this thing through Germany! Why can't you leave it with me? I'll give it to Professor Sandwich!"

"I don't know for certain that he or anyone else is coming, and I can't wait for a confirming telegram. Besides, what if Beck changes his mind?"

"I won't let him," Lubienski declared.

She didn't want to explain that she couldn't dare count on him. "No," she said simply. "And I don't want to fight with you in our last precious minutes."

"Neither do I." He gave up.

"Good." She put her head against his chest.

They stood that way, still and close, while around them other passengers scrambled to board the train.

"Look," Lubienski pointed to the shafts of light appearing under the eaves of the vast steel roof that spanned the railway station. "The sun is coming up red in the east. That's always a sign that a storm lies ahead. My career is probably finished. And my life is not worth much as you are going off to the west. Someday, I will find you, even if it takes me twenty years."

She could not respond, for she knew of nothing to describe how she felt.

The conductor called the all-aboard. At the steps to the

wagon-lit they embraced for the last time and Elizabeth silently climbed up into her car. Lubienski stood on the platform watching her lips form the words "I love you" through the window. The locomotive began its heavy breathing, and her coach began to slide away. He ran after it until he reached the end of the platform. He then continued staring after the train until it was well out of sight. She was gone.

As he walked downcast back through the station, he heard his name being called. Lubienski looked up to find a young lieutenant from BS–4 rushing toward him with a slip of paper.

"We just decrypted it from SD traffic."

BEGIN TEXT:
TO: UNIT 107 POZEN
FROM: GESTAPO-AMT BERLIN
1089/s/O7/19/39–11:24
SECRET
POSSIBLE POLISH/BRITISH AGENT ELIZABETH PACK
TRAVELING WARSAW–PARIS VIA BERLIN EXPRESS
JULY 20. ESTABLISH SURVEILLANCE AND AWAIT
INSTRUCTIONS.
END TEXT.

Chapter 32

Polish-German Border—
July 20, 1939

Elizabeth was lunching alone in the dining car when the Berlin Express crossed the German frontier and stopped at Pozen for customs. The border police and customs officers entered at the far end of the car and began their methodical check of the passengers' papers. She picked at her food, too keyed up to eat. Relax, she told herself. Stop worrying. Your papers are all in order. The hard part's over. All you have to do is to act natural and mind your own business.

To distract herself, she watched a long freight train pulling out of the station. The cars were half the size of the big boxcars she remembered as a child rolling across the prairies of the Middle West. With their arched roofs, the little European freight cars looked like a Gypsy caravan. Elizabeth felt like a homeless Gypsy herself.

She had spent the morning in her compartment seated on her velvet banquette with its lace antimacassar while she gazed backward at the retreating landscape. Wanting never to forget Poland, she tried practicing her "aloneness." But the act of remembering made her last days with Lubienski seem like something already distant.

The border guards had reached Elizabeth. They examined her diplomatic passport and transit visa, then looked back and gave a quick nod toward two men in black leather trench coats standing near the door. She had not noticed them come in. Handing back her papers, the border officials moved on, but the two men in black seated themselves a few tables away. They did not take off their hats, and they did not take their eyes off her.

358

As calmly as possible, she finished her meal. The men had to be Geheime Staatspolizei. But why were they watching her? The *bombe*? She told herself not to panic. The Gestapo did not need a reason to watch anyone.

When the train moved out of the station, she stood up and, trying not to hurry, headed toward her compartment. Swaying down the corridor, she sensed that she was being followed. Suddenly, it dawned on her that they might have already searched her room. Still, she kept her pace slow and deliberate. Reaching her door, she quickly stepped inside and looked around. Nothing appeared disturbed. She threw open the closet. The green trunk was still there.

Her relief was short-lived. Outside, in the corridor, she heard steel-tipped footsteps approaching her door. They stopped. What would she do if they knocked? What *could* she do if they demanded to come in? She heard whispers. Then the steps moved on. When they finally died away, she was able to breathe again.

Feeling exhausted, Elizabeth rang for the porter. He pulled down the bed from the wall and closed the shades. As soon as he left, she climbed up into the bunk, and still fully dressed, shut her eyes and let the train rock her swiftly to sleep.

When she awoke a few hours later, a rainstorm darkened the German countryside. Her nap had made her feel more composed. Her fear had subsided. Of course she was being watched by the Gestapo. It was only *natürlich*, as the Germans would say. Britain was threatening to go to war with Germany if Hitler attacked Poland. Elizabeth was traveling on a British diplomatic passport and had to expect to be watched by the Nazis as a potential enemy alien. The important thing was to do nothing suspicious or provocative. Stay out of sight as much as possible, and play the part of a demure British diplomat's wife.

She planned to remain in her compartment when the train reached Berlin. There, her car would be switched to the *Nord Express* departing at six-thirty. Later that evening, she would order dinner in her compartment from the porter. That might seem defensive and arouse the Gestapo's curiosity, but it was safer than taking dinner in the dining car and leaving the trunk unguarded. Keeping the *bombe* in her room now seemed like a big mistake.

Elizabeth recognized the outskirts of Berlin flashing by in the rain and could feel the tension rising in her chest. Berlin would be an important test. If she was wrong and the Gestapo had something unpleasant in mind, this was where they would make their move.

Hitler's pride and joy, the autobahn, ran parallel to the tracks for several minutes. The headlights of the cars gleaming off the wet pavement made the ribbons of concrete look like glass. Then came the tiny garden plots, no more than a few square meters of cabbages, that the working-class Berliners escaped to on weekends. Large industrial plants followed and soon covered the entire landscape. It was late afternoon; the day shift should have been over, yet smoke still poured from the tall stacks that towered above the miles upon miles of corrugated metal buildings. In time, plain brick apartment blocks started to appear among the factories, and the city began to take form.

Rattling over viaducts and dipping under bridges, the train finally began to slow as it approached the *Banhof*. The rails rapidly divided and multiplied until it seemed that the train had emerged onto the delta of a steel river. Elizabeth could feel her coach lurch from one track to another as the Berlin Express switched toward its final arrival platform.

As the passengers disembarked, she watched the two Gestapo agents get off the train. Any second she expected them to return with a squad of Hitler Youth to break down her door. But nothing happened. The railroad police on the platform showed no interest in boarding. After a few minutes, she felt the welcome sensation of moving again as her car tolled out into the switching yard where it would be joined to the *Nord Express*. So far—she crossed her fingers—so good.

For the next half hour, Elizabeth's coach shuttled back and forth about the yard. She must have dozed off once more, because she awakened with a jolt when her car coupled up against the train for France. The platform for the *Nord Express* was already crowded with eager passengers; among them she spotted the two men with leather raincoats. They stood huddled with a group of officers in black military-style uniforms. To her shock, she realized that she knew one of them.

It was her old acquaintance from the Wasserspiele night-club, Colonel Kruzel. He was saluting a taller and more formidable-looking officer with the insignia of a gauleiter, who then turned and began to make his way toward the steps of the train.

The knock on her door came almost immediately. When she opened it, Elizabeth had another surprise. It was not the Gestapo. She was confronted with a lean, wiry man in a tweed cap and a Burberry trench coat.

"You're Mrs. Pack?" he asked in English.

She nodded.

"I am from the Passport Control office of the British embassy. May I see your identification?"

Elizabeth checked her sense of relief and prayed he was genuine. "If I can see yours."

"Quite."

They exchanged papers. He spoke with a knobby York-shire accent. Another ex-Royal Navy officer to the rescue, she guessed.

"I've a message for you"—he lowered his voice—"from Broadway." He handed her a slip of paper.

SECRET/MOST URGENT.
4:27P—20/7/39
FOR BERLIN STATION. BROADWAY SENDS 2142
PASS FOLLOWING MESSAGE MRS. ARTHUR PACK ARRIV-
ING THIS PM FROM WARSAW ON BERLIN EXPRESS
BOUND PARIS. WORDING AS RECEIVED FROM POLES. AS-
SUME PACK UNDERSTANDS SENSE.
BEGIN TEXT: GESTAPO AWARE YOUR TRANSIT [STOP]
TAKE EXTRA PRECAUTIONS [STOP] JETTISON YOUR DES-
SERT [STOP] END TEXT.
C.

Elizabeth read the message again, then lit the paper and put it in an ashtray. "I have a small trunk that you must send to Broadway in the diplomatic pouch." She opened the closet.

"What's in it?"

"There's no time to explain." The conductor had just called the all-aboard. "But it's vital, I'm afraid the Germans will get it."

He shot a glance out the window and then tried to lift it. "Sorry, but there's Gestapo all over the platform. If I get off draggin' this thing, they'll clap me in irons."

"But you've diplomatic immunity!" she pleaded. The conductor called the second all-aboard.

"I've no seals to put on the trunk. They'd be in their rights to open it."

"What can I do then?" She was growing desperate.

"I dunno. But you've got to excuse me. I must go ashore."

In a moment he had gone, and again Elizabeth was alone, trapped with the *bombe*. The train began gliding gently out of the station. Soon, it was hurtling across the Spree River, past the massive new Olympic stadium, and through the leafy Berlin suburbs toward the night.

The order to appear before Gauleiter Manfred Ochs arrived in an envelope pushed under her door. The note inside invited Elizabeth to supper in the dining car. She could hardly refuse, but what could she do with the *bombe*? Moving it to the baggage car would only draw attention to it. The answer, Elizabeth decided on careful reflection, was to take a shower. She rang for the porter.

"Is the *Dusche* free?" she asked. He nodded. "Good, will you help me with my trunk? I didn't know what to bring, so I packed everything." She worried that the weight might make him suspicious.

"*Frauen*," he muttered as he hauled it away on his dolly to the shower room at the far end of the car.

In addition to a stall shower, the bathing compartment also held a sink and an enclosed water closet for the toilet. The room was small. She had to maneuver the trunk around in order to open the door to the WC. As she had remembered, it was not like American trains. When she flushed the toilet, she could not look straight down onto the tracks. Some sort of plumbing was involved.

She showered for ten minutes. After drying herself and

putting on her robe, she wadded up one of her hand towels and stuffed it into the toilet. Then she pulled the handle. The bowl filled up. She did it again and the toilet overflowed. Once more, and the water ran under the sill into the corridor. Finally, with slippers soaking, Elizabeth pushed the emergency button. The porter came running.

"Toiletten kaputt!" she cried helplessly.

The porter became frantic. Toilet mess was an unspeakable blot on the honor of the German railway system. He rushed away for something to wipe the floor, hurrying back with bed sheets and a mop. When he was done cleaning up, he put a sign on the water closet declaring KAPUTT—EINTRITT VERBOTEN. BROKEN—ENTRY FORBIDDEN. With profuse apologies, he offered to help Elizabeth back to her compartment with the trunk.

"Never mind," she declined. "I'll manage, and I still must get dressed."

As soon as he was gone, she opened the water closet and wrestled the trunk inside. But then she could not get the door to close. It was enormously heavy, but with the strength of desperation, Elizabeth managed to hoist it up on top of the seat. The train lurched and the trunk slid to one side, crashing against the wall. She pushed and yanked. It was stable. She could close the door.

Elizabeth took several deep breaths. There was no way to lock the toilet door from the outside. If someone ignored the *VERBOTEN* sign, the *bombe* would be discovered. She just had to count on the Germans' horror of bodily waste and their compulsion to obey orders.

She had steeled herself for an interrogation but this was worse. Gauleiter Manfred Ochs was trying to be charming. With his albino-colored hair and porcelain face, he looked utterly humorless, except for the Halloween decorations on the lapels of his uniform—miniature human skulls surrounded by lightning bolts. How could a grown man wear such things?

They were seated in a special compartment in the dining car, which afforded them both luxury and complete privacy. The walls were mahogany and mirrors, with the glass etched with idyllic scenes from Teutonic mythology. Ochs could pull out her fingernails and none of the other diners would hear her. However, he worked hard at being congenial and showed no interest in why she was on the train. He introduced himself as Colonel Kruzel's superior. He talked about how lovely she looked. How much he appreciated her gracious acceptance of his invitation to dinner. He recommended what she should eat and drink. He behaved like they were old friends. She found it all quite ominous.

Elizabeth defended herself with smiles, flattery, and by listening intently. All the while, she was anxiously trying to figure him out. What did he want? Did he know about the *bombe*? The message from the Poles had suggested as much but didn't really say so. And how could he, unless . . . unless Beck told them. No, that was unthinkable. Beck might be a fascist, but he was a *Polish* fascist. So why was he here, pursuing her, measuring her? Maybe he knew about the incident with the van! Stop, she warned herself, you're letting your guilt run wild. You don't know what he is up to, but you'll find out soon enough.

"With dessert we shall have a 1934 Eiswein," he announced, concluding his review of the wine list. "The grapes are left on the vine long after the others have been harvested," he explained, "almost becoming raisins. They're picked with the first frost. The peasants hurry out into the vineyards to pluck them while they are still covered in ice. The wine is a tribute to patience and sacrifice."

And like clockwork, with the arrival of the main course, the cultivated Ochs became the secret policeman.

"So, what have you been doing in the past year?" He nodded to the waiter to begin pouring more wine.

Elizabeth explained that she had remained in St.-Jean-de-Luz with her husband after being evacuated during the Czech crisis.

"Why did you not go back to Warsaw like everyone else?"

"My husband was not well."

"He had been sick for a long time. A stroke, wasn't it? And yet you had remained in Warsaw."

Ochs knew more about her than she had expected. This was a dangerous line of questioning. She took refuge in the truth. "To continue our allowances, we wanted to maintain the impression that he would soon return."

"They are not generous with your husband?"

"Not the British Exchequer."

"So shortsighted." He seemed pleased. "Then what brought you back to Warsaw at this time?"

"Why, Herr Gauleiter, I believe you're interrogating me!"

"Not at all." He smiled a tiny-toothed smile. "Why did you go back to Warsaw?" he said again.

So much for the Scarlett O'Hara defense, she decided. "I had to collect our household goods."

He looked at her with frank disbelief.

"And how was Count Lubienski?"

It was a natural question, but it alarmed her. Perhaps Ochs planned to use her against Lubienski in some way. "That's all over."

"Was it difficult to say good-bye?"

"I think you misunderstand our relationship," she said warily. "Count Lubienski compromised me. He pledged his love and then manipulated me into spying on the British embassy. Lubienski's a cad. As far as I'm concerned, Poland should be wiped off the face of the earth!"

"My Führer's exact sentiments, Elizabeth." He took a sip of wine. "And will Britain try to stand in the way?"

"Does your Führer care?"

"He believes that the German Reich and the British Empire have a common interest in eradicating the threat of Russian bolshevism."

"So you expect Chamberlain to continue to cooperate?"

"We hope he will be persuaded by our strength."

They toasted. Elizabeth had a hard time swallowing.

"So tell me, Mrs. Pack"—he patted his lips with his napkin—"if you feel that way about Count Lubienski, why did you spend every night with him while you were in Warsaw?"

She had made a mistake. Lying was playing his game. "You seem very well informed."

"We have our sources."

Elizabeth felt sick with fear. If he knew about the *bombe*, why didn't he simply arrest her? Seize her baggage? Search everything? But no, that was not the way of the intelligence officer. They never proceeded in a straight line. They hated direct questions and answers, preferring instead to tease out the truth, winkle out morsels of fact. They placed far more faith in information contained in a contradiction than in a frank answer. It was ego: Intelligence officers assumed their quarry were skilled at lying, but never clever enough to tell the truth.

Elizabeth was looking down at her plate. She had eaten little. Ochs's milk-blue eyes had noticed.

"Perhaps you will find dessert more to your liking," he said.

As her pancakes with chocolate sauce arrived, Gauleiter Ochs changed direction again. He became friendly and confidential. He leaned across the table, and put his hand on hers.

"The Reich is extremely grateful for what you did in Prague."

"Herr Henlein was pleased?" Elizabeth had been afraid to raise the subject.

"Very. Everything worked out beautifully. Czechoslovakia is ours."

"Herr Henlein," she said sweetly, "is a pig."

"He has had only kind things to say about you." Ochs drew back.

"I had to tell him Colonel Kruzel was my boyfriend to keep him from attacking me!"

Ochs laughed, his eyes coming alive for the first time. He took her hand again. "Yes, he asked me about that. I assured him that the Gestapo had a relationship with you and that it would continue."

She tried not to register her shock. "In what way?"

"Wherever your husband is assigned next"—he squeezed her hand—"I am sure you could provide invaluable services to the Reich. And we, of course, could solve any financial worries you may have."

Elizabeth forced herself to blush. This wasn't about the *bombe*! The bastard was trying to recruit her!

"We're going to Chile," Elizabeth demurred.

"There are many Germans there. Hitler has great plans for South America. And in time, you can encourage your husband to ask for an assignment to Washington. . . . ''

"Herr Gauleiter, I'm trying to leave all that behind."
Elizabeth was surprised at her own sincerity. "I just want
to be a wife and mother again."

"Frau Pack." Ochs allowed himself a mocking smile,
"Isn't it a little late for *Kinder, Küche, und Kirche*?"

My God, did he know that she was barren? She wanted
to stick her fork in his throat.

"But these are mere details. We have all night to discuss
this matter." His voice purred like a cat with its paw on a
butterfly. "Join me for brandy in the club car." It was an
order. "I have arranged some entertainment from the renowned Sacha Guitry."

A place of honor had been reserved for them. The furniture in the wood-paneled club car was rearranged so that
all of the leather sofas faced forward toward a small area
with a single stool lit by a spotlight. As they sat down,
Sacha Guitry stepped forward. Playwright, actor, and a famous *boulevardier*, he was tall and thin with a hawklike
face and penetrating black eyes. He began by reading a
series of sketches from *Le Soir d'Austerlitz*, the locale for
Napoleon's crushing victory over Hitler's Austrians.

The irony was not lost on Ochs. "The French have such
artistic talent," he said irritably, "but no sense of propriety.
Germany will know how to bring such talent to heel."

As the reading proceeded, Guitry seemed to direct his
performance directly at Elizabeth. But she could barely sit
still, let alone focus on him. Even if Ochs knew nothing
about the *bombe*, her situation remained extremely precar-
ious. She kept imagining more and more passengers using
the shower room, and one of them, out of an excess of
Germanic technical curiosity, opening the water closet and
finding the trunk. At any moment, she expected one of
Ochs's aides to appear and whisper in his ear. The gauleiter's faint eyebrows would rise sharply, and he would stand
up, Luger in hand, to announce that she was under arrest.
Her brandy was disappearing fast.

If everyone respected the *EINTRITT VERBOTEN* sign, she
still was not safe. German efficiency made it certain that
when the train stopped in Frankfurt, someone would come

to fix the toilet. She had to do something before then. Could she simply throw it off the train? Menzies and his team would soon arrive in Warsaw and get everything they wanted from the Poles. Or, would they? She'd had no confirmation from Broadway that the meeting would take place. And previous ones had been a bust. For all she knew, she and her trunk were it. A *bombe* in hand . . . Elizabeth cursed her stubborn pride in not turning over the *bombe* to the British embassy in Warsaw.

The audience was laughing and clapping. "Thank you, ladies and gentlemen," he said as the applause died down. "In particular, I want to thank Herr Ochs for the invitation to appear before you tonight." His stress on the word "invitation" made clear that it had been a command performance. He bowed and stepped away from the light.

"Do join us, Mr. Guitry," Ochs insisted.

The Frenchman glanced over at the men and women in his entourage who waited at another banquette.

"For only a moment, if you don't mind," Guitry replied and sat down. "It has been a difficult and long day."

"You were wonderful," Elizabeth said.

"Having you right in front of me was an inspiration, mademoiselle." His eyes twinkled with interest.

"Do you often perform in Germany?" Ochs cut off any reply.

"In the past. This time, I was merely helping a friend, an impresario, for the benefit of his family."

"He passed away?" asked Elizabeth.

"He was arrested. He is a Jew."

"I'm sure it was for his own safety," Ochs said blandly.

"If you will forgive me." Sacha Guitry rose. "Mademoiselle, when you are in Paris"—he handed her a card—"I hope that you will give me the pleasure of being inspired by you once again."

Ochs was left with an annoyed smirk on his face. The club car was beginning to thin out.

"I'm exhausted," Elizabeth said. She didn't want any more third degree, and she needed time to think. "Thank you for your hospitality, but I really must retire."

"I'll accompany you."

Just what she feared. Mercifully, he had to walk behind

her through the train corridors, which kept conversation to a minimum. On the way to her compartment, they passed the shower room. The door remained closed and the sign in place. Next, came a suite of rooms occupied by Sacha Guitry and his entourage. Their doors stood open. Inside, a party was already under way. They were drinking and laughing and singing while someone played a concertina. Guitry waved. Ochs frowned.

When they reached her compartment, Ochs offered Elizabeth a cigarette. She declined.

"You must take my proposal seriously." He stepped forward. "You would be an invaluable asset to the Reich."

"I'll think about it, of course."

"I hope so." His voice took on an edge of menace. "Scotland Yard or your Mr. J. Edgar Hoover might not understand your collaboration with us in Czechoslovakia. What would happen to your husband's career? What would happen to you?"

Elizabeth made herself look suitably intimidated. "And if I agree to your proposal?"

"We would want you to delay your departure from Germany for a few days to receive proper orientation." He took hold of her arms. "You have until tomorrow morning when we reach the French border to give me your answer. In the meantime . . . " He lunged forward to kiss her.

She turned her head. Would wonders never cease? On top of everything, the fearsome Gestapo gauleiter wanted into her pants! That, at least, put her on more familiar ground. Elizabeth placed her hand on his chest to keep him at bay.

"My dear Manfred," she said invitingly, "I would love to get to know you better . . . "

His eyes shone with anticipation.

". . . but I'm having my period."

And before he could think to shut his mouth, she had disappeared inside her room.

She leaned against the inside of her door and tried to calm her nerves. Incredibly, she herself had now become a major threat to the security of Broadway's code-breaking effort. She had to handle Ochs's proposition carefully, whether she said yes or no. Otherwise, she could wind up under severe questioning and might reveal enough to compromise all that the Poles and British had achieved against the Enigma. Elizabeth saw no alternative; she had to find a way to get both herself and the *bombe* out of Germany on that train.

Chapter 33

It was two o'clock in the morning before Elizabeth re-
emerged and tiptoed quietly toward the shower compartment. The doors to Sacha Guitry's suite were now closed,
but she could still hear music and voices. The rest of the
compartments were dark and silent. Elizabeth had stayed in
her cocktail dress, reasoning that if questioned, she could
claim that she had been at Guitry's party.

Entering the shower room, she found that the *VERBOTEN*
sign remained fixed on the door to the water closet. Inside,
to her relief, the trunk continued to squat crazily on the
toilet. Struggling, she managed to deposit it on the floor
with a heavy thud. Breathing hard, she waited to see if the
noise brought any reaction. There was none.

Carefully, she opened the door to the corridor. No one
was in sight. Pulling on one of the leather handles she began to haul the trunk toward the front of the train, hoping
that the dragging noise would be muffled by the sound of
the train.

She passed by her compartment. It was not a safe place
to hide anything. When she had closed her door in Ochs's
face, she half expected to find her compartment in a sham-
bles. But superficially, nothing seemed to have been
touched. On close inspection, however, she could see that
everything had received a thorough going-over. Each object
in the room had been disturbed just enough to let her know
that she had been systematically searched. Her toothbrush,
she noticed, had been moved to the opposite side of the

sink. She refused to think of what would have happened had she not stashed the trunk in the shower room.

Stopping to rest as she neared the front of her car, Elizabeth saw that a light burned in the porter's compartment. Peeking through the window in his door, Elizabeth could see him methodically going over his receipts on an adding machine. She crouched down and began to inch the trunk along under the window. Suddenly, there was a screeching as it scraped against the wall. The adding machine stopped. Elizabeth held her breath. What would she say if he came out and found her on her hands and knees? What was she doing with her trunk at this end of the car? At this hour of the night? Dressed in her cocktail outfit? After what seemed like enough time for the train to cross half of Saxony, the adding machine started up again. Slowly and carefully, Elizabeth slid the trunk past the porter's compartment to the door to the landing between the cars. She pushed it open.

The sound of the rushing train filled the corridor. As she stepped through and pulled on the trunk, it caught on the threshold. She yanked. It wouldn't come loose. The train traversed a bridge, the hollow clatter booming through the car. She could see the shadow of the porter in the corridor. He was standing up. Desperately, she twisted and pulled at the trunk. He was moving.

With all her strength, she pushed and lifted and jerked the trunk free. The door slammed, and she fell back onto the swaying platform. In the passing lights, she could make out the face of the porter pressed against the window, peering into the dark with a perplexed look on his face.

She rolled to one side, tucking herself into a shadow, hoping he could not see the trunk, praying he wouldn't open the door. They entered a tunnel and everything went black. When she could see again, his face was gone from the window.

Picking herself up, Elizabeth discovered that she was shaking. You've no time for this, she said silently, and proceeded to wrestle the trunk over the sliding steel plates that coupled the cars. But before hauling the trunk into the next coach, she decided to go ahead to check. Thankfully, everyone seemed asleep. That enabled her to stand up as she dragged the trunk down the corridor. When she reached the next porter's office, she was relieved to find that it was closed and dark.

Her destination lay just ahead. She had decided that the only place to put the trunk was where it belonged—in the luggage compartment at the front of the train. Once she had gotten it inside, she again stopped to catch her breath. Despite the window in the door, it was too dark to see. She had to risk turning on the lights. It took her several minutes to find the switch, and even longer for her eyes to adjust and to locate her household effects. She found them hidden behind the trunks, equipment, props, and scenery of Sacha Guitry's show.

As Elizabeth tried to maneuver her trunk into an inconspicuous place, she had the sudden sensation of the train rapidly slowing. Then she heard the brakes start to squeal. Concerned, she ran to the door and looked out. The train had entered a marshaling yard and was quickly coming to a halt. She checked her watch; had they reached Frankfurt already? To get a better look, she stepped out onto the platform between the cars. Ahead, in a pool of light, she saw a contingent of soldiers. The moment the train stopped, they fanned out and began climbing on board.

Panicked, Elizabeth retreated into the baggage car. She snapped out the light and then groped her way toward the trunk. Struggling to push it against the other baggage, she saw flashlight beams waving outside the window. They were coming her way! Taking an extra minute for one last effort to conceal the trunk, Elizabeth then dashed to the other end of the car and out onto the landing just as the soldiers threw open the door.

The next coach was the mail car. Inside she could see German postal workers busily sorting mail into pigeonholes. That was no place to hide. The light came on in the baggage car. Standing back in the shadow, Elizabeth anxiously watched as the soldiers worked their way through the luggage. Every few feet, they would stop while one of them examined a baggage tag and the other made a note on a clipboard. To her dismay, they seemed to spend an inordinate amount of time inspecting the documents on her household effects.

Finally, they moved on, but that only brought them closer to her. Would they stay in the baggage compartment, or continue into the mail car? She could not chance being discovered. Elizabeth desperately tried to think of an alternative, but there wasn't any. The train was stopped. She would have to get off and hope to find an unguarded landing farther back where she could again climb aboard.

Her leap to the ground in high heels sent her tumbling. She got up and brushed herself off. Holding up the hem of her dress, she began to make her way back toward her coach, staying close to the side of the train. But something seemed strange, wrong. At first, she thought that her fall had made her confused. She hurried faster and faster but appeared to make no progress. Good God, she realized, the train was moving! Backing up! Backing away from her! She began to run, but it moved even faster. The baggage car went sliding by. Then the mail car. Then the engine.

To avoid the headlight, Elizabeth ducked behind an empty switching station. Helplessly, she watched as her train retreated farther and farther into the night and fog. A string of freight cars rolled in front of her, blocking her view. When they had passed, her train had vanished.

Wildly, she looked around. In every direction she found a sea of crisscrossing rails that stretched away until they disappeared in the misty blackness. Here and there, floodlights created small islands of illumination where boxcars and locomotives moved slowly through the ground fog, groaning and creaking and wheezing like unwell monsters. Every few minutes, their agonies would be halted by a shattering collision, as the cars coupled in some nightmare mating dance.

Fighting hysteria, Elizabeth began to run, tripping and falling, in the direction that she had last seen the *Nord Express*. She tore her stockings and snapped the heel off her right shoe. She thought she saw her train stopped in the distance, but as she stumbled toward it, a long freight materialized out of the night to her left, cutting her off. Frantic, she could do nothing but wait as it leisurely rolled by. When the last car moved past, she anxiously leaped across the track only to find another engine bearing down on her from the other direction.

Her broken shoe stuck between the ties. She fell. Transfixed by the locomotive fifteen feet away, everything seemed to go into slow motion. Like a hideous dream, her legs wouldn't move. She could not get up. Her mind faltered. She saw herself trapped in the German communications van as the Baltic Zephyr smashed into it. Then her hands found the rail. It stung with the vibration of the oncoming train. She pulled, pulled with all her might.

The locomotive was upon her. She rolled off the track as it lumbered past, a sharp pain piercing her ankle. She looked down at her foot. It was still there! It had been a glancing blow. And she was alive!

Staggering upright, she looked around. Not far away, a passenger train moved gracefully across the yard. In agony, she limped toward it. As she got nearer, she could make out the words lettered on the side of several cars, *WAGON-LIT*. Salvation! It was the *Nord Express*! Then for a moment she hesitated. What if it wasn't? But she had no money, no papers. If she were caught in a railroad yard at night she could be shot as a spy. Better to take her chances with the train.

She had to run hard to intercept it. As she drew even with the moving coaches, Elizabeth leaped for the handrail next to the door. She missed. The damn train was accelerating again! She jumped a second time and caught it, swinging her feet up to the steps which were tucked under the door. Hanging away from the train, she tried to open the door to the landing, but the handle would not give. The train was traveling faster and faster. A signal pole brushed by close enough to snatch at her hair. Ahead, she could see that she would soon overtake a parked freight. She would never fit between the two trains.

With all her remaining strength, Elizabeth pulled on the handle, but still the door would not open. Now the train was moving too fast to jump. Desperate, she released her grip on the handrail, and put her entire weight on the door handle. It cracked open. But then slowly and inexorably, the door swung wider and wider—with Elizabeth clinging to the outside.

Dangling out over the side of the train like a sack of mail, she was hurtling toward the stopped freight. No matter how she jerked and wriggled, she could not get the door to swing back. Extending her left leg she managed to reach around and hook the toe of her shoe under the handrail. Slowly, she managed to pull the door closer and closer to the train until at last she was able to get her right foot onto the bottom step. Then she was stuck. The other train was no more than fifty feet away. In terror, she let go of the door and grabbed for the handrail, twisting around just as the door hit the back of the parked train. With a crash, the door slammed shut, knocking her into the car and across the landing.

Stunned and dazed, Elizabeth tried to stand but fell against the bulkhead. She heard shouts and the clatter of boots and realized that soldiers were coming. On her hands and knees, she crawled to the door of the next car and pulled herself up. Through the window she could see no one. Pushing the door open, she staggered into the car. Finally, she was in luck; it was her coach. But as Elizabeth turned into the corridor, her luck ran out. At the far end, soldiers knocked at a compartment, demanding to be let in. They were searching the train.

She was trapped. The soldiers were closing in on her. How could she explain one shoe gone, the other broken, her stockings torn and her dress ripped and soiled, a bleeding ankle and skinned hands and knees. It was too late to duck into the shower room, and they would surely check it anyway. Elizabeth felt exhausted. She wanted to give up.

The soldiers ahead of her stepped into the compartment. She had a chance to make a dash for her room. But before she got halfway to her door, one of them backed out into the corridor again. She would be caught! The next compartment was Sacha Guitry's. She turned the knob, and the door opened. Before the soldier could turn around, she slipped inside.

"*Qui est là?*" He put on the reading light, then he smiled. "It's late, but you can still join our little party." He was nestling in bed with two women.

Elizabeth could hear the Nazis knocking on another compartment nearby. "I haven't been able to sleep, thinking of you," Elizabeth whispered. In the half dark she quickly shed her tattered clothes.

"Come here," one of the women said, holding up the sheet. In the corridor, the German soldiers cursed and shouted like angry geese. As Guitry put out the light, Elizabeth sought sanctuary in the labyrinth of their bodies.

Skin moved against skin. Hands and lips explored her most secret places. She felt spent, helpless, without a will of her own. Entwined in the undulating mass, Elizabeth could not tell who was who, and she didn't care.

A sharp bang on the door and they all stopped. It flew open, and two soldiers stood outlined in the low light of the corridor. One of them was an officer. He spoke.

"*Achtung!* Who is in here?" It was Ochs's voice.

Sacha Guitry again put on the light. The gauleiter failed to conceal his shock.

"Frau Pack! We thought something had happened to you!"

"You can see that I'm quite safe."

Ochs's expression wavered between envy and disgust. Clicking his heels, he bowed. "Be advised, Monsieur Guitry, decadent sexual acts receive stiff punishment in the new Germany!" The other two girls began to giggle. "As for you, Mrs. Pack, I shall see you in the morning." He stepped back and slammed the door.

Guitry put his hand on Elizabeth's cheek. "I believe you have made our *Eisenbahnführer* jealous." One of the other girls began stroking her shoulders.

"Pity," was all Elizabeth could find to say, and with a sigh, she fell asleep in the security and comfort of their flesh.

Chapter 34

The Franco-German Frontier—
July 21, 1939

With the dawn, her fear had come back like morning sickness. Elizabeth awakened with the realization that she had done the one thing she shouldn't: make Ochs into an adversary.

She slipped out of Sacha Guitry's bed and returned to her room, her mind in turmoil over how to respond to his proposition. Her instincts told her to refuse. After all, what could he do to her? She was a diplomat traveling under diplomatic immunity. He had no grounds to detain her.

However, as the train slowed approaching the German border, her resolve began to waiver, for when she opened her door to go to the W.C., an SS storm trooper with a submachine gun blocked her way.

"You are confined to your compartment under the orders of Gauleiter Ochs," he informed her. Her anxious protests were met with armed indifference. Humiliated, she had to use the sink in her room to relieve herself.

As soon as the *Nord Express* came to a halt on the German side of the frontier, another platoon of SS guards boarded and began forcing dozens of passengers from the train, making them line up in front of the dingy railway station. From her window, Elizabeth watched with growing apprehension as one by one, the passengers were brought before Ochs. He sat in the middle of the platform behind a large makeshift table like a judge at a kangaroo court. After a brief exchange, he would nod his head one way or the other and they would either be allowed to reboard the train or be marched off to several waiting trucks.

Many of the passengers would hand Ochs bundles of
cash, often whole briefcases full. Soon, the banknotes piling
up on the table spilled onto the platform. Women, in desperation, would reach beneath their dresses to draw out
strands of pearls or diamond necklaces from their underwear. Sometimes the bribery worked; sometimes it did not.
Occasionally, Ochs would indicate that only one or two
members of a family could reboard the train. Through their
anguished gestures, Elizabeth could see parents and chil
dren, husbands and wives, beg one another to leave them
behind. If they failed to decide before the gauleiter got
bored, he would order them all hauled off to the trucks.

Elizabeth felt angry and ashamed: angry that she could
do nothing to help them; ashamed that she had a diplomatic
passport that would protect her. A heavy banging on the
door announced that it was her turn to confront the gauleiter.

"Your travel documents." Elizabeth handed over her
diplomatic passport to the storm trooper who had been
guarding her door. "You must disembark."

As she stepped down to the platform, the SS guard gave
Elizabeth a shove in the direction of Ochs's table with the
butt of his gun.

The Gestapo gauleiter sat there studying her passport,
making notes. "What is your answer?" He did not look
up.

Behind him, the SS were unloading the baggage car,
dumping the possessions of the people in the trucks onto
the platform. Farther on, just past the locomotive, a concrete bunker and a fence topped with rolls of barbed wire
defined the French border. Beyond that, barely a hundred
yards down the tracks, she could see the town of Mars-la-
Tour shining in the morning sun. A tricolor flag flapped
briskly against a bright blue sky. She could imagine the
smell of café au lait and croissants. France was so close
she ached.

"I hope you didn't put on this display for my benefit."
She didn't care how much of a beast he was; if she was
going to negotiate, Elizabeth was going to start tough. She
only hoped the quiver in her voice wouldn't give her away.

"I want your answer now," he demanded.

She would have loved to spit on him, but her mouth was too dry. Then the shouting and swearing of the SS guards drew her attention back to the baggage car. Suddenly, she recognized some of the trunks and crates. They belonged to her! The storm troopers were removing her household effects from the train!

"If I refuse?" Elizabeth was almost talking to herself.

"I'll have to keep you here for questioning." Ochs raised his head and looked at her. His watery blue eyes were blank.

"And if I agree, you said you'll keep me here for training and indoctrination?"

"One is better than the other."

"I'll know the difference?" She struggled to be flippant but sounded fatalistic.

"You can ride with me"—he pointed to an open Mercedes-Benz touring car—"or with them."

Elizabeth glanced at the trucks. Her bravado collapsed. Why not join the others? Her position was as hopeless. As one of the trucks pulled away with its doomed cargo, a Daimler had driven up, and a sweating red-faced man in a black suit and homburg had gotten out. He was hurrying toward them. Exactly what I need, Elizabeth thought bitterly, Gestapo reinforcements.

"So your offer is a ruse," she said, angry and dispirited. "You're going to keep me here no matter what."

"Only for a little while." He surprised her by smiling magnanimously. "We don't want to create undue suspicion. You can cable your husband and say you're briefly delayed. I'm sure he's used to that."

Could she believe him, or was this more of the technique held used on the other passengers; intimidation, terror, and just a ray of hope to keep everyone docile? Did she have any choice but to capitulate? "What do you really want from me?"

"It is as I have proposed. But first you must establish your bona fides."

"And how do I do that?" The man with the homburg had gathered up an entourage of SS and was fast approaching.

"By telling us everything you know about Poland." He

paused. "And of course everything about British activities as well."

By the time they were through with her, Elizabeth knew, she would have told them everything about everything. The sooner she was dead the better.

"I say, who's in charge here?" interrupted the man from the Daimlier. He was English!

Shocked, Gauleiter Ochs clicked his heels.

"Well, what's going on?" the Englishman demanded officiously. He was built like a fireplug and looked about as bright. "Who are those people?" He pointed to the trucks.

"Jews and Communists, and none of your affair," Ochs snapped. He had recovered his composure. "Who are you, and what is your business?"

"I'm the British consular agent in Metz. I've got instructions to locate a Mrs. Arthur Pack. She's supposed to be on this train."

"I'm Mrs. Pack!" Elizabeth shouted. Ochs looked like the consul had just snatched away his autographed copy of *Mein Kampf*. Bless Broadway for being on its toes for once!

"Can I see your passport?" the consul asked.

"He has it." She pointed to Ochs.

"This woman has no passport," Ochs declared. "That is why she must remain here."

"But you took my passport!" Elizabeth cried.

"Why would I do that?"

How could she explain? The consular agent looked stumped. A conductor called the all-aboard.

"I am a British diplomat's wife," she insisted anxiously. "I'm traveling on a diplomatic passport with a valid transit visa. No matter what trick they're pulling, I've diplomatic immunity, and I demand to be allowed to go to France!"

"But you've no proof of who you are," Ochs pointed out.

The consul, who appeared irritated at having to be up and working so early in the morning, seemed ready to go along with him. "I must say, madam, you don't sound British."

"I'm not! I'm American! But I can explain. . . . "

The consul looked at the gauleiter, who shook his head. The train conductor shouted out a second all-aboard.

"Christ, this is absurd!" Elizabeth fought not to sound hysterical. "I've got other identification, photographs, in my baggage." She gestured toward her household effects, which were now piled up by the side of the track. Then she realized that the SS had begun to pry open her crates and trunks.

"Stop them!" she demanded.

"We must examine everything carefully," Ochs insisted.

"You've no right. . . ."

"He does, actually," said the consul unhelpfully. "Personal things aren't under diplomatic seal, you should know that." He looked at her with growing suspicion.

"This is a hostile act against His Majesty's diplomatic service! I demand you stop the train and put my things back on board!"

"Let's not get carried away, madam." The consul frowned. "We've problems like this every day. Remember, we're guests in this country."

"I'm sure we could work everything out," Ochs added soothingly. "You could be on the next train." He smiled. "Otherwise, I can't tell you how long it will take to go through your baggage."

The conductor called the last all-aboard. Panic broke loose in her again. Control yourself, she ordered. Something was wrong with this picture. What was it her father used to say about the Germans? They're either at your feet or at your throat. Why was Ochs trying to *persuade* her? How far was he authorized to go?

The locomotive let out its shrill cry. Elizabeth looked at her baggage; she had to choose. She looked at Ochs; she had to gamble.

"Keep my luggage." She smiled icily at him. "I hope you enjoy wearing my dresses." Turning her back, she headed for the train.

"Stop!" Ochs commanded. He had taken out his Luger.

She whirled on him. "What are you going to do, Gauleiter, shoot me? Kidnap me? What about the consul here? He'll have to report to London. Or are you going to shoot him too?"

The Englishman began stuttering, "No, no. . . ."

"Will murdering two British diplomats"—she stared

Ochs in the face—"help the Führer keep Britain out of your war on Poland?"

Ochs's eyes were blinking furiously. Elizabeth again turned away from him and began to walk purposefully toward the train. At any moment, she expected to feel a nine-millimeter slug smash into her spine.

"You'll regret this!" he shouted after her. "I promise you!"

Elizabeth jumped on board just as the train began easing away from the platform. From her compartment window, she watched her household effects being plundered by the SS. All she had left were the clothes in her closet, but she was grateful beyond words for that. She took out her raincoat and then tore away the lining. Her most precious possession was there. She pressed her old American passport in the name of Amy Thorpe to her breast as the *Nord Express* carried her away to safety.

Station Wicher, Pyry Forest, Poland— July 25, 1939

Dilly Knox, Commander Denniston, and Colonel Menzies (presenting himself as Professor Sandwich from Oxford) sat on one side of the table along with Captain Gustave Bertrand, chief of French radio intelligence, and two of his staff. The Polish team facing them was led by Colonel Stephan Mayer, chief of intelligence, the Polish General Staff, and consisted of Colonel Gwido Langer, head of the Cipher Bureau; Major Maksymilian Ciezki, chief of BS–4, the German section; and Antoni Palluth, chief engineer of AVA. They were gathered in the same blank underground conference room where Elizabeth had confronted the Polish general staff only a week earlier. This was a technical-level meeting; Beck, Lubienski, and more senior Polish officials were not present.

"We arrange everything like so." The cherubic Ciezki was lining up a stack of enormous sheets of paper, twenty-six of them to accord with the number of letters in the alphabet. Each sheet was marked with squares, fifty-one on a side. Some of the squares were perforated. "When the hole goes all the way through the stack, we have found one letter of the key. We call the holes 'females,'" he added with a blush. "It is a pun in Polish on 'same places,' not a biological reference."

"Very creative," Dilly Knox allowed. For two days, the British had been listening to the Poles describe how they had cracked the Enigma: how they had deduced the wiring of the rotors, the reflector board, the ring settings, the keyboard, using extremely sophisticated mathematics, group theory, and permutation analysis. They displayed their tools—the perforated sheets and "grills"; a device called a "clock" that determined the order of the rotors; and a cyclometer, which eliminated the complexity of the reflecting board. But the Poles said nothing about the *bombe*, and while the rest was technically interesting, without the *bombe* the British were essentially bored to tears.

"The climax of all of these efforts," Colonel Mayer began to sum up, "was to produce an Enigma of our own." From a cabinet behind him, he took out a machine and put it on the table.

"My God!" Knox exclaimed. "We must tell London immediately!" He was laying it on thick. "Get our mechanics and electrical people over here right away to examine it!"

The Poles beamed with pride.

Menzies nudged Denniston. "Tell Dilly not to overdo it," he whispered.

"Sending experts won't be necessary," Colonel Mayer was saying. "As a token of good faith, I have one for each delegation." Major Ciezki lifted two more Enigma machines onto the table.

"Isn't that marvelous!" Dilly gushed.

"You're too kind," Denniston added.

"How shall we ever get it back to London?" Dilly wondered.

"I volunteer the French diplomatic pouch," Captain Bertrand spoke up. "It would be an honor."

"But we must emphasize," Colonel Langer continued, "that breaking the Enigma is not a single event. It is a duel, with the Germans constantly making changes. In a real sense, we must break the Enigma anew each day, finding the keys, decrypting the messages. That is why collaboration is so essential. We look forward to working with you.''

As the meeting broke up so that the British could catch their flight, Antoni Palluth approached Colonel Langer.

"I don't understand," he said. "Why do we not give them a *bombe*?"

"The first rule of intelligence cooperation," Langer explained, "is always to hold something back."

Prae Wood, St. Albans— August 16, 1939

The steel door clanged shut behind her. Elizabeth lay down on the cot, exhausted but unable to sleep. Her basement room had no window, so she had no sense of day or night. This part of the Prae Wood mansion had been off limits when she was there before studying tradecraft. Now she knew why. It was a detention area for agents under suspicion of having been "turned."

Elizabeth had managed to get back to London on July 23, in time to brief Menzies and the others on what had happened to her and the *bombe* before they flew to Warsaw for their meeting with the Poles. Everything seemed fine. She was given a room at a modest hotel on Birdcage Walk not far from Broadway and a small office at SIS headquarters to write a report. When the team returned from Warsaw she was told she was meeting them at Prae Wood. But when she arrived at the mansion, she was greeted by a far different team. It was from counterintelligence. She had been under interrogation ever since.

Her principal inquisitor was a large, barrel-chested, bald man in his mid-forties who looked like he should shave three times a day. Elizabeth tried to estimate whether it was morning, noon, or night by the length of stubble on his face. She never learned his name or that of the others who questioned her. They called her Cynthia. No physical force was used. They didn't have to. After her initial outrage, she had settled into a state of perpetual panic. It was clear she would never leave the basement of Prae Wood until she said what they wanted to hear.

As the hours, days, and weeks passed, Elizabeth had been required to go over every moment of her time in Spain and Poland. They went into her childhood. They wanted the names of every foreign diplomat who ever had come to dinner at her home in Washington, D.C., and she had to remember every classmate when she had gone to school in Switzerland. Finally, after what had seemed like a month, the chief interrogator had just revealed what they wanted her to admit.

She was seated across from him in the same bare white room where all the questioning took place. The table between them was bolted to the floor. So was her chair.

"The plans that Lubienski supposedly stole from AVA," he began, "who altered them? You? Lubienski? The Poles? Your German control?"

"Nobody," she said wearily. "The camera was broken. . . . "

"And the Enigma machine you allegedly stole from the Germans, it was already obsolete. What made you think that we wouldn't figure that out?"

"I warned Broadway about the changes!" she suddenly yelled at him.

"And this so-called *bombe*," he continued calmly, "who besides yourself has ever seen it?"

"Our man in Berlin!"

"He saw a green metal trunk. Nothing more."

"Ask Denniston, Menzies, Knox! The Poles must have told them something about it!"

"Not a word. Why do you think you're here?"

"So you think that I conspired with the Nazis and Count Lubienski to give you fake plans, a bum Enigma machine and made up the story about the *bombe*?" She couldn't believe it!

He looked at her evenly. "Would you like to make a confession?"

Elizabeth let out a scream. It was a scream of frustration, terror, and hopelessness. And it didn't stop until they dragged her back to her cell and slammed the door.

Now, she was sitting on her cot, her legs drawn up, her arms around her knees. She realized that this had been Dilly

Knox's theory all along—a vast and subtle deception orchestrated by the Gestapo to keep his code breakers one step behind, off balance, wasting their time trying to solve malevolent riddles secretly created by the Germans.

If only she had gotten the *bombe*! She thought that she had outwitted the Gestapo. When she was in the baggage car of the *Nord Express*, she had taken one of the tags off Sacha Guitry's equipment and put it on the trunk containing the *bombe*. But when she arrived in Paris, the attendant at the baggage room said it was not with his luggage. For a hundred francs, the attendant also explained that a portion of Sacha Guitry's baggage was destined for his new show in London and had gone directly to a closed customs shed in Le Havre, where it would await onward shipment. Before being locked up at Prae Wood, Elizabeth had written to Guitry saying that one of her trunks might have been mixed up with his luggage. Elizabeth had also urged her inquisitors to have Bertrand check with French customs. She had heard nothing back from anyone. Maybe, thought Elizabeth in despair, the Gestapo had discovered the *bombe* on the train after all.

A discreet knock rattled her steel door. She was startled. They had never bothered to knock before. The door opened. It was Captain Lance in a tuxedo. He had a silvery formal dress in one hand and a pair of high-heeled shoes in the other.

"All that Guitry's letter to you said," Captain Lance explained as the car worked through London traffic snarled by a downpour, "was that his boat train would arrive at Victoria Station at eight-ten this evening, and that he looked forward to seeing you." There was a clear note of concern in his voice. "You'd better hope he's got the *bombe* with him."

"Otherwise?" Elizabeth asked.

"Otherwise, it'll only be a question of whether you've been a witting, or unwitting, accomplice to the Gestapo."

"You don't believe that! You can't!"

"Elizabeth, understand. Because of you, I'm under a cloud too!"

She felt utterly confused. "I can't understand why Bertrand couldn't find out from French customs whether the *bombe* was with Guitry's things in LeHavre."

"We didn't ask him."

"What? For God's sake, why not?"

The car had arrived at Victoria Station. It drew up next to a pair of Bentleys at the curb.

"I'm joining Knox and Denniston in the second car. You're to get in the front seat of the first. Menzies is in the back with Stephenson. Ask them."

"If there is a *bombe*," Menzies sniffed, "we're certainly not about to let the French get it first. We did, for security, arrange for Bertrand to accompany Guitry on the boat train. Neither of them are aware of this of course."

"Then why is Bertrand coming?" Elizabeth asked.

"He's delivering the Enigma machine the Poles gave us. That's why we're all in these monkey suits." Like Captain Lance, Menzies and Stephenson also wore tuxedos. Menzies fingered the red carnation in his lapel. "Bertrand wants to celebrate afterward at the Savoy."

"What I can't understand," Stephenson said, "is why Beck would give a *bombe* to Elizabeth, but the Polish intelligence people would say nothing about it to you."

"Quite," Menzies growled. It was clearly a sore subject.

"Politics," Elizabeth insisted. "Rivalries. The left hand wants to solidify the alliance with Britain, the right wants to protect its 'privates.'"

"Of course we don't really know that Elizabeth got a *bombe,* do we?" Menzies smiled at her menacingly. "How are they treating you at Prae Wood, by the way?"

"Just great," she replied.

They all fell silent. The tension in the car grew thicker. The rain had stopped. Elizabeth rolled down her window. The station clock struck eight.

Menzies and Elizabeth got out and waited in the damp summer twilight. After several more minutes, people and carts piled with luggage began pouring out of the old brick train station. Through the crowd, a stout balding man with another red carnation in his lapel emerged carrying a suitcase. Menzies greeted him warmly.

"Monsieur Bertrand, it is an honor to welcome you to London."

"Ah, Monsieur *Mengeez*,"—he pronounced his name with a Gallic hiss—"I have the honor to present to you our first victory over the Germans!" He handed over the Enigma machine.

While this ceremony was taking place, Elizabeth had her eyes trained on the entrance. Stephenson, Knox, Captain Lance, and Denniston also got out of the cars. The wave of passengers from the 8:10 began to subside. Elizabeth and Stephenson glanced at one another anxiously. Denniston lit his pipe, and Dilly put on a grim smile. Suddenly, flashing lights lit up the inside of the station. A knot of photographers appeared. It had to be Sacha Guitry.

Elizabeth pushed into the throng. Through the popping flashbulbs, Guitry saw her. Diving past the reporters and photographers, he reached out. But before he could get to her, another young woman threw herself at him, clinging to his neck. More flashbulbs exploded.

"Welcome to London, lovie!" She gave him a kiss, then raised her skirt to show her legs for the photographers. The reporters yelled questions at them. Looking harried but amused, Guitry called out to Elizabeth as she was being elbowed aside by the press.

"I've missed you! Come along with me!"

"Can't! I'm here with friends!" she shouted back. She saw him being swept away. "Wait! The trunk!"

"I thought you came to see me!"

"Don't joke!"

He merely waved his hand as the mass around him moved off toward a fleet of waiting Rolls-Royces. "Stop!" she begged. "Please!" Her cry was lost in the din. She was helpless to halt the tide of his departure.

" 'Scuse me, mum." The cockney whine came from behind her. "I was asked to fetch this for yer."

She whirled around. A porter stood there with a cart. On it was strapped her green metal trunk.

"Oh, God! Please, take it to my car," she said excitedly, pointing at the second Bentley. She stumbled after him, her legs wobbly with relief.

As soon as the trunk was loaded into the back of the car,

Knox was eagerly opening the lid. He gazed at the *bombe* in wonder. A few feet away, Menzies continued to distract Bertrand with flattery. Stephenson cracked a magnum of Pol Roger and the chauffeur handed around the glasses. Reluctantly, and with a beatific smile on his face, Knox closed the trunk. He and the other men joined Bertrand and Menzies. Standing in the street, they raised their glasses in a toast to Bertrand and sang, "For he's a jolly good fellow!"

And as they did so, Stephenson stepped aside and whispered to Elizabeth, "Good work, girl."

Aboard British European Airways Flight 302— September 1, 1939

From her seat on the left side of the airplane, Elizabeth could see the Pyrenees rising above the clouds. In a few minutes she would be landing in Biarritz. She hoped Arthur would meet her. There was so much to tell him.

The previous two weeks had been completely schizophrenic. Despite her ordeal at Prae Wood and paucity of subsequent praise, Elizabeth felt exhilarated at her success. She also had the pleasure of being able to shop for a new household, courtesy of the British Exchequer. In contrast, everyone else felt deepening gloom over the growing certainty of war. It all seemed unreal until the day she was passing through Piccadilly Circus and saw that they had carted off the statue of Diana for safekeeping.

She also got an allowance for a new wardrobe. Standing in front of the mirror at Harrod's one afternoon, Elizabeth took a good look at herself. Physically, her body remained young and attractive. Only she knew that inside, she was no longer complete. It had been a long time since she had thought about that. As an intelligence agent, she felt proud and fulfilled. And yet she could not help wondering where her life was leading her. The "boys of Broadway," as she liked to call them, hinted that they wanted her to stay and work there. Menzies had actually apologized, and whatever resentment she may have sensed before had evaporated.

Dilly Knox even drove her out to Bletchley Park to see the monstrosity of a grand Victorian manor house where the Government Code and Cipher School planned to relocate in time of war. Over a pub lunch, he gave her a baton of rolled-up paper covered with numbers and letters with which he had tried unsuccessfully to crack the Enigma.

"I surrender my sword to the victor," he said gallantly.

She also had a chance to see her son. There was no question that her visits were causing a strain with the Porters. Tony was now old enough to be intensely curious about Elizabeth. The whole arrangement was becoming unfair to everyone.

The steward moved through the aircraft cabin announcing that they were about to land. Descending through the clouds proved frightening, but the landing was smooth. The shock came when she entered the little bathhouse-style building that served as the terminal, and saw the black headlines at the newsstand. Hitler had invaded Poland. Her heart went out to Lubienski and all the proud Poles she had come to call friends. Sometimes they were their own worst enemy, but they didn't deserve this.

As she half expected, Arthur had sent their old driver to pick her up. Elizabeth buried her disappointment and gave him a kiss on the cheek as he loaded her bags into the car.

"The captain's much better," he said. The son of a Basque pirate, he had a way of giving Arthur's army rank a nautical air. "Sound as a gold doubloon, but tires easily," he explained as they made their way down the coast road toward St.-Jean-de-Luz. "I think he wanted to save himself to be with you this evening."

Elizabeth looked forward to seeing him. She had called several times over the last few weeks, but usually talked with Barbara Brasswell. She was still loyally nursing him back to health. Elizabeth had bought her a cashmere sweater set to show her gratitude. She felt guilty that she hadn't a gift for Barbara's husband. Though he had, in effect, gotten a promotion out of it, Tom still had been a saint to let his wife devote so much time to Arthur's rehabilitation.

As the sea came into view, Elizabeth's thoughts turned to Lubienski. She hoped that he would be safe. Arrangements had been made for him to evacuate with his family through Romania, then Yugoslavia and Italy, and ultimately into France. But while she prayed for him, she had to put aside the hope of seeing him again. It was time to pick up the threads of her life and try to make something of them. She had already fought her war. Now, she had her own responsibilities to fulfill.

Arthur expected her to go with him to Chile, and after long and painful thought she had concluded that she would. But only on one condition. She wanted her son to join them. It was the only way she would ever have a family. Elizabeth knew it would be difficult for Arthur to accept, but it was high time that he broke out of his Victorian straitjacket. The world was changing. Hell, she said to herself, the world was at war!

The Villa Ttirritta seemed exactly the same. The chauffeur unpacked her bags as she climbed the steps to the foyer. As ever, the view across the living room and the terrace, to the sunlit sea and the hills of Spain, made her pause. Arthur sat alone in his wicker lounge chair listening to the radio. He looked up.

"Heard the news?" he asked her.

"Yes, we're at war."

"Nazis beating the Poles to a pulp. I always said they were all flash and no fight."

"Arthur, do you think you could say hello?" She bent down and gave him a kiss on the cheek. He twisted around uncomfortably.

"There's something important we need to talk about," he announced. She heard a strain in his voice.

"I've something important to discuss with you too." Elizabeth drew up another chair and sat down. "But I thought it might wait until dinner."

"I want to talk now," Arthur insisted.

"All right. Go ahead."

"Elizabeth"—he took a breath—"I've had an affair."

"I know, Arthur, you told me." Since the stroke he sometimes forgot. He also could become inexplicably emotional.

"That's why I went to Poland."

"So you said." She nodded patiently.

"To get over her. But I couldn't. . . . "

"Arthur, I know I've not been much of a wife. I've been unfaithful and I've abandoned you. Frankly, you haven't been much of a husband either. But I thought we could put all that behind us. . . . "

"I'm afraid not."

She looked at him. He seemed in full command of his faculties. Elizabeth felt a growing sadness. "Do you hate me so much?"

"You needn't flatter yourself," he said angrily. His face was so red, she feared he might have another stroke. "I want a divorce!"

This was too much. Why was he being so disagreeable when she had just arrived home? "Don't be ridiculous," she said curtly. "It's against your religion, not to mention your career."

"We've never stopped loving each other!" he raved. "We want to be married!"

"Love? Married? We? Arthur, who on earth are you talking about?"

Arthur looked over her shoulder. Elizabeth heard footsteps behind her. She turned to find her good friend Barbara Brasswell coming across the terrace toward them.

PART
FIVE

The intelligence which has emanated from [Bletchley Park] before and during this campaign has been of priceless value to me. . . . It has saved thousands of British and American lives and, in no small way, contributed to the speed with which the enemy was routed and eventually forced to surrender.

I should be very grateful, therefore, if you would express to each and every one of those engaged in this work from me personally my heartfelt admiration and sincere thanks for their very decisive contribution to the Allied war effort.

—Letter from General Dwight D.
  Eisenhower to General Stewart
  Menzies, July 1945

I hope and believe I was a patriot.

—Elizabeth Pack

Chapter 35

Euston Station, London— September 11, 1940

"Leading Aircraft Woman 1069833," Elizabeth gave her rank and held out her hand to William Stephenson. He stood at the curb next to an olive-drab Rover with the lights painted out.

"Well, to me you'll always be 'Cynthia.'" He helped her into the backseat of the car. "How was the trip from Bletchley?"

"I felt a little awkward in this fancy dress and everyone else in uniform." She was wearing an ivory taffeta gown with a black velvet cape around her shoulders. "But now I feel underdressed. All my jewelry's in storage."

"You look just fine."

The car pulled into the street, then turned left onto Tottenham Court Road heading toward Covent Garden. In the gathering dusk, not a light was visible in the city.

"I don't mind telling you I'm very nervous. I've only been in London once since the Blitz started." She could see the block wardens patrolling to enforce the blackout. "After Madrid, I found I couldn't bear loud noises. In a bombing, I'm afraid I'll lose complete control of myself."

"We'll be safe where we're going," Stephenson assured her.

"And where is that? I'm dying with curiosity."

"I'm maintaining top security, until the last possible moment." Stephenson smiled.

"Well, I only hope they're not serving fish and chips. It's the only thing not rationed, so that's about all they serve at the Bletchley canteen."

"How are things going there?"

"Good. Chaotic, but good. I'm helping Denniston handle the administrative load. We've thousands of people working there now. First, we built huts all over the place, and now we're putting up some more permanent buildings. We're short of everything. Today, I traded several truckloads of bricks for a carload of paper."

"And the Enigma?" he asked.

"Are you cleared?" she teased. "It's going like gangbusters. Do you know Alan Turing? Well, he's this whiz from Cambridge. He's built a much improved *bombe* called Agnes and we're getting ready to turn them out like sausages. We're cracking the Luftwaffe Enigma on a regular basis. There's going to be a big raid on London tonight," she added anxiously.

He squeezed her hand. "You must be very proud to know that all that's the result of your work in Poland."

"Yes." A rueful look came over her face. "But it's a little hard to sit and listen to some of our senior 'inmates' at BP talk knowingly about how we got the Enigma from a Polish mechanic working in a German factory. It's really an absurd cover story when you think about it. As for the *bombe*, people simply assume Turing invented it."

Elizabeth looked out the window to try to determine where they were going. They had passed Leicester Square and now were headed toward Trafalgar.

"But morale is good?"

She nodded. "Churchill came up to visit, and I escorted him around. At lunchtime, we were standing on the steps of the mansion with Denniston as all these gawky mathematicians and consumptive logicians were parading by, and Churchill said, 'When I ordered you to leave no stone unturned to get the people you needed, I didn't expect you to take me quite so literally'!"

Stephenson laughed. The car was approaching Admiralty Arch. The gates were open, and the car passed through it and onto the mall.

"I do hope you realize"—Stephenson turned serious—"how vital your work has been. The only thing stopping Hitler from invading Britain is the Royal Air Force, and we're hopelessly outnumbered by the Luftwaffe. It's the

Luftwaffe's Enigma messages revealing their attack plans that give us a fighting chance.''

"Can you tell me what you've been doing?" Elizabeth appreciated the compliment, but it made her uncomfortable. She found herself becoming more like the English every day.

"At Winston's direction, I've been organizing a backup SIS in America. If the Germans overrun Britain, we'll carry on the fight from there. I'm also working on bringing the United States into the war. As Winston says, drawing an ally into the field can be more vital than a dozen victories.''

Elizabeth looked pensive. "I never imagined that the Germans would actually invade England until a few days ago when the government sounded the 'Cromwell' alert. Within an hour a score of yellow school buses showed up at BP, ready to take us to Bristol for evacuation to Canada." She shook her head.

"You're thinking about your son?" Stephenson guessed.

"I'm not leaving him behind," she said defiantly.

"How is he?"

"I see him every weekend." She brightened. "He's growing like a weed. I've worked things out with Mrs. Porter. She's Mama and I'm Mummy.''

"And Arthur?" He didn't know how to frame the question.

"I'm giving him a divorce. He can charge me with adultery. I don't care, and it'll do the least damage to his career. My mother's furious. She says it will ruin my reputation and my chance to hook another man." Elizabeth shook her head. "Actually, I'm quite off men altogether. When Arthur first asked for a divorce, I was surprised how lost I felt. But I've found that I still have myself.''

"Any word of Lubienski?"

"He was interned in Romania for the longest time, then made his way to France. When France fell, he was evacuated from, of all places, St.-Jean-de-Luz. Now he's with some supersecret unit here in England. His family is here too. I've not seen him.''

"Well, I'm sure that this evening, he would want you to wear this." Reaching under the driver's seat, Stephenson brought out a flat box covered in velvet. When he lifted the lid, she could see, even in the dark, that it was dazzling.

"A diamond tiara!"

"I'm sorry that I can't let you keep it," he apologized. "I wish I could."

"So do I!"

They both laughed. Where *were* they going, she wondered. Elizabeth fastened the tiara on her head with a few bobby pins. She could not imagine how it looked with her military bob, and blackout regulations prohibited turning on the interior light. While she struggled to see her reflection in the glass to the driver's compartment, she suddenly realized that the car was hurtling toward a massive iron gate.

At the last moment, the gate swung wide. The car crossed a half acre of gravel, passed through an archway in the facade of a massive building, traversed a vast courtyard and drew up in front of a two-story colonnaded entrance. Liveried footmen with white gloves opened the door. Elizabeth stepped out and looked around. She had arrived at Buckingham Palace.

The grand staircase and corridors of the palace were dimly lit as a gesture to save electricity. This made it difficult to see the paintings in the picture gallery for which Buckingham Palace was renowned. Still, Elizabeth saw that the king's residence was far more modest than Versailles, Vienna's Beauborg, or countless other royal palaces she had visited on the Continent. The rooms were on a scale befitting a global empire, yet they were so beautifully proportioned that she did not feel lost, even in the dark. The space, the design, the details of moldings and decoration inspired a sense of measure and balance rather than excessive grandeur and pomposity. Perhaps, Elizabeth concluded, that was why Buckingham Palace still had a royal family to occupy it.

"What is this all about?" she whispered to Stephenson.

"You'll find out," he said happily.

They were ushered into a brightly lit salon where the floor-to-ceiling windows were covered with blackout curtains. A dozen other guests were sipping sherry. The only one she recognized was Colonel Menzies. Elizabeth had not seen him in almost a year. She congratulated him on becoming "C," chief of SIS, after Admiral Sinclair's untimely death.

The other guests were a surprisingly varied lot: a few Indians, a couple of Levantines from Egypt and Mesopotamia, several varieties of Central Europeans. Elizabeth detected a Polish accent and something else Slavic. She was introduced to two other women, an Argentine and a Frenchwoman, both very beautiful; the former dressed quite flashy, the latter elegant but drab.

Sometimes they gave only their first names and often only their last. "Christine," said the Frenchwoman; "Singh," said one of the Indians. "Li," declared a Chinese. Stephenson told Elizabeth to use her code name: Cynthia.

A pair of double doors opened and a herald appeared in eighteenth-century livery.

"The king!" he announced.

He emerged from the darkness of the hallway in a military uniform and began greeting his guests. He did not shake hands. The men bowed; the women curtsied. Elizabeth said, "It's an honor to meet you, Your Highness."

"The honor is mine," he replied.

When the introductions had been completed, Colonel Menzies raised a toast. "To the king."

George VI did not take a drink. Then he took a glass of sherry and they all drank "to the Commonwealth."

For dinner they moved into the state dining room. Its crimson walls and carpet glowed majestically in the candlelight. The grandeur of the ornate ceiling threatened to dwarf the modest dinner party. Elizabeth was amazed to find that her place was to the right of the king. Stephenson was shown to one end of the table next to Colonel Menzies. Elizabeth could not decide if she were more excited by sitting in the place of honor or by the magnificent four-foot sturgeon that arrived as the first course. She found herself diving into her food like a trencherman.

"Forgive me for playing the starving Armenian, Your Highness." She paused to apologize and gulp down a mouthful of 1927 Pol Roger. "But to me a treat is a Woolton pie." That was a concoction of unrationed root vegetables named after the minister of agriculture.

"How d-dire!" the king responded. He then leaned over and whispered confidentially. "I p-particularly wanted to meet our Cynthia. This evening was d-designed mostly for you." He smiled. "The others d-deserve recognition too, but it started with you."

Elizabeth could only mumble, "Thank you."

As the table was cleared for the next course, George VI rose to salute his guests. The champagne in his raised glass glittered from the light of the chandeliers. He spoke slowly, and with evident pleasure.

"The p-purpose of this d-dinner is to express the appppreciation of a grateful nation, commonwealth, and empire. We can't t-talk about what you've d-done, with the exception of Bill Stephenson who's g-getting us arms from America."

They all burst into applause.

"B-But even then," the king continued, "we can't t-talk about how he's doing it."

Elizabeth joined in the laughter. Stephenson seemed to be blushing.

Just then, the air raid sirens began to wail. Elizabeth could feel herself growing alarmed. A palace guard appeared and led everyone down a stone staircase to a comfortably appointed bomb shelter with padded leather walls. They all arranged themselves according to the protocol at the dining table. A gramophone somewhere piped in martial music to cover the noise of the antiaircraft batteries. But it could not obliterate the sound of thudding bombs.

Sitting next to the king, Elizabeth felt safer but more anxious too. The bombs were landing closer. What if she couldn't control herself? What if she behaved like a fool? Like a coward in front of the king?

She could feel the building shaking, her panic rising. The blood, the blasted bodies of Madrid came rushing back to her. She was going to disgrace herself, but she couldn't stand it. She had to get out of there! The explosions seemed almost on top of them! She started to rise. The king reached out and drew her down again.

"I know how you feel," he murmured.

At that moment they were stunned by a huge detonation

that tossed everyone onto the floor. They waited for the final blast that would end it all, but it never came.

"W-what a mess they made of our ch-ch-ch-chapel," the king stuttered as firemen and palace guards ran madly in every direction. When the all-clear had sounded, the king had led them out of the bunker to inspect the damage to his palace. The chapel was not so much a mess as that half of it was gone. In the moonlight, Elizabeth could see that the altar still stood but that much of the stone and plaster work had been shattered by the blast. All the windows had vanished and she could see past a missing wall right into the royal gardens. Most of the floor was a massive hole in the earth.

"Shouldn't you move to some place safe till the Blitz is over?" Elizabeth asked the king.

"I'm simply n-not moving out," he responded, "until the b-b-b-bombing stops. Nor am I going to repair the ch-church," he said angrily. "I want the p-people to know I'm sharing their hardship and d-danger."

The king insisted that they all return to finish their dinner. He picked up his toast where he left off.

"M-Most of you soldier on without recognition. Only your g-grandchildren will know of your exploits and m-maybe not even them. B-But you know what you've d-done. I want you to know you also have the thanks of a g-grateful sovereign."

When the king sat down, he shocked Elizabeth by putting his hand on her arm for a second time that evening.

"You've d-done so much for Britain, Cynthia. You can't know the p-pressure we've been under to sue for p-peace. The Enigma has given us the courage to struggle on. We'd have had no chance to survive this tempest without you."

Elizabeth floated through the rest of the evening. The king went on to confide his frustration at not being able to lead men into battle as some of his ancestors had. As they continued to talk, her sense of being appreciated made her feel that whatever ordeals lay ahead, she was ready. She looked forward to them. Elizabeth knew who she was, and she knew what she was fighting for. The world might be torn apart by primeval and uncontrollable forces, but Elizabeth believed that, at last, she had her destiny in her own hands.

At the end of the table, Stephenson and Menzies were watching Elizabeth with the king.

"Your Cynthia has done us all proud." Menzies said quietly. "I only hope this business with Arthur Pack stays under control."

"I didn't know there was a problem," Stephenson said with a note of concern.

"As you know, we arranged for Barbara Brasswell to accompany him to Chile. We wanted her to keep things going through the divorce. She wouldn't have to actually marry him, but we wanted to be sure that Elizabeth would be completely free of him. But now Tom Brasswell's acting up. He wants a post that's come open in Rio and the Foreign Office is balking at holding it available for him until Arthur Pack's divorce is final."

"If anyone deserves a decent posting after what they've done," Stephenson declared, "it's the Brasswells."

"I'm going to take it up with Halifax personally," Menzies assured him.

"Good. Just so long as Elizabeth's free for further assignments. I'm going to have a lot of work for her in America."

They both looked down the table. The king seemed to be pouring out his heart to her. Stephenson smiled. Menzies put their shared thought into words.

"She's really got the gift."

#1

HIS THIRD CONSECUTIVE NUMBER ONE BESTSELLER!

James Clavell's

WHIRLWIND

70312-2/$6.99 US/$7.99 CAN

From the author of *Shōgun* and *Noble House*—
the newest epic in the magnificent Asian Saga
is now in paperback!

"WHIRLWIND IS A CLASSIC–FOR OUR TIME!"
Chicago Sun-Times

WHIRLWIND

is the gripping epic of a world-shattering upheaval that
alters the destiny of nations. Men and women barter for
their very lives. Lovers struggle against heartbreaking odds
And an ancient land battles to survive as a new reign of
terror closes in . . .